Book 3 of The Crash

Children of The Crash

A New Humanity

PATCHIN
PICTURES®

Published by Patchin Pictures, LLC.
Patchin Pictures, Las Vegas, Nevada

Paperback ISBN: 979-8-9899902-2-1
E-Book ISBN: 979-8-9899902-3-8

"Rain Black, Reign Heavy" lyrics are used with permission from Crippled Black Phoenix, lyrics by Belinda Kordic. Copyright © 2018, Season of Mist.

Thank you to Justin Greaves and Crippled Black Phoenix for the amazing music.

"Sheep"
Words and Music by Roger Waters
Copyright ©1977 Roger Waters Overseas Ltd.
Copyright Renewed
All Rights Administered by BMG Rights Management (US) LLC
All Rights Reserved Used by Permission
Reprinted by Permission of Hal Leonard LLC

Thank you to Dr. Jordan B. Peterson for bring into the light numerous ideas and concepts that have been held hostage in darkness for too long.

Thank you to Colleen for always staying beside me so I can do my insane stuff.

Author photo by Athena Patchin.

Books by Steven S. Patchin:

Backfire Crash, A Mind-Bending SF Thriller
Beyond The Crash, The Cosmic Consciousness
Children of The Crash, A New Humanity
Derelict Dreams, An Illustrated Novel
Burnt Ends, Fucked up Stories

For Athena. Because you are you.

Book 3 of The Crash

Children of The Crash

A New Humanity

by Steven S. Patchin

CONTENTS

Thus Far   1

Part I: Exodus   3

Chapter 1: **Eternal**   5
Chapter 2: **Childhood**   9
Chapter 3: **Strike**   15
Chapter 4: **Collapse**   21
Chapter 5: **Interlinked**   27
Chapter 6: **Lucid**   31
Chapter 7: **Stock**   37
Chapter 8: **Adjustments**   43
Chapter 9: **Aliens**   47
Chapter 10: **Departure**   57
Chapter 11: **Confluence**   63
Chapter 12: **Remembered**   73
Chapter 13: **Priorities**   79
Chapter 14: **Committal**   89
Chapter 15: **Cortege**   97

Part II: Communion   103

Chapter 16: **Commencement**   105
Chapter 17: **Lies**   111
Chapter 18: **Leader**   119
Chapter 19: **Fight**   129
Chapter 20: **Tribe**   139
Chapter 21: **Coyotes**   151
Chapter 22: **Repel**   161
Chapter 23: **Between**   165
Chapter 24: **Threat**   175
Chapter 25: **Magic**   181
Chapter 26: **Playground**   191
Chapter 27: **Pursuit**   203
Chapter 28: **Precedence**   211
Chapter 29: **Spies**   219
Chapter 30: **Reinhard**   223

Part III: Annihilation   233

Chapter 31: **Separation**   235
Chapter 32: **Coordination**   241
Chapter 33: **Timeline**   247
Chapter 34: **Physics**   257
Chapter 35: **Psychology**   267
Chapter 36: **Ben**   273
Chapter 37: **Assurance**   283
Chapter 38: **Adolescence**   291
Chapter 39: **Org**   297
Chapter 40: **Aim**   307
Chapter 41: **Fireshots**   311
Chapter 42: **Nexus**   319
Chapter 43: **Apocalypsis**   329
           Afterword: 333
           About the Author: 339

Thus Far

In Book One of "The Crash" trilogy, *Backfire Crash*, we saw that the world was devastated by a mental contagion called The Crash. Most people in the world were killed as a result. The Family and Ben Stoffer fought our way to Ben's underground lab at the Rocky Mountain Arsenal National Wildlife Refuge in Denver, Colorado. We initially succeeded in outwitting and even outfighting the troops that were trying to take Ben into custody. In the lab, we developed a technological antidote to The Crash, which we called the Beep, a Brain Electromagnetic Pulse (BEMP) transmitted from a Jeep. It worked on a very small number of survivors in a nearby neighborhood. We, the Family and Ben, believed we were on our way to creating a large-scale answer to the problem of resetting crashed brains all around the world.

In Book Two, *Beyond The Crash*, the Family were surrounded in the neighborhood by troops from Upstream Security, the enforcement arm of Genetrix, which was a partner company to Ben's Stoffer Enterprises, and was involved in distributing the Stoffer Solution. It was Genetrix that was responsible for altering Ben's Stoffer Solution, which led to The Crash. As these troops tried to capture Ben and the Beep, Ben hit them with a non-lethal pulse from the Beep and knocked them out.

The Family captured these dozens of troops and held them for ransom at the lab. Our goal was to structure a truce so that the troops would allow the Family and Ben to do what was needed to help more survivors. After we successfully negotiated with Upstream authorities who had set up headquarters at the nearby Space Force Base, the troops were released. During this time, Ben and his crew had been working on an expanded BEMP designed to have a much wider range and effect for the purpose of resetting the brains of more people who were crashed. Ben and the Family worked with the Upstream troops at the base to reconfigure bombs, which we called BBs, and which would release the larger BEMP when dropped from a B-52 military plane.

Meanwhile, some of us in the Family had been working on a newly-discovered method of mentally reaching people around the world, a practice and an ability that we named Iter Anima. We found that the combination of Jason's and Glenda's unusual bond, along with my own unique capability to reach into people's minds, allowed us to make connections with people far away. In these mind travels, we met survivors throughout the world, including a young girl named Jaguar and her Zo'é tribe in the Brazilian rainforest, a shaman grandmother named Kallik who traveled with her family and their reindeer herds in Siberia, and many others of various religions and spiritual beliefs.

We also discovered that forces of higher authority than Upstream Security were not interested in working with Ben and the Family, and instead, were determined to take the technology and use it as they pleased. The combined strength of the now-cooperating Upstream troops and the Family, initially defeated these Genetrix soldiers. We managed to set off the BBs, which reached around the world.

We accomplished this by combining Ben's technology with the mental connections of the Family's Iter Animas. Without this integrated approach, the effects of the bombs alone would have reached only the city itself. Instead, their waves traveled around the world, sending their healing BB frequencies to the few survivors who remained.

But, during the process, someone from the outside infiltrated our transcendent mind connections and took Lauren from me, leaving her lifeless body next to our meditative fire.

This left me devastated as I returned to the lab without her and faced our empty room and Daisy, Lauren's gentle pit bull.

And the story continues . . .

Part I
Exodus

"The day the child realizes that all adults are imperfect, he becomes an adolescent; the day he forgives them, he becomes an adult; the day he forgives himself, he becomes wise."

- Alden Nowlan

Steven S. Patchin

Chapter 1
Eternal

When I heard the "Hello" in my head, I slowly recognized that it was Jaguar. Facing Lauren's death, I was crawling toward a precipice, ready to fall into my deepest depression or something worse. Hearing Jaguar stopped me. A fissure split my mind, and light burned through. Jaguar waited for me to respond.

I wanted to tell her to go away, but I also knew I couldn't do that. The song Lauren had played for me that had come to mean so much, echoed in my mind: "Rain Black, Reign Heavy." Two lines kept repeating: "I choose to bleed, I choose life. I choose to live, I choose to fight." *How could I turn away from that?* It would be like turning away from Lauren, and it was Lauren who had found Jaguar's tribe, the Zo'é.

Mustering as much strength as I could and facing the light that burned through the granite of my mind, I finally responded to Jaguar with a question: "Are you okay?"

"We are safe, but we feel your loss. She was with us before."

Jaguar was referring to Lauren, and this made my throat tighten with grief. After an empty pause, I said, "Yes, Lauren is gone. Something happened when we traveled, or something went wrong with the bombs and the waves they created."

"In our tribe, those who die are always with us, because they are part of eternity, the always now. They can never truly be gone, even if we do not see them anymore."

Her statement felt meaningless to me. Even while facing the warmth that Jaguar brought, Lauren was gone. She was *not* still with me. I didn't really care about philosophical ideas at the moment. So I asked in deflection, "What did you feel with the waves we sent out?"

Jaguar replied, "When you came to us this time, we saw others, through you, who seemed lost. And we also saw those who were like the ones who wanted to attack us, those we had to kill. We felt the waves and helped them along, helped them reach these others. Some of the people were close. Some were far. We saw the waves reach them."

"That was our intent. Thank you," I said. "From what we felt, we think this is what happened throughout the world. We all did our best, and I hope it will make a difference. We don't know the full effectiveness of it yet, though."

"Don't you see?"

"See what?"

"Where and who we are."

"What do you mean?"

"Stop thinking."

"What?"

"It's there. It's not words. It's not thought. It's there."

What the hell was she talking about? As the light in my mind glinted, I was slipping again anyway, wanting to crumble to the floor of this room and stay there until something changed, but I didn't want to make the change, myself. I was tired, lost, and getting pissed, losing patience. But here I was having this conversation. *Could I escape to Ben's library and finish one of his best bottles of Russian vodka? Did he have a shitty bottle of vodka? Would this girl leave me alone?*

She was right, though. I needed to stop thinking. I pictured a bottle of vodka, which looked and sounded pretty fucking good right now. That's what I wanted to see and hear for real instead of philosophical thoughts projected into my mind by a child. If I left my room and headed for Ben's library, would Jaguar follow me? *Of course she would follow me. She was in my mind. Fuck!*

An image grows: viridescent eyes, penetrating. Dark fur. Piercing moonlight. Intense focus. Rippling muscles. Iron claws. Shoulders spread. Back arched. It gathers into a force, into concentration that lives without thought. Pulling me with it, making me become it. Darkness curls around me forming a tunnel that twists into saturated green and purple strands.

I see through the emerald eyes now. They are me. And I stop moving. I breathe with intent. Silence echoes. I feel everything around me falling away until I smell the damp soil, the sultry greenery cooling in the azure moonlight. I crouch on the jungle path.

The silence becomes insects buzzing, calling for mates. Frogs crying. Life grows to a symphony throughout the speckled shadows, calling. It's here. We're here, bigger and bigger, all around.

I stand. Daisy stands. Jaguar stands. Calmness flows.

The path lay before us. Darkness swings away like curtains revealing a grand play. Light rains down through the leaves. I can not shrivel and hide. I am brought up to see again. What we accomplished was not for nothing. This was not a mechanical exercise. This was not an obligation. This was a stepping through, and I can not go back.

I continue my controlled breathing, the air flowing through me, my eyes seeing farther, my ears wrangling sounds deeper, my nose filling me with wholeness, my skin feeling everything: cold shivers, warm stretches, slick openness, strength ready. I taste life.

In my room. Jaguar is there. *The* jaguar is also there, in me and me in it. Daisy pants calmly next to me. I come back to myself.

Jaguar says, "Now you see the eternal now."

Steven S. Patchin

Chapter 2
Children

I would not be hunting down one of Ben's bottles of vodka after all. A lot had happened, and it could take me a lifetime to process only part of it. The world had changed, and I would need to embrace our new reality or float away like driftwood in a lazy river. But what was I to do in these dark morning hours? Daisy could use a visit outside, so that's where I went, taking the gentle pit bull with me. I drove an electric cart up the tunnel, Daisy in the seat at my side.

Jaguar left the dog and me to ourselves. Daisy didn't know that Lauren was gone, but over time, she would adapt to her absence. I, however, knew I would not see Lauren again. Even with the reality of the eternal now, actually feeling it and understanding it on a deep level, I still faced the loss of what I had envisioned for our future. These clashing thoughts churned in my stomach.

Lauren and I had discussed the little things – or maybe they were the big things – that we wanted in our lives. Art and music had been shoved into the dusty crevasses of society as The Crash brought down civilization, but Lauren held them in her heart and mind, and on her phone. As long as the technology lasted, as long as recordings and images remained accessible on various media, as long as her phone lasted, we could still experience the human creations of the past. We had talked about saving those things that Lauren felt were the nucleus of humanity, the art and music that revealed our inner selves, expressed our pain and desire, inspired our vision going forward. I wanted to experience more of it, beyond what Lauren had shown me, and I had imagined those experiences that Lauren and I would have.

Daisy romped away across the dirt lot and into the long grasses of summer. The half-moon watched from high among the stars. I could see a good distance to the east, a hill rising close by, no hint yet of the coming sunrise. It had been only two days since Lauren and I stood out here watching Daisy run. I continued thinking of what I had imagined our lives could be, our finding a house not far from here, maybe in sight of this wildlife refuge that had become so important to our survival, to our hearts and souls. We could have found our own functioning vehicle, explored the museums and galleries in Denver. I could hunt. But we would have needed to address the littered dead that had collected throughout the city like debris blown by the wind. We would still need to do something about that problem, and even more importantly, we would need to help the survivors.

For now, this would be my life: helping the crashed survivors who likely had been diverted from The Crash by the BBs and our Iter Anima, looking for other survivors who had not been crashed, and all of us working together to build a new society that could be so much more than the one that we had lost. There was much to do and lots of promise to inspire us. But with Lauren gone, I didn't want to think too far into the future. I would need to look at my footsteps and the ground in front of me, only letting in glimpses of what lay along our new path, because seeing all of it at once was more than I could bear at the moment.

Daisy barked, not a playful yip, but a sound of warning. She bounded out of the grasses, rushing past me, barking more urgently. I turned toward the raised entrance to the tunnel that was behind me and watched Daisy run to the left of it.

In the open dirt lot, a group of figures approached slowly in the dim moonlight. Daisy reached them and barked viciously, growling and snarling. They stopped and stood still. They were people, small in stature. Children.

"Daisy," I called. "It's okay, okay. Take it easy. Come on back here." I didn't really know that it was okay, and I feared one of them might harm her if she continued barking. Or, she could attack with her iron jaws. It wouldn't take much for her to crush a child's bones.

The dog stopped barking but still growled. I called out to her again, and she came to me, reluctantly. I didn't know what to think of this group, which numbered a couple dozen or more. Obviously, they had come here for a reason. They weren't acting crashed, either.

One of the taller children, a boy, stepped forward and said to me, "You were trying to help, but you had to fight those soldiers." It seemed neither a statement nor a question.

I replied, "We did fight them, but we're working together now."

Some of the children behind him began to fidget a bit, while others stood completely still. Children. We had wondered why we hadn't seen any children since The Crash exploded throughout the world. None of the Family had mentioned having children of their own, either. Now, this group of children had approached our tunnel entrance, not just by chance, but with purpose. They all wore backpacks and carried odd-shaped sticks and other items that, I assumed, were weapons.

The boy said, "We saw what you did, that you traveled, and there were waves. We tried to catch up to you, but you were too far away."

This was getting deeper. "Oh. We didn't see you. How did you see us?"

"We just did. We could see. It happened when you adults went crazy."

"You began seeing those kinds of things in your mind when The Crash happened?" I was not expecting anything like this. We had worked hard to discover and use Iter Anima, and this child seemed to be saying that they just did it naturally.

The boy said, "Yes." It was a simple truth to him.

"Oh. So, did you see where we went, the people we visited?"

"No. We didn't see where you went. But we saw the waves and the clouds. We wanted to stop you. We tried to hide from the waves, many of us around the world. But we couldn't. The waves hit us when you came back. That's why we're here now."

"Did they hurt you? What happened?"

The boy seemed angry, as though he had a simple request, and a parent had denied him what he wanted. He said, "You took away our friends, other kids like us. We can't find them anymore. Your waves hurt us."

I asked, "You're saying that what we did made you unable to see people through your minds like you did before?"

"That's it. And we want you to fix it."

Ah shit! Nothing happens without consequences, and often, those consequences are not what we intended. We knew this when we started trying to "fix" the problems we saw with The Crash. Ben knew it, too. It was a risk. We hadn't even known where any children were, and we certainly hadn't thought that what we were doing would cause this kind of harm, or at least we had pushed those thoughts aside.

I recalled a surgeon friend I had met through the motorcycle shop. I did a fairly simple repair on his bike, and we wound up going on a couple rides together. One of the last times I saw him, he told me about a surgery he had performed on an infant. I couldn't remember the specifics, but he had finished addressing the problem that required surgery when he saw a tiny spot on one of the baby's organs. He thought it was possibly something left from their procedure. He touched it with a piece of sponge so he could pick it up, intending to fix an inconsequential problem, and the area started bleeding. His efforts escalated from simply finishing up from a successful surgery to trying to stop an organ from bleeding, to trying to stitch the organ, and finally failing completely, him and his team unable to control the situation, and ultimately watching the infant die.

The man wouldn't forgive himself for the infant's death. He stopped riding, and I only saw him once more. He had resigned from his residency. It made me think that sometimes, with our good intentions, we fail to admit that we are not gods and fail to see that what we think we can control is more complicated than the climate itself, that we can't control it, and when we try, there are repercussions.

From what the boy was saying, our attempts at managing and "fixing" the brains of humanity had harmed the children. And here we were again facing a dilemma of what could be done, because this group of children expected us to fix the problem. Fuck!

I asked, "How many are there of you? How many children?"

"Many."

"Where do you live?"

"Everywhere. We go where we need to."

"How do you eat?"

"We find what we need."

The boy didn't want a conversation. He wanted a solution. And I could see clearly that we didn't need any more solutions. I couldn't imagine Ben coming up with yet another iteration of the brain electromagnetic pulse and blasting more brains with it. I didn't know how to reply to this boy.

I asked, "Where are the others who you reached around the world?"

"They are around the world. You know, this is why we had to hide from you adults. You never could see. And maybe you're still crazy."

I understood his point. I looked around at his group, which numbered a couple dozen and were spread out behind the boy. He was among the oldest, and I guessed he likely wasn't much older than 10. He didn't seem to have reached puberty yet. I saw some very young children in the shadows, younger than five possibly.

"To start," I said, "I need to introduce you to Ben. But he's at the Space Force Base. How about you come inside with me, and all of you can rest until morning, get something to eat. We can take you to see Ben later."

He replied quickly. "How about we wait up here, and you go get Ben now."

I felt that I was outside my element. I didn't know how to talk to children. Maybe Lauren – No. Sophia? Ah, Glenda! She might know what to do.

I said, "I'll go back inside and see what we can do. Make yourselves at home among the bison."

Steven S. Patchin

Chapter 3
Strike

I took Daisy back to our room and sought out Glenda in her room with Jason. Sophia would have been a good choice, too. Both were very empathetic, Sophia naturally so, but Glenda was growing into her position as the mother of the Family. Sophia was more of the care-giver. She had attended to the 12 original survivors and always found a way to comfort people when they needed it. She also had been instrumental in helping us connect with Filipe from among the soldiers who we had held prisoner here after they tried to take Ben and the Beep Jeep. Without that connection, we still could be fighting Upstream troops.

But I decided to consult Glenda because many in the Family looked up to her as a leader, a mother figure, and because I wanted Jason's take on this, too. Jason answered my knock at their door. He appeared to have been sleeping, and was dressed in a rumpled pair of shorts and a t-shirt. He showed no irritation at my imposition. Instead, he looked concerned. I saw Glenda sit up in bed behind him.

Jason asked, "Hey, are you okay? Is there something we can do?"

I knew he was thinking about Lauren, but I wanted to stay on task.

"Uh, we have a strange situation that I thought you guys could help with. We're all going to have to deal with it, really. I took Daisy up top to run in the grass. A group of children are up there. Only children. A couple dozen, as far as I could see in the moonlight. And it seems that our BB waves did something to them, and they want us to fix it."

Glenda sat up and said, "What? Children? What did the BBs do to them?"

Jason gestured for me to come into their room, which I did, and he shut the door behind me.

I said, "A boy spoke for their group and said that they had been connected to other children around the world and that our waves took the connections away. They were doing something like our Iter Anima, I think."

They both looked surprised at what I told them, which I had expected they would be. Jason sat on the edge of their bed that was two singles pushed together like what Lauren and I had done. He indicated a chair that I could sit in, but I ignored it.

Glenda said, "My god! Are they still up there?"

"Yes. They want us to do something immediately, as if we could flip a switch. I told them they needed to talk to Ben, that he was at the base. The boy said we should go get Ben now. I invited them down here, but they wanted to stay up top."

Jason rubbed his face in angst. "This has become a dangerous slope we're sliding down. Maybe it always was. I thought we did the right thing with the BBs, but now we have another problem already."

"I think we did do the right thing," I said. "But I don't believe we can keep hitting people with the BEMP. It's just too complicated, and we don't know what the other consequences might be." I looked directly at Glenda. "I was thinking we should try to talk to the children so they aren't so determined to have us fix this. We might not be able to fix it anyway, and I really don't want Ben thinking about coming up with another BEMP setting. Can you talk to them?"

Glenda thought for a moment. "I can talk to them, but I'm not a child psychologist."

"We don't need a psychologist for this. I could have gone to Craig for that. We need to develop trust and make a connection. And they certainly don't trust us right now, except that they expect us to fix their problem."

"Yes, I'll talk to them. We can go up there now," she said.

"Are they dangerous?" Jason asked.

"They didn't appear to be violent. The boy was fairly calm until he got frustrated that I wasn't doing what he wanted right away. I would say that we can go up and talk to them. But keep in mind, he doesn't really want a conversation. I doubt they want anything to do with us except for getting us to fix what they think we broke."

"Alright," said Glenda. "Let's go." She got out of bed and slipped into a pair of jeans and a long-sleeve shirt.

They both put on shoes, and we set out to have yet another conversation with a group that was not happy with us. This unity stuff was not easy.

The Beep Jeep sat outside the trash collection room. We took a different Jeep up the mile-long tunnel. As Jason drove, Glenda sat in the other front seat, and I sat behind her.

I said, "And uh, something else happened, too."

They both turned and looked at me with concern.

I continued, "Jaguar contacted me."

More surprise on their faces.

"She spoke in my head the way I do in their heads through our Iter Animas. I don't know how she did it. She said she knew about Lauren." I had to stop and collect myself before speaking further. "And she showed me something, made me feel something. I was in the jungle, a jaguar. I was a jaguar. And I felt my being, something beyond thought. Sort of like some of the moments I feel in our Iter Animas, but different because I didn't feel like myself. Well, I felt like myself and everything else at once. I don't know . . . ."

They didn't say anything for a while.

Glenda replied first. "Whatever's happening to us as people is deeper than we can comprehend. Look at what we've been through, what we've accomplished. We actually found a way to communicate with other people through our minds only. Then we helped deliver the BB waves. And we all saw what Jaguar did, how she went inside that tree, how she made those two guys see multiples of herself, how she became a jaguar and diverted those crashed men running through the jungle. And now she's showing you that she can do even more than that."

Jason said, "I've been trying to put all this together into something that makes sense, but maybe we need to stop trying to make sense of it using the same reasoning that sent us in the wrong direction to begin with. It was reason, the logical idea of messing with our brains, that opened the door for The Crash. It wasn't just Ben's fault. Our whole society had been headed in that direction for quite a while. But it wasn't reason that gave us the ability to travel with our minds. Maybe it was intuition and something else that we can't explain. We've experienced a lot that we can't really explain. Maybe we should stop trying to explain it, and just go with it. That's how we travel. We don't sit around and look at maps and try to find the best route to get where we want to go. We feel our way there."

"Just going with it is about all I can do right now, anyway," I said. "I'm too tired to try and sort it out. I'll just keep going with whatever is happening and see where it takes me."

"You're both right," said Glenda. "But we do need at least a little bit of discussion so we can keep navigating through this. The best way is balance. Remember that the Taoist monk described the Way as a blending of opposites. It's not either/or. It's both. It's activity and quietude at once.

It's reason and intuition together. It's both halves of our brains working in concert."

I could certainly go with that, too.

We arrived at the tunnel entrance. I had left the tunnel doors open, and we drove outside. The children were over to the south about a hundred yards from the entrance, sitting in the grass. They didn't stand when we drove up to them. The approaching sun was washing away the stars, and I could see the children clearly now in the brighter blue of pre-dawn. Their clothes were typical of what children used to wear, t-shirts, shorts, jeans, things usually found in stores. Most were relatively clean, too, the clothes as well as the children, themselves. I would have expected a group of children who were barely surviving to have been scruffy and dirty. But why was I assuming they were barely surviving?

We got out of the Jeep and walked closer to the group. The boy I had spoken to stood up but didn't say anything. He had dark, almost black, straight hair, the length just below his ears. His eyes were intense, deep blue. He wore fairly tight jeans, as though he had grown into them, and his shirt was black with a rustic American flag across the front.

I asked him, "What's your name?"

"Sam."

I introduced myself and said, "This is Jason and Glenda."

They both said hello to Sam and the children.

"Are you going to fix what you did?" Sam asked, flatly.

I replied, "It's not really something we can do anything about, ourselves. Ben's at the base, and—"

I looked to the south toward the base and realized I had been hearing the sound of a distant plane, a large jet such as a B-52 or 747. That was a sound we hadn't heard over the city in many weeks except for when the plane that carried the BBs flew for our mission to distribute Ben's BEMPs. As I scanned the sky, I saw brightly reflected sunlight glinting off a plane high above the base as it flew east. I wondered why they would be flying anything right now. We had just finished our mission with the B-52 delivering two BBs. Where would they be going now?

Then I saw the explosions. The concussive sounds hit us soon after. A cluster of explosions peppered the horizon where the base was located. The booming sounds rolled over us as if they were from the climax of a fireworks show. The sky brightened above the exploding blooms of flowers that were obviously bombs detonating on impact. Fire and smoke spread a wide swath across our southern view.

The children were standing now, and the explosions stopped. The plane got louder, and I searched for it in the sky. It flew closer to us and banked out of the southeast, doubtless turning toward us.

"Run for the tunnel. Now!" I yelled.

The children gazed at each other and at Sam, but didn't move.

"That plane's coming here," I screamed. "It's going to bomb us! We have to take cover! Get in the tunnel!"

Jason and Glenda began pushing some of the children in the direction of the tunnel, and we all ran for the opening. We were looking at a helluva hundred-yard dash with more than that to get down the tunnel. All of us ran, but some of the children were so young that they couldn't keep up. Most of the older kids ran ahead, but some stayed back to help, picking up the smaller kids. Jason, Glenda, and I each picked up children, with Jason and me grabbing two each. I didn't think to use the Jeep until we were already past it, and then I knew it would have been more awkward to drive it anyway, because we all couldn't fit in the vehicle. It had to be all of us together getting to the tunnel or none at all.

I carried a boy and a girl, each aged five or younger. Jason reached the tunnel entrance where some older children were gathered. He stopped there, still carrying a boy and a girl, himself. He began directing the kids inside, telling them to run and keep running. Glenda and I caught up to him, and we guided the rest of the kids inside. The plane was very close, high above us, coming in directly from the east. I shut the tunnel doors, and we began running down the tunnel, we adults staying back to make sure none of the kids fell behind.

We ran and ran until the bomb explosions slammed us to the floor and crashed through our eardrums. A heavy rush of air and dirt billowed into us as the tunnel behind us collapsed. Soon after, another dust cloud hit us from the other direction. I realized the north entrance to the underground complex had been hit, too. We were strewn through an intact section of tunnel amidst a dense cloud of dust. The lights went out.

Chapter 4
Collapse

An emergency light clicked on ahead of us revealing the deep haze of dust in the air and kids lying on the floor, spread out forward for a couple dozen yards. Some of the children cried and coughed. The two I had been carrying had landed on their butts when I fell and were sitting up looking confused. Others began rolling onto their knees or sitting up, depending on how they had landed. Glenda was ahead of me, and Jason was behind, another emergency light glowing beyond him. The dust hit my lungs and made me cough. We all began coughing.

I said loudly, "Cover your mouths with your shirts so you don't breathe this dust. Let's head down to the lab."

We stood up slowly and collected ourselves. The crying died down to grumbles and sniffs. Glenda began leading us toward the lab, walking carefully. All of us covered our mouths with the tops of our shirts or our sleeves. We walked at the pace of the youngest children, and after quite a while of walking in silence, we arrived at the service entrance to the trash collection room. The door was closed, and I knew someone inside would have closed it – because we hadn't – likely to keep the dust out, I thought.

I pounded on the door twice to let anyone inside know we were there, and then I opened it. Emergency lights glared from the opposite wall. The air was clearer here. I recognized Renzo and Craig inside near the door to the lab hallway. Glenda and I directed everyone through the outer door, and Jason followed us inside with the last of the children. I shut the door quickly to keep out as much floating dust as possible.

Craig rushed over to us. "What's going on? What happened?"

"They bombed us," I said. "The base, too."

"Who bombed us? Who are these kids?"

"The kids were up there when I went outside. We saw the plane banking toward us after they hit the base, so we ran down the tunnel. It collapsed farther back. The same with the north entrance, I assume, from the second rush of dusty air that hit us. We barely made it."

Others were crowded in the main hallway outside the door, trying to see what was happening. Craig and Renzo stared at us, trying to take in what they were seeing and what I had told them. I noticed how dust-covered we were. We looked like we had been in a cave-in, which we had.

Craig said, getting a better handle on the situation, "Okay. Okay. It's knocked out our power, maybe even the generators themselves. We have to assess that situation. Let's get these children cleaned up first."

Sophia shuffled through the crowd and into the room, immediately beginning to look over the children, which Glenda had already started doing, herself. None appeared injured. Sam stood toward the back and stared at me as if this were my fault.

I said, "Let's get them into the Great Room and see how everyone's doing."

We filed through the doorway, past the others of the Family who were in the hallway, and into the Great Room. A pair of emergency lights cast long shadows across the tables and chairs inside. We slid some chairs away so the children could sit on the large tables, and we began looking closer at the children. They gathered in subgroups near their closest friends from among the larger group, showing keen familiarity with each other. I counted 26 kids.

Ginny came in with damp towels, and we began wiping faces and looking for injuries. It seemed that everyone had weathered the ordeal unscathed aside from getting covered in dirt and dust and getting a few scratches. The children had taken it mostly in stride, maybe because they had been experiencing life-threatening situations for weeks, and they'd seen worse. We all knew about the hell that was out there. Though they were initially cautious of us adults, they warmed to us quickly except for Sam, who stood apart. As I wiped the grime from the two kids I had carried, I noticed Jason approach Sam.

The boy showed neither interest nor apprehension, his expression neutral as Jason stood above him and then sat in a chair next to him.

Jason said, "You have a tough group here."

Sam nodded.

"We want to help you. As you saw, we have a big problem. We're trapped down here, and we may not be able to get the power back up. We don't know who bombed us, either."

To everyone, Glenda said, "Ben was at the base. Who else was still there?"

Craig replied, "Douglas, Danielle, and Andrew. Is that it?" He looked around. Sophia nodded, and Aiden, who was just coming through the door, agreed.

"Who would bomb the base?" I asked.

Jason asked, "Did you see the plane? What type of plane was it?"

"Just before we went into the tunnel, I could see it pretty clearly. It looked like a B-52."

"Ours?"

"No idea. Gray like the one we used."

Craig said, "Aiden, can you come with me? Let's go have a look at the generators." He and Aiden left.

Glenda said, "So, we're trapped in here."

"Wait," Jason said. "Javier and Ellen. They went through an air intake vent. They got out of the lab that way. Are they here?"

Someone called for them in the hallway, and they both stepped into the room. They had become a couple recently, and they were the ones who had figured out that the Upstream troops were stationed at the Space Force Base.

Jason asked them, "Can we all get out of here through that air intake tunnel you found?"

They both nodded. Ellen said, "If it wasn't bombed, I don't see why not. It seems designed for easy access as long as it's not locked. We sawed the lock off. It's a steep climb, though."

"Do we want to leave?" asked Glenda.

"I think we should consider it," I replied. "Even if we get the generators working again. Obviously, someone knows we're here and wants us dead."

"Maybe they'll think they took us out by hitting the two entrances," said Jason.

"True," I said. "And we are pretty well set up here if the power's still working. But if they see us using that air vent as an entrance, we're dead. Assuming whoever it is has troops on the ground."

"At least, we need to go up and check out the situation," Jason said. "We should go see how bad the base is, too, if we can. Maybe there are survivors. Maybe Ben . . . ." He sat, thinking for a while and didn't say more.

"Yes, we should go see," Glenda agreed.

Sophia asked the children, "Would you like something to eat?"

They all either nodded or said yes, except for Sam, who stated, "I'll go up top with you."

Jason stood up. "Okay. Ellen and Javier, can you lead the way? Who else is going?"

I said I would go, but Glenda wanted to stay and help with the kids. It was just the five of us going up. I told Daisy to stay. We brushed ourselves off and headed out. We collected rifles and flashlights along the way. Ellen and Javier led us to the generator room, telling us that the air access branched off from the air handlers near there. Craig and Aiden were checking a breaker panel when we entered the generator room. Trong was with them. One of the two massive generators was running, but the power it was supposed to provide was not getting out to the lab.

Craig said, "A main breaker is tripped, and it won't reset. We have a problem down the line somewhere."

"Is there anything we can do?" I asked. "We want to go out through an air intake to see what's up top."

"We don't know what to do, ourselves," he replied. "I think we'll follow some of the lines, if possible. I don't know much about this."

The rest of us didn't know much about A/C power grids, either.

I said, "We'll help troubleshoot after we have a look above. If we can't get the power working, we'll have to leave the lab sooner rather than later, so we need to know the conditions up top."

The air handling units were in the room next to the generators, and they were not operating because the power was off. They had multiple large air intakes, some for circulating internal air only, and one that led up to the surface for fresh air. One also had a door. Ellen opened the door and shined her flashlight into the darkness. With our flashlights to light the way, we all ducked inside the small space and found a very tight stairway inside a metal pipe leading up, with room enough for us to climb the stairs single file. A wide air duct ran inside this larger pipe we had entered, running below the stairs, possibly for venting exhaust out. Initially, the slope maintained one continuous angle with landings every half story or so, and eventually, it turned to the right at a landing, and then, after a while, turned to the right again. I assumed we were climbing the same distance as the stairs at the north entrance. That was 14 stories, approximately 200 feet.

This meant that the climb took a healthy amount of effort. Finally, we reached the top of the stairs at a longer landing that arched up before going down again, where a drain sat below an opening at the top of a ladder. The duct pipe that ran below the stairs shot off in the opposite direction. I could see light coming through a bend in the pipe above. Ellen climbed the 10-foot ladder to reach the bend, where she crawled sideways out of sight. We followed her. Past the bend, a heavy metal grate covered a wide opening to the outside. To the left of the grate was a small door, which Ellen swung inward. We exited to find that the opening outside was backed by a mound of dirt, and we stepped down to the ground below it. I checked out the mound around the exit pipe and found that the whole construction was covered in grass and bushes. From a short distance away, it would look like a small hill, not an entrance to an underground facility.

I heard the sound of a vehicle from the southeast and told everyone to get down. I peered over the mound, and saw a Jeep. It stopped where the road became rubble, more than half a mile from us. Just beyond that was where the raised entrance to the main facility tunnel had been. The whole area was now churned up and covered with overlapping craters. Four people got out of the Jeep. The distant figures stood surveying the damage.

Steven S. Patchin

Steven S. Patchin

Steven S. Patchin

Chapter 5
Interlinked

We huddled behind the berm, and I watched the four people who were at the edge of the rubble in the long shadows of the rising sun. They didn't appear to be soldiers and weren't wearing fatigues. As I studied them from this distance, I realized that one of them seemed to have the familiar attributes of Ben Stoffer, that perfectly round head of his and the not-so-buzzed buzz cut that had grown out since I met him almost two months ago. I decided that this was Ben along with the other three who had stayed back at the base when the rest of us had returned here after our BB mission.

"It's Ben!" I said, and stood up.

I began trudging toward them across the mottled plain. The others followed me. To the northeast, the ground was churned up and pockmarked just like the area over the main entrance. That had been the north entrance to the underground facilities, now destroyed, too. The group next to the Jeep didn't see us until we were almost upon them as we approached them from behind. I was excited to see them, especially Ben.

What a difference from when I had first met Ben on the street near my apartment. I had been wrapped up in the insane derangement surrounding Ben, all the ridiculous anger and hatred focused on him, which was really the beginning of The Crash. I had bought into it myself, and I had not been happy to see Ben standing in the street with parachute lines connected to him as he demanded my help. At the time, I had wanted to go back to my apartment and continue wallowing in vodka and girls in magazines. Instead, I had gone with Ben to help him and had wound up on this even more insane adventure. It seemed like a whole lifetime had passed since then.

"Holy shit! You made it!" I said. I went straight to Ben and hugged him.

He seemed just as happy to see us, especially me. He leaned back from the embrace and looked me in the eyes. "How the hell did you survive this?" He waved his hand toward the rough and uneven ground where the tunnel entrance had been.

"The lab is still intact, everyone's fine, but the main tunnels collapsed. We just came up through an air intake access back there. But what about you? Why weren't you hit in the bombing?"

"We were on our way here when we saw the plane. We stopped in a neighborhood to see what it was doing, and that's when it bombed the base. Then it hit the lab too. We stayed where we were and watched it fly off to the west. When we thought it wasn't coming back, we drove here."

Douglas, Danielle, and Andrew stood next to him. I greeted them, and the others exchanged greetings, too. The bandage on Ben's face was dirty, and a dark stain seeped through the center. I now realized that Ben's speech had been muffled and lispy. His gunshot wound had gotten worse, and his shattered teeth were likely infected, too.

We stood studying the destruction, and Ben noticed Sam. He looked at me and then at Sam.

I said, "Ben, this is Sam. He has a group of children with him, and we just met. They're down in the lab."

Ben extended his hand to Sam.

Sam said, "I know you," then shook Ben's hand perfunctorily.

"A lot of people thought they knew me and got pretty upset about it. I hope you withhold judgment."

"They said we should meet you."

"Right," I jumped in. "It seems the children saw us in our Iter Anima, and they were already connected around the world with other kids. But the BB broke that communication."

Ben shook his head. "We try to fix one thing and break another." He looked at Sam. "I'm sorry."

"They said you could fix it."

"Uh," I said. "I didn't say we could fix it. I said we needed to talk to Ben."

We waited for Ben to reply, but he only stared silently across the up-turned field.

As I was about to give a further explanation, Ben said, "I really can't fix anything. The chain reaction that led to The Crash apparently hasn't stopped. We tried to fix the distorted brains, but we've only made things worse. I don't—"

"I wouldn't say that," I interrupted. "I need to tell you about the girl in the Amazon rainforest, Jaguar. She—"

"You know about Jaguar?" Sam said, wide-eyed.

"What? You know her?"

"The girl in the jungle. She's like a cat. Jaguar. Yes."

Okay, these kids were more connected than I thought. But how could they know about Jaguar, even if they communicated with other children around the world? What were the odds?

"I guess we both know her," I said. "I kind of gave her that name . . . ."

Sam was still in awe. He said, "We don't know her, but some of us dream about her. She's with her tribe, and they're headed out of the jungle."

"Yep, that's her," I said.

Ben looked perplexed, glancing between Sam and me.

I said to Ben, "I talked to Jaguar recently. Shit, just a couple hours ago. She said . . . she *showed* me what I hadn't seen before, that our minds can be open. That the BBs worked. That what's left of humanity is changing. You really did make a difference, Ben. We all made a difference, even beyond resetting some twisted brains. There's something else happening, and it's helping us connect with each other more deeply than we had anticipated. It's different with these children, too. Maybe all children."

Ben stared at me, thinking. "The troops at the base who appeared to have had the isolated variant of The Crash did seem better when I checked them after the BB. We were going to test them at the lab later . . . I guess that's a moot point, now."

He was noticeably drained and not enthusiastic, even while talking about his success, but we all were facing the likely loss of everyone at the base, too.

Ben said, "And we were going to go out to look for survivors in the city later. But here we are with more problems of our own. And these children . . . ."

"Yeah," I said. "And we were having power problems down in the lab when we came up here. A generator was running, but power wasn't getting out to the facility. I don't know if they got it fixed. We came up here to see what we could see, and we found you. You said the plane didn't return. We don't see any troops around, at least not yet. Maybe we should go back down to the lab and see about the power."

I turned to Sam. "We don't know what to do right yet. We've got to sort out our situation. But I do want to talk to you about Jaguar." To everyone else I said, "Shall we go back down into the lab?"

Everyone agreed.

Ben said, "I didn't know there was another way in besides the two. It's an air vent?"

Jason replied, "Yes, Javier and Ellen found it. It's a lot of tight stairs. And we shouldn't leave the Jeep near here, either, in case someone figures out we have this other way in."

Javier volunteered, "We can take the Jeep further over by the dirt road where the main tunnel entrance was, leave it in one of the bigger craters. Ellen and I can walk back."

"That would be great," said Jason. "Thanks."

Chapter 6
Lucid

We went back down through the vent access and then straight to the generator room. AC power to the lab still was not working, but various battery-powered emergency lights continued to provide some illumination. When Craig saw Ben, the relief showing on Craig's expression was so strong that I thought he would cry.

Craig set down the power meter he was holding and strode straight to Ben with a smile and his hand extended. They shook hands, both glad to be alive and glad to see each other. Everyone acknowledged everyone else and exchanged brief explanations of what had happened to them. Then, they got back to the task at hand, which was figuring out why electricity wasn't getting from the generator to the rest of the lab.

Technology wasn't easily accessible to the rest of humanity anymore, either, I thought. Could it be that technology had run its course? The idea crossed my mind, and I put it aside. Determination could fix anything, right?

All of us poured ourselves into the problem. We started at the generator, searching, studying, analyzing every wire, every connection, every circuit. We found nothing broken. We worked outward from there, along main power lines, opening panels, checking fuses and breakers. We followed lines from room to room, and checked electrical boxes we hadn't even known were there. They hung from walls like ghouls waiting for Halloween.

Line after line, room after room, we followed the pathways, but those pathways remained empty of electricity, and no removable roadblocks to power showed themselves to us. We went over all we could. We checked junction boxes and distribution boxes, control panels and breaker boxes. We found nothing we could fix. And with the power elusive, we couldn't conceive of how we could remain down in the lab facility for long. We would get no fresh air, and the loss of refrigeration would soon spoil a lot of the food. None of Ben's inventions would work without power. All we had left was ourselves and what we could carry.

Finally after spending all day trying to find the problem and failing,

Ben declared, "We don't have a solution, here. Let's get a few hour's sleep and figure out what to do in the morning. I think we'll have to leave the lab."

That night, I found myself with Jaguar's tribe. Sam had mentioned that some of the children in his group had experienced dreams or conscious connections with them. I went to sleep thinking about that until I knew I was doing something more than dreaming. I hadn't fallen asleep until a few hours before dawn. In Brazil, where the Zo'é tribe were forging their way through the jungle with the goal of reaching the eastern seashore in a month, dawn broke through the fog. The tribe, with its 38 members, were packing for another day of travel.

Jaguar immediately knew I was among them in spirit and said, "Welcome."

The emotions I felt upon hearing that single word involved everything I had lived through during the past two months. The fights, the killing, the insanity, the danger, the pain, the sorrow, the love, the music, the connections, the people, the successes, the failures, the deaths. They flooded my soul.

I thought of Lauren, and through the hazy morning sun, she walked tall in the jungle. Light danced in dazzling rays that flickered around her beautiful form, creating a halo of hope. A monkey called in the distance. Bright green leaves glowed with an uplifting luminescence. Mist shifted, a shimmering vapor.

I held out my arms and brought myself closer to Lauren. We embraced. Air coursed through my lungs without breath. I existed with no desires, no needs, no fears, nothing wanting. The eternal now. It persisted, a note played by an orchestra, the first note of a symphony, a note that never ended. I gave myself to it.

Time traveled apart from me and came back. Lauren was gone. I found myself moving with the Zo'é tribe. They were very efficient in negotiating the dense jungle even while carrying their belongings and various pets. It was a choreographed dance among the copious shades of green vegetation and shifting shafts of sunlight. They kept a steady pace but were not in a hurry. A few of the adult men had taken point and watched out for danger. Jaguar remained near the back. I joined her.

"You've met some of the children where you are," she said. "And they're the same ones we've lost in our connections."

"Yes," I replied. "We only recently found out that you were connected and that they knew you specifically."

"It was a few days ago for us that I found other children around the world, and then some of them disappeared when we sent the big waves. Those were near you, and now I see them through you. They came to you, and you have met them."

"Yes. But our waves stopped their connections. They want us to fix it."

She walked in silence for a while. "The craziness that infected the world did something different to the children."

"But not to your tribe," I said.

"Not to everybody, but to all the children."

"*All* the children? How do you know?"

"Because I'm a child. I saw it late, but I did see. I have been trying to guide them, but I also have my tribe. None of the adults here caught the mind sickness, and we are leaving the jungle with much ahead to do. I try to help the others when we aren't traveling. I'm seeing more and more children when I reach out."

"And you know of Sam and his group . . ."

"He is like you. And like Jason."

"What do you mean?"

"Trees have roots, trunks, branches, and leaves. All are connected. Our bodies have brains and hearts. Arms, legs, hands, and feet. All are connected. The Earth has a center, and mountains, lakes, forests, sky. All are connected. The sky has the sun, the planets, and the stars. All are connected. Life has its essence, its smallest parts, and insects, plants, and animals. All are connected. But most people do not know how they are connected. They just *are*."

I waited open-minded, knowing she had more to say.

She continued, "Most are not *aware* how deep the connections go, even though the connections are there. They might see when they sleep, but they awake and forget. They might remember from before they were born, but they think it a dream. It is hidden from them because they are busy walking, staying warm, getting food, eating, staying safe. Fighting, loving, dying. They don't remember. It is *behind* what they know.

"Recently, most have died because their connections were torn apart, even though they did not know the connections were there. These were different connections within themselves and among other people and them. They knew something was gone, and they only wanted to find what was lost. They forgot about food and sleep. They saw only lies that their minds told them, what was *not* there, and they could not see what *was* there. They lost the connections, tried to take back what was lost that they did not understand, and blamed others for it. They died because they lost these connections and fought to get them back, not even knowing what they were.

"Now, those who remain are finding some old connections again. For them, they are finding connections they did not know were lost. And when they find them, they understand that what they did not know was hidden. What had been hidden from them is becoming known. And some help show the way to others. Some are like wind in the trees, water over the rocks, but also like birds who call warning and lead the rest to safety, becoming a big wing in the sky, flying as one.

"You are like wind, water, and birds. You flow among it all and help the others see, then show them the way. You and Jason and Sam . . . and others. The people *hear* you."

I understood Jaguar's meaning because I *saw* the things that happened. I had experienced what we had done. I said to her, "And they hear you, too."

"They do." It was a statement without ego, a fact of reality.

"How did you discover all this?" I asked.

"I showed you the tree as it showed me life. From the very smallest of the small through every part of the Earth and to every living thing, the tree showed me our essence. And you showed me, too. Without you, I only *saw*. With you, I saw what to do."

She was telling me that I had made a difference. *We* had made a difference by finding our way to her and her tribe, and that was also thanks to Lauren, too. The connections really did run deep. The tree had helped her see the essence, part of which was DNA, something she did not have a word for.

"Okay," I said. "Yes, we do see the connections. We see the *Cosmic Consciousness* and know that we are part of it. And we know that we lead others. But where are we leading them?"

"We are coming out of the jungle so that we can find that answer." she replied.

I took her to mean that coming out of the jungle was what she and her tribe were doing literally, but that the rest of us were doing the same, coming out of the jungles where we had been entangled in order to find ourselves again. And I agreed with her.

As I moved along with the tribe, staying close to Jaguar, I began to feel the presence of the tribe as part of myself and something bigger than myself. I lost the point of focus that kept me near only Jaguar and now felt bigger as I perceived this place through multiple viewpoints at once, as if my body were expanding to the size of a grove of trees or a mountain lake. I knew it wasn't my body that was expanding but my mind. I was feeling the connections becoming wider-reaching, growing toward a wholeness that had always been there, but that I was only now touching.

I resolved to be more conscious of reaching these connections intentionally. It seemed that we might not always need to follow the involved process of gathering around a fire and drumming in order to reach these new connections. I had just gone to Jaguar and her tribe through the state of partial wakefulness and partial sleep. And she was making her connections without even using that delicate balance of mindfulness.

As I had these thoughts, my mind went its own direction again. I swung into a state of ideas and images jumping around me. Along the way, I must have slept, because I eventually found myself becoming aware of having been asleep.

. . . .

I awoke to Daisy lying beside me, peacefully sleeping, and Lauren was there, too. I felt her presence in my being.

Welcome. So be it.

The room remained completely dark, no emergency lights. I put my arm across Daisy's back and did nothing.

The world lives in darkness and nothingness. My thoughts returned through nothingness. I imagined the light. It was a moth fluttering in dead stillness, searching, straining for direction, beating its wings against the night. Alighting on freedom and unity, the right place. And I waited, suspended. I felt the Cosmic Consciousness.

I sat up in bed. Daisy stretched. I felt her muscles quivering through the mattress as she prepared for whatever was next. I stood. Daisy jumped down to the floor. I clicked my flashlight on and saw the closed door in the ring of illumination.

I could go through it. I *would* go through it. And the world would not be the same.

Chapter 7
Stock

We met in the Great Room, the space as full with people as I'd ever seen it. I had taken to making notes to myself about what we were going through, having decided that I would write about all this, so I counted everyone. I had even begun writing in a used notebook that I had found before I got some fresh notebooks out of the office supplies cabinet. At the moment, I just took mental notes.

To start, the core of the original Family, in addition to Ben and me, as well as the active lab people, numbered 16. We had lost four recently, including Chieko, Victoria, Leon, and Lauren. There were two crashed lab people, Asami and Jackson, who had, until recently, remained in isolation while they recovered. There was one person, Phillips, who we had found hiding in the Genetrix section of the underground facility, and we had locked him in a room because of his dangerous attitude. We released him to participate with us or not. There were the five scientists who we found locked up and forgotten by Upstream, all of whom had been instrumental in helping Ben develop the Beep and the BBs. There were the 12 survivors from the neighborhood who we had saved with the Beep. And now, there were 26 children.

This brought the total number of people in our group to 62 and one dog.

Who was "officially" part of the Family and who wasn't in this unique cluster of people was unclear. There really wasn't an *official* anything. The Family had originated with Jason and Glenda and, at first, consisted of only those who joined the couple in the city during the earlier days of their crashed afflictions. Ben and I joined them but were not considered Family until sometime later. I still wasn't sure if Ben was technically thought of as Family. I became accepted as one of them during the situation when I joined most of the Family in the tunnel to address the troops who were up top. This was when I first consciously felt our connection, and we had created an explosion that leveled the troops and everything around the tunnel entrance, evaporating or burning what was up there, including the building that had housed the entrance, leaving only the entrance structure itself.

When Lauren joined our group, not being crashed, she hadn't become part of the Family then. But sometime along the way, she did become a Family member. As for those in Ben's crew, some of them had become Family through osmosis. Certainly Craig, Ben's closest assistant, and Renzo, the ever-inventive and handy lab tech were both included. And Trong, the highly skilled electronics tech. But the Genetrix people we found hadn't seemed to be Family, and neither were the survivors we had rescued.

Given the evolution of the Family, with new members joining naturally rather than subscribing to it as though it were a club, I began to wonder who among our current group would not be considered Family. Phillips wasn't Family. And it was too early to consider the children as members, but maybe they could be, though I doubted they would agree. At least Sam wouldn't. But maybe the survivors we had rescued could be Family.

Our Iter Anima with the BBs was an integration of technology and minds, an infusion of people around the world. During that transcendent experience, we all had felt that the Family could include everyone who was willing and able to be part of it, certainly the groups we had touched with our minds.

This left me with questions about definitions more than it revealed concrete designations. What constituted the Family? And what defined a Family member? In the strict sense, based on how the Family was formed, its membership might be very narrowly defined. But in a wider sense, the Family could be Humanity itself. That begged the question of what was Humanity, a question I was in no position to try to answer.

The Great Room accommodated everyone in the lab, but there were not enough seats for all of us. A few had to stand. Only a few of the children took seats, most of their group having gathered together along the left wall. Everyone was eating, even those who had to hold their plates while standing.

Sophia, Javier, Jon, and Ellen had set up food, orange juice, and coffee at the back of the room, including plates and plastic utensils. Using a couple small gas camp stoves they had found, they made French toast from the last of the bread, which had been thawing in the walk-in freezer, and from powdered eggs. They brewed coffee in multiple small pots and filled two large plastic dispensers, which they set up along with stacks of paper cups.

I fed Daisy. We all ate and chatted in the dimming glow of the battery-powered emergency lights. Someone had smartly gone around and disconnected many of the lights so that we could use them later as needed. Even so, with these lights reconnected, they were fading fast. They weren't intended to last more than a few hours, and the lab's power had been out for a full day.

The children remained standoffish. Even the younger ones didn't seem interested in associating with anyone but themselves, although they tolerated Sophia and Glenda, who made sure they got something to eat and had helped them get settled in a room last night.

Ben stood up front and waited while everyone quieted down. He was pale and weak. When he had our attention, he said, "We see no choice but to leave the lab. The bombing disabled our power, and we can't stay here. Our only exit is through an air vent service tunnel. It involves negotiating very narrow stairs that lead up 14 stories to the top from the west end of the lab complex. There are others of you who are much better qualified than me to lead us out of here. I would suggest we organize into smaller groups so each group can have a different responsibility and carry certain equipment or supplies. Craig and I will oversee the lab crew. But I defer to someone else to take the lead of the whole group."

He looked directly at me, as if to say that he wanted me to step up, but didn't think I was ready at the moment. I certainly could have done it, but the better choice was Jason. Ben turned to Jason, who was not far from him. Jason stepped over next to Ben.

Jason said, "Ben's right about organizing into smaller groups with different tasks. Our primary groups are the lab crew, the original Family, the neighborhood survivors, and now the children.

"I suggest we organize this way: As Ben said, he and Craig, along with the Genetrix techs, will work with the lab crew, as they always have. Survivors from the neighborhood, it appears you have recovered a lot and gotten stronger, but I don't want to put too much on you. Carry what you can, and Ginny, if you will help them, I think that would work pretty well."

Ginny was typically quiet, but she was also very helpful and intuitive when things needed to be done. She nodded to Jason and walked around a table to stand next to most of the survivors who were sitting at two of the tables.

"And Sophia, you've been with the survivors all along. You know what you're doing."

Sophia replied, "We might need a little help getting some of them up the stairs."

Mitchell, who was one of the survivors, and who had volunteered for the task of monitoring the Jeep radio when we had begun working with the Upstream troops, said, "I can help with that. I'm feeling pretty good."

Jason said, "Excellent. And for the children, Sam, they're your group. But I suggest Glenda stay close with you, and Aiden, too."

Aiden was already standing next to Sam. He was only a few years older than Sam and was just getting past puberty. He had learned a lot since our journey began. I had spent time with him, showing him what I could, giving him responsibility and tasks that he always accepted and performed well, even though he made a few mistakes, one leading to the deaths of two Upstream prisoners. He had become good with a rifle, too. Along with Glenda, the two of them would offer protection and emotional security for the children, if they needed it.

"The rest of the Family," said Jason, "we all need to be on the alert for whoever might want to attack us. We have no idea who bombed the base and the lab. We don't know if they have troops on the ground. We don't know if the crashed, those who are still alive, are dangerous or recovering. So, we will do what we've done so surprisingly well: We'll be armed, alert for danger, and we'll deal with things as they come. And we'll fight when we have to. We need to spread out among our other groups and work as their protection. That's a start."

He paused to see if anyone had anything to say.

I said, "Makes sense. We'll just have to adapt to what we find out there. Should we discuss where we want to go?"

"We were concentrating on getting away from Upstream until we found a way to work with them," Glenda said. "And our main goal was to help the crashed. Once we got here to the lab, we didn't have to worry about food or a safe place to sleep. When we leave here, survival will become our priority. Without the lab and what they had at the Space Force Base, we won't be able to help survivors much, because we'll be trying to survive, ourselves. I think that pretty soon, we'll need to decide how we want to live."

I recalled what Lauren and I had discussed. We had envisioned a life for ourselves, maybe on the outskirts of the city. Of course, we didn't get deep into the difficult parts. It was an idealized vision of living peacefully in a country-like setting. We hadn't imagined the particulars, yet. The particulars are what life is made of.

Glenda continued, "We are not just a group of people simply trying to survive an apocalypse. With our Iter Anima, we've made connections throughout the world." She looked at me. "And it's likely that the mind connections and communication are becoming more fluid."

She was referring to how Jaguar had contacted me yesterday, and I hadn't even discussed with them what I had experienced with Jaguar this morning. I knew Glenda was right about becoming more fluid. A lot had happened to us, and we had been so focused on task after task that we hadn't spent much time considering the wider effects that Iter Anima would have on our lives. Really, our having discovered Iter Anima and connected with so many people in so many places had changed everything, even though we hadn't discussed it much among ourselves.

She said, "I don't see us going out there and just surviving. We can't carry on as though an apocalypse hasn't happened. We can't ignore the problems that caused the apocalypse, either. We can't do what we had been doing before. We also can't turn away from what we have discovered and just survive. But we do need to remember the good things humans have done that have brought humanity this far. We can't abandon thousands of years of tradition. It's a lot to think about."

Craig spoke up. "Then we need to decide what it means for us to live in this new situation. The world has changed. Humanity has changed. What does that mean to us?"

Ben remained standing to the side, looking tired and in pain. His face was puffy and his eyes sunken. I was worried about his health and was about to say something to him when he leaned forward and sat on the floor. Glenda reached him first. The others up front stooped down next to him, too.

Ben said, "Sorry, sorry. I'm okay, just tired."

Glenda felt his forehead and said, "Ben, you need more than sleep. Let me see your teeth."

He opened his mouth, and Glenda looked inside.

"My god. Your whole mouth seems infected. I don't know how you're still walking around at all. You need antibiotics, at the very least."

"I was taking some–" Ben passed out.

Steven S. Patchin

Chapter 8
Adjustments

Glenda and Jason caught Ben before his head could hit the floor.

Craig pushed aside some chairs. "Let's get him on a table."

They lifted him onto the closest table and laid him down, putting someone's jacket under his head. Ben opened his eyes but didn't talk.

Craig said, "He was taking an antibiotic before, but he really needed to have a couple of those broken teeth pulled. We can't do that now. I'll go see what other antibiotics we have in our medical supplies."

Craig left the room. Ben mumbled something I couldn't understand and then closed his eyes. He seemed to be sleeping. There wasn't much else we could do for Ben, ourselves.

I thought of Craig's last comment about what all the recent changes in the world might mean and what Glenda was saying about our connections to the good things in the past.

I said, "Our Iter Anima does mean something new to humanity. And the way the communication works might mean it's more accessible than we thought. We put a lot of effort into making it happen. We didn't know another way to try, but it worked. I had wondered if we could make connections like that naturally and possibly more casually. Could we have used it to talk to someone at the base, for example? Or someone in the next room? Did we really need to get together around a fire and create a rhythm first?

"I believe my questions were answered yesterday when Jaguar reached out to me from the Amazon forest, and I didn't get the impression that she had gone to great lengths to do it. It seemed to me that it was an obvious and natural thing to her, much like simply talking to someone next to you. I assume that if she can do it, others can, too. So, if you want to talk about what all this means and how we want to live, we are looking at a massive leap in human ability. We need to keep that in mind. And, Iter Anima isn't just about communication. It's also about a new way for us to see the universe. I can't explain what it means, but we do have to consider it."

Jason said, "We certainly have many things to consider, and I don't want to disregard our newly discovered abilities, but we're not going to decide everything at once. We got here one step at a time. Now, with Ben so unwell, we can't all march into the city and start fresh. He can't travel like this. Someone needs to stay here and help him. And that means we need to be more careful about not being seen leaving the lab. We need to adapt constantly while keeping in mind that we have new abilities and resources at our disposal."

Javier said, from the middle of the room, "We should choose a place to go first, even if it turns out we can't stay there. Ellen and I didn't see anyone outside when we left the Jeep up there. But we don't know what it's like farther into the city. There's a school pretty close, but maybe that's too close."

"We need to get farther away from the park in order to avoid potential troops who might be watching the area," said Jason. "We can assume that the BB set the crashed straight, but we have to be prepared in case it didn't. And with a group of this size, I think we should go into the city rather than away from it, because of the resources that are in stores."

Jason looked over to the group of children and said, "Sam, you've been out there all this time. Can you suggest a place to go?"

Sam sat on the edge of a table with his arms crossed. He said, "We just want to leave if you can't fix what you broke."

"I'm sorry about what happened. We want to help, but we need somewhere safe to go first. Can you work with us so we can get set up somewhere else? And then we can try to help you?"

"You said we needed to talk to Ben, but he's sick."

"You're right. He's not well, and we're trying to help him, too. Everything we do depends on doing something else first. Nothing's simple. And we can use your help."

I thought Jason was working on two levels here. He wanted the children's trust, and though we could find somewhere to go without Sam's suggestion, he wanted to turn things around and show that we needed the children as much as they might need us. I didn't think Jason saw this as manipulation. He likely thought it just made sense. I probably wouldn't have bothered. If the kids wanted to leave, they were free to do so. This was yet another reason why Jason was a good choice to take charge, even at his young age, barely in his 20s.

Jason asked Sam, "Are there places you stayed that you think would be good for all of us? Where did you go during all these weeks of The Crash?"

Sam relaxed some and put his arms to his sides. "We didn't stay in one place. We wanted to keep away from the adults. We even saw you out there when the helicopter crashed. You knocked out all those soldiers. It didn't hurt us then, but when you used the plane, we lost contact with all the other kids everywhere else. Why do you have to keep messing with everyone?"

That was the question of the decade, maybe the century. There sure as hell wasn't a good answer for it. I could have told him that what we did worked, for a lot of people anyway, and that our minds could see further than ever before, but what good would it do for the children? We didn't even know yet what good it would do for us. We had made a mess of the world, tried to fix it, and had taken away what the children had only just found.

Jason replied, "I can't deny that everything seems to be a mess. But if you work with us, we'll do what we can to help you."

Craig returned with a small medical bag and went straight to Ben. Elizabeth went up to help him. He took out a syringe and a vial of liquid.

Craig said, "I found Amoxicillin."

He gave the syringe and vial to Elizabeth, and she dug into the bag to retrieve an alcohol wipe. Craig took out a blood pressure cuff and stethoscope, then waited for Elizabeth to administer the antibiotic. When she finished, he strapped the cuff around Ben's arm, put the stethoscope's earpieces in his ears, and held the bell to listen for the pressure. He followed the blood pressure procedure, pumping up the cuff with the ball, and then pulled off the earpieces, looking very concerned.

"Eighty-eight over fifty-eight. His blood pressure's too low. He's probably in sepsis. Let's get him back to the lab so we can hook him up to oxygen and put a fluid drip in him."

Jason, Aiden, Javier, and I took hold of Ben and carried him to the lab hub. Elizabeth, Sophia, and Glenda followed. We placed him on a gurney and rolled him into a medical room. Craig and Elizabeth went about treating Ben, and the rest of us stayed out of the way. When Ben was set up with oxygen and IV fluids, neither requiring any electricity, Sophia rolled a chair over to his gurney and settled in to attend him. She had been instrumental in taking care of Glenda after Glenda had been shot. She had nursed the survivors back to health, and generally served as the physical health backbone of our entire group. Without her, many of us would have been worse off, and Glenda might have died.

Craig said, "Elizabeth, Sophia, and I will stay here with Ben. We can't leave."

We all agreed and understood that they were doing what they could for Ben. The rest of us returned to the Great Room and gave everyone an update.

Jason sat at the corner of a table up front and addressed Sam, who was still at his table. "What do you say? Can you work with us for a bit, so we can get settled somewhere else?"

Sam stared at him with a forced neutral expression. "Okay."

Jason stood up. "Alright. Let's gather all the supplies we can carry, any containers or backpacks you think will work. Take things we can't likely find in stores, but also bring food that won't spoil. We'll stick to the group structure we discussed. A few of us will get together and pick an initial destination. Can we leave this evening when it's dark?"

We all agreed. Jason pulled me aside. We went over to Sam and invited him to sit down with us while Glenda escorted the other children out of the room, and everyone else left, too. We sat at one of the long tables.

Jason asked Sam, "What's it like out there? How did you kids find each other?"

Chapter 9
Aliens

Sam was hesitant at first, but began his story and became more enthusiastic in the telling as he continued. I found that he was pretty sharp with describing details and giving his impressions of what had happened. I began to see an older soul that, at first, appeared incongruent with the child before me, but soon, he reminded me of Jaguar with the wisdom she possessed beyond her physical years. Was it actually *younger* souls that had more wisdom than us older people? Or was it something else that I was seeing?

The beginning of his story brought me back into the hell of The Crash, someplace that I didn't want to go. It reminded me of Jason's story but with a colossal difference: Sam didn't go insane. It was quite the opposite. But he was surrounded by the crashed, which he discovered in one wild moment of horror.

. . . .

Sam's father pounded on the door of his room and then swung it open. "Fuck that," the man yelled at Sam and his brother. "You little motherfuckers. You think you can hide from me? You do whatever the fuck you want, don't you? You little pieces of shit. It was you who called those people here. I know it."

Sam was sitting on his bed playing with his action figures. His little brother, Shane, was on his own bed closer to the door, doing a puzzle. Their parents had been arguing a lot lately, and the brothers had heard yelling a few minutes ago but were trying ignore it. Everyone seemed irritated lately, the adults anyway. Sam and his brother avoided them as much as they could. They liked it when their parents were at work, partly because it was summer vacation, and their parents had let them stay home instead of putting them in a summer program, but lately, they liked their parents being gone because their parents were making them nervous with their yelling and complaining. When their parents were home, the brothers either stayed in their room or stayed outside. They wouldn't go near their parents until they were told to do so.

On this summer Saturday, Sam and Shane had been outside most of the day and had only recently come into their bedroom, closing the door behind them. They had heard yelling down the street and felt uncomfortable being outside, a feeling that had been growing stronger in the past few days. But it wasn't better inside.

When their father opened the door of their room and cussed at them, it was the first time Sam had ever heard their father cuss directly at them, and with such harshness behind his words. It didn't seem like it was their father who was standing there, but rather some chaotic force that had taken control of their father. Sam immediately felt repelled by this man, not just sickened by his anger and dangerous demeanor, but physically repelled.

It came as a wave of pressure hitting his vision, rolling down through his body. And although it made Sam want to pull away from his father, it also gave him a strange feeling of calm, which didn't make sense, considering the cussing man before him. The conflicting feelings swung back and forth inside him, and he couldn't decide what to do. He couldn't move.

After yelling, their father stepped into the room. He turned toward Shane, picked up their wicker clothes hamper and slammed it into Shane's face. And again, and again, slinging blood across the walls and onto Shane's sheets, killing the boy.

Sam hadn't moved as all this happened. He was stunned, horrified, and not believing what he was seeing until his father turned back to him. Then, all he could do was yield to his own reflexes. The crashed muscular man brought the grisly hamper above his head, and moved to bring it down on Sam, but Sam flipped himself away and hit the screen of the open window behind him. He fell backwards out the window and crunched onto the dry branches of a bush. He scrambled away from the bush and the window. His father threw himself into the window opening and began crawling over the window ledge.

Sam ran toward the front of their house, through the backyard gate, and out by their kitchen window. He saw his mother through the window. She lay bloodied on the floor, not moving. He couldn't think about what he saw. He kept running and came around to the front of their house. People were outside screaming and fighting. One pounded on their front door. Others were scattered up the street, and some lay on the ground. A woman close to the corner of the house saw him and screamed. She carried a potted plant.

She yelled, "You can't leave. Your job's not finished." She threw the pot at Sam and ran at him.

Sam stumbled and threw himself forward, running, running, legs swinging and arms flailing. He didn't think; he didn't cry. He just kept moving. He kept running, passing more crazy people in the street, some of them chasing him, but he kept going. He turned a corner and saw his elementary school ahead. He ran toward it and into the teachers' parking lot, then reached the chain-link fence of the playground. Nobody was near him now. He jumped onto the fence and climbed over, swinging down and landing in the basketball court. He checked behind him again, saw nobody there, and ran to the outdoor breezeway where the drinking fountains were installed. The breezeway opening didn't face the fence, so he could hide there in the shade and not be seen from the street.

Sam sat next to the drinking fountains for hours, shaking at first, crying a lot, and finally calming down, then sliding into a stupor. He couldn't think about what had happened. He didn't want to think about it. His mind slipped into nothingness, but not sleep.

With his eyes closed, he saw fire. It began with a distant hint of light and became a single tiny flame in the distance. The flame doubled, and those two doubled, and this repeated. It reminded Sam of cell division, which he had learned about in science class. It wasn't a roaring fire, but multiple, individual flames, dividing and becoming more and more. He lost track of the individual flames as the fires surrounded him. Now, they bled into each other, and the mass churned and bubbled around him. The individual flames became lost in the mix as the fire pulsed and billowed.

He felt the heat, but it didn't burn him. He heard its sounds, which were like a massive waterfall. He smelled it, not a burnt smell, but fresh like air in a meadow on a spring morning. And it tasted like the honeysuckle he'd once tasted in his yard. Its warmth cuddled him, a blanket of comfort and safety. He felt it in his heart and mind.

The sound of chains on metal pulled him out of the vision. He sat up and took a drink from the fountain. The sun had just set, and he peered around the corner to see if anyone was there. He saw a boy clinging to the fence and looking behind, panting, scared. A woman screamed from across the street. A man screamed from somewhere along the fence, and the boy turned to climb the fence, but his feet kept slipping out of the fence holes. The woman ran toward the boy, carrying a can that rattled as she ran. She would reach him in seconds if he didn't get over the fence.

Sam yelled at the boy, "Come on. Grab up higher. Cram your feet in there."

The boy was surprised to see Sam and found more resolve with Sam's directions. He jumped, gripped the fence above his head, and stuck his shoe into an opening. He heaved himself up and reached the top. Sam climbed up from his side of the fence and took hold of the boy's arm, helping pull him over. The woman slammed herself into the fence as the two boys jumped down the other side.

"You fucking insects," the woman screamed. "You should be exterminated."

She sprayed what was in the can she carried, not bug spray, but yellow spray paint. Sam felt that repelling feeling again, a magnet pushing back, pushing him away from the woman this time. They backed up from the fence after getting misted with the paint. Sam guided the boy into the breezeway, and they stood out of the woman's sight, breathing hard. The woman yelled incoherent babble at them, and after a few minutes, stopped yelling. A man screamed and the woman screamed back. Then, both of them were screaming at each other. The fence rattled, and Sam thought they were fighting. Three, then four loud bangs against the fence and silence.

Sam considered the boy now. He had seen him in school before but didn't know his name. The boy was in third grade, two grades behind Sam. He wore a small blue backpack.

The boy asked, "Why was she chasing me? What did I do?"

"Nothing. But why did you come to the school?"

"My parents made me go to school, even though it's Saturday. I told them it was Saturday, but they screamed and pushed me outside and said I had to go to school."

At least the boy's parents weren't like his own father had been, Sam thought. He tried not to think of his little brother and his mom. He felt close to puking and wanted just to sit under the drinking fountain until the nightmare ended. But he couldn't.

"Something bad has happened," Sam said. "Did you see anyone else on your way here?"

"I saw some kids around the corner. Anthony was there, and I wanted to say hi, but they all ran into Avery's backyard. And I had to go to school."

"Did you see any grown ups?"

"Only one before that lady chased me. He was driving a car and almost hit me on the sidewalk."

"Okay. But he didn't hit you. Good," Sam said. "People have gone crazy. And you don't have to go to school, either. I think we need to hide from the adults."

"That will be cool. Should we hide at the school? Since it's Saturday?"

The boy had no clue how dangerous the adults were, and maybe other kids were dangerous, too. He saw it as a game. Sam thought that letting him pretend it was a game was good for now.

Sam asked, "What's your name? I'm Sam."

"Liam."

"Okay, Liam. How about we see if we can find those other kids you saw?"

"Sure. We can go to Avery's house. Maybe they're in the backyard still."

The street lights blinked on as Sam looked around the corner. The woman lay crumpled and motionless on the other side of the fence. He didn't see anyone else outside across from the school, so he led Liam to a different part of the fence away from the woman and boosted him over, then climbed over, himself. He let Liam show him the way to Avery's house, but he kept vigilant for any people. They walked slowly and stopped often next to cars and trees, trying to avoid being seen. Two cars raced down the street at insanely fast speeds in a neighborhood. The first one crashed into a parked car a couple blocks away, and the second one crashed into the first. People came out of their houses and ran screaming toward the crashed cars. The boys ran down a different street.

After two more blocks, they arrived outside Avery's house. Sam didn't know anyone named Avery, but he assumed she attended their school. Nearby traffic noise was louder than usual with engines roaring, tires screeching, and various bangs and crashing sounds. Shouting and screaming echoed from a distance throughout the neighborhood. The boys walked up to Avery's wooden backyard gate and stopped. They listened for talking from the backyard but heard nothing.

Sam decided to open the gate and go back there. They entered the yard quietly, moved along the house in the darkness, and saw a wooden shed at the back of the small yard. Sam thought this would be where he would hide. If the kids were in there, he didn't want to surprise them, and he also didn't want anyone else to hear him if he spoke. He and Liam crept up to the shed's door.

Sam whispered close to the door, "Hello? Hey, is anyone in there? We're just two kids out here."

They waited for a response, and the door squeaked open a crack. Sam couldn't see inside.

A whisper from inside: "What do you want?"

"We're trying to hide from the crazies, and we knew you came back here."

The door creaked open more, and a girl approximately Sam's age stuck her head out. She recognized Liam and said, "What are you doing here?"

Liam said, "Hi Avery. My parents sent me to school, but it's closed, and it's summer vacation, Saturday even."

Sam said, "We were running from some adults by the school, and Liam said he saw you come back here. We were hoping you weren't crazy."

The girl carefully swung the door open wider, warily looking out past the two boys, and said quietly, "We're not crazy. Come in, quick."

Sam recognized her from school now. She was in the same grade as him but a different class. They entered the cramped shed to find three other kids in addition to the girl. She pulled the door closed. The shed smelled of cut grass and gasoline. Sam could barely see the kids outlined in the minimal yard light filtering through a tiny window at the back. Sam was taller than all the kids in the shed, and he assumed he was likely the oldest, too, except maybe for Avery.

"What's going on out there?" Avery asked, sounding very worried and scared.

"Everyone's gone crazy, running around and driving around like they're nuts," Sam replied.

"Yeah, that's what we saw. Nobody is acting normal. That's why we hid in here."

"What about your parents?" He tried not to think about his own parents, but that didn't work.

"I don't know where they are, but if everyone is crazy, I didn't want to go in the house in case they came back, in case they're crazy, too."

"Not everyone is crazy." He meant the group of kids in the shed.

"Is it just the adults?"

"I don't know. I only saw adults, except for you guys. All of them were fighting each other and screaming, or running after Liam and me."

"That's what we saw, too," she said, sounding jittery. "Henry was outside his house, sitting by the street, and he's only in preschool. He had blood on his face when me and Raya came out of her house and found him crying in his front yard. Raya's parents were yelling at each other, so we left to come to my house. We just thought her parents were arguing again. We didn't know people were going crazy. When we saw Henry, we tried to take him back inside his house, but he wouldn't go. He started screaming. At least the blood on his face wasn't his. Then, Mrs. Pinkton was running down the street. She had a rake, so we grabbed Henry and hid behind a car. We got to my block and saw Anthony running out of his house. His mom was throwing pots and pans at his older sister. That's why we all came here."

"Wow," Sam said, and didn't have more words, because he thought of his brother and parents.

"What about your parents?" she asked.

Sam didn't want to talk about it, so he just said, "They're dead." Maybe his father wasn't dead, but he didn't want to see him again.

"I'm sorry."

Sam didn't want to stay in the shed, even if it was safer there. It felt stuffy, like it was closing in on him. He wanted to run and keep running. He didn't want to worry about these other kids, either. He wanted to get his little brother and hide in a fort by the dry creek, but his brother was dead. They could have built up some rocks and bushes and made a fort down there the way they had many times. They could have pretended to be heroes saving Earth from the alien invasion. They could have planned how to kill the aliens with the aliens' own weapons after they captured one of their ships. They could have taken back the neighborhood and saved everyone.

Sam said, "I have to go."

He pushed at the shed door, but Avery grabbed his arm and pulled him back. The door thumped closed.

"Where're you gonna go?"

"I'm going down to the dry creek."

"Why?"

"Because I can't stay up here in the neighborhood. There's nothing up here. There's crazy people up here. I just want to go." He also didn't want to explain what he wanted to do, because he really didn't know what he wanted to do except run, get away from all this.

"We're here, and we're not crazy. And we can all go." She sounded desperate, like she didn't want to be left behind.

Liam said, "I thought we were going to hide from the adults together. That's why we came here." He sounded scared too, starting to realize that it wasn't really a game.

Sam considered their situation and couldn't think of a reason they all couldn't go together. Maybe he didn't really want to be alone, either. He said, "Okay. I guess you can come, too."

Avery replied, "What do you want to do down there?"

"I said you could come. I don't know what I want to do. You can stay here. I don't care." What Sam didn't want was to explain things right then, because he couldn't explain it. He only knew he needed to keep moving.

"No, we'll come," she said, her voice rising. "Let's go."

Sam opened the door and checked the yard. It was small, so he thought he would have heard anyone who might have been out there. Nobody was. The house remained dark inside. They would have to go back out through the side gate. He crept quietly around the house and to the gate. The others followed. He pulled the gate open enough to look out and stood eyeing the street, listening for danger. It appeared clear, so he pushed the gate open more, then moved along the house while Avery held the gate so the others could go through. Sam stepped out to the edge of the house, still seeing and hearing nothing to indicate danger. He relaxed a little, walked out to the sidewalk, and continued along the street. The rest of them followed.

The distant traffic noises mixed with the arguing and screaming voices had gotten worse and louder. Sam thought their group could reach the train tracks and the dry creek bed without going out of the neighborhood where all the noise was clamoring. From the sound of it, the craziness seemed to be spreading wildly out on the bigger streets.

He looked back at the other kids as they marched in a line like soldiers going to war. Liam was directly behind him, followed by little Henry, who Avery picked up and carried. Next were Raya and Anthony. Maybe they could fight the aliens after all. Maybe they could take back their neighborhood and even the whole city. It sure sounded to him like an invasion out there.

Sam thought of the soldiers and the people from the wildlife refuge, us, as he told his story. He paused in the telling.

.   .   .   .

Sam looked at us cautiously, remembering what worried him the most, now.

He said to us, "So, the one watching us wasn't one of you, was it?"

"What do you mean?" I asked. "Someone was watching you?"

"I thought it was one of you at first. It was after we saw you with the soldiers and then found other kids with our minds. Someone else was back there in our heads, watching. At first, it was like a bright diamond. Then, it was like a shadow, but when I tried to look at it, it moved just behind me. Like in a bad dream." Sam seemed genuinely scared as he spoke of this.

It gave me a chill. I asked, "Was it there when you saw us doing our Iter Anima, our last mind travels that cut you off from the other kids?"

"Yes, that's why I thought it was with you. It was there, and I almost saw it more clear the last time."

Jason said, "There wasn't anything like that from the Family. I didn't see it."

"No," I said. "I didn't either. And we were reaching out to so many people. I was talking to so many, learning so many stories. But I didn't see you either, though you were there. And it was *behind* you?"

"That's what it seemed like." His voice quavered. "But it wasn't always behind us. It also seemed like it was up with you once. It was like dirt in a tornado. I couldn't keep track of it. One of your people went with it, too."

"What?" My chills were turning ice cold.

Sam said, "I couldn't see any of you like I see you here. It's not like that. But you said it wasn't with the Family, so I can tell now that it was different from you, that you were different from it. You were like the white clouds, and it was like a thunderstorm. I saw a white cloud spin into the dark storm. That must have been one of you going with it."

Lauren!

Steven S. Patchin

Chapter 10
Departure

We put off hearing more of Sam's story so we could prepare to leave. I went about organizing my things and taking care of Daisy as though I were in a trance. I did what I needed to do, but I also felt as if I were watching myself from afar. I couldn't stop thinking about the shadowy presence Sam described . . . and Lauren. I was sure it had been Lauren who Sam had seen spinning away with this shadow. *What the fuck was it? How had it taken . . . killed . . . Lauren?*

I had never bought into the idea of ghosts or spirits floating around and fucking with the living. Even with all that we'd been through in our Iter Animas, I still didn't perceive any of that as being like paranormal horror movies. I didn't believe in evil as manifested through monsters and ghosts. There was enough evil in humans that monsters didn't scare me. But this shadow. How could it be anything but evil? Sam felt it and feared it, even though he'd stood up to what was attacking him during The Crash, and he'd endured awful horrors. The thought of this thing would live with me until I could find it.

I had asked where they put Lauren's body. They had placed her in the storage room where Taylor had been locked up when we captured her. Ginny and Sophia had wrapped Lauren's body in white sheets and covered her with a blanket. She lay on the small bed. I went into the room, pulled the chair over to the bed, and sat with her for a while, not thinking of anything in particular, but trying to feel Lauren's presence in my life. She had made a difference to me in the short time we had been together. I regretted that we could not bury her, considering our circumstances. I resolved to take care of her burial when we returned for Ben and the others.

As for the group, we needed to get away from the lab without being seen, and we needed to hide a good distance away. We chose to go northwest, exiting the park via 88th, the entrance we had used when we first came to Rocky Mountain Arsenal National Wildlife Refuge, the gate we had been using when we went to and from the Space Force Base. We planned to travel up Highway 2 and eventually cut directly north and work our way toward Longmont. It was more suburban than the center of the city and also might have useful stores for supplies and homes where we could eventually stay. We didn't want to go toward downtown, because we thought it would be safer on the outskirts, not knowing if any crashed were still about, and we didn't want to face too many survivors who we couldn't help much yet, anyway, at least until we could get ourselves situated and evaluate the conditions out there.

We guessed it was at least 30 miles to Longmont, and to avoid attracting too much attention from whoever had done the bombings, we wouldn't use vehicles for the journey. So, it might take a couple days. We weren't in a hurry, and we could stop almost anywhere along the way. We had a plan and a start.

It was important that we were able to leave the park without being seen, even though we didn't know if anyone was out there to see us, anyway. Craig, Elizabeth, and Sophia stayed behind with Ben. I intended to go back for them if we found that it was safe to do so. When I returned, we could drive away with the Jeep that Javier and Ellen had left in the crater, or I could bring another vehicle with me on the way back.

We set out after 8 p.m. There were 58 of us and Daisy, who we would have to lift up the ladder in the last section of the tunnel. We navigated our way through the lab, into the air handler room, into the access tunnel, and up the stairs. I took the lead through the gate and emerged in the cool, quiet night. A silver sliver of moon stared down from the southwest. Stars shined brightly like I'd never seen them in Denver before, not a wisp of clouds in the sky or light to spoil the view. I immediately sought out the Big Dipper, as I had always done when out in nature. I rarely bothered to do this when I was in the city before The Crash because the light pollution had mostly stolen the stars, and I didn't care to face a muddy sky. But this time, I found the north star straight off the Dipper's cup, and it made me feel at home.

The plains were dark, and no lights survived in any direction, even in the west toward the industrial edge of the city. If someone was watching the park, they would need night vision to see us out here, and they also would need to suspect that we were here in the first place. I thought the chances of that happening were very slim. I told the others to come out. Soon, all of us stood in the dry grasses and organized ourselves as we had planned. In a loose line, we began the new journey. Angling toward the exit gate, Daisy staying next to me. After a half hour or so, we filed out of the park and onto Highway 2.

Abandoned and crashed vehicles littered the pavement intermittently, some of them spilled into the wide shoulders of the road. Bodies lay here and there among it all. Often, we knew we were approaching a body because we smelled it. Our eyes adjusted to the darkness, and we could see our way fairly well.

We all carried some collection of provisions and weapons in backpacks or other improvised luggage. I had found a large tool bag with a shoulder strap and had cleared out most of the tools so I could make this my luggage. In it, I carried water, packaged snack food, some first aid supplies, a few basic tools, a small knife, and a good stock of pistol and rifle ammunition. My pockets were filled with a variety of smaller items, including more ammo and a flashlight. On my belt, I carried a long knife in a sheath and a pistol. Over my other shoulder I carried an M4.

I wondered what we were headed to as a group and as part of a new-found world society, if that really was possible. I still had trouble mustering enthusiasm about it, because I felt that my future had been stripped from me when Lauren died. I knew I had to keep going. I forced myself to think beyond myself while taking each step. What we had done was to find new ways to connect humanity. Maybe they were old connections rediscovered, but they had brought together people around the world and given us a glimpse of a new existence. I felt we had a responsibility to continue our efforts. And now Jaguar had shown me that those connections could be more versatile than I had thought. It was as if we were headed for a grand revelation, if only we could keep going.

We moved through the night as we had planned but without Ben, Craig, Elizabeth, and Sophia. Jason took point. A few from the Family stayed near him, and Glenda and Sam kept the children together. They were followed by the other subgroups with armed Family members scattered about. I hung back near the rear, and Aiden took up the job as sweeper.

We kept to the highway for a short time and then began worming our way west and north as the roads dictated based on how clear they were and what felt safe. We took 120th west, and Ginny said there was a Walmart Super Center a few miles away, off Quebec Street. We made that our new destination, somewhere we could stop for the night. On the way, I saw no live people nor signs that survivors had been out recently. But we did see and smell the dead, who, we saw after we left the highway, remained in the odd piles like those we had seen only in areas outside of neighborhoods. We speculated that something in people's behavior had led them away from their homes and out to commercial and industrial sections of the city. That's where most of the dead had accumulated in piles, usually against buildings or in corners where fences joined. I was grateful for the darkness so I didn't have to see the rotting details, even though not seeing the horror added its own unnerving trepidation.

With Daisy, I worked my way up to Jason and asked him, "Since we're away from where any troops might be looking for us, and we apparently delivered the BBs to reset the minds of any crashed out here, do you think we really need to worry about anyone attacking us, now?"

Jason remained alert but had to keep his pace slow so everyone, especially the youngest children, could keep up with him. He said, "We need to be prepared for the possibility of someone attacking us, but I'm not worried about the crashed, no."

"I doubt any crashed survivors would have the strength to do us much harm, anyway," I said. "But I do still wonder about people who were never crashed. We know they exist. Lauren wasn't crashed."

"They don't have a reason to attack us, and yes, they are out there. I can feel them, along with crashed survivors. Since the BB Iter Anima, I can see them in my mind. It's like the connections with the Family but on a scale I can't quite comprehend. I've been trying to get it right in my head, because it's too much at times. I hear their voices, or rather their thoughts, and I can't separate them and understand any of them. They're all different. It's not like a crowd at a baseball game, all cheering at once. It's more like a mob of individuals all shouting something different.

"It's not like this with everyone, though. I do feel clarity with the groups we contacted, the ones you communicated with. And there are others like them. They already had a unity before the BB. It's the vast majority of everyone else who I'm trying to reconcile. And I think a few are watching us right now."

I looked into the darkness, as if I would see people following us, but we weren't near any structures or homes at the moment, and I didn't see anyone out there. I said, "Do you think they're a threat?"

"I don't know. My mind's buzzing right now. I can't get it straight."

We walked in silence. Staying on the road, we crossed open space, the South Platte River, and reached Quebec Street. We turned north and arrived outside the Walmart at a few minutes past midnight.

The store was dark, as we expected. The parking lot was a deserted battleground with burned out and crashed vehicles denying the order of the tidy parking lines. Some of the vehicles contained bodies, and other bodies lay here and there on the bloodied asphalt, as if the people had died for a cause. The glass of one of the doors on the grocery and pharmacy side of the store was shattered and lay in nuggets around the opening.

We had the group and Daisy stay in the parking lot to the side of the store while Jason, Javier, and I went through the door to see if it was safe for everyone to go inside, and to see if there was anything left that would be of any use to us. We entered with our M4s ready and flashlights shining. We found that the store had not been ransacked. Some items were strewn in the aisles, but overall, the shelves remained eerily intact. I imagined that if the lights were on, the store would not seem too out of the ordinary, visually. However, the lingering sweet staleness of rotting meat hung in the air, a reminder that things were not normal. We didn't know if the stench was from spoiled food, dead people, or both.

We kept alert and combed through all the aisles to make sure there was nobody in the store who might want to hurt us. We checked every door and all the stockrooms. We found nobody and were amazed at how well-stocked everything was. The meat and cheese that had been left out in the deli and sat rotting in the meat display cases turned out to be the source of the pervasive odor, which was not as strong on the opposite end of the store, away from the food section.

We decided that because we had accomplished our main objective of getting out of the lab without being seen (we assumed), it made sense to stay in the store for now and get some sleep. After that, we could get more provisions and decide where to go from there. I went outside and invited everyone in. We took up residence in the home goods section of the store, where there were plenty of blankets, sheets, and towels so we could set up places to sleep. Some found comfortable spots on couch and bed displays, and some went straight for the outdoors section to get camping mattresses or lounge chairs. We generally kept close to each other, though we were spread throughout different aisles. Javier and Ellen volunteered to keep watch on the shattered glass opening in the front door, which was the only easy access from outside.

When everyone was mostly settled in, I took Daisy with me and found Glenda and Aiden with the children. They were talking to Sam. Some of the kids had sleeping bags from the camping section of the store and were organizing them so they were next to the people of their choosing. One girl of eight or so came over and petted Daisy, who was happy to get the attention. The older kids were helping the younger ones make sure they had what they needed. Jason came down the aisle and joined us. I wanted to hear more of Sam's story, and so did Jason and Glenda.

Chapter 11
Confluence

In the aisle of the Walmart lit by flashlights, amid settling children, we listened as Sam told more of his story. He seemed as wide awake as Jason and me.

. . . .

"Should we get a gun?" Anthony asked from the back as they marched in a line down the neighborhood sidewalk toward Dry Gulch.

Sam stopped. Everyone stopped behind him, and Sam turned to Anthony, who was close in age to Liam, eight or nine.

"I know where my dad's gun is," Anthony offered.

"Wasn't your mom crazy? What about your dad? Where is he?" Sam asked.

"My dad's at work. I think my mom was crazy, but my sister could go with us, too, if she's alright. My dad keeps the gun in a box under the sink in their bathroom."

Sam thought that a gun could be useful, but he'd never held a real gun, only the ones they'd made out of sticks. He asked, "Do you know how to use a gun?"

"No. I just know where he keeps it."

"Does anyone here know how to use a gun?"

"I do," said Raya. "At least a little. My uncle in Las Vegas showed us last summer when we stayed with them. We went to a shooting place in the desert."

Raya was 10 or 11, almost Sam's age. She was in Avery's class, and Sam remembered seeing her run during track and field days. She had been the fastest of the girls.

Sam considered the idea. No adults were outside at the moment, and he said to Anthony, "Show us the way."

Little Henry said, "Want Mommy."

Avery, who was still holding Henry, said, "You're going to stay with us for now, just like when I babysit."

"Want Mommy."

"I know, sweetie," Avery said. "We'll have to see when she gets home. But you can have fun with us. We're going on an adventure. It will be fun."

They continued walking. Henry lay his head on Avery's shoulder, dried blood still on his face. Sam knew there wasn't much hope that Henry's parents were sane. They traipsed through the eerily quiet neighborhood that seemed like a ticking bomb waiting to explode, surrounded as it was by chaotic noise in the distance. They came upon a black truck that was T-boned into the side of a small white car in the street. The driver was hunched over the steering wheel, and Sam guided everyone to the other side of the street. He noticed a few open front doors and open garage doors at some of the houses, but saw no people in the shadows of the streetlights and porch lights. Sam wanted to get down to the dry stream bed, Dry Gulch, where he would feel safer, but he also liked the idea of having a gun with them.

They drew closer to Anthony's house, and the front door was open there, too. Sam held out his arms, signaling for everyone to stop. Anthony began charging across the lawn toward the open door. The darkness in-side the house yawned like a throat ready to swallow an oyster, or worse, a shark ready to swallow a kid. Sam reached for Anthony to stop him from going in, but Anthony trotted up to the door the way he was used to when-ever he came home.

At the open mouth of the house, Anthony inhaled with a yelp and cried, "No!"

Sam ran up to him and saw a girl lying inside the doorway. Her head was mis-shaped, flattened, and Sam didn't want to look closer. A heavy fry pan lay deeper inside the house.

Anthony moaned and stammered, "It's Janet. My sister. Janet. What happened? No!"

Sam pulled Anthony away and shuffled him back to where the other kids stood. Raya hugged the boy as he cried. Sam took a couple deep breaths, started toward the menacing orifice, and went inside. He slipped past Anthony's sister's body, not looking down, and reached the back wall of the living room where a doorway led to the kitchen. He found the kitch-en light switch and flicked it on, then evaluated the layout of the house. A hallway led down to the left, and with focused resolve, he found another light switch, flipped it on, and trudged across the worn carpet toward the master bedroom.

He didn't expect that anyone was back here, having decided that the crazy adults were making a lot of noise, and the only thing he heard here was the low rumble of a floor fan in the first bedroom. At the end of the hallway, the master bedroom door stood open. Sam found the light switch inside and hit it with angry determination, turning on the lights in the room.

A man lay on the bed staring at the ceiling. Sam flinched, knocking his arm against a tall dresser and toppling a vase of plastic flowers over the side. The vase and flowers bounced on the carpet.

The man was dead, a thin piece of plastic sticking out of his neck, blood soaked into the sheets all around his head.

Sam turned away and saw the bathroom. Light shined in from the bedroom enough that he didn't need to turn on another light to see the cabinet under the sink. He entered the bathroom, plopped down onto his knees, and pulled open the cabinet door. A perfumy mixture of nail polish remover, old soap, and musty wallboard odors hit his nose, causing him to gag. He saw the small wooden box past a cluster of plastic bottles. He pulled it out roughly, knocking over the bottles, and placed the box up next to the sink. It had a single latch, which he clicked open and used to lift the lid. Inside, a black handgun rested on a linty piece of brown towel. Six bullets lay in a cluster in one corner.

He snatched up the gun and the bullets, crammed the gun in one pocket, the bullets in the other, and ran out of the room, headed for the front door. Outside, the kids waited on the sidewalk, leaning against a car parked along the street. He trotted out of the house and up to the group. Their expectant faces stared wide-eyed.

"I got it," Sam said.

Anthony was the only one not looking at him. Instead, he sat on the car's hood and gazed down the street.

Sam said, "Okay, let's go."

"Do you think there are other kids like us?" asked Avery.

"Could be," Sam replied.

"Then shouldn't we try to find them?"

"Where?" Sam only wanted to get going. He wasn't thinking of other kids. Her question annoyed him, so he said, somewhat sarcastically, "Do you want to search all the neighborhoods?"

"No. But what if they went to the school, like you and Liam?"

"I guess we can go check at the school," he said.

They headed toward the school, which was a few blocks away. It wasn't too far from the path that led to the dry creek, anyway, so Sam didn't see it as too much of a diversion. Anthony trailed behind the group but not too far back. When they turned the corner by the school, they saw the woman with the spray paint still lying by the fence. Farther down, a boy sat against the fence, and two other kids stood near him. Sam's group walked up to these kids, who watched with apprehension as they approached, but didn't run away.

Before he recognized who was sitting there, Sam said, "Don't worry. We're not crazy." And then he added, "I don't think."

The boy sitting against the fence stood up. It was Theo, a kid who was in Sam's class and who Sam hung out with during school. He hadn't seen him since school let out for summer. The two who were standing, a younger boy and a girl, were in first or second grade.

Sam said, excited, "Theodore, man. You're here."

Theo wasn't as enthusiastic, but he replied, "Yeah. I'm here. What's up with you guys?"

"We're going down to Dry Gulch. There's something seriously wrong with the adults out there."

"Yeah, I noticed. A guy killed my parents and my brother Jim. I barely got out of the house." He stated this without emotion, though Sam knew it tore him up. Sam felt the same way about his own situation and wasn't surprised by Theo's statement because his own experience was similar.

"Man, I'm sorry. My mom's dead, and so's my little brother. It's really messed up. I just want to get out of here."

Theo perked up a bit, hearing this. Sam thought it was because Theo felt a connection to Sam and what had happened to them. Maybe he liked that Sam had a goal, too. For Sam, the goal of where to go might have been the main thing that kept him from crawling back under that drinking fountain at the school and doing nothing.

Theo said, "There's more kids inside the school grounds. They jumped the fence." He called out to them, "Hey guys. Hey. Get up here. Let's go with Sam."

Sam didn't see anyone at first, but slowly, kids came out of the darkness from different directions behind the fence. Soon, a dozen or so kids gathered by the fence and began climbing back over. They all were at least age eight except two, who were in kindergarten and needed help climbing the fence. Sam began to realize that they were looking to him for direction. But all he wanted to do was leave. They were welcome to come, but he was no leader, he thought.

Sam knew only a few of the kids, because most weren't in his grade or his class. They were an even mixture of boys and girls.

Avery asked him, "Glad we came here?"

Sam didn't feel glad, but it was good to find Theo. And maybe Avery was right. Having a bigger group could be safer. He had a gun, which he hadn't looked at since shoving it in his pants pocket, and he figured it would be good if they got other things to protect themselves, even if they were only sticks. And there were sticks in Dry Gulch.

Sam said to everyone, "If you want to go with us, some of us are heading for Dry Gulch so we can figure out what to do and hide from the adults. You can come with us."

Everyone gathered closer to Sam, some of them saying they wanted to go. All of them demonstrated by standing ready, that they didn't want to stay behind, as if they were awaiting orders. Sam didn't know how to give orders, nor did he want to, but he did like having the bigger group together. He realized he hadn't been thinking of the homeless who lived along the railroad tracks and near the dry creek. Usually, when he and his brother went there, they just avoided the tents and odd thrown-together shelters. But if these people were still there and were crazy, this group of kids could be in for problems instead of safe hiding places. Sam began getting frustrated because none of this was part of his plan. He had wanted to go alone.

Loud car engine noises screamed from down the street, and suddenly two small cars skidded around the corner, lights flaring, speeding directly toward the group. Everyone scattered, and one of the cars raced over the sidewalk and slammed sideways into the chain-link fence where they had been standing, taking out one of the fence poles and crinkling the fence up under the car. It revved wildly, broke free from the fence, skidded, and crashed into a tree across the street. The driver, an older teen, threw his door open and flopped out, screaming.

"Ahhh! You crashed my car! It's your fault!"

He ran at some of the kids he had narrowly missed hitting, but they tore away and disappeared down the street. The other car had already crashed into a small truck, and that car's driver was running at another splinter of kids. Sam found himself between the two groups and the two careening cars. Now, he saw everyone running in different directions as he ran, himself, straight up the street, thinking of reaching one of the pedestrian bridges that crossed the train tracks a few blocks away. He saw Avery with Henry and slowed down so they could catch up to him. He took Henry from her, and Henry screamed at the change of transport, but Sam couldn't stop to console the child. They were running behind one of the crazy drivers, who split left to chase two other kids. Sam, Henry, and Avery sprinted up the street, and looking back, Sam saw Liam following them. Again Sam slowed, and Liam caught up. They kept running for the bridge, and Sam wondered why he'd chosen the bridge as his destination.

They cut to the left and then a quick right and found themselves running out to the road parallel to the gulch trail. They took a left on the road and came to one of the bridges. On the way, Sam had decided they should hide under the bridge and watch for other kids, who he hoped would be heading for the train tracks and Dry Gulch so they could all meet up again, even if they came out from different streets. He also thought about the gun, that he wanted to figure out how to use it, and he decided he could have a look at it, but he'd want Raya to be there to give her input. Some of the other kids might know something about guns, too. But without some time to understand the gun, he feared trying to use it. He felt his thinking speed up as he considered multiple things at once.

To get under the bridge, they had to climb over a sagging chain-link fence. It was harder to negotiate than the solid one at the school. Sam helped Avery over and then boosted Henry up so Avery could help him over. When Sam and Liam reached the other side, Sam immediately noticed how dark it was down past the fence. A single street light back by the road cast a dim light toward the bridge, and another on the bridge illuminated the path, but below the bridge, darkness loomed. Sam wished he'd thought to get a flashlight from somewhere.

He asked Avery, "Do you have a phone?"

"Yes, why?"

"We could use the flashlight."

She pulled her phone out from her back pocket and turned on its light. With Henry holding Avery's hand, she shined the light below the bridge, seeing nobody there, and the four of them eased their way down. Sam didn't want to go too far, because he hoped that other kids would show up along the gulch, but he also wanted to hide from any crazies who might be nearby. He guessed it wasn't even midnight yet. It would be hours before sunrise. They crouched at the edge of the bridge where the ground sloped down to the dry stream bed. Sam gazed around and saw no other movement. Very few lights showed through the apartment windows on the other side of the bridge. The houses on their side were mostly dark, too, except for a few porch lights.

They were multiple blocks away from bigger streets that surrounded them on all sides, and yet, the sounds of traffic, car horns, crashes, and even screaming voices reached them, much noisier than what Sam was used to hearing on a typical day. And then there were the screams. All of it made him flush with apprehension, and it gave him a feeling that he needed to fight. But who would he fight? He knew this was nothing like his imagined alien invasion. It was far worse. The people they were supposed to trust were either dead or crazy. And the crazy ones were the aliens who they would have to fight, including people they might know. If it was an alien invasion, people's bodies had been taken over. That wasn't the kind of invasion Sam wanted to think about. He wanted it to be simple, with slimy monsters jumping out so he could shoot them.

He wiggled the gun out of his pocket and studied it. A cylinder intersected the gun's barrel, and the cylinder had holes in it. He realized that would be where the bullets went, and the gun was not loaded, at least as far as he could see. He'd heard that he should be careful if he ever found a gun – though he didn't know where he'd heard it – and that any gun could be loaded. He remembered thinking how stupid it sounded that he might find a gun. Where was he going to find a gun? And here he was holding one.

He shoved it back into his pocket, which wasn't easy because of how bulky it was. He'd been carrying it during all the running, and he now felt bruises where the gun had banged against his leg while he ran.

Liam said, "I think I see Anthony."

Sam and Avery turned in the direction Liam was looking. Down along the gulch path, a line of kids moved toward them in the darkness. Sam could make out Anthony, Raya, and a few others who had been at the school. He stood up and waved. They saw him and picked up their pace. Sam scanned the area and saw Theo and some other kids coming from the other direction. They had already seen him.

The groups came together with nobody missing. They had evaded the crazy guys who had been chasing them. Sam felt less tense with everyone back together. He was starting to realize that he didn't want to be alone after all. There was something really cool about being part of this group.

He knew that nothing would be the same again, but he didn't know just how much the world would change and how quickly. He did know that they had each other, however, and that they were bound by their recent experiences with the crazies

"Okay," Sam said in general to everyone, "Looks like we need to stick together."

They all climbed over the fence and gathered on the hill that sloped down from the bridge. Sam, Theo, Avery, and Raya were the oldest at 10 to 11, having finished their last year at the elementary school but not having started middle school yet. Most of the rest were in the seven to nine age range, such as Liam and Anthony, with two in kindergarten, and Henry, the youngest, in preschool. Sam figured there were a couple dozen kids in all. If he was going to keep them together, Sam thought that he would need to make up some rules for the younger kids. Rules for all of them, really.

Sam said, somewhat quietly, looking at the oldest kids, "If you'll go along with me on this, I think we can keep everyone together. And I do think we should keep everyone together."

They considered him with quizzical expressions and shrugs of approval.

He continued loudly so everyone would pay attention. "Hey guys, hey. Um, we've all been through some really bad stuff, I know. And that's why we should stick together. I wanted to come here because it was close by but also away from the big streets and houses. We should be able to see anyone coming. And the first thing we should do is make weapons in case we need them. We have one gun, but we need more than that."

Liam asked, "How do we make weapons?"

"With sticks and stones. Like the cavemen."

"Yay, cavemen," said Liam.

"And later, we can go find better weapons in stores or houses. That's how we got this one gun." He noticed Anthony staring at him, and then Anthony nodded.

"We can find sticks and stones to make weapons in the dry streambed," said Sam. "There could be some metal spikes laying around by the railroad tracks. But watch out for trains. I don't want any of you younger kids to go anywhere alone. Always be with one of the older kids. You have me, Avery, Theo, and Raya. And Raya, can you help me with the gun? But everyone else, stay close to one of us. If you want to go down there and get sticks, stones, and any other things you think will work, go ahead. Watch out for the homeless, and stick together. Bring everything back up here."

In a big group, they descended to the dry stream bed and spread out a little before beginning their search. Raya stayed back, and so did Anthony. Sam took the gun out of his pocket. Raya said it was like one of the guns her uncle had shown her. She thought it was called a revolver, and she showed them how to load the bullets one at a time. All six bullets fit in the gun. She said to keep it aimed away from anyone unless you wanted to shoot. You could pull back the hammer and fire, or you could just fire. And there was the safety, of course. You had to switch that off before shooting the gun. It all made sense to Sam and Anthony. Sam tucked the now-loaded gun back in his pocket with the safety on. If he needed to shoot someone, he'd have to remember to switch the safety off first.

He watched the kids not far below, collecting things. He saw an image of his dad smashing his brother's face. His mother lying in oozing blood. People running at him, screaming. Cars barreling toward him. Maniacs trying to grab him. Fire blazing across the sky.

Dizziness flooded through him again. It felt like the flu but not. A calmness eased through the dizziness, and his face grew hot. The world wobbled and spun. He thought he would pass out, but the feeling faded, and something different spread into his mind. His whole body tingled, and he felt himself reaching out toward the stars while still seeing what was around him, too. This *something-new* spiraled through him, through his body and mind, twisting from his feet up to his head and expanding out from inside him, past his cheeks, and streaming wide, away from him while not letting him go. He breathed deeply, and it all pulled back to him. He felt different, at ease, but ready. And clear-thinking.

Calmly, he watched the other kids. It didn't take long for them to return with their booty and place it on the path. They settled around, sitting near the pile of sticks, stones, and metal junk. They didn't seem interested in chatting or asking questions. Silence floated across the group. They waited for him.

Sam stepped over to the pile. "Listen," he said.

The distant sounds of chaos in the streets penetrated the quiet of their gathering, rumbling and screeching, zipping and zooming, crunching and crashing. They looked from one to the other, worry creeping into their faces like clouds passing in front of the sun.

Sam said, "I think those are the sounds of the world ending out there."

Now surprise spread through the group. The younger kids gaped. The older kids looked around as if searching for what to think of it all.

"But it's not *us* ending. For us, we'll fight. For us, it's war first."

Their expressions changed in search of resolve and determination. Upstream from the group, out on Sheridan Boulevard, an explosion boomed, and orange light flashed under the wispy, low clouds. The kids didn't flinch. They remained focused on Sam.

He continued, indicating the junk pile. "These're our first weapons. And we'll find better ones. We will not let another crazy force us to run. We will stop these invaders when they attack us. We will fight. And when we're done fighting, there is something more . . . ."

To Sam, the faces of all the kids were fire burning and spreading, on them, through them, around them, and outward. He knew this meant he was seeing *inside* them, and he also knew that they would see the same things he saw, very soon.

. . . .

Javier interrupted the story, saying, "There are people outside."

Chapter 12
Remembered

After picking up our M4s, Jason, Glenda, and I followed Javier to the front of the store where we shut off our flashlights and found Ellen peering out through the open door to the dark parking lot.

She whispered, "We saw movement in the parking lot, but I can't make out much, only shadows against the sky if you get down low enough."

Ellen pointed out to the right, between two burned-out trucks. We knelt down with her. There did seem to be people a few dozen yards away, standing where she pointed.

"I think there are four or five of them," she said.

I could make them out now. Five, I thought. Before I could say anything, Jason set down his M4 and climbed through the door frame. He stood in the entryway very briefly and then walked out to the people. He got within a few feet of them and sat down, cross-legged in the parking lot. It reminded me of what Ben had done when he first met Jason. They had sat in the street amidst abandoned cars, and Ben had begun his dialog with Jason. Now, the five who were across from Jason sat down as he did. I could hear that they were talking, but I could not make out what they were saying, though I could tell, somehow, that these people were no threat. Maybe they were some of the people Jason had told me he had felt talking in his mind.

I thought of asking Javier and Ellen what the Family connections felt like to them outside of Iter Anima and apart from what we had done when we had tested channeling the song from me through Jason. A realization like an electric current zapped through me, raising the hairs on my neck.

I had forgotten to bring Lauren's phone with me. It had all her songs on it!

Lauren and I had discussed things that were important to us, and she had mentioned how much she loved having her songs, which were on her phone. She had played some of the songs in her collection with me, and I had intended to bring her phone with me when we left. It was the most important item that I wanted to bring, and so it was the thing I had left behind. I believed that Lauren could live with me through her collection of songs. It would be a way I could get to know her without her being here any longer. I didn't care about anything else, right then. *I needed to go back and get her phone right then.*

To myself, I justified going back, thinking about Ben and that I had intended to go back for him, anyway, when we had everyone else safe, and he had recovered. It seemed that the group were in a good place, but I knew Ben hadn't recovered in just a few hours. Still, I didn't hesitate to leave.

To Glenda, Javier, and Ellen I said, "I have to go back to the lab." I didn't give them time to respond.

I went back into the store, collected my gear and Daisy, and told Aiden what I was doing. Aiden asked if I wanted him to go along, and I told him that I would be better off alone.

On my way out, Glenda said, "Shouldn't you wait until we're ready to go back for Ben?"

I looked at her with fiery determination. She understood.

"No, I guess not," she said. "Please be careful."

The dog and I headed out, first to the parking lot to find a car. Jason and the five new people were still sitting in their same places. I skirted away from them and began checking cars to see if they would start.

The first few I checked had the keyless button ignition. Some doors were open and some were closed but unlocked, though their former owners were not nearby with the necessary key fobs. I began checking older cars that would require keys. The ones with the doors open would have dead batteries because the interior lights would have drained them long ago. So, I chose to look for older cars with their doors closed, which meant I would need to choose the ones with dead people inside, or they weren't likely to have keys inside to start them. This also meant I would have to endure the horrific stench of the dead after removing the bodies.

I pulled out two dead drivers before I found a car that would start. I dragged a young woman out and away from her old PT Cruiser. She had been inside rotting for who knows how many weeks of summer. Fluids from her decomposition had pooled on the seat and left a sticky gel. Without sitting down, I reached inside and turned the key. The engine tried to turn over, but needed more gas, so I balanced myself and reached my right foot inside to the gas pedal. After a few cranks, the car started.

The putrid stench the woman left behind was almost unbearable. On the garden side of the Walmart, a full pallet sat, stacked with bags of lawn fertilizer, the load having been forgotten before being put away. I ran over and took with me two bags of the white granules. I dumped one bag into the car, tossing handfuls throughout the interior. I placed the other bag on the driver seat to cover the rotting gel and then sat on the bag. After adjusting things as best as I could, I opened the passenger door and let Daisy in. She didn't seem to mind the stench as she investigated it with her nose.

I could turn off the car headlights but the running lights stayed on. I wanted to drive with no lights so the car wouldn't be seen easily, but apparently those who stole from rotting dead women couldn't necessarily get everything they wanted. And I was going to suffer the smells, too. I drove the car out of the parking lot and navigated the streets, retracing the same path we had taken to get to the Walmart. This involved avoiding crashed cars and dead bodies. Compared to the four-hour trek on foot, the drive was quick, only taking a half hour for me to arrive outside the park.

Because of the car lights possibly attracting attention, I didn't want to drive it directly inside to the access tunnel, so I parked it near some other cars across from the big gate. We walked from there, a distance of about a half mile to the access tunnel.

As it turned out, my caution didn't help me. Just as I swung the tunnel gate open, four armed men in military fatigues sprung from the darkness of the summer grasses. Two of them took hold of my arms, the other two aimed their rifles at me. Daisy attacked the man who held my left arm and who was relieving me of my M4. Growling, she bit his lower leg and began pulling on his pants. One of the others swung his rifle down, aiming it at Daisy.

I yelled, "No!" to the soldier and to Daisy, "No! Daisy, back off. Daisy, off!"

Daisy let go of the man but continued growling.

I held my hands up and said to the soldier who was aiming the gun at Daisy, "Please. You don't have to shoot her."

He wobbled in his stance as though he were trying to remain standing and slowly processed what I said. He lifted his gun to aim it at me again. The man whose pants Daisy had bitten took my handgun and knife. His breath smelled of alcohol, a lot of it.

"Upstream?" I asked.

"Not exactly," the bitten guy replied, looking back and forth from me to Daisy.

Then who? I wondered.

They all backed away from me, and the soldier who had almost shot Daisy said, "You might remember me from that interrogation with the ink spots. I sure remember you."

I recalled that ridiculous day of psychological testing. Afterward, Ben and Kenner had used Upstream soldiers as subjects for their BB test with a real bomb. They had locked soldiers outside, under the drop zone. They justified doing this by saying that the soldiers were isolated-crashed. They wanted to see if the BB worked on them.

"I remember," I said. "You guys were test subjects?"

"Just me, but I got out of there before the bomb went off," he replied. "I think it got me anyway."

I remembered that one of the soldiers had escaped. I knew who this guy was. "You felt the BB?"

"If that's what it was called. A little more than a BB, I'd say. I felt different after that thing went off. And then you did it again. And then another time, really big. And then you bombed the base."

"No," I said. "Someone else bombed the base. And the lab. It's all gone." I gestured out toward the churned-up ground above this depression by the hill.

"Not you huh? Then why are you still here? Where does this access lead?"

The man didn't know the full story. He was trying to figure out things. So maybe he wasn't here for Ben or anyone in the lab. Maybe he hadn't seen our group leave here.

I said, "I think you have things all wrong. I do remember you, but not your name?"

"PFC Michael Terry."

I told him my name and said, "What they did to you was fucked up, no doubt. That was really on Kenner, though."

"Yeah, and these guys tell me Kenner went crazy, himself. Got himself shot."

That had been me. I looked at the other three and said, "You guys must have left just before we did the big BB. And I can't blame you."

They nodded.

Terry said, "I met up with them at Steel Tips Bar. It's where we used to go before all this shit. I was there for more than a day before they showed up. It was only us, and we watched that last thing you did from that B-52. We felt it, too. And we want to know what the hell it was."

"My god. They didn't tell you?"

Terry stared at me quietly, so I continued, "It was a pulse we were using to clear The Crash from people's heads. I know it worked on some level, but I didn't hear the details of how it affected people. My . . . a woman . . . My friend was killed. And then they bombed the base, and bombed here too."

"So you believe it cleared our minds?"

"That's what we were trying to do, yes."

"I don't think my mind was muddy before. But I do feel like something has changed. We all do. It's like we can hear other people, and they're lost. Or we're lost. I don't know. That's why we came here. The base is as good as gone. We didn't know they bombed the lab."

"Okay," I said. "I understand. We're still trying to figure it out, too." I couldn't yet tell whether or not these soldiers were dangerous, and I didn't want to say too much. "The lab is fucked, too."

"Then what's this gate? An alternate access? There must be something left or you wouldn't be here."

"There is. But everybody's gone. I came back to get something."

"What?"

"A phone with songs on it."

"Really?"

"It's important to me. I forgot it when we left."

He studied my face, but I doubted he could make out much of my expression in the darkness. I smelled the alcohol from all four of them and figured they had been enjoying lots of drinks at the bar before they came out here. I almost laughed, thinking of what I was like at bars and what might have happened with these guys. *Hey, it's two a.m. The apocalypse has happened. They bombed our Space Force Base. They hit us with some kind of special explosion. How about we go over to the wildlife refuge and see what's up?*

I said, "I can try to explain it to you. The BB pulse might have helped you, or changed you, even if you weren't crashed. All of us were exposed to it. And those people you hear in your heads are real. It's one of the results of the pulse, which is a method of mind connection we discovered that we shared with the rest of the world. We found a new way to communicate with people. It's a new connection, or an old connection rediscovered. You said you feel it."

"We do, but it's all jumbled up, hard to think with it. Can't get rid of it with a bottle of tequila, either."

"Yeah, that's something we're trying to work out. I think Jason was making some inroads on that when I left everyone and came back here."

"To get a phone," he said flatly.

It annoyed me to have to justify myself. I didn't care if he thought it was trivial.

"Yes, to get a phone with songs on it."

"Where did your people go, then?"

I didn't get the feeling that these soldiers wanted to do us any harm, but I also didn't want to lead them to our group. And I didn't want them to know that Ben was down there in the lab. Terry would certainly recognize Ben and Craig from the inkblot test they had administered on him. He might even feel considerable resentment for how that went down, and if they were drunk, they could react with violence.

"We went out into the neighborhoods," I said. "The lab down there has no power, and thus no fresh air. We couldn't stay."

They looked at one another, trying to decide what to do with me, what to do with themselves. The alcohol that had spurred their outing to the lab was wearing off, but I didn't know how much. I tried to drive the conversation.

"How did you get here?" I asked.

"We took an SUV from the parking lot at the bar. It's over by the rubble. We heard you drive in."

"Okay, then if you want to figure out what's going on in your heads, we should go talk to Jason. He seems to be getting a handle on this. But I need to go down into the lab and get that phone first."

I wasn't sure it was safe to take them to the group, but wanted to get them away from the lab, and taking chances was how we got here, anyway. We weren't going to build a new society by following the sure path that was already marked with all the proper road signs. We couldn't keep running, either.

Terry said, "I'll go down there with you."

That, however, wasn't a turn I wanted to take.

Chapter 13
Priorities

I wasn't leaving without the phone, and maybe that was stupid and short-sighted. I didn't want Terry to think I was hiding anything down in the lab, so I tried to make it seem like it wasn't a big deal.

I said, "It's just dark down there. And a lot of steps, a steep confining access tunnel. I'm only going to my room and coming back up. That's it."

"No problem. I have a flashlight," said Terry.

What could I do now? Apparently, he trusted that I wasn't outright lying to him, which I was and wasn't, but he wanted to verify it. I hoped that the others with Ben down there didn't make any noise, so we could just get the phone and leave.

"Alright," I said.

I opened the gate and gestured for Terry to go ahead of me. He declined, so I entered the tunnel with Daisy following me. The others stayed where they were. Terry, Daisy, and I descended. Terry had to help me get Daisy down the ladder, which seemed more difficult than getting her up. By then, she had stopped growling and let Terry help. Terry remained wary of her, though.

As we continued down, I tried to come up with a plan. To get from the access tunnel to my room, we would have to pass through the hallway by the lab hub where they were tending to Ben. There wasn't another way. And if they had the main door open, Terry would see them.

In the dark narrow tunnel, both of us using our flashlights, we worked our way down the stairs.

I said, "You know, Ben was trying to help when he ran those tests on you. Kenner thought you were crashed. They needed to know if the BB worked."

"Sure. A human sacrifice."

"I don't think they believed it would harm you. And it didn't. You even said that you feel different now. That's what we were trying to do. The BBs reset people's brains. For all of us. And if you see what we've discovered, I think you'll understand that it was for the best."

"For the best, huh?" he grunted. "What do you know about it? You weren't used as a guinea pig."

"Actually I was."

"Right."

"I was the first to be tested using the Brain Electromagnetic Pulse in the Jeep. We called it the Beep." I didn't want to tell him about the glitch that had caused an unintended result, even though it led to my being able to communicate with people through Iter Anima.

"Did they lock you up to do it?"

"No. I volunteered. And I get it. You were forced. I still think that was fucked up. Kenner lost his mind. Maybe he was crashed. And Ben wasn't thinking clearly, either. He'd been shot. He wanted to get his invention working as quickly as possible in case he couldn't function anymore. He was shot in the face."

"Yeah, I know about that."

"And he did get sicker from it. So . . . I told you that everyone left the lab . . . Actually, Ben is really sick. He had to stay here. He's still down here with Craig, Sophia, and Elizabeth. They are taking care of him."

Our steps on the metal stairs echoed in the tight stairwell. We continued descending.

"Then we'll have to pay them a visit while we're down here," he said.

"Uh huh. That's why I told you. I need to check on Ben, anyway."

I couldn't tell by his tone how irritated he was at hearing this news and finding out that I had lied. What would he want to do to Ben, a man who likely wasn't even conscious? I would be ready for whatever happened. I wasn't going to let Terry harm anyone.

We exited through the access door, made our way through the air handler room and out to the hallway. Walking up to the lab hub entrance we heard talking. We entered the door to the hub where dim light spilled out through another door from the room where they were taking care of Ben. We stepped in, and I saw that a sheet had been pulled over Ben's body.

Ben had died.

We startled them when we walked in. They looked up at us in surprise. Craig's face was pale and glistening with sweat. Elizabeth seemed lost, staring at the white sheet over Ben. Sophia appeared defeated, as if all her efforts were not enough, and Ben's death was her fault. When Craig saw me, the tension in his face turned to sorrow, and he began to cry. Sophia put her arm around him, while Elizabeth turned her head back toward Ben. Terry shuffled sideways but didn't speak.

I felt my energy drain away. I wanted to sit down. My ears rang, and my sight grew dim. As if from a distance, I heard voices . . . no, they were thoughts from somewhere else. I couldn't make them out clearly. They faded to the background. The ringing turned to the sound of openness like still air among the trees in the mountains. I saw Ben in a tux, parachuting as he had when I first saw him. No sounds of machine gun fire this time. Just the open stillness. Ben was close to me, and he waved, smiling as if he knew something I didn't. I realized he wasn't coming down in his parachute. He was going up. And he was laughing with wry amusement.

I felt the presence of the Family. They knew about Ben, too. And they were saying their farewells. Jaguar entered my mind with respectful acknowledgement. Kallik was there, too, the old woman projecting peace to us all. Thoughts and faces hovered around, a warm embrace. I felt Ben's death, but I also felt his life. And even more, I felt everyone's connection.

I found myself gazing at Craig, Elizabeth, and Sophia, who were gazing back at me and at each other. They felt what I did, not with surprise, but with an awareness of something they had known was there. It had been just beyond their sight. This didn't stop the tears, but now the tears fell not just for sadness but also for the realization of what we had together. I stepped over and reached toward them, across Ben, and the four of us joined hands, closed our eyes, and let the moment exist. I thought of nothing, and I don't know how long we remained that way, so present in the moment that I didn't feel or think, my ego completely gone.

I came back to myself as a recognition of the silence in the room, and I heard the sound of Daisy's toenails clicking on the floor. The openness had shrunken back to this closed room. I heard my own breathing. We released our hands and turned our resolve to the next obvious task, that of burying Ben.

"I think we should leave him down here," said Craig, trying to gather himself into a purpose. "Right here in the lab hub with his inventions."

I began to see that leaving Ben's body in the lab made a lot of sense. This was where he had made many of his discoveries and created numerous inventions. And even though he had gone too far, delved too deeply into manipulating the human mind, he had served humanity while aiming for the greater good. He had tried to tilt the world towards heaven.

Craig continued, "This could be his tomb. It's already sealed except for one way in. I recommend that we wrap his body and place him in the middle of the hub. Humans and other hominids have been using tombs, even improvising with caves, for hundreds of thousands of years. I think it's fitting."

I thought it was more than fitting. It was exactly right. I said, "Should we consider destroying the BEMP technology so nobody can ever access it again?" We couldn't get rid of the billions of Stoffer Solution devices themselves, but those were specific, manufactured items, not the designs and functionality behind the technology itself.

Elizabeth replied, "I think we should destroy it, yes. I know that Ben planned to destroy as much of his equipment, diagrams, and notes as possible after he confirmed that the BBs worked. That will mean destroying his computers and the BEMP we have down here."

I asked Terry, "Do you have any grenades?"

"No, but the other guys do."

"Could you help us with this?"

Terry seemed conflicted for a moment but quickly saw his place in the situation. He had come to the park, perhaps, to get revenge on Ben. And now, he was in the position of destroying Ben's work, but for another reason altogether.

"I'll go up and get the guys," he replied. He turned slowly, and left.

"I think we should find a way to close off the access tunnel when we leave, too," said Craig. "We'll need something more than grenades for that."

I said, "I don't know what explosives might be left at the base, but I agree with you. We could start with grenades and come back another time to finish the job."

Sophia said, "Okay, then let's find something to place Ben on, not just the floor. A gurney would work."

I said, "I'm sure there are some crates in the equipment room. We could cover them with something . . ." Then I thought of Lauren. I wasn't going to leave her down here.

"Yes," Sophia said.

"But I want to take Lauren's body up and give her a proper burial." I said.

"You're right, we should," Sophia replied.

We set to work organizing Ben's entombment. Craig and I went to the equipment room to find some crates to use as a platform while Elizabeth and Sophia prepared Ben's body. By the time we drove a cart back with two crates, they had wrapped Ben tightly in white sheets and even included a piece of decorative gold fringe that Elizabeth had removed from a dress she had in her closet. We placed the crates in the center of the hub, behind the circular counter, arranged more white sheets over the crates, and then laid his body across that.

Elizabeth went in and browsed through Ben's library for a particular book and for a particular bottle of spirits. She brought out a large, heavy book written by C. G. Jung called *The Red Book*, and balanced a bottle of cognac along with it. I found it almost funny to see that particular bottle of cognac being carried in such a precarious way, but the book was so big that Elizabeth didn't have a choice if she wanted to carry both at once. I had first seen that bottle when I had enjoyed a few drinks with Craig just before we discovered the power of our mental connections and wiped out the troops outside the south entrance. It was a Louis XIII, worth more than $3,000. Priceless now. Perfect choice.

She said, "These were a couple things that meant a lot to him. Carl Jung was a big inspiration for Ben, especially with Jung's spiritual explorations of the mind and his artwork in this book. It's an elaborate account of an unbelievable trip that I still can't get my head around. And the cognac, that speaks for itself."

"Perfect," I said. "How about we leave Ben with all this cognac and we toast him with Scotch?"

"I think that's a good idea," Craig replied.

"I'll get it," I said. "Hey, were you aware of Ben writing anything long-form by hand?"

"No. I only saw him working on computers. Why?"

"When I saw him parachuting outside my apartment, he had a briefcase with handwritten papers in it. They were lost when the biplane shot at him. He later told me that those papers were very precious to him, that it was a story he had been working on for years. I got the impression that he might start over and write it again. Maybe he did."

Elizabeth was surprised at this information. She knew about his jumping out of a plane and that whole situation but didn't know about the handwritten papers. Craig apparently did not know about the papers, either.

"If he wrote anything by hand," Craig said, "he likely would have done it in his library. He spent some time in there once in a while, recently, when we had all the soldiers locked up. There are sections around the bar area and even other parts of the bookshelves where he could have kept papers like that if he wrote anything. Do you want to go have a look?"

This made me realize that I had forgotten more than Lauren's phone. By then, I had filled two notebooks and part of a third with my own notes, and I'd left them in my room, too. I had been so focused on leaving the lab and taking care of Daisy that I had not remembered what should have been the first things I wanted to take with me.

"Yes, let's go look," I said to Craig.

With our flashlights, we entered the pitch-black library. When the lights worked, it had been beautifully lit, spotlights on the books creating a glowing colorful ambiance, and backlights behind the spirits highlighting the extensive collection of whisky, bourbon, rum, vodka, tequila, and other liquor. Now, as I saw the place in the beams of our flashlights, it reminded me of videos of the Titanic in the spotlights of underwater ROVs. I felt the loss of what had been, and a respect for leaving it as-is. In many ways, we would be leaving it as the Titanic had been left. I hoped that nobody would discover this tomb like they had found the Titanic.

We shined our lights throughout the room, and I went to the liquor cabinets first. I chose the Highland Park 18 Year Old Viking Pride Scotch and lifted it out of the glass case. I also collected eight lowball glasses and set them aside.

Craig explored the bookshelves. The books were separated into fiction on the left and non-fiction on the right, all arranged alphabetically by author. The bookshelves filled the entire back wall and part of the wall on the right. I was no literature expert or bibliophile, but I did recognize literary classics from authors such as Shakespeare, Tolstoy, Dickens, Dostoevsky, Twain, C.S. Lewis, Orwell, Hemingway, Steinbeck, and others from more contemporary authors. I didn't recognize many names in the non-fiction section, which ranged in subjects from history to psychology and philosophy. But I did know Freud, and because of the book Elizabeth had brought out, Carl Jung. One whole shelf was dedicated to Carl Jung's work.

The liquor cabinet was set behind glass doors between the bookshelves on the back wall. Cherry wood cabinets anchored the display, topped by a long, narrow counter for drink preparation. A variety of chairs and tables took up the rest of the room, some with green banker's reading lamps hunched like small statues in the darkness.

Craig said, passing his flashlight beam across the beginning of the non-fiction section, "If he didn't want someone reading what he wrote, I don't think he would have put it out with the books. I think he would have had a place for it that was out of sight."

The bookshelves did not have much ornamentation other than the top cornice and a simple leaf design on the vertical divisions. Looking in the base cabinet below the liquor, I saw only glasses and items related to mixing drinks. As I studied the wood panels inside the cabinet, it occurred to me that Ben had been too practical to stash his papers in just any hidden cubby.

"A desk might make the most sense," I said, shining my light across the tables and chairs.

"I think you're right." Craig turned away from the books and lit a desk in the corner where the non-fiction section ended on the right. "I saw him sitting here a couple times."

We stepped over to the desk, and Craig pulled open the drawer in the center. There lay a thick stack of handwritten papers, exactly what we were looking for. Next to the writings sat a partial ream of blank paper. Craig carefully took the stack in hand and set it on the desktop. He stood back reverently, as though he were witnessing the discovery of a copy of the Gutenberg Bible. Handwritten on the top page was the title, "Remembered and Told Again," and below that, "Benjamin Lee Stoffer."

I thumbed the stack. Ben's handwriting was tight and precise, no cross-outs or other corrections, and the writing across the unlined pages was perfectly straight. I estimated that he had filled more than 300 pages with his writing.

I said, "Let's get something to put these in."

"I think there's a valise in his room that will work. I can go get it."

Craig picked up Ben's papers, and I collected the scotch and the glasses. We left the library, both of us pausing outside the door to look back at the room and its contents one last time. Would anyone ever see this again, this physical representation of one man's mind?

In the center of the hub, Sophia and Elizabeth had set up candles around the counter but had not lit them. They also had cleared away everything from the counters and the whole hub area. The hub was now an austere circular room that would serve the purpose of a tomb. Ben's body lay prone across the crates, outlined with branches from artificial plants the women had found somewhere. This was becoming a proper resting place for Ben.

Daisy sat patiently in front of the door labeled BEMP. I arranged the lowball glasses along the counter and opened the scotch, lightly sniffing for its unique aroma. I poured a shot's worth in each glass and stood back to think about how quickly life can change directions or simply end. Ben had changed the course of humanity by trying to make life better for everyone but had his efforts corrupted by people trying to control everyone's mind. He had tried to fix the damage as best he could. In the process, more had changed in the Collective Consciousness than anyone had imagined could be possible. We still didn't have a handle on what it all meant or the extent of our new mind connections. Now Ben was dead, and so was Lauren. Others of the Family, too. Not to mention most of the world's population. The Crash had come like a storm of death and cleared to reveal a hopeful morning sunrise.

Craig returned carrying a small leather valise which now contained Ben's writing. He showed it to us and explained to Sophia and Elizabeth that we had found Ben's handwritten story. Eventually, Terry returned with the other three soldiers. We all stood silently, looking at Ben's body, each pondering the situation, each finding a different meaning.

I asked Terry and the other three men, "Will the grenades cause too much damage or start a fire?"

The shortest of the four replied, "They aren't incendiary, so they won't start a fire, but what do you mean by too much damage?"

"Could they cave in the room?"

"No, they aren't powerful enough for that. But they'll be loud."

Elizabeth said, "I'll get earplugs for everyone." She went inside the medical room and then returned with a handful of earplug packages which she then distributed.

I asked her, "Which of the lab sections do we need to destroy?"

"There are nine sections, but you only need to destroy four of them. STD, MS, EEG^2, and TMS+," she said.

I knew what all the acronyms represented. STD was Stoffer Transcranial Device, the earpiece Ben had created, used by billions, which was the interface that had caused all the problems when Genetrix altered it at the manufacturing level. These devices were the mechanical catalyst for The Crash, though they weren't the only method of transmission of what became a mental contagion. MS was Memory Scribe, the invention Ben designed to record people's memories and transcribe them into written words. EEG^2 was the electroencephalogram, improved by Ben, the device he used to record highly specific brain activity. TMS+ was the transcranial magnetic stimulator, another existing technology that Ben had expanded on. It was the core technology behind the Stoffer Transcranial Device, and it was this that led to all the trouble.

Elizabeth said, "If you destroy the equipment and computers in these rooms, you'll destroy most of the key technology Ben invented that related to The Crash. I'm including Memory Scribe in this because, if you want to stop the technological intrusion into people's minds, this one stands out as a prime candidate for destruction."

Memory Scribe had been used to recover memories from crashed people, especially Jason. I would not know his story in detail if it weren't for Memory Scribe. Ben also used it on me to reveal that what I had thought had happened to me when I was deep inside The Crash, was not the same as what had actually happened. I would be dealing with that incongruity for the rest of my life. *For better or for worse,* I thought, *it should be destroyed too.* It certainly could do a lot of good, but if people ever found themselves in a position to get technology back up and running, and they discovered Memory Scribe down here, it would leave open the opportunity for the type of meddling in brains that might better be left behind.

"Let's take out all four," I said.

"I think that's the way to go," Elizabeth said.

"I agree," Craig put in.

"I'll go prepare the rooms," said Elizabeth. "I'll move the computers closer to the other equipment and leave the doors at the end of each hallway open, so you can throw the grenades in."

"I want to go get Lauren's body so we can take it up with us," I said. "We can have a service for Ben when I get back. Craig, can you come with me and help?"

"Absolutely."

We drove in the cart to the room where Lauren's body was kept. I tried not to think too much about the task of moving her. I didn't want to think of her as a stiff dead body. I wanted her to live in my mind, and facing the reality of her physical death made me cringe. Still, the task had to be done. We would need to move her and get her up the access tunnel.

I put my hand on her shoulder. I did not feel Lauren there. It wasn't her. I had to imagine her, who she was, what she meant to me, what she would always mean to me. I nodded to Craig. He took her legs, and I took her upper body. As expected, the body was stiff. We placed her across the back of the cart and drove to the entrance of the lab hub. We had been gone for only a few minutes. Each of the soldiers had checked out one of the hallways for the rooms we designated for destruction. Elizabeth and Terry exited the TMS+ door, and the others soon returned from their sections.

The soldiers nodded at each other, and Terry said to the rest of us, "We're good to go. We have eight grenades. We can double up on two of the rooms and save two grenades for up top. The room I just looked at, the TMS+ room, has a big piece of equipment in it. We can hit that one with two." He asked Elizabeth, "Which other room should we give some extra treatment?"

"Memory Scribe, MS. That one's got big equipment, too."

"Okay, that's the plan," said Terry. "The rooms are all through door-ways to the right of the hallways. Each of us can throw the grenades into the rooms and take cover outside the doors. Do you want us to do this now?"

"Let's have our service for Ben first," I said.

Everyone agreed.

The soldiers stepped back to give us room. Elizabeth took the huge volume of *The Red Book* and placed it under Ben's head. She set the Louis VIII cognac at his right side. Sophia lit the candles with a lighter. I distrib-uted the lowball glasses to everyone, shots of Scotch in each. We gathered inside the circle of the counters, the soldiers stepping up near the opening to the center area but staying slightly back from entering the circle itself. Daisy sat at my feet. Craig stood at the top of the circle, just above Ben's head. We shut off our flashlights to let the candles illuminate the room. The flames wobbled slightly as we settled into our places, and then they stopped moving. Their warm orange light reminded me of our Iter Ani-mas around the fire, and I felt the irony that Ben had never experienced even one of those connective explorations. Our delivery of his Brain Elec-tromagnetic Pulse through the BB had been our primary goal for bringing people out of The Crash, and the fire had been key to that process.

We stood solemnly in the silence, waiting.

Chapter 14
Committal

Craig had retrieved a suit jacket and tie from his quarters when he went to find the valise for Ben's handwritten papers, and he now appeared as a proper officiant for this service. He was not only ready to speak, but he was also reaching out to those who were elsewhere. I realized what he was doing: He was silently calling for an Iter Anima. And it was working. The tiny candles around us swelled, overtaking the room in penetrating orange light.

I didn't feel my eyes close, if they did. The warmth of the candles swelled and passed through me with their light. Jason appeared first. His presence came like eyes rushing up to my face and expanding beyond me. Then came Glenda, Aiden, and the others. The whole Family. Now the climbers. Now Kallik. And Jaguar, with her tribe. The room was gone, and we encircled Ben's body. I felt them all, even a spark from Daisy. We were connected around Ben and open for what Craig would say. I knew I would not need to be a conduit, nor would I have to translate. Everyone would hear and understand.

Craig began speaking humbly and reverentially but soon showed a colossal resolve and insight that I had not expected: "Ben was dedicated to helping humanity. He focused his work on making life better for people. He designed his inventions to help us live better lives, to help fix problems in our brains, to help us see ourselves better. Perhaps his biggest mistake was not recognizing the extent to which some narcissists and sociopaths will go to serve their own egos. It wasn't so much that his invention was misused, and that it became the catalyst for The Crash, but rather that he underestimated the sick evil that lives within the human mind. He . . . we! . . . believed that people generally wanted the same things, that they wanted peaceful co-existence, the freedom to pursue their positive creativity, the enjoyment of associating with those who made them feel more alive, the excitement of discovering the world and living peacefully to their fullest. He believed that humanity was in accord with these ideas.

"And as a whole, maybe he was right. But these ideals did not apply to everyone, and it only took a very few, who wielded too much power, to upset the foundations of humanity. Ben failed to see that some people don't want the same things as the rest of us, that some people kept control and destruction closest to their hearts, and that they did not consider freedom and abundance for the whole world to be sacred ideals. At their best, they only cared for themselves and their own power. They were perfectly comfortable pursuing further control of everyone, even in the face of The Crash. At their worst, they wanted this destruction that now exists throughout the world. It could very well be that destruction itself was, and still is, their goal. These inhuman embodiments of evil may yet survive, or at least their mindless servants may live on to further the destruction. Someone is still out there putting effort into stopping us from carrying on with our lives, even now.

"What that means for us, we will have to figure out. What that meant for Ben was the poisoning of all his efforts and the corruption of his inventions, turning them inside out and using them for evil rather than for good. What that meant for Ben was his demise.

"Ben was not just a colleague to me. He was a friend. Many believed he was a horror, a sociopath, an ego-driven megalomaniac. These perceptions were constructs of the nefarious forces that have driven society into the ground. They were wrong. I saw his soul. I understood what he was doing. I knew the truth." He looked at Elizabeth. "Elizabeth knew, too. We worked with him to bring his vision to reality. And it was a great vision. But we failed to see that not all of us in the world want the same things from life. Not all of us want what is best for humanity. Some are nothing more than evil. And the price we paid for our failure to see was this destruction we are experiencing now. Ben paid for it with his life.

"As goes Ben, so goes the world. Unless we commit ourselves to stopping it. The Stoffer Solution became the catalyst for The Crash, so let Ben's death become the catalyst for ending the evil that drove The Crash."

Craig paused. I knew he was right. We had already joined together, even brought together many around the world to pursue a greater purpose for the betterment of humanity. We had already committed to stopping the destruction and sought greater connections among people. What Craig was saying was something more. Craig was proposing that we actively fight it. We had already taken our slow steps through negotiations, and we had found a way to send Ben's healing pulse, barely. With the kind of evil Craig was speaking about, we could not negotiate. The Crash had not been an accident. And the evil behind it would not go away if we yielded to it or if we pretended it was not there. We could not be sheep in a pasture being led to slaughter.

"I am not a soldier," Craig said. He looked at the four soldiers who stood just beyond our circle. "Most of us are not soldiers. But I will fight. And I appeal to everyone to join me. There are others here who can lead, but I offer myself as a new recruit in the war.

"And here before us now, Ben has offered himself to humanity." He lowered his head and closed his eyes. Bringing his hands together, he whispered to Ben, "Thank you, my friend. You will be missed, but you will never be forgotten."

I heard the sounds of openness again, a wide expanse. We let it exist around us.

Jason, who had been there with the others in spirit, now came forward in our minds, and actually spoke to us, something he hadn't tried before. We heard him clearly, and it seemed a natural extension of what we had already experienced with him. "If I may . . ."

Craig replied, "Please."

"I know we've all felt this evil, and we've obviously experienced its destructive forces. I would not be so presumptuous as to think we can defeat evil itself. But we can fight the evil that thrusts against us and seeks our destruction. Craig is right. We can not negotiate with evil. We barely survived our encounters with those who were sent to eliminate us. We underestimated their power. But they underestimated our ability to fight. Now, we will go for them. We don't know in what high castle they reside, but we will find them."

I knew he was talking about that shadow in the storm, the one that had also taken Lauren. Was it one person or a few? Jason was saying that the specifics didn't matter. We all knew it was there, and we weren't going to find it by traipsing across the countryside and breaking through bolted doors, seeking out dark figures wearing black capes. The results of their deeds were all around us. And though their ways of thinking may have been beyond our understanding, and we knew they didn't see life the same way we did, we now understood that they were beyond any further benefit of a doubt.

Jason continued, "We will find them through their blind minions or through their own egos. And we will give no quarter to those who attack us or stand in our way. We have fought them before, and we will do it again. We are forming our human alliance. We will reach more and more people, and we will need many. Until we unite enough of our numbers, we will fight separately to come together. And as we come together, we will grow stronger. Know that violence is not a choice. It is a truth. We either accept it or we die."

I felt our combined understanding. It flooded through us, through the Family, through Kallik in Siberia, through the climbers in Canada, and through Jaguar with her tribe.

Kallik came forward and said, "Violence against people is not our way. Though it is the way of others. We can not deny it. We will not flee from it. We will confront it."

The climbers didn't speak and were the most hesitant to the idea, but they were not resistant. It seemed that they were reserving judgment, which was a reasonable response that I expected would be common throughout the world. I knew we had a big task before us, not just the fight against evil itself, but the fight to accept what must be done. The fight to show everyone that life was worth fighting for, and we had no choice but to fight.

Jaguar said, "Fight is in the sky. In the trees. In the animals. Fight is in our hearts. We are not prey. We are predator."

Jason said, "And we still have our battles in front of us. Those battles, we each have to fight in our own ways. But know that you are not alone. We are together."

I heard the candles breathing again, as if they had exhaled and needed a breath. Their light contracted slowly.

Jason said, "Ben, you brought me out of The Crash and showed me what I hadn't seen. You were a friend, and I honor you."

I felt that I should say something, though I didn't know what. I was fully committed to the Family and agreed completely with Craig and Jason. I would be there with them and for them. Thinking of Ben's absence was almost impossible. He had become the center of my will, the force that pulled me away from The Crash and allowed me to live again. Without him, I likely would have died of vodka poisoning in my apartment or from some nonsensical crashed rampage that got me killed. The intensity of our adventure had defined my life, not just during the past couple months, but for time going forward. I had met Lauren and lost her. I had met the Family, and they were still with me. I had no final words to say out loud for Ben, because I could not imagine Ben in any final way. I had plenty of thoughts that would play in my head for years.

Nobody else spoke. I heard Daisy's soft panting below me. The room shrunk back down to its own size. The candles fluttered dimly.

I held up my shot of Scotch. The others raised their glasses. I said, my throat tight, "To Ben," and took the shot. The others followed in kind, toasting to Ben and taking their own shots.

Craig threw his glass over the counter and against the wall. It shattered with a pop and shimmer. He stepped away from Ben's body. I moved around to where Craig had stood and threw my glass at the same spot on the wall, adding more shattered pieces to the tribute. Everyone else did the same.

Silently, we all agreed it was time for the grenades. The four soldiers lined up outside their designated doors. The rest of us inserted our earplugs and left the lab hub to wait outside the room. We closed the door behind us, and leaving Lauren's body there on the cart in the smaller hallway, withdrew to the larger main hallway, taking our guns, packs, and Ben's papers with us. We stood facing each other and waited.

The first explosions were two almost on top of each other, dull, dead thuds that shook loose dust from the ceiling. After a minute or so, two more close together whumped, and then two more a couple minutes apart. Those were the six. We returned to the hub door and waited for the soldiers to open it. Terry swung the door wide in a whoosh of dust. The other three followed him out, their flashlights swinging beams of dirty light within the haze. Though they were covered in dust, they appeared unharmed. They removed their earplugs, and we did the same.

Terry said, "That took care of it." The shortest soldier nodded in agreement behind him.

I remembered two things then. One was that I had come here to get Lauren's phone and my notebooks. The other was that we had left the Beep Jeep in the outer hallway, and it would need to be destroyed, at least its controller.

I said, "We forgot about the Beep Jeep. We need to destroy the controller."

"Damn!" Craig said. "That would have been a pretty big oversight on our part."

"Yeah. I can go take care of it. I need to get Lauren's phone, anyway. I can walk out there and shoot the shit out of the controller first."

I excused myself, leaving Daisy with the others and carrying my M4 with me. I took the long walk down the hallway to the trash room exit that led to the main hallway which previously had run all the way to the surface. The Beep Jeep was just outside the door, sitting in the dust that still lingered in the air.

I needed to shoot the controller, which we also called the football. It was the key to making the Beep work when it was connected to Ben's laptop. I found it inside the caged front of the Jeep and disconnected it. It was a bit larger than the size of a football, and it had a box shape. I took it out, placed it in the hallway about 10 yards from the Jeep, and knelt to get a more stable aim with the M4. Just before firing, I remembered to put my earplugs back in my ears. Then, I fired, emptying my magazine into the controller. It had enough weight to it that the rounds didn't cause it to tumble away. They shredded the case and its insides as if it were a living thing being executed.

The Beep Jeep, sans controller, sat quietly in the haze of my flashlight, its 12 foot long pipe antenna angled upward, now useless like an arm without a brain to direct it. This invention had been the beginning of our successful efforts to send the BEMP to reset people's brains from The Crash. It had also been the source of the BEMP glitch that had given me the unique ability to see into history, especially the histories of individuals. The best way to describe what it had done to me was to say that it had given me the tenuous ability to read people's minds. I knew that I would need to exercise this ability so that I could strengthen it and put it to greater use. But I also feared what this would mean and what the negative consequences would be.

After I disabled the Beep Jeep, I headed back down the large main hallway, then made the left turn to my room. Lauren's phone and my notebooks were on the small table we had pushed over next to Daisy's floor papers. Her phone was turned off, and I held the power button and waited for it to turn on. When the power cycle finished, I swiped the screen and saw that the charge was at 52 percent. I also saw that I would need a PIN to access the phone. I held the power button, shut the phone off, and found the charger. I placed those and my notebooks inside my pack and returned to the group.

Everyone was ready to leave.

I drove the cart, Daisy beside me, Lauren's body on the back. I kept it slow, and the others walked behind us. We proceeded through the hallway and into the air handler room. At the opening to the access tunnel, I had to think about how we would carry Lauren's body up all those stairs and then up the final ladder. I gave my rifle to Craig so he could carry it up. He slung it over his shoulder. He also carried the valise with Ben's papers in it, and the only thing he carried of his own was his baubin drum. Sophia and Elizabeth each carried their own large shoulder bag with a few personal items.

I turned to the soldiers and asked, "Can you guys help me with her?" indicating Lauren's body.

They agreed and were willing to help. Any previous animosity they had was gone now. Being part of Ben's service and working with us to destroy Ben's technology seemed to have cleared their thinking and smoothed their attitudes toward us. I realized I didn't know the names of the other three.

I introduced myself and said, "Sorry, I don't know your names."

The shortest soldier stepped up to me and extended his hand. "Gerald," he said. His expression was friendly and determined. He also appeared to be the youngest of the four, barely into his 20s.

"Moore," the man behind him said, extending his hand around to me. "Sorry about your loss." In terms of age, Moore seemed to be the most senior of the four, and he was also the tallest and most sturdy looking, but he did not bear the countenance of a leader. I got the impression that he would be the man who did what he was told with every ounce of his energy, and that in battle, he would be one of the first picked for a mission to engage the enemy.

The fourth man said, "Santiago," and shook my hand. I couldn't get a read on him other than no negative vibes. I didn't worry about him, but I wasn't sure of his dedication to the other three, and thus was unsure about the extent of his desire to cooperate with us.

All four wore the desert fatigues of soldiers. I assumed that because Terry had not been armed when he escaped from his guinea pig status, the rifle he carried now was the one he had taken from me. Terry was not wearing a sidearm, though he did have my pistol and knife in his pockets. The other three each carried rifles and wore sidearms.

"Okay," I said, and prepared to pick up Lauren's body from the torso. Terry took hold of the legs, and we lifted. I realized immediately that two of us carrying her would be awkward going up the stairs. Moore saw this and got under her midsection, lifting with us. It seemed that three of us at a time were needed, working together to get her up the stairs. The others could trade off, but I wanted to carry her the whole way up. We entered the tunnel and began the climb, Daisy keeping close by. Gerald and Santiago followed, with Elizabeth, Sophia, and Craig at the back.

I steeled myself for 14 stories of stairs and then tried to forget about how far we had to go. I carried Lauren by holding her shoulder above my shoulder, and the other two took similar positions. This put Lauren's body close to the ceiling of the tunnel, and we had to navigate her around the curves. As we climbed, Terry traded positions with Gerald and Santiago every few flights, but Moore carried his burden without wavering, apparently determined to make it the whole distance. As I realized that he wasn't going to share the load, I felt a camaraderie with him, and this gave me more strength. My shoulder and back ached, but the effort felt good. I was accomplishing something important, and my body was responding in kind.

We made it to the ladder and lifted Lauren's body up to the landing, laying her across the length of the concrete floor. Then we helped Daisy up. While we waited for the other three to get up the stairs and ladder behind us, the soldiers and I sat momentarily, taking a breather. I looked toward the tunnel grate and noticed that it was not pitch-black outside. Gray light filtered in as if to say that regardless of what we humans went through, the sun would always rise and it would continue to do so even when we were gone.

I was closest to the door next to the grate, so I opened it, at the same time feeling the cool fresh air of morning. I smelled the grasses of the plains and the churned earth from the bombs. When we were ready, we took Lauren outside and laid her along the rocks that surrounded the tunnel opening. The sky was flat and cloudy, the sunrise not far off but also likely not to give a dazzling show through these dull clouds.

I trudged up the short incline of the berm to have a look at the coming day and to stretch my aching back. The soldiers waiting for us up there already had their rifles raised and ready. I quickly estimated that there were eight of them.

Chapter 15
Cortège

These newly-arrived soldiers wore solid tan fatigues. These were very different from what the Upstream troops who took over the Space Force Base wore, including the uniforms of the four troops who had joined us. There was no camouflaging what they were here to do. They stood a dozen yards away. Instead of being resigned to this situation, I felt anger welling up, ready to explode from my core.

Daisy barked, and I started to turn toward her so she wouldn't run out and get shot. Automatic gunfire erupted around me. The rifles that had been eyeing me like a mad octopus swung wildly as the troops flailed and fell. My ears rang with a growing, stinging echo.

Immediately, all the tan-clad soldiers lay dead, peppered with tattered holes and oozing with blood. The soldiers in our group ran out to the newly deceased, kicking and prodding them to make sure that dead was really dead, which it was. I looked behind me and saw that Sophia, Elizabeth, and Craig were on the ground, not shot, but taking cover. They were lifting their hands away from their heads and starting to sit up. Daisy had not been harmed either, but she sat hunched up next to the tunnel grate, obviously frightened by all the gunfire. I made a cursory check of my own body and saw no holes. Sounds were muffled, but I could hear the muted voices of our soldiers, though I could not make out what they were saying.

Looking back out toward the carnage, I saw that they were shouting at each other, not from anger but just to be heard above the ringing in their ears. Their tension relaxed, and they came over to us, glancing around to see if we were hurt. If there had been any question as to what side they were on, the question clearly had been answered. I wondered if Craig's and Jason's speeches had made the difference. No more negotiation. No more hesitation. My legs gave out, and I sat down abruptly. Daisy ran up to me and licked my face. The ringing in my ears was decreasing, and my hearing began to clear.

Terry stood over me, and I looked up at him. He shook his head ruefully. "Those fuckers came directly from Genetrix, not Upstream. They weren't part of our contingent. We saw Genetrix troops in the beginning when we moved into the Space Force Base and then after you wiped out everyone outside the tunnel. I still don't understand how you did that, by the way. They came in a small detachment with a guy in a suit who met with Captain Taylor. I heard you guys killed the man in the suit, at least he never came back out of your facility. That's what I heard. Some of those Genetrix troops were back by the park gate when you destroyed everything above the tunnel entrance, so they were out of your range. They reported to Captain Taylor what happened here."

Dixon, I thought. He had come down the stairs at the north entrance, climbing over the dead troops there, and had presented himself outside the lab when we were under siege by Upstream troops. He had been Ben's Genetrix partner, and he had believed he could talk Ben into cooperating with Genetrix and Upstream. Ben was having none of it, and Jason had shot the man, killing him.

"Fuck. I didn't know there were other Genetrix people around now," I said. "How many could there be?"

"I don't know. I saw a couple dozen back then with the man in the suit. Part of our contingent was still at the base, too, when Mr. Suit came here, including us four. Good thing, or it sounds like we'd have been killed with everyone else when you hit them."

He was right about that. Anyone nearby or in our line of sight when we sent that explosion outside the tunnel would have been evaporated, too.

I didn't want to get into that right then, so I turned back to our immediate situation. "Where the hell did they get a bomber with bombs? And a pilot?"

"I have no idea. Maybe the same place they got the other B-52. They could have landed it at Denver International and attacked from there. Or it could have been from somewhere else altogether. Or, these could be all that's left."

"Well, I'm sure as hell glad you guys were here this time. Who knows what they would have done with us. I don't know what the hell they want either. How about we throw those last two grenades into this tunnel and get the hell out of here?"

"We can do that. I don't think the explosions will do much to the concrete tunnel, but maybe they'll break the ladder enough to make entry more difficult."

Craig, Sophia, and Elizabeth were standing now, staring out at the dead troops. I heaved myself up and got my balance back. I looked at Lauren's body. *Where could we bury her now?* I walked out past the berm and saw two Jeeps parked not far away, out of direct sight of the access tunnel.

I called back to everyone, "We have Jeeps up here. Let's just take those and Lauren, and go."

We moved Lauren to one of the Jeeps and stayed back as Gerald threw the two grenades into the tunnel. The explosions cracked and echoed out of the tunnel, and a good amount of dust and concrete fragments shot out of the hole. Terry went down to the opening to look inside and inspect the damage with Gerald.

When they came back up, Terry said, "It caved in part of the concrete, but the tunnel's not sealed. Maybe we can come back another time with bigger explosives, if there's anything left at the base that we can use."

We collected the dead soldiers' weapons and drug their bodies into the depression near the tunnel access gate. We drove the SUV that Terry and the soldiers had driven and left it out on the paved road. We drove out of the park in the two Jeeps the Genetrix soldiers had brought. I drove one Jeep with Craig, Sophia, and Elizabeth joining me, Lauren's body across the back and Daisy squeezed between the front seats. Terry followed us with the soldiers in his Jeep.

Damn it! I thought. *When is this shit going to end? Why don't these people stop trying to control things?* And how many of them could be left? They had already caused the deaths of most people on Earth, maybe 90% or more. And they still send out soldiers on missions to make sure nobody is doing anything they don't like. Here I had Lauren's body in the back of a fucking Jeep. It was absurd!

I hit the brakes and stopped. I kept pressing the brake pedal, mashing it to the floor, pushing it down as though I could grind it through the Jeep and into the ground. My leg shook. I put the vehicle in park, let go of the brake, and sat rigid in the seat.

"I can't do it," I said. "Lauren's body needs to be buried. I'm not driving her to Walmart in a fucking Jeep. I'm taking her back in there and giving her a proper service."

Craig was sitting in the seat next to me. He nodded. "I'll go with you."

"Yes," said Elizabeth.

"I'll go, too," Sophia added.

I got out of the vehicle and walked back to the soldiers, telling them,

"We're going to take Lauren's body back into the park and bury her, give her a funeral service."

They nodded. "We'll go with you," Terry said.

I went back and turned the Jeep around. We drove very slowly on the access road and onto the churned-up, bombed ground. To me, these two Jeeps became a funeral procession, the best we could do in the situation. Two overlapping bomb craters gaped where the facility entrance had been, no sign of the raised door entry structure. I angled the Jeep along the shallow slope of one crater and reached the broken ground that was part of the intersecting dirt road going north and south. I turned south, passed the former tunnel entrance – the Jeep Ben had arrived in, sat down in a crater there – and maneuvered my Jeep through the ground debris until the road smoothed out. We had buried the other Family members not far from here, and I could bury Lauren in the same place.

After a few minutes of slow driving, I was relieved to see that the bombs hadn't damaged anything this far from the lab, and the cottonwood trees stood overlooking the graves of Victoria and Chieko, a few fluffy, cottony seeds still clinging to the tree branches. The excavator that Leon had used to dig the graves was parked farther down the road, and two shovels were leaned against it. We had not brought Leon's body from the base, thinking we would go back and get him after we rested up from the BB experience. Now, assuming he was buried in the rubble at the base, we could not give him his own service.

I parked near the graves, then walked over to get a shovel. I wanted to feel the exertion of digging the hole, making the effort part of the healing, part of my showing respect for Lauren.

The soldiers stood by their Jeep, waiting to see how they should be involved.

As I returned with a shovel, Craig eyed it, flicked his gaze back to the other shovel, and said, "May I?"

"Of course," I replied.

I started digging. Craig retrieved the other shovel and joined me. Elizabeth and Sophia searched around the tree and in the grasses, looking for late summer flowers. The sun was up, but the pervasive clouds kept the sky a uniform diffuse gray. The soldiers stood distant, knowing we had to do this ourselves.

I didn't think. I just dug. I felt my muscles performing their duty, working in unison, straining and stretching, my hands getting blisters. It was right.

I don't know how long it took, and we didn't talk as we dug. Eventually, the hole was deep enough. Elizabeth and Sophia had gathered some long grasses with a few weedy flowers mixed in. The sky hadn't changed. Moore helped me lay the body into the grave. I stood to the side looking into the hole. Seeing the body down there didn't make me feel better, but it was right.

I searched for something to say. I thought of the vision I had had of Jaguar's tribe and of seeing Lauren. It had been some solace to me. My feelings ran deep, but I didn't have words enough to match. I tried anyway. I said softly, "In the short time I knew Lauren, she showed me new ways of seeing life. It changed me and will always live with me. I will miss her.

"I've never been religious, but what we've experienced together with the Family has made me reconsider some of my thinking. We met people around the world who have beliefs I knew nothing about. It makes me want to know more. And I feel Lauren in all of this. We didn't discuss any religious beliefs she may have had. I don't know if she felt a personal connection with God. But I feel new connections, myself, that I need to explore. Lauren will be there with me when I do. That is only part of what Lauren means to me.

"So it is right and proper that we give her this respect today. We commit her body to the ground and carry her spirit with us always."

As I said this, I also felt the others in the Family joining us, just as they had with Ben's service. It showed me how important these traditions are. For those who are close to us, for those we love, we need this acknowledgement when they die. It's part of our psyche, part of our collective human memory. It is yet one of many things that make us human.

Craig, Elizabeth, and Sophia gathered close to me, and we closed our eyes. For the second time in a couple hours, we found ourselves together to honor our dead. The connections among the Family, and many others who we had reached, were revealing their natural order. I began to understand that humanity was meant to connect in this way, that it was natural, and as we experienced it more, the connections were happening with less effort. It was like lost memories that, once recalled, become easier to recall again and again. Exercising the connections was making the pathways easier to use. I wondered why humanity had forgotten them and why the children now found them so easy to access, at least until the BB got in the way. It could be that the BB was like humanity's overall technological evolution, or revolution, an intrusive alternative that invaded our minds and overtook many of our natural dispositions, replacing what we did naturally with its own seemingly logical solutions. Even while technology helped our existence overall, and brought so many out of poverty, it seemed that it also made us forget our own abilities. But we were finding them again.

All these thoughts flashed through my mind as I considered what Lauren meant to me. We were headed into a new humanity, or rediscovering in ourselves what had been lost. I knew that our efforts to reconnect the pathways in our crashed minds had made all the difference. And, ironically, none of this would have happened without The Crash. It was an opportunity, and I was playing an important part in driving us in the right direction. Lauren would continue to be my inspiration.

We released our hands and stepped apart.

Craig said, "Lauren will be missed but not forgotten."

Elizabeth and Sophia echoed his words.

I took up my shovel and began burying her body. Craig did the same. Elizabeth and Sophia arranged the grasses and flowers at the head of her grave. When we finished the burial, we stood silently for a moment, and the soldiers stepped over with us, bowing their heads. I felt the presence of the Family, too. This was not a last goodbye to Lauren. She would remain with me.

I inhaled deeply and felt invigorated by the morning air. "Thank you," I said to everyone.

Now it was time for us to continue our journey.

Part II
Communion

"I maintained that God did not exist. I was also very angry with God for not existing. I was equally angry with Him for creating the world."

– C. S. Lewis

Chapter 16
Commencement

By having Lauren's service, we had taken the chance of being seen by Genetrix troops. It was a chance we all were willing to take, because we were not willing to let them stop us from doing the things that were important in life. We were not going to let them control us. We stood at ground zero, literally and figuratively. Ben's lab was where The Crash began, if we consider the development of his technology the beginning. Now, the area had been bombed and left in ruin. It led me to remember the attacks on and the destruction of the World Trade Center on 9/11/2001. The physical destruction was vastly different, but what it meant was similar. There were those who did not accept our values, and they sought to destroy us because of it. They could not accept our continued existence. For them, life was not about the freedom to pursue adventure and work toward a greater human good. For them, life was about control and destruction. Whoever was behind Genetrix, and whoever had reached into our minds and taken Lauren away, was no different. They were dangerous, and we could not let them reign.

"Do we want to take care of that access entrance now?" I asked the group.

The soldiers looked at each other. Craig and the women pondered the idea.

Terry replied, "I'm willing to."

I asked, "What kind of explosives did they have at the base? Do you think anything could have survived the bombing?"

Gerald said, "Explosive Ordnance Disposal handled that. C4 or RDX with a long detonation cord is what you need. If the storage bunkers weren't hit directly, it likely would not have exploded. And if we can still get into the facility to reach it. Those are the ifs."

"Do you know how to use it?"

"Barely. I did some basic training with it, but I'm no expert. It's fairly simple, though. The plastic is easy to mold, and you use blasting cord to detonate it. It's safe to handle."

"Do you want to go to the base and see if we can find any?"

"We can," said Terry.

I looked at Craig, Elizabeth, and Sophia. They nodded and shrugged their shoulders, indicating they were okay with going. And so, our journey continued with a goal of stopping the destruction by using destruction to fight it. A little irony never hurt anyone. Wasn't that what war was anyway? Escalated destruction to stop destruction?

Let's hope that the destruction can be contained, I thought. *There's an idea that nobody at war has ever thought of before.*

We drove in the two Jeeps, following our familiar route to the base. As we approached the gate, we could see the devastation. The guard shack was caved in. We removed some rubble from the entrance and held up the gate so we could drive onto the base. We followed the troops in their Jeep. To the right, the white spherical housings for the radar lay broken in pieces like orange peels torn from their fruit. To the left, the runway was pockmarked with craters, rendering it unusable. We drove on the road for a while but soon had to divert around bomb craters. Most of the buildings this far from the center of the base still stood, though some were damaged. Toward the center where the aircraft were stored, the destruction was more extensive. The grouping of F-16s was a broken shambles, and the hangars were gaping shards of metal.

Farther out on the tarmac, the B-52 lay flat, its wings splayed out and touching the ground, its back broken. Among all this, a few bodies were scattered about and burned. Considering the early hour when the bombing had occurred, I assumed that most of the troops would have been in the barracks, which were now an L-shaped, blackened, smoldering, mound. Other buildings in the distance had similar fates. We worked our way farther south to where the helicopters were parked, all of them now piles of twisted metal. We drove past the wasted copters, across the pockmarked runway, and over to a fenced area surrounding bunkers that were spaced many yards apart. The gate stood ajar, and we parked inside the fence, next to a moderate-sized utility or office building.

The soldiers stood back from the building's entrance, and Moore fired a few rounds from his M4 at the entrance door's lock, shattering it along with part of the door. Gerald entered the building, and after a couple rounds of gunfire from him, he returned with multiple sets of keys. He told us to wait in the parking lot, and they took their Jeep across a dirt road and over to a curved, paved road that led to three different bunkers, which were hills split by the road. They parked between the hills of one bunker out of sight from my view.

Sophia asked, "Do you think there are any survivors on the base, maybe trapped in buildings or some of the rubble?"

"There could be, I guess," I replied. I didn't want to think about injured survivors in there. We weren't equipped with any means of helping them if there were, and I wanted to get off the base, finish the job with the access tunnel, and get back to the rest of the Family.

"Shouldn't we go look?"

I understood her concern, but I also thought it would be a futile effort. I'd seen news clips of searches through collapsed buildings. Very few people were ever pulled from the rubble, and those who were, usually were dead or badly injured. We couldn't even help Ben. How could we help anyone trapped in a building that had been bombed?

"No, I don't think we should," I said.

Sophia looked at me with growing astonishment.

"How could we help them, anyway?" I said. "And we don't want to get caught in here if anyone from Genetrix comes by."

"Sadly," said Craig, "I think he's right. If we see someone as we drive back out, we will certainly try to help, but we can't go searching every building. And there isn't much we can do if anyone is severely injured, anyway."

"But there could be people who we can help," she said, almost pleadingly.

"I think they're right," Elizabeth added. "We can help if we see someone, but it's really beyond us to start a search. It's just too futile and dangerous. I understand your concern, though. This whole situation is a mess, but sometimes there are no good options."

Sophia sighed, and we sat in silence, waiting for the soldiers to return. After what seemed like a half hour or so, I was getting antsy and thinking that this was taking longer than it should. Eventually, their Jeep emerged from within the bunker hills and returned to the parking lot.

Gerald said, "We're stocked up."

"I'll say you are," I replied.

The back of their Jeep was filled with military green ammo boxes of various sizes. I imagined something setting off the whole load of those explosives at one time. It seemed to me that it could take out a whole city block. But I didn't know anything about explosives. It just looked like a lot of explosive power.

"We might need it for other things," Santiago said.

"Fair enough," Craig added.

We worked our way back through the base and onto the streets, heading for the park. Along the way, I saw a few people in the distance here and there. Each one slipped out of sight as we passed. Outside the park gate, we stopped. I didn't see or hear any sign of Genetrix troops or anyone else approaching us.

Terry said, "We'll go take care of this. It's best that you stay out here."

They drove in to do the job, parking near the access tunnel, dropping off some explosives, and then moving their Jeep a few dozen yards away. I knew Gerald was the one who would set off the charge, and the others sat on the other side of the Jeep waiting for the explosion. Gerald would be in the tunnel, packing the plastic explosives into cracks and on the ladder, then wiring all of it so he could trigger the blast. Finally, in the dead silence, under the cloudy sky, I heard Gerald's distant shout to notify everyone of the pending explosion.

After about 15 seconds, we heard the whoomp and saw gray smoke puff up from below the berm. The three soldiers by the Jeep walked over to check the damage. Soon, all four emerged and got in the Jeep. They drove up next to us outside the park.

"That took care of it," Gerald said. "Dropped the back of the tunnel. It'll take some heavy machinery to open that back up."

And thus, Ben's tomb was sealed.

"Thanks, guys," I said. "How about we head over to Walmart so you can meet the Family?"

Terry smiled. "That sounds good."

I saw two bison standing side by side to the northeast, beyond the cratered ground. They stared at us, and I wondered if they were glad to see us go.

We still wanted to avoid attracting attention on our way back, but we figured driving two vehicles wasn't much of a danger, so we drove and kept an eye out for any sign of movement on the ground as well as in the sky. I began to feel a calmness that I hadn't expected. It was as though I had settled in for the evening with my first sips of vodka, but this time, there was no vodka, and most of the day was still ahead. We had big problems to deal with, and we had just said our goodbyes to two people who had become very important to us.

But instead of feeling tense and upset, I felt as though the difficulties were something shared, not my burden alone. It had been easy for me to forget the world outside my apartment and exist in my own stupor. But The Crash had pulled me back into the world, made me face reality, and now I had found the comfort of a unifying purpose. I had found others who wanted the same things. We had discovered that we could affect a positive change in what was left of humanity. I imagined the energy of our potential flowing in me like the rumble of a finely-tuned motorcycle. It was not a smooth hum but a vibrating, cycling rhythm of a machine waiting to be thrown into gear and used to its fullest, ready to tear down the street at high speed, drive deep into our hopeful future, not alone, but with an ever-growing number of others on an infinitely widening path with no boundaries.

We stopped a few blocks away from the Walmart and shut off the Jeeps, then spread out, watching and listening for any approach of a vehicle, aircraft, or a person. We had passed various piles of the crashed and the dead, people who had lived their last while fighting and clawing at each other, then died together, forming mounds that turned to festering masses of decaying flesh. The stench wafted through the city in waves as if it were an entity itself. I imagined it as a gray mist, though we couldn't see it. When we passed through a wave of it, I thought of the smells creeping into my lungs and spreading their poisons, trying to infect me. I had to push these thoughts away and focus on the waves of clean air that survived in between. This was our reality in the city. I realized that I had barely noticed these same smells when we had fled the lab in our large group, but now they were hitting me as reminders that we could not march blindly into the future without facing what had been. What had drawn my attention more? Was it the waves of stench that were standing out so strongly, or was it the clean air in between that was providing a hopeful alternative?

We waited quietly for quite a while until we felt that nobody was watching us and then finished driving to the store. In spite of the scattered dead who had been rotting in the parking lot, the air smelled fresh here. The area had been cleaned of the dead.

In the parking lot, the Family and others were clustered in a large, loose circle. Everyone sat facing the center, but nobody commanded the focus of the circle, which was occupied by a healthy fire that had been burning for a few hours. *I would need to discuss the fire situation with Jason and Glenda.* I also saw the children, along with the new people who Jason had been speaking to when I left. Jason was close to the fire calmly staring into it, Glenda next to him. Part of the parking lot had been cleared of vehicles and other debris and was now adorned with blankets and pillows from the store. It looked like a sit-in from the 60s, but I knew that this was no hedonistic drug trip and that these were not hippies. This was something new.

As we approached in our Jeeps, everyone turned toward us, but none looked concerned that we might be a danger. Jason stood and threaded his way out to where we parked a good distance from the group. Craig, Elizabeth, Sophia, and I got out of the Jeep, Daisy staying by my side as I stepped down. The soldiers got out of their Jeep and came over next to us.

"Our circle is growing," I said to Jason, observing the situation in the parking lot.

"That it is," Jason replied. "And it's not the only one. There are others, and they are all forming an even bigger circle throughout the world. It seems that our awakening connections are expanding and becoming stronger."

"Yeah, I feel it. I look forward to seeing where this goes."

"We do have a problem to face, though."

"I know about that, too. But I don't know what to do about it. I don't even know where it is or how to find it." *A shadow without a light,* I thought, *hiding beyond the corner of our eyes, waiting to trip us up and create another crash, something that could throw us all off a cliff and leave us dead in the dark abyss. All hidden behind a deception.*

Daisy growled, and Jason spotted something off to his right. He said, "I think it may be paying us a visit."

A single figure stood at the south entrance to the parking lot. It was a child, a young girl with long brown hair, dressed in faded jeans, a clean white T-shirt, and dirty red Converse. She looked 11 years old at the most. But it wasn't a girl. It was something else. It was a lie personified, a facade of innocence, a broken chromosome in the mind of humanity. It raised its hand in greeting, and I immediately wanted to sight it down with my M4 and empty my magazine into it.

Chapter 17
Lies

My rounds tore through the girl, cutting her to pieces, her white shirt shredding and mixing with the spattered red of her blood, pieces of her flesh shooting off in all directions, her legs fracturing, head splitting, body dropping to the ground, blood squirting across her red Converse, making them look clean in contrast to the stringy mess on the pavement. These images flashed through my mind, but my Carbine had remained in the Jeep, doing no harm.

What the hell was going on? Where did this visceral, visual reaction come from? How could I have such a strong need to destroy her? How could I know that she was not what she appeared to be? *It* was not what it appeared to be. But I *knew*, and so did Jason. When Jason shot Ben's former Genetrix partner, we all had had enough of the bullshit. Killing that guy didn't accomplish much, but at least he wouldn't be able to continue with his lies and manipulation. This "girl" was different. Our senses knew it, and killing her would only take a life, the wrong life, at that. But it would not stop what was hiding behind her like a trapdoor spider ready to ambush its prey, paralyze it, turn its insides to liquid, and suck it dry.

She approached us with an inhuman mixture of confidence and innocence. If I let go of my emotional and instinctual gut reaction to her, I might have seen a precocious young girl who wanted to meet us and become a part of our growing Family. Instead, I saw a horror that twisted my insides while smiling because the weather was nice.

"Hell-oh," she said brightly.

I couldn't reply. Daisy growled viciously, snarled, and began barking. I knelt down and held her around the neck, trying to calm her, wanting to make sure she didn't rush the girl. As I petted her, she quieted down and stayed still.

Jason said to the girl, "Is this a game to you? Nothing more than a competition to win?"

"I don't know what you mean."

"Sure you do."

She narrowed her smile to a grin and her eyes to a squint. "You're the ones playing with people's minds."

"Is that so? You turn the world upside down, we try to pull it back upright, and we're the ones playing with people's minds?"

"I didn't create the Stoffer Solution. I didn't go into people's heads and try to manipulate their minds. I didn't set off bombs to twist people's brains."

Such logic, I thought. She wasn't wrong about what we had done, at least technically. But she could not have been more wrong about the truth. Such twisted lies she told by playing with the truth as if it were a watch that required tuning, as if noon and midnight were the same.

Instead of getting wound up by these manipulations, Jason relaxed like a soldier at ease, not fully geared up for an immediate fight, but ready to take action if needed. He did not reply to her, and I stayed quiet as well, straining to keep my violent vision from becoming a reality.

The girl looked around at us and everyone in the parking lot, then said, "Quite the gathering you have here. Can anyone join your club?"

Jason said, "This is the Family, and we are growing stronger."

"Is that a yes or a no?"

"The Family can be all of humanity, but we will not put up with the nefarious manipulations of narcissists, psychopaths, and sociopaths."

"Then perhaps you should look closer at the people in your group." She gazed up at Jason with her eyebrows raised and a mocking pout on her lips.

Jason smiled, not allowing the girl's provocations to succeed. "I see you've skipped simple manipulation and gone straight to possession." He was referring to the girl, herself, who clearly was not the one speaking to us.

"Ah, we have discovered some new shortcuts in human communication, ourselves."

"This goes beyond communication. So you must have something important to say to us. What do you want?"

She held her arms out sideways and raised her hands as if she were being open and truthful with us, as if she were an emissary who had come in peace. "Are you not the invaders of the New World? Am I not the innocent native who has met you on the shore to discover who you are and why you have come here?"

"You know who we are, and the only innocence here is this girl you are controlling like a puppet."

I was relieved that Jason was the one who was conversing with her, with *it*. I wouldn't have been able to abide such nonsense without losing patience, and my replies to it likely would have involved scathing sarcasm, not the directness Jason was employing. He had tempered his temper, having gone from having no tolerance and reacting immediately with violence, to having enough patience to dance around this bullshit.

"Are you so sure she's a puppet?" it said. "There are no strings. And I have no reason to control anyone when there are always people willing to offer themselves up in service of the greater good."

"How can this young girl know anything about the greater good if all she sees of you are lies?" Jason was now struggling to keep his anger in check.

"Lies? Do you think you have an exclusive on the truth?"

"Obviously I don't, with you hiding behind this girl. How could I see past your lies to get at the truth when you are afraid to show yourself?"

"I don't have to hide. I'm right here!" Some impatience on its part showed through.

"Then what do you want?"

"I wanted to warn you that you're hurting people by messing with their minds, and this is a threat to the ecosphere of the world," it said. "The Crash made most everyone go crazy, but those who are left were getting better until you set off those bombs. People were supposed to heal naturally. What you're doing with these mind travels will only confuse people and upset nature's balance. You think you're helping, but you're making a mess of things."

Finally, getting to the source of The Crash, I thought. Whoever this was speaking through the girl was implying its involvement with the altered Stoffer Solution and was almost admitting that changing the STDs, the Stoffer Transcranial Devices, had been done on purpose. I wondered if they had expected The Crash to happen the way it had, if they had intended the mass deaths. This person was claiming that the crashed were better off without our help. Given all this, it, and whoever else was with it, was still trying to control people.

Why? Why the hell did it matter to them what everyone else did? There were so few people left alive that we all could go our separate ways and not bother each other. Why couldn't these people just let go, forget about running things, and live their own lives, leaving everyone else to live theirs? I wanted to yell at it, but I knew that would be useless. I left Jason to continue the conversation.

Jason said, "So, you came here out of concern for your fellow humans. That's so considerate of you. Do you want to tell us your plan to help humanity now that we're beyond The Crash?"

"We want nature to be nature and humans to be humans. The two don't mix. Just leave everyone alone. Stop these mind meetings you've been having. When you connect, you're harming the consciousness of the world. There's a natural order to things, and you're ripping into it. You're going to tear apart what's left of the world with what you're doing. Humans aren't supposed to have their fingers in everything. It's not natural."

Jason nodded. "Not natural, like using a girl as a puppet?"

"How could I reach you otherwise? Some of us need to take shortcuts for expediency and efficiency. I can't call you on the phone, and I can't get in a car and drive over to meet you. But it is important that you know what you're doing to the world."

"And zapping people's brains with the altered Stoffer Solution was natural? That was okay?"

"We didn't make the Stoffer Solution. We were trying to bring people together by *adjusting* it, so that they could have access to what they wanted much easier. It would have unified societies around the world, bringing together all the diverse populations and people into one connection that helped them find, buy, and experience anything they wanted, helped them see what would make their lives easier and better so they knew what was best for them. And we were going to give them what they wanted. They would have understood that what we could provide was exactly what they wanted, and it was the right thing for everyone."

"Then why didn't it work? What was The Crash?"

"The Crash happened because people didn't do what they were supposed to do. Things weren't supposed to go that far. We just needed to adjust the tech a little more. We were almost there. If we had the opportunity to do it exactly how we wanted, you would see now how successful it could be."

"And you see this *adjusting* of the tech as natural, but our biological connections throughout the world aren't?" Jason had become very calm and patient again.

The girl frowned. "Sometimes we have to intervene, just to set things right. People had already impacted the world. We could have soothed everyone, given them what they needed in order to stay in their places. And the world would heal."

"Just a little more time, huh?" Jason said. "A little more tweaking, and things would have been fine. And you believe this. You don't see that you were the cause of The Crash. But you expect us to stop bringing free people together so we can form a better society. This is what will split the world apart, is it?"

The girl's frown became impatient displeasure. "We knew you wouldn't understand. But we had to give you a chance to stop your destruction. We can still set things right, and we're going to do that whether you agree or not. There is still Ben's tech that we can use to put things right, and Ben will help us, like it or not. This world isn't yours to play with."

Jason started to reply, "And it isn't yours–"

"Raya?!" Sam interrupted. He had come up near us, and I hadn't noticed him until he spoke. He was addressing the girl.

Avery stood next to Sam and said, "Raya, what happened to you? Where were you?"

The girl turned to them with some hesitation and a brief look of confusion. She said, "Hey guys. Uh, I–" Her expression dulled, and she continued on a different track. "Okay, I'll leave you to look a little more closely at the lies you tell yourselves. I suggest you prepare to do what we need you to do. We'll be coming for that tech – we know you still have it – and you'll be handing it over, along with Ben, too. Or we'll take more of your people like we did that woman."

Raya relaxed her arms, and her shoulders drooped. She looked around, eyes darting as if she were re-thinking something she had decided previously. She said, "Uh, I was . . . I thought I was helping. But I couldn't even feel my body. He said there were people trying to control our minds, that he could stop them . . . ." She trailed off, looking confused.

"Did you see who went into your mind?" Sam asked.

"No. It seemed like a man, though. He led me away from our group like he was talking to me, and like I was thinking to myself at the same time, like it was my idea to leave, but I know it wasn't."

Avery said, "But you disappeared days ago. Where have you been?"

"Days? I don't know. I remember walking here. I thought I needed to go into a store for food, and I was talking to these men here." She looked very nervous, afraid. She glanced at Jason and me, then back to Sam and Avery.

Jason asked her, "Do you remember our conversation?"

"Yes. And I'm not playing a game. You asked me that. If I was playing a game."

Jason shook his head. "I was talking to the one who was in your mind."

"Then I don't know." She reached her arms toward Avery, who ran to her, and they hugged.

Jason said, "I'm sorry this happened to you. We are trying to figure out who it was and what he's after. We don't want him to do this to anyone else."

"I'm sorry," Raya said, crying on Avery's shoulder.

"You don't have anything to be sorry about. It's not your fault," Jason tried to console her. "The rest of your group is here. You can join them again."

"I know. I know. But it *is* my fault." Raya pulled back from Avery to address us. Craig stepped in closer to listen. She said, "He was following you. He said you were getting into people's heads, and you caused everyone to go crazy. And you were going to do it again. I was there. I believed him. You were in the clouds, and I don't know how I was there with you, but I was. And I know it was you because of how you looked then, the same as now when we were talking, he was talking to you." She swung her arms in frustration.

She was fighting to remember and grasp what had happened to her. And she also wanted to tell us something more.

"When were you with us before?" I asked.

"You had bombs. He said you were going to kill us."

"You saw us with the bombs?"

"Yes. It was like when we talk to other kids and see them, sort of. There was something beautiful in there, like a giant diamond. I wanted to go to it, but He pulled me away. He told me, he *made* me, he asked that woman to stop. I asked that woman to stop. When she turned, he took her. I couldn't follow after that, not anymore. After he took the woman. That's how I knew you weren't trying to hurt anyone, that he was lying, when that man took that woman."

I understood that she was talking about Lauren. It didn't surprise me. Maybe I knew there was a connection, and that's why I had reacted to the girl the way I did. I kept these feelings inside. I didn't want to make Raya feel any worse.

I asked, "When he wasn't with you. What do you remember?"

"Sleeping. But he was always with me, even when he wasn't inside me. I was so tired. There was this house, and I found food. It was clean. Nobody had been there or died there. And I slept."

"Did you stay there for long?"

"I don't know. I think so."

Jason asked, "But when he controlled you, you were on the move, right?"

She thought for a moment. "Yes, I was always walking."

Jason looked at me and shrugged. "I don't know what it means. Just trying to match up time, see what she remembers."

Raya said, "He's gone now."

I took that to mean he wasn't lurking nearby, somehow. I was glad that I hadn't made the horrific mistake of using my M4 to kill her, and now I wanted to track down whoever had been messing around inside her brain. With fewer people on Earth, the narcissists had fewer options to manipulate people, but the changes that The Crash had caused, and what our BBs had done, had apparently created a new avenue for their manipulations.

That the law of averages had not eliminated these people altogether in The Crash was infuriating. How many could there be? We were trying to make the world a better place, but these psychos wouldn't go away. Whether they were members of Genetrix or some other organization, or they weren't even working together, they needed to go. Not only because of what they had done to Lauren, but because of what they would continue to do to any society we might form.

Some of us had, in essence, made a pact down in the lab that we would not tolerate these sociopaths anymore. And Jason and Glenda would need to get us caught up on what was happening with this bigger circle they had formed here in the parking lot.

Avery hugged Raya again.

Sophia stepped over to them and said, "Let's get you a place to sit down."

Avery, Sam, Raya, and Sophia worked their way toward the circle, Ginny joined them, and I introduced Jason to the four soldiers we had brought with us.

"What now?" I asked. "They don't know Ben is dead. They think we still have Ben's technology, and they don't know we destroyed it. But that's not good enough. What do we do about this piece of shit who still wants to rule the world?"

"We chase him down," Jason said. "But we're going to do it carefully, deliberately. We can't rush in wildly. He knows we're coming."

Chapter 18
Leader

The women and Avery comforted Raya as they sat by the fire. The four soldiers who arrived with me made places for themselves not far from their Jeep. Sam stood near Raya, looking concerned. The fire added a familiar reassurance under the hazy gray sky, even though the day was very warm.

Jason asked Sam, "When did Raya disappear?"

"A few days ago, after we started looking for your group again."

"You were looking for us?"

"Yeah, we had just found Jaguar in our minds, or she found us, and we had lots of connections with other kids around the world." Sam looked resentful but was trying not to show it too much. "We didn't know you had found Jaguar too."

He stopped and thought for a moment before continuing. "We were looking for you because we watched what you did with those soldiers in the neighborhoods, back when you knocked all of them out . . . and the helicopter crashed. We hid from you at first, and we didn't see where you went after that. A long time later, weeks I think, we saw that big plane fly over us. There hadn't been any planes since the adults went crazy, so we wanted to see what was going on with this plane. It looked like it was landing, so we went in that direction. We found you in the park first.

"We didn't want to talk to you or anything, and when we found you, there were soldiers around, so we kept away from where you were. But after that, you exploded those bombs, and it messed up our heads. We couldn't find the kids in our minds again."

"I'm sorry that happened to you," Jason said. "We were trying to help the crashed. That's what we call the people who went crazy. We *did* help them. But we didn't even know about you. By the way, we call the mind connections or mind travels Iter Anima. It took us some effort to discover how to do that. We start with a fire and drumming."

"You do drumming? Wow. That's not how we do it . . . before you set off those bombs that messed up our heads. It all just went away. We lost everyone then."

"You were still in contact with other kids until we set off the bombs?"

"Yes. We knew you were doing something big because Jaguar told us. When we went into our minds the other night – the Iter Anima? – we saw lots of the children at once. Then we saw you, and whoever was behind that glowing diamond, I think. Sounds like it was the one who was inside Raya just now."

"Can you tell us about how all this happened? How did you even survive against the crashed that were everywhere when you got together?"

"Yeah. We had to fight them."

"How did Raya disappear?"

. . . .

The group of kids walked in the neighborhoods east of Denver. They knew something was going on with some adults who might not be crazy, the same ones they had seen when soldiers had surrounded these adults' trucks, and somehow, the soldiers had gotten knocked out. They didn't know anything else about the group. They only knew that something was going on with them, and Sam was thinking that they should find out what it was.

They had stopped to get some food from a convenience store, and they discovered that Raya wasn't with them. They retraced their path and spread out in a search across a few blocks of houses and businesses, but they didn't find her. They even waited overnight in case she returned, but she didn't. Finally, they chose to keep moving. It would be only two days before the BBs would explode over the city.

Weeks before, the group had gathered together for the first time after having escaped the crazed and murderous adults by their school. Most didn't know each other yet, but they had collected a pile of items from down in Dry Gulch, things they might use as weapons.

The fire burned in Sam's mind, and he saw it on the faces of all the kids. They were ready to follow him, even the older ones were, and he knew he needed to lead. The noises of chaos continued in the distance. He had wanted to come here to the dry gulch, because it was a place he was familiar with, a place where he could clear his head of the bad things that had happened to him. He hadn't considered what he would do after he got here, and he hadn't imagined having a group of kids with him. He thought of the insanity out there as an alien invasion, but something else had happened to him while he stood on the sloping bank of the gulch, watching the kids gather their weapons of junk.

He felt purpose and direction forming in his mind, the excitement of adventure, not just a child's game, but life itself. He had felt a moment like this once before, and it had happened near where he was standing now. He saw the world differently from then on. It wasn't something he could describe to anyone so that it would make sense.

Before the world went crazy, he and his brother had sat on one of the footbridges over Dry Gulch. It could have been the one next to him at this moment. They had found a couple of long branches that had dropped from a dead bush, and they had fought each other, using them as if they were swords from the times of knights, or lightsabers from Star Wars. And then they had decided that they didn't need to fight, that they were brothers in arms, instead. He'd even thought of the Dire Straits song, "Brothers in Arms," that he had heard on a music app and had even downloaded. It gave him comfort to feel this camaraderie with his brother.

It had been a quiet, cloudy Saturday afternoon. A thunderstorm had overtaken the distant mountains, covering the familiar peaks. The grayness of the clouds wasn't ominous or dreary. Instead, it was like the curtain in a movie theater just before the movie started. He'd only seen one movie where there was a curtain in front of the screen. His family had gone on vacation in Hollywood, and they went to see a movie, because that's what you did in Hollywood. He had wondered why the theaters in Denver didn't have curtains. When the curtains opened to reveal the screen, Sam knew that they had been hiding the potential for something great. He couldn't even remember the movie, only the feelings he'd had as the gathered cloth parted to reveal what waited behind it.

The clouds over the mountains were like those curtains had been. They were a sign that something great was back there, and it was coming toward them. This feeling, combined with the easy familiarity of being with his brother, had made him believe that life was an adventure he could embrace if he wanted to. And since then, seeing clouds over the mountains had always given him that same feeling.

He couldn't see the clouds over the mountains in the darkness now, as he stood looking at these kids, but he could smell the coming storm. He knew the clouds were there, and he could feel the adventure waiting behind them. It was his to take or leave behind. He knew he would follow the call for adventure. He knew that these kids with him, both boys and girls, were his brothers in arms. He even thought of the word *arms* as both weapons and actual arms that they could use to hold each other or fight attackers.

The pain of what had happened, what was still happening, would not disappear, but the hope of their adventure would give them purpose and direction. Sam smiled. *This is a good beginning*, he thought.

"Pick your weapons," he said to the group. "We have things to do, and we're not hiding down here."

All of the kids converged on the pile and combed through the items, selecting the things they wanted for weapons. Even little Henry participated, picking a strip of thick black cord. Most of what they had collected were various branches from dead bushes or broken pieces of tools, crates, and fences, small stuff that had gotten mixed in with the rocks and brush and had become part of the scenery. One of the kids had dumped a pile of rocks among the collection.

With growing interest, they chose their items, nobody arguing over the choices. Quickly, the group were armed, as best as children can be by improvising, which once had been a specialty of children whose imaginations had not yet been buried in the endless flood of electronic entertainment and virtual images. This was physical and real.

The kids stood in a loose group, checking out their chosen items, getting a feel for how the things they chose would work as weapons, and making adjustments with their clothes so they could carry what they had chosen. Most had picked up two or more items each. Theo had picked a long narrow board with part of a hinge on the end, along with a few rocks. One of the younger girls had loaded up her pants pockets with rocks, and kept out a large one to carry in her hand. Avery stood apart from everyone, swinging a long thin branch like a whip. Liam had picked a ragged piece of aluminum. He tore his T-shirt with it, ripped off the bottom section of the shirt, and tied it around one end of the metal, giving him a comfortable handle and creating a usable knife in the process. Raya picked a small shovel with a broken handle. All the others found their arms. Such was this small army.

Sam said, "I know each of you has been through a lot of bad things, and that's why you ran. But you're here now. We're all here now, and we can stick together. The way I see it, we don't need to hide inside anywhere for too long unless it rains. It's not too cold at night yet. So, the next thing we need is food. From the sounds of it out there, lots of adults are going crazy in the streets. I don't think anything is normal anymore. With this many of us, we need a lot of food. So, I say we sneak out to the big streets and see what it's like. If we can, we'll go to a store."

A younger, tiny girl, whose name he didn't know yet, said, "But I don't have any money."

"You won't need money," Sam said. "We'll have to take whatever we need. That's how it is now. And we have to be ready to fight. That's what the weapons are for. If this is the end of the world, if adults are all crazy, then we need to grow up fast so we can fight them if we have to."

They regarded him with growing determination on their faces. He tried to imagine how they could fight, a bunch of kids, most of them less than half the size of most adults.

He said, "There's a Walmart a few blocks from here. We can follow the gulch for a while first. We're brothers . . . and sisters now. If anyone tries to attack us, we will fight them. You have to use your weapons to stop them. We have to protect each other. You have to hit the crazies however you can. Just keep hitting until they stop."

Sam saw nods from some of them, and the rest seemed to be letting go of any hesitation they might have had. They were coming together.

"Let's go."

They kept to the trail along Dry Gulch, following the train tracks and passing under Sheridan Boulevard. The trail and the tracks angled up until it joined with 13th where they left the trail behind. At Wadsworth, they turned north and marched up the boulevard past the train station. Initially, they saw no people. A few cars sat abandoned in the street, some of their doors open, engines still running. It was only a couple blocks until they reached the Walmart Supercenter. Here, they found chaos.

Sam didn't want to run everyone straight into a fight. He wanted to get food and supplies, and then find secure shelter. But the parking lot looked like a war zone, something he'd seen in a movie. Instead of intimidating him, the sight energized him. He felt his sweat steaming out in the cool night air like it does on a racehorse at full speed. He knew he needed to harness that energy and turn it into successful results.

He looked back at Theo, who was right behind him. Theo's eyes widened as he saw Sam's expression, felt Sam's energy, knowing that Sam would lead them, and that following Sam was the way.

Sam also saw the faces of the other kids, a mixture of excitement and apprehension. Down in the parking lot, past a line of pine trees, cars skidded to and fro, some crashing into each other. People screamed; guns cracked and popped; screeching and clunking noises resounded off the surrounding buildings. An explosion erupted from near the farther store entrance. Most surprising to Sam, however, was the fact that nobody seemed to be raiding the store. The crazies were busy fighting each other. Two women near the closest entrance were slamming shopping carts into the side of the building repeatedly in a competition of futile destruction.

Sam said to his group, loudly enough for everyone to hear, "Get ready, and follow me. We're going into the store."

He stood tall and walked calmly down the driveway past the garden center, straight toward the central entrance. The other children followed. The chaotic activity continued in the parking lot, and the two women who were slamming their carts into the wall didn't notice them. The sliding front doors were partly closed, blocked by an overturned shopping cart, and the doors looked broken. Sam didn't hesitate and climbed over the cart as a matter of course. Soon, everyone was inside, the store lights flat and white, bathing everything in pale pallor.

A scream tore at them from directly ahead, and an old, bearded man charged up the wide aisle in front of them. Sam calmly pulled the gun from his pocket, aimed at the charging man, and waited. The man continued screaming as he got closer, until he was almost upon Sam, and Sam fired the gun once – not wanting to use all his bullets – then sidestepped to let the man pass. The round impacted the man's chest and blew through him, causing him to stumble, but it did not stop his progress. Theo hit the man with the hinged board he'd brought from the gulch. The rest of the children converged on the man as he fell, and they whaled on him with their new-found weapons until the screaming stopped.

They stood in the now-quiet store, winded and nervous. The man lay bloodied and still.

Sam addressed them: "We had no choice. This is how we protect ourselves, and you did what we needed to do. You stopped the alien. Now, let's go get backpacks first, and then pick supplies to take with us. We need to keep an eye out for anyone else who might be in here, and anyone who might come through that door. Someone grab some carts, too."

Raya went back to the entrance and wheeled a cart up to them. Avery did the same, along with Anthony. They used the carts to help them organize the things they picked. As a group, they filed through the aisles and gathered supplies, filling backpacks with flashlights, batteries, first aid kits, lighters, and other potentially useful items. Some of the kids grabbed baseballs, footballs, tennis balls and rackets, and one thought to get an air pump for the larger balls. Others picked up various smaller toys that they liked. In the sporting goods section, they smashed the knife display case, and each child chose at least one knife. Some took up large knives that required belts for easy carrying, and they went off to get the belts.

Sam looked closer at his gun to see what kind of bullets it used. Ruger .357 was stamped into the short, chrome barrel. He found matching ammo on the shelf, and shoved four boxes of it into his backpack. He then smashed the gun case with a pair of dumbbells and told Theo, Avery, and Raya to pick guns. They did so hesitantly, and Sam pulled down matching ammo for them. Theo picked a .45 auto, and Avery chose a smaller 9mm auto. Raya picked a 9mm, too. Each of them also took extra magazines. Together, under Sam's and Raya's direction, they loaded their guns and switched the safeties on. Avery and Raya put their guns in their packs, while Sam and Theo found holsters for their guns, which they threaded onto their belts. Raya suggested they all choose some jackets, too, even though it wasn't cold yet.

Having outfitted themselves fairly well, they regrouped and hit the food aisles. Many of the kids stocked up on candy bars and chips. Avery tried to get them interested in healthier things, but most didn't listen to her. She wanted them to carry some canned meat and vegetables, but that didn't go over well. They were more willing to pick up apples, oranges, and other fruit, though. Some even took cartons of milk or cold sodas. Others had chosen sturdy water bottles and filled them from plastic bottles of water in the food section.

At the front of the store, they came together and evaluated their pickings. The two carts still had a few things in them, which were scooped up as the kids finished outfitting themselves. Most still had their original improvised weapons and were proud to keep them. Sam stood back to have a look at this crew. He was impressed with their setup. Even with the multiple colors and patterns on the backpacks, some with superheroes or cartoons on them, Sam thought they looked like a valid army squad, a new colorful squad instead of the camouflage versions the adults had. Henry stood among them like a little caboose at the back of a train, but one who knew he had an important position on the line.

"Alright then. You look pretty badass," Sam said. "For now, the store seems like a good place to stay for the night. We can find a way to lock the front door so nobody else gets in. And we can eat the food that's here, too. At least we're ready to leave if we have to. How does that sound?"

Everyone either nodded assent or agreed verbally. Sam found a way to shut and lock the doors, and they went about organizing places to sleep in the home section, using the abundant mattresses, pillows, and blankets. Then someone brought over lunch meats, cheeses, and bread, so they could have sandwiches, and someone else brought a cart full of chips, crackers, and condiments. It was a crazy-looking feast in the bright aisle of a department store, and Sam had to laugh as he thought of survival TV shows. They had done exactly what participants do on those shows, which is come up with a plan, assure a safe location for themselves, get water, make shelter, and then get food. But this store version of survival looked almost comical. He imagined it would make a good TV show, if TV survived whatever was happening.

And that's when Sam had a chance to stop and think about their situation without having to make decisions that required immediate action. He sat on a blanket at the end of an aisle that overlooked most of the kids. They were in good spirits, nobody yet fully feeling the horror of their situation. He figured that some homesickness would kick in after they settled down to sleep. He knew what that was like from the first time he spent the night away from his family at a summer camp when he was six. He had awakened in the middle of the night wanting to go home, but he couldn't because his parents had gone out of town for the night themselves. He had cried to himself for most of the night, barely sleeping. In the morning, he had felt better when there was more to do to keep his mind off the thought of going home.

Sam also wondered how he could be so sure that the world was experiencing a full-on alien invasion, even if it was one without real aliens. But he somehow knew. They had only been through a few blocks of neighborhoods and a few more blocks of stores, but it seemed obvious to him that this was not just a local occurrence. There were no police. There were no sane adults about, trying to stop the insanity. And very strangely, there were no insane kids among the chaos. The world had changed, he was sure of it, and they would have to accept this new reality.

Along with that, he would learn to embrace his new place in this new world. He felt the call to lead. But what were the visions of fire that had threaded through his brain at the dry gulch? They weren't like destructive fire burning things down, but rather they were like flames of life bringing the children together. He felt those flames reaching beyond their group, reaching out to kids who weren't nearby. *Did anyone else feel this?*

What were they supposed to do now? He felt the adrenaline that had been carrying him forward running out. His muscles relaxed, and his heartbeat slowed. The lights on the ceiling flared until all was white, and Sam forgot what he was thinking about.

Steven S. Patchin

Chapter 19
Fight

We listened intently to Sam's story. I thought about how it was different from our stories, the stories of us adults, because we had had The Crash. And troops in helicopters had been chasing us. But in terms of pure survival, Sam had led his group to do what we had done: stock up with supplies, and get ready to fight.

Sam continued.

. . . .

Orange and red flickered in the brightness, resolving into flames that danced on deep blue. Tiny yellow sparks swelled out along the darker flames and rode to their peaks before bursting brightly and shooting away. The yellow sparks shot in all directions like sparklers on the Fourth of July. He could see more detail in the sparks that came toward him, and there within the yellow were faces, children turning and glancing, spinning into the distance. Voices reverberated through the flashing colors. At first, he couldn't make out any individual faces as they blended together and bounced off each other.

He felt himself among everything, not separate like an outside observer. The warmth of the fires, the children themselves, surrounded him, and he began to draw himself deeper inside. He fell into the sparks and jumped with them, seeing kids everywhere, alone and in groups.

With directed effort, he held onto one spark so that it did not jump away from him. He went with it, and heard clear voices now.

Run the other way . . . around that car . . . they're in back . . .

He saw kids huddled next to a large trash bin. His vision waved and shuddered. Strings of people ran wildly in the distant road, some crashing into each other or bouncing off each other, others tumbling to the ground, rolling, and getting up again. With screaming everywhere, the three kids next to the trash bin in the shadows of a dim street light remained hiding from the melee. Someone approached from behind, a woman with small garden tools.

Instinctively, Sam yelled, "Behind you. Run!"

Somehow, they heard him and scattered. The woman, now screaming, smacked her claw and shovel onto the trash bin. With the metal on metal sound, Sam jumped to another spark, another place, another group of kids. Sounds rumbled around him like wind and thunder, but he felt no air movement.

This group were running in the middle of a street, glancing back and trying to keep together. There were five of them dodging the random clutter of cars and other debris as they ran. Their long shadows drew out behind them as if the shadows were chasing them, too.

Bang! Spark!

Sam spun into a different place just as a group of adults reared back from each other like the petals of a flower opening in time-lapse. Two men in the center of the group flailed their arms wildly, hitting some people, missing others. One child in the crowd crawled away from this roiling mess of humanity (or un-humanity?) and flung himself out toward safety.

Another jump!

A large group of children on a school playground, adults whaled on them, smashing faces and arms and stomachs, the kids crashing to the ground, overrun by the chaotic carnage. The adults then turned on each other.

Jump!

Hit, crash! Faces and voices mixing, flying, spinning. Sparks flaring. Flames jumping. Sam felt dizzy. The roaring sounds overtook him. Everything spun. And stopped.

He faced an Asian girl as if she were sitting close in front of him. She gasped. Sam gasped.

She said, "What?!"

Sam said, "Uh!"

It wasn't a word that he "heard." She said something else. Instead, it was the idea of the word that came through. He understood the word "what" as an exclamation of surprise. In his mind, he felt that he "heard" the word "*nani*".

After he quickly recovered from the jolting moment and guessed what was happening based on the context, he spoke to her: "You really heard me . . . and you see me."

She spoke words he didn't know, but he understood their meaning: "Yes, and you see me," she said.

He asked, "Did you see a fire in your mind?"

"Fire, yes!"

"See anyone else?"

"No. Well, yes, but not like you but far away."

"That's what I saw at first, everyone far away, then lots of kids all around, closer. Are there other kids with you?"

"Yes. Look."

Sam *turned* and saw a large group of kids the size of his own group, all of them Asian, most standing, some sitting on the floor. He said, "Your group is like ours. Are you safe?"

"Right now we are. We hid in this shrine."

Sam noticed the dark, polished wood floors, red wooden pillars, and backlit white panels with black grids in front. It was a very tidy place and felt calming.

He said, "I'm Sam. What's your name?"

"Himari."

"Good to meet you. I guess you're seeing crazy people everywhere, too, right?"

"Yes, we are. Do you know what's happening?"

"Only that people are going crazy, adults, anyway."

"I know . . . Only adults."

"All the kids I've seen who are still alive were not acting crazy."

"Same here too."

"Where are you?"

"Fukuoka, Japan"

"I'm . . . *we're* in the United States, Denver. It looks like the craziness could be everywhere."

She didn't say anything for a while. Sam took in the sights of this cool room, a place where he could imagine having a sword fight.

"Then we are . . . we kids are . . . on our own," she said.

"That's what I'm thinking. Our group has prepared ourselves, but I'm not sure what to do next."

"How are we talking like this?"

"That's another thing. It could be that whatever happened to the adults happened to us in a different way. I felt some strange things in my mind only a few hours ago after my dad . . . after so many adults . . . went crazy. My group came together, and I saw fire. And then I saw even more fire just now, spinning pictures in my head. Lots of kids. And you."

Sam had begun this head journey after wondering what to do next, and now he had seen all these kids, and then talked with Himari. He was back to thinking about what to do next. He didn't have the time or the inclination to consider all the fun potential for a head trip like this.

Himari said, "I started seeing the flames and the kids, too. We will prepare ourselves as you have. Maybe there are other mind connections to make, too. Are we supposed to work together somehow?"

"I think it's up to us to figure it out. I don't see how it will hurt if we keep talking, or whatever it is we're doing, if we can, if we can find each other again. We could help each other."

"Yes."

"I think we should see where these jumps take us, but I'm really getting tired now. I'm going to go back, if I can figure out how, and sleep. I hope that's what the others in my group are doing, sleeping."

"Okay, see you again."

"Yes."

Sam concentrated on going back to his group. He tried to open his eyes, but they seemed to be open already, though he wasn't seeing what was physically around him. Everything in his vision pulled together and stretched toward a point. He saw the faces of the kids in his group emerge from the streaking colors. He didn't know all their names, but he felt himself connecting with them one at a time and then all together. Some names he did know: Liam, the boy he met first at the school; Avery, the girl with the group at the shed; Henry, the littlest one; Raya, Avery's friend, who was a year younger than Sam; Theo, Sam's friend who was also Sam's age of 11; and many others, boys and girls of various ages and attitudes, 27 in all, and each one was connecting with him and each other, their minds finding new ways to see.

Sam's eyes really opened now, and there before him were the actual faces of the kids in his group, those not blocked by the shelves that divided the aisles. They were looking at him with expressions of surprise and interest. They all knew that something unique was happening, that they were forming a bond unlike anything they had experienced before. Children came over from other aisles and stood behind those who were in Sam's aisle, everyone now within sight of each other.

Sam studied them all. He stood and said, "You feel this, don't you? It's new to me, new to us. And I think it will help us work together. I just saw kids in other places, too. It felt like I was flying or jumping around the world to meet them. Some were in trouble, getting killed by crazy adults. Some were running, and some were getting organized like us. This means something. It might mean that we're all supposed to come together. That we're supposed to help each other."

He waited to see if anyone else wanted to speak.

Theo said, "I didn't see other kids besides the ones here, but I felt what just happened right now. I was seeing through everyone's eyes at the same time and hearing voices . . . or thoughts that weren't mine. Then it settled down. And now you all are like a hum in my headphones, like I can change songs and video channels whenever I want to find you. This is crazy." He looked puzzled and pleased at the same time. He rubbed the top of his head, flipping his short, reddish-brown hair.

Avery spoke up. "I don't think this is crazy. It looks like it's the adults who are crazy. And *we're* the ones who aren't crazy. Kids aren't fighting each other and crashing cars into things. We're *fine*."

"Yes, we're fine, and *that's* what's crazy," Anthony said.

"But we're not fine," said Raya. "Look at what's happening."

"I don't think he means that everything's fine," Sam said. "Just that we're not crazy."

"But how do we know?" Raya replied. "I'm scared. I don't know what to do out there. And I don't want to go home." Her arms shook, and she looked lost.

Theo said, "We have each other. That's what's fine. We can stay together and not let the crazies get us. That makes a difference."

Sam said, "It *does* make a difference. It means that we know we're not alone and that this is happening all around us. The adults are crazy but we kids can be stronger than ever. Raya, we have your back. And I'm sorry about what happened to everyone's parents. But you helped me with the gun. We can all help each other."

Sam didn't want to make a speech, so he backed away to see how everyone would react to their changing situation.

Avery, who didn't look much more confident than Raya, worked her way over to Raya to comfort her. They both sat against a stocked shelf. Some of the kids began talking about what they wanted to do together. Others began rearranging their sleep areas. A few of the little ones who didn't have phones had found toys to play with, including some electronic games. The kids with phones discovered that voice and text apps weren't working, but some of the game apps were. Several of the older kids started organizing their packs. Sam continued to feel tired and wanted to sleep. He laid out a sleeping bag and pillow on his blanket one aisle over. Without anyone else speaking to the whole group, they all settled down, and eventually, it got quiet again.

They slept, and for Sam, it was a fitful sleep, the past few hours replaying in his mind and churning through him, thoughts of what the group might do now. Eventually, his mind calmed enough that he slept more deeply. He awoke in the morning to find some of the others already awake and talking quietly among themselves.

They had survived their first night, and now they could build on that. He strolled out to the glass front doors, passing the dead crazy man on the way. The parking lot was wet from rain that had poured heavily during the night, but the sun now shone brightly against a stark blue sky. A scattering of people lay throughout the parking lot, presumably dead, among the crashed and abandoned cars. He saw no movement. *What next?* he asked himself.

He didn't want to hide in the Walmart. They would need to go see for themselves how bad things were. Their first big confrontation with the crashed would come later that day.

They left the Walmart, heading north, then east. Sam wanted to go to the high school and see if other kids were there. On the way, they saw some crashed screaming at each other or just running through the neighborhoods. At Jefferson High School, they found only quiet sports fields and empty parking lots. They circled the school to make sure nobody was there and then set out toward downtown Denver.

At Sloan's Lake, a couple hundred acres of water surrounded by businesses and neighborhoods, they got a clear view of downtown in the distance, reflected in the lake. The surrounding streets were littered with crashed vehicles, some in the water. Very little space remained for any car to navigate the road. Crazies rambled around individually, generally heading in the same direction toward downtown. Sometimes, if a crazy saw another crazy, they would fight each other. The group of children kept a safe distance from these crashed people and adjusted their movements to mirror those crashed who were simply walking east. They also used the cars for cover when possible.

Past the lake, it was only a few blocks to Mile High Stadium. They had to sneak around bushes, trees, and cars in the neighborhood to keep hidden. Once, a man inside a house saw them and pounded in fury on the front window, but he didn't come outside. The crashed who surrounded the stadium clashed with each other on the sidewalks and parking lots, no vehicles to get in the way within the stadium's barriers. Some of the crashed lay dead on the ground. A few piles of them had accumulated against chain-link fences and other walls, churning like ants on carcasses, individuals lost in the melee.

A screaming woman brought attention to the children's group as they tried to skirt to the south of the stadium, and they had to accept their first fighting challenge. During their journey, they had been as ready for an attack as a group of kids could be. But they weren't real soldiers, and they didn't have an idea of tactics. What they did have was The Crash itself and how it affected them.

They also had Sam, who didn't have experience with fighting or organizing defenses, but he did have a greater connection with wild instincts from the past.

I'll provide some perspective from Craig, here: This is a topic that he and Ben had discussed a lot. Craig thought that Sam appeared to exhibit something like an epigenetic reaction to his situation. Epigenetics is a DNA expression caused by an experience or environmental stimulus. This concept applied to Jason, too. In theory, certain DNA characteristics could be triggered by environmental factors. The Crash is a powerful example of this. Craig hypothesized that Sam and Jason responded in unique ways to The Crash, such that certain unexpressed characteristics in their genes expressed themselves as a result of The Crash and other new experiences that they had.

For Sam and Jason, this appeared to result in a newly discovered mental thread that tied them to an accumulation of successful survival behaviors that had been developed throughout human history (though they weren't consciously aware of this). One might call this instinct, except that it wasn't prevalent in most people. The Crash had opened this in them. Sam also had a unique connection with the other children, especially those in his own group, just as Jason did with the Family.

When the woman screamed, everyone turned to see her flailing toward them. It wasn't just the woman who was a problem. It was her screams that started the skirmish by attracting the attention of other crashed and bringing them charging toward the group. All of this triggered something in Sam's mind that gave him new vision. He said to his group, "Don't use your guns yet until you know how to use them safely. I'll do the shooting for now."

Everything slowed for him, and he suddenly saw the situation clearly, the positions of the coming attackers, the attitude of the children, the relationships of attackers to children, and the potential abilities of the children to defend themselves and even take the offensive.

He briefly thought of a chessboard, though he knew little about chess. Then he thought of his tiny plastic soldiers and alien monsters organized in the sand and grass in his backyard. The throng continued approaching. As he imagined the toy soldiers moving into defensive positions, the real kids did what he imagined, and they did it with such speed when compared to the mob, that their movements were blurs. They readied their weapons as the crashed got closer, ever so slowly.

His child army fanned out on two sides with him in the center. He began firing his gun, taking his time to aim carefully at the attackers' heads. His six shots quickly dropped five of the charging horde. He backed away to reload as his soldiers converged on the ragged line. While he ejected the six empty shells from his revolver and popped in six new rounds, he was aware of the repeated swings, hits, and throws erupting from the kids as though they emanated from him and finished with them.

Dozens of the crashed fell over themselves to get to the kids as the child army assaulted these crazed people who didn't stop their attacks in the face of surprisingly greater strength. They kept coming with no regard for their impending doom. The small defenders became like a massive harrow with arms, rolling and swinging, cracking into and flattening everything in its path.

The kids climbed on the bodies of the fallen crashed and violently addressed each new assailant that threw itself at them. Sam continued shooting and reloading. The kids kept hitting and kicking. Soon, the disparate speeds of the slow army and the fast attackers evened out, and everyone's movements appeared normal again. What remained was a tattered pile of squirming or dead crashed surrounded by a blood-spattered group of children who were breathing heavily and discovering that they had nobody left to hit.

The only crashed still walking were on the other side of the stadium at the moment. The kids began to realize what they had just done, looking around at the carnage with dawning understanding that they had stopped dozens of crashed from harming them. They had just killed these crazed adults who were once regular people but who had become sick, dangerous creatures that had to be stopped.

This was a clear indication that civilization itself had changed drastically and was still changing. Sam began to realize that a search for sane adults wasn't likely to reveal sane adults. He wondered how many kids were out there trying to escape the adults and how many were getting killed. How could they find them? What could they do to help them?

Sam considered trying to find other kids in his mind as he had found the others, without actually looking, as he had earlier that morning. Could he bring his group together this way and find more kids nearby? They would need to get to a safe place, somewhere they could use as a base or even a home, somewhere close to food, too.

For now, he chose to continue leading them east. Something pulled him toward downtown, as it seemed to be doing for the crashed, too. He now felt disconnected from what they had just done, though he understood the horror of it and the need for it. He had to turn his back on the horror and keep the group moving.

.   .   .   .

As we listened to Sam's harrowing account of their fight, we adults were shocked. The children had been subjected to something that should have been unthinkable, but it actually had happened. They had emerged unscathed, at least physically, and this was perhaps more surprising than the power of Sam's Iter Animas.

Chapter 20
Tribe

Sam kept charging forward with his story.

He took his group farther south of the stadium and found access to Colfax Avenue, an elevated road that ran above the neighborhoods. The road was jammed with vehicles of all types, but very few people. The cars and trucks had been abandoned, many left running in what was now a perpetual traffic jam. Sam thought that the group would be safer up there because it was an elevated road, no stores or houses directly connected to it where crazies could hide. It also would take them into downtown.

The bright sun threw lengthening shadows in front of them as the group weaved between the hunks of plastic, rubber, and metal that had once been useful transportation. Dead bodies lay interspersed among the mess, evidence that extensive violence had happened there. The children were becoming used to these conditions, and generally took the horror as a new reality. Some even chatted about things they liked and disliked, including games, TV shows, and sports teams. Maybe some were Denver Broncos fans who felt something positive from their experience with killing people in the parking lot of the team's stadium.

From their higher vantage on the avenue, they saw the writhing chaos below them, crazy people fighting each other, smashing things, and even starting fires in vehicles. It looked like a riot, but it was not directed, nobody cooperating to accomplish anything, such as looting stores. Bodies accumulated in clusters and piles as the crazies wrestled with each other and became indistinguishable within the masses. After crossing over the highway, the avenue eventually dropped down level with the surrounding businesses, and the children had to defend themselves again. This time, there were so many crashed raging about that the movement of their group didn't attract particular attention. Instead, they mainly had to fight off those who happened to be near them as the kids walked in an extended line.

Sam knew he was putting them in danger by being there, but something inside him said they needed to see this, experience it in order to accept what they had to do, face it like a fear that would get worse if not confronted. At Broadway, he took them north toward the skyscrapers. Within a few blocks, the masses of crazed people had become too intense. Sam wanted to get away from the ceaseless encounters. The children were getting physically tired from having to stop the random attacks.

In front of the extremely tall Republic Plaza building, two crashed men ran at the group from across the street. A few crazies wandered up the steps of the building, but they weren't paying much attention to the kids. Sam directed the group toward the rotating glass doors of the building, and they ran up the steps to reach them. They waited for the two screaming men to get closer, allowing Theo and Liam to stop the men with their now-bloody weapons before trying the doors, which were not locked. The kids scrambled through the rotating doors and found an empty lobby that was relatively tidy, given the situation, except for a few items of clothing, spilled paper coffee cups, and fast-food trash lying here and there. The quiet gave them some peace after all the intensity of their trek. No crashed followed them inside.

Sam grabbed one of the lobby chairs that sat near the entrance doors and jammed it into a door opening so that the door would not rotate. Avery and Anthony did the same on the other doors with chairs and a small table, and they now had the entrances blocked. At least it would be more difficult for anyone to get inside. Sam did find it strange that the lobby was empty of people, but the Walmart had been the same. It appeared that the crazy people had a desire to go outside and fight each other, and they also had been drawn to the center of the city, as his group had been. Sam began to feel that he might have a touch of the "crazy" himself, having guided his group here. At the same time, he also believed that they had come here for a particular reason, even if it didn't make sense yet.

Might as well check out the place and settle here for a bit, he thought. He figured there would be plenty of rooms where they could camp out. And, considering the height of the building, maybe they could get on the roof and see the whole area. *Where better to have a look at the city?*

The lobby was huge, a couple stories high, and the lights were still on. Outside, the crashed went about their insanity, wandering, screaming, attacking each other, and generally throwing fits. Inside, Sam wanted to give everyone a break. He peered down the escalators that led to a lower level and then rode the moving steps down to see what was there. He found an elaborate fitness center and multiple lounge areas. He went back up and let everyone know that this would be a good place to stay. Then he went looking for food. Theo joined him.

Some doors were locked, but many were unlocked. As they searched for food, they found only office refrigerators with some leftovers, no stocked kitchens. Back down in the fitness center, Raya told them that she had noticed a noodle restaurant around the corner before they came inside. That would be something they could explore later, as well as other restaurants that were likely nearby. They had enough food for the present.

Sam wanted to get on the roof and have a look around. Theo went with him, and Avery joined them. They took an elevator to the highest floor the security system would allow, and then entered the stairwell on that floor in order to climb the rest of the distance up. They had to climb a few stories, and finally they arrived at the top, where a sign declared, "WARNING! OPENING DOOR SOUNDS ALARM. NO EXIT"

Sam pushed the bar and opened the door. They heard no alarm. Theo laid his belt across the threshold so the door couldn't close, and they stepped out onto the rooftop. The sun was low to the northwest, and the sky was still clear, as it had been all day. Sam smiled upon seeing the familiar mountain range to the west. To get a better view, they walked over to the low parapet along the edge of the roof. From there, they could see the closer buildings, as well as everything in every direction. They realized that this was the tallest building in sight. They had to shift over to each wall to look at all the closest buildings. What they saw nearby was clogged streets, hordes of people, and extensive chaos. The thought of going back into that hell gave Sam the shivers.

The view astonished them, especially when juxtaposed against the quiet that came from being up so high. They didn't hear the crashed and all their crazy activities below. Only the slight breeze and their footsteps made sounds. It was as if everything was okay, and what they had been through was only a dream. But they knew this wasn't true.

Sam said, "I wanted to see how bad all this was. It's pretty bad out there. But we made it here without getting hurt, and it looks like this is the worst of it, like downtown is the center of something."

Avery replied, "Yeah, the crazies were headed this way, but what are they going to do here?"

Theo said, "I don't think they know what they're doing at all. Those piles of people are really weird, like they're searching for something by crashing into each other. And they don't seem to come back out of the piles. It's like rugby but with lots more people and no ball."

"You watch rugby?" Sam asked, surprised.

"I've seen a bit of it, but I still don't understand it."

"Then, this is more like rugby than we thought."

Theo laughed. "Talk about not understanding something. What was that with you controlling us when we fought those crazies at the stadium? What *was* that?"

"Yeah," said Avery.

"I don't know how it works, but you know we connected in our minds at the Walmart. It just happened. And I think I'm supposed to get more kids together with us. Like I'm supposed to do this stuff on *purpose.*"

Avery said, "I wasn't as scared when you did that. It's like they were going to kill us, and then I wasn't alone, and we were all together, and we killed *them!*"

"I know," said Sam. "I didn't plan it, but we had to do it, and we did."

"So, how do we find more kids and help them?" asked Theo.

"I talked to this girl in Japan. Her name is Himari. All the way in Japan. When I did that, I was seeing other groups as I jumped around, getting dizzy. And then I thought I could jump and stop. So I did, and I talked to her. That's how I know there are other groups like ours. When our group got together, we helped each other. What I don't know is what happens to kids who don't work together. We still haven't seen any kids who are crazy. There aren't any kids out there in those piles. What if the adults are killing them? What if we were just lucky?"

Avery opened her mouth in surprise and covered it with her hand. "Oh no! What can we do?"

"I think we need to try to reach other kids through our group. When I found the groups in other places, I thought I was going to sleep. Then the lights in Walmart started glowing, and they turned to fire colors, like orange and red. That's what I saw when we were in Dry Gulch, too. I saw fire on all your faces. What if we get everybody together and concentrate on lights or something?"

"How about making an actual fire? Like the Indians used to." asked Theo.

"Yes! We could make a fire. A campfire," Sam agreed.

"But where?" Avery asked.

"Right here!" said Sam. "Right here on the roof."

"Wouldn't it burn the roof?" she replied.

Sam stomped his feet. The surface felt as solid as the ground. It was covered in hard, gravelly sand mixed with tar, and seemed really thick. "I don't think it will burn through."

"How big of a fire are you talking about?" she asked.

"I don't know. We can go see what there is to burn in the building, and take it from there."

Avery didn't seem convinced, but shrugged her shoulders in resignation.

Theo said, "This could be really cool!"

Sam smiled. He thought it would be really cool, too, even if they didn't jump to other kids out there. He gazed around at the machinery on the roof. Big air handler fans blew straight up on the east side of the roof. Near there, a raised section sat at the top of short stairs. He went up the stairs, and the other two followed him. To the south side, two heavy, metal sheets of some kind took up a good section of roof.

"Hey," he said. "We could make the fire on these, so it won't burn the roof as much."

"Yeah," Theo replied. "That should work."

They had a better view from this higher portion of the roof. To the northeast lay the plains, and beyond that, the airport. To the south and north, extensive neighborhoods stretched out for miles. They could see the crashed approaching from all directions, as if they, themselves, were at the hub of a wheel on top of this building, and the crashed were converging on them from the rim. To the west lay the foothills and the mountains. And to the southeast, the Space Force Base rested silently, just like Denver International Airport did farther northeast of it. A short distance north of the base, the wildlife refuge waited calmly, with its summer grasses and Ben's lab. Sam wasn't familiar with a lot of the specifics of what they were seeing around Denver, including Ben's lab and the Space Force Base, but he certainly saw the horde approaching. He understood the physical threat they posed, but he believed the bigger threat was whatever had caused this insanity in the first place.

What were he and the children supposed to do? Just survive by living in this skyscraper? He would need to figure that out. To start, they would bring their group together, build their fire, and see who or what they could find through it.

They took the long trip back down to the first floor and then the lower level where the kids were resting and eating.

Sam said loudly from the middle of the fitness facility, "We're going to build a big fire on the roof of this really tall building. You'll be blown away by the views up there. Be careful at the edge, though. It would be easy to fall. Anyway, we could use some volunteers to help gather things that we can burn up there. It's a long way up in the elevator and then in the stairwell. Who wants to help?"

All of the kids who were with Sam in the beginning volunteered, including little Henry, Liam, Anthony, and Raya, along with Avery and Theo. Most of the others did, too, but some were obviously too tired or too anxious to do much more than stay where they were. Sam had no problem with that. He felt that they would all find their places among the group, eventually. This experience was already beyond anything any of them would have imagined before.

Sam said, "We need some small stuff to burn that you can carry in your backpacks, but we really need big things, too, like chairs, maybe some boxes of paper, whatever looks good to burn. I don't think anyone will be needing much of what's left around here in the building. If you find something big to burn on another floor, just leave it by the elevator, and we can get it on the way up."

They spread out to various parts of the building, and eventually returned with full packs and larger items ready for pick up. When they were ready to make the fire, Sam sent some kids upstairs while he stayed back to make sure nobody was left behind. When the last ones were ready to go, they took an elevator up with Sam. At the highest elevator floor, they arrived to find most of what everyone had gathered. There were lots of boxes of new paper and old files. Also included were a few wooden broom and mop handles, one big desk with a wooden top, three wooden chairs, and an assortment of odd knick knacks that looked to be flammable. All of this had to be huffed up the stairs, the desk being the most difficult to maneuver. By the time they got everything outside and up the short steps to the raised section of the roof, the sun was winking out behind the mountains.

Theo had found a lighter in a desk somewhere. He and Sam started the fire in a box of loose papers, adding more and more boxes until the fire burned strong enough to ignite a chair. When the chair began burning, they added the big table, knowing the metal legs would not burn.

Everyone took a place around the fire platform and the expanding flames. The moon wasn't visible yet, but Venus, the ever-present summer sunset planet, stared at them from the west. The sky grew darker blue, and the fire became strong and confident. The south parapet on the roof was very close to the fire platform, and Sam sat on it, overlooking this collection of children around the fire, a soft breeze blowing at his back. The kids remained at comfortable distances from the fire, forming a half circle, facing the fire and Sam.

Sam said, "I want to try something with you. I think we can find more children with our minds, and we had this idea to use the fire, a bright, warm light for us to stare into and lead us. That's kind of what happened to me at the Walmart, but those were only lights in the ceiling. This is a living fire." He looked at Theo. "Like what the Indians had, you know, when they used to dance around the fire and see spirits? That's what we want to do, but we're not looking for spirits. We're looking for other kids."

Nobody else said anything in reply. They were already looking into the fire, wanting to lose themselves in it, not thinking about the bad things that had happened to them but seeking a new direction. Sam wondered how he would go about making any of his new ideas for finding other children happen. When he traveled before, he had just jumped away with sparks that shot off the flames he saw in his mind. He didn't know where those flames came from. Now, he assumed that having real flames might help him expand on what had happened and let him bring the group together for the experience. That, combined with the power of what they had done at the football stadium, could be like extra shots of energy working in unison, a couple Cokes and some candy bars giving them a big *zing* into the mind. *Or whatever,* he thought.

Then he stared into the fire. It glowed directly in the faces of all the other kids, like the vision he had seen the night before at Dry Gulch. He liked the fire's warmth. One of the chairs settled deeper into the burning boxes, and sparks shot up, catching the breeze and flying away from him over the children. He watched the sparks fly and forgot what he was thinking about.

One spark grew bigger in his view, and it left trails of other sparks like a comet. It twisted into spirals with its streaming embers spinning into the mix. Flames from the faces of the kids around him jumped and blended into the sparks. He heard voices from every direction, different languages and tones, all those of children. He began to understand some of the words, and then he felt the understanding. His group spun around him, and they began to understand, too. He aimed for one of the smaller sparks, so he could branch away from the "comet." His direction turned toward the tiny glowing ember, and he joined with it. Particular voices became louder than others. He understood what they were saying.

The spark became a ring that opened to a vision, and this view stabilized, his group there with him, seeing the vision, too. They were above a nighttime city street, somewhere far away from Denver, bright and colorful lights glaring around them, and in the distance, tall buildings stood as if nothing were wrong in the world, as if civilization were thriving, people were out there going about the business and enjoyment of life as they always had. But closer in, down on this street, a mob of crazies were attacking a small cluster of children, and the children were fighting back.

Sam's instinct was to help them, but he didn't have any idea how. The children in the street were fully engaged with the attackers, and they had formed a defensive circle, a dozen of them working together to keep the crashed at bay. They all had hockey sticks and were expanding their circle as they cracked the sticks across the faces of the crazies. Some adults lay scattered on the street around them, and a few lay at their feet. Four crashed continued clawing and screaming as two kids dodged away, and the others beat them until they stopped moving.

These kids stepped back and checked for more crazies as though they had dealt with these kinds of encounters before. Seeing that no more attacks were imminent, they relaxed some.

Sam reached out to them, saying, "Good to see other kids fighting."

They stood still, and a boy aged 10 or so replied, surprisingly quickly, "Do you fight, too?"

"Yes. And nice to see you can talk in your heads like us."

"I haven't talked to someone in my head before, but we were starting to hear things from each other in our heads. Where are you?"

"I'm in Denver, Colorado. I think there could be many others like us, but you're only the second . . . well, third . . . group I've talked to beyond my own group. I saw others, and I think the sparks could be more groups of kids, too."

"Sparks?" the boy asked. He was very short in stature, and his thoughts were intense but also friendly.

"That's what I see when I fly out . . . my mind flies out . . . to look for other kids."

"It's just kids, isn't it? Only kids who aren't crazy."

"I think so. We haven't seen any adults acting normal. And I brought my group with me now, by the way. They're here with us."

Sam's group had been listening to the exchange patiently and with curious interest. They now tried to speak (so to speak), and they yielded a variety of results, similar to what they would have if the meeting were in person. Some expressed a clear "hello," and others a more simple "hi." A few barely mumbled.

The boy replied, "Hello?"

Sam said, "I'm Sam."

The boy replied, "Mateo."

"Good to meet you. What city is this?"

"Montreal."

"I also met a group, a girl, in Japan last night. I saw others and warned one group that a crazy was charging at them, but mostly I only saw the kids instead of talking to them. Some were getting killed by adults. It's scary."

"Yeah," Mateo said. "Some of our friends were killed before we got these hockey sticks. And before that, our families were killing each other."

"I'm sorry," Sam said. "I think we've all lost someone. And that's why we need to connect with each other. I have a feeling that we can be stronger together . . . but I don't know what we can do . . . yet. We can figure it out together, I think."

"We've been closer to downtown, and we had to come back here. More adults were there, fighting . . . piles of them. But we haven't seen any more kids since we found each other."

"Neither have we," said Sam. "Except this way, in our minds. We made a fire so we could do this . . . and it seems to help me focus. I've been thinking that if we keep connecting to more and more kids, we can help each other. I think we're supposed to do something . . . like it's our responsibility to do something. That's why I'm looking for groups like yours. Maybe when we've found enough kids, we'll figure out what's next."

Mateo thought for a moment. "Okay. I'd rather have something to do, too. I mean, we can have some fun playing around almost anywhere we want, but I don't want to do that forever, really. I want to know what happened. I don't just want to just play games."

Sam had a look at the other kids around Mateo. They were paying attention to the conversation, though Sam wasn't sure what they understood. He looked further to see if he could hear them, and yes, they were there in his mind, too. They were mostly quiet, waiting. He thought that Mateo was the default or designated leader of their group. *Were these tribes?* Sam wondered. Is that what his group was? A tribe like an Indian tribe?

Sam said, "Maybe you can try reaching other groups, too. My group, or tribe, is going to look for more tribes right now, and we'll come back here to you eventually. I think it will make sense to keep doing this."

"Okay," Mateo replied. "I'm in for that. Do you think that whatever happened to the adults made us like this? Made it so we can talk this way?"

"I do. Could be that the adults went crazy, and the kids got something more, something that will help them do better . . . survive better . . . see things we haven't dreamed about. Anyway . . . I'm starting to think that's what happened."

Mateo smiled. "I like that. We'll work on it, too."

"Great," Sam said. "See you again."

Sam led his group away. He was beginning to get a feel for this as though it was natural, like learning to walk. But it didn't necessarily seem natural to many others yet. He thought it might become more comfortable for them eventually, though. He saw the visual movement of images in his mind as something that made sense. It started with the fire, broke off to become a spark, and the spark flew, becoming something he knew to follow. The spark led him to groups of kids who he could talk to. So, to keep traveling, he just needed to find a spark. As for how he could figure out a way to pick the sparks and go where he wanted, he would need to learn more, he thought. Maybe it was like the flames he saw on the faces of the kids in his tribe. Could he learn to recognize the different patterns of flames, and the different patterns of the sparks? Could that help him choose where to go, who to seek out?

He followed another spark that appeared when he looked for it, as if his desire to see the spark allowed him to see it. It took him to another tribe of children, this one more relaxed than Mateo's tribe. A couple dozen or more children sat on playground equipment in a park. They, too, had various items that were clearly weapons. Sam "sniffed out" the leader, a skinny redhead boy of 12 or so. *This was getting easier.* Sam introduced himself and had a conversation much like the ones he had with Hamari and Mateo. He did this three more times, making new connections, before coming back to his own fire.

The fire had burned low but was very hot. Stars covered the dark sky as though they had been formed from the sparks Sam had been following. The breeze had stopped, and Sam felt a surprising sense of calm. All the kids in his tribe were relaxed and apparently content. Sam had a deeper connection with his own tribe now, too, and he felt no strong dissatisfaction coming from any of them. They weren't just passive fellow travelers, but they weren't agitated, either. They seemed to be real brothers and sisters in arms. Sam couldn't imagine being more satisfied with their situation, considering how bad everything was beyond the building. He would give them this victory of peace without pushing them any further tonight.

They all sat and enjoyed the fire. Eventually, some began talking among each other, and Theo came over to join Sam on the parapet. They smiled at each other.

Theo said, "How did you know you could do all this? How did you know you could lead everybody?"

Sam had been wondering about these very questions, but he hadn't paused to think about them deeply. Now, what came to mind weren't *great* explanations, but they were all the explanations he had. He replied, "Did you see that movie *Braveheart*?"

"Yeah, the Scottish warrior who fought the big British armies with swords."

"That's the one. Remember how he just wanted to live his life? He had a wife, and they killed her?"

"Uh huh. That was terrible."

"Then he didn't have the life he wanted. So he had to fight to stop the armies who were killing his people."

"That's why I like that movie," said Theo.

Sam nodded. "That guy? Nobody ever told him he was the leader. He just k*new*. He did what he had to do because doing nothing was worse. And when he fought back, people followed him. That's what I feel, myself. I wasn't trying to tell people what to do. I just did what needed to be done. I just knew I had to do it, like I was *supposed* to do it."

"Wow. That's amazing."

They sat quietly for a while. Then Theo asked, "But what about this floating around on fire in your head? And taking us with you? Where did that come from?"

"Theo, man. That just happened, too. I was sitting in the Walmart . . . ." Sam laughed at the mundane ridiculousness of it all.

Theo laughed, too, but kept staring at Sam, waiting for an answer.

"A damn Walmart, man," said Sam. "I saw fire in the lights. It just happened. I don't know where it came from. So, I thought the fire we could make up here on the roof would be even better . . . and it was. And here we are."

Theo shook his head. "I don't know what all this is, but I'm glad you're at least taking us somewhere. I think I would still be at the Walmart, eating candy and playing video games or something, if you hadn't led us out of there."

"I never played those electronic games. I always played with toy soldiers, instead."

"Good thing. Fighting the crazies really isn't like the games with zombies attacking you, so that wouldn't have helped you know what to do. We were killing somebody's parents out there. They weren't just drooling monsters or bad guys from an enemy army. They were *people.*"

Sam said softly, "Yeah, I know what you mean. Toy soldiers aren't like people, either, but maybe they're more real than a bunch of pixels." He sat up straighter. "Ya know, those games will eventually stop working without being charged or having new batteries? Especially the ones on phones? With the adults going crazy, stuff is going to stop working. The power will go out. All we'll have is real stuff. And the real stuff is even more crazy than the crazies. The real stuff is—"

. . . .

"Hold on a moment. Look over there." Jason interrupted Sam's story.

He pointed to the west end of the parking lot. Three coyotes stood in a row, staring as if they knew something we didn't. Two were equal in size, and one was slightly larger than the other two. All stared intently down their sharp noses, their triangular ears twitching, and bushy, black-tipped tails swaying behind them.

Chapter 21
Coyotes

The coyotes were ominous. It was as if they hadn't approached on foot but had appeared from nowhere. I realized that coyotes hunting and scavenging in the city should have been expected. With so few people alive and so many dead bodies to eat – more toward the center of the city, according to Sam – it made sense for them to be here, but these seemed out of place.

"I haven't seen coyotes in the city before," I said.

"We've seen them a lot in the past couple weeks," said Sam. "They don't come too close, but it's weird the way they follow us sometimes."

Jason said, "These three are pretty intense."

"Just before we met you in the park, there were a lot of them watching us, like ten or more," Sam said.

"Shit!" I said. "That could be dangerous. But they have plenty of food, with all the bodies around. Why would they be watching you . . . or us?"

The rest of the people in the fire circle were now looking at the coyotes with curiosity. I watched the faces of the animals. Except for the intensity of their stares and their twitching ears, in their stillness, they almost didn't seem real.

Jason got up and began walking toward them, his right hand lingering near his sidearm. He wasn't trying to scare them away; it appeared that he wanted to see how they would respond to his approach. They didn't move until he got within 20 feet of them. Suddenly, they spun in unison and trotted away in three different directions, one heading directly back, and the other two going to the left and right. All three disappeared from view behind cars in the road and then behind buildings.

When Jason returned to the fire, I said, "For some reason, the coyotes made me think of something. Those of us who survived being crashed, and those who weren't crashed but also survived to join us, have connected, and we now have become the Family. But seeing the coyotes reminded me that the odds of all survivors connecting and getting along are basically zero. Those animals stick together, yes, and they're also good at tricking their prey, luring them out as if they want to be friends, they want to play with others, as though they aren't a threat . . . just before they kill.

"We've always known that there could be other survivors, besides the soldiers we encountered, who might not see things the way we do, who might be more interested in fucking up any harmony we've found instead of joining us or even living peaceful lives, themselves. Obviously the person who controlled Raya is one of them. But these coyotes make me wonder how many more people there could be who are like coyotes."

"A lot, I would say," Craig commented. "Throughout the world, at least, if not just here in Denver."

"Coyotes, and people who are like coyotes, they'll always survive." Jason replied.

"Yes," I said.

Jason said, "Sam, I want to get back to your story, know more about your Iter Anima. But first we need to organize the Family and address this situation with whoever it is that took control of Raya."

He raised his hands to get everyone's attention and said, "It's time we stop wondering how or why we can do the Iter Animas and start looking around to see more about who else is out there. Those who might not want to participate with us or who might want to do us harm. We did great with the BBs, and that was a huge effort. From what Sam here just said, I think the Iter Animas might not need as much focus and effort as we've been putting into them. It could be that our minds are open enough now that we can go into them much more easily.

"As we just saw, someone was actually controlling this child, Raya, with his mind. He spoke to us through Raya by actually taking control of her mind and body. We hadn't considered that possibility, because slavery wasn't in our intentions. But this person had no qualms about doing it. This is a big problem. We can't just let this slide. We can't just live and let live while people like this exist. We have to stop them. And we'll have to do it through Iter Anima. No bombs this time."

The group – could everyone here be considered the Family now? – were paying close attention and giving all consideration to Jason. The soldiers remained somewhat separate.

"What we've done in our minds so far is not magic. It's a natural ability that has always existed. We only rediscovered it. But not everyone has the same level of ability. The difference with us is how we make it stronger by working together. And that's what we should keep doing, working together.

"I propose that we take the offensive and hunt these people down. We have something this enemy doesn't . . . if everyone here will agree to join the Family." He looked at Sam and held his hands out in a welcoming gesture and addressed Sam: "We can help each other, your group and ours. I think you already see that. The first thing I want to do is get your mind connections back."

Sam didn't look surprised at Jason's statement. He replied, "We want that, too. But how? Can you use your machines again?"

"The machines are gone and so is Ben. We can't use machines. We'll have to find it within ourselves. And I'm thinking Jaguar might help, too."

I was glad to see that Jason was bringing things together. So much had happened so fast, and now we found ourselves gathered in the parking lot of a Walmart, considering how we might fight an enemy we had yet to see, with help from children who had been more mind-connected than us but who may have become disconnected because of something we did to help save the world. That was the summary that shot through my head, along with the thought that I hadn't slept in quite a while.

Jason stepped up to Sam and said, "Can you tell me how your connection worked with the other kids? Especially Jaguar?"

"Well . . . it's mostly what I just told you, that's where it started. We did good with the fire on the roof, and we did that a bunch of times. We were starting to make a bunch of friends out there, like a web, sort of. Then, I started seeing the sparks without a fire, so I could go to other kids real easy. I was teaching the kids in our tribe how to do it, too."

"And you didn't have any problem finding food? Staying safe in that building?"

"Not really. We got food from some restaurants nearby. There were lots and lots of crazies . . . *crashed?* . . . out there. The streets were buried with them in places. But they didn't bother us much downtown. They were too busy messing with each other. At first, we had to distract them to get them to move out of the way if there were too many around. One of us would start screaming so they would chase us, then someone else would distract them in a different direction while the rest of us slipped through. The crashed got slower by the time we left the building."

Jason was listening intently. He asked, "And your connections with the other kids, in this web, what were you doing with them? You said you started finding other kids so you all could work together. What did you do?"

"We started watching each other's backs," Sam said thoughtfully. "Helping each other fight. The crashed that were downtown didn't fight us as much. Maybe they were looking for something, but didn't look as hard once they got downtown. The crashed in other places were really bad, though, away from downtown and in the places where other kids were. So we helped the kids."

"How did you help them?" Jason looked fascinated by what Sam was saying.

"We *saw* for them, warned them. And then we figured out how to yell at the crashed when we weren't even there in those places. It was pretty funny. Then the kids could beat them easier because the yelling distracted the crazies, and the kids started to find ways of seeing differently, themselves, and yelling, too."

"So, what happened when you lost all that?"

Sam's eyes narrowed. "We came out of that mind storm you made with the bombs, and it was gone. We were following you. The bombs went off. We shot back home and couldn't connect after that."

"But didn't you say you saw someone else in there? Maybe whoever had Raya?"

"Yeah, there was something beautiful, like she said. We didn't see Raya in there, but she said she saw . . . like a diamond. We saw that, too. It seemed beautiful and dangerous."

"Could that have done something to you instead of the bombs?"

Sam looked pensive, then thoughtful. "Uh . . . wow," he said.

"Did you follow it, go past the diamond, behind it maybe?"

"Sort of. Yes, I guess." He thought about it for a while. "We were going further around it, because I was worried about what was back there, behind, and we didn't see what it was. Then the bombs went off. We saw the bombs."

"You saw the bombs, so you were there after they went off. They didn't break your connections. Right?"

Sam hesitated, and then nodded, understanding Jason's point. "You're right. It wasn't the bombs. We were still there . . . and then something rushed out of the diamond. *That* was it! It came from the diamond!" His eyes were wide with realization.

"I don't think it was the bombs," Jason said. "Because they helped people, and they didn't hurt us, either. I think it was this *person* who took Raya. Now, if that's true, and he deceived Raya, maybe he deceived you, too."

"What do you mean?"

"What if you didn't lose anything, but only think you did?"

"But we tried to go back out in our minds. We couldn't. We *can't*."

Jason wasn't just asking questions of Sam; he was *guiding* Sam somehow. It reminded me of what Ben had done during Memory Scribe sessions.

"Think some more. What happened exactly? Remember what Raya said, that she thought she was going into a store when she was taken, but you all really *were* going into a store. She must have gone somewhere else right then. This guy, whoever it is, made Raya see a lot of things that weren't true. Could he have done that to all of you?"

Sam searched his memory. He looked around at the other kids who were close-by. They seemed lost and worried. He said, "Yeah. I do remember what was back there. It was behind the diamond. The giant shining diamond." He thought about it some more. "It was a baseball diamond, too. We were playing *baseball!*" The other kids looked surprised and scared.

Jason said, "Tell me what you see."

"We're playing. All of us . . . well, some of us are waiting in line to bat, like it's a line to buy a movie ticket. But others are also out in the field. We're on both sides, both teams. Except the pitcher. I can't see the pitcher, and I'm at bat. The pitcher is blurry and smudgy, dark. Wait . . . he's throwing the ball–"

Sam flinches and shakes his head. He looks at Jason, confused.

"I was helping you see what really happened," Jason said. "Or see something else that you thought happened. Does anyone else remember anything like this?"

Theo said, "Yeah. That's it. I was at third base. The pitcher was throwing at *me!*"

"Yeah," said Audrey. "I was way out in the field. The ball was falling from the sky, straight to me. But . . . ." She stopped.

The other kids were nodding their heads. They mostly kept close to each other, though a few were scattered a little farther away.

Jason said, "It's like having The Crash. That's what happened to me. I remembered things that were different from what really happened. Ben helped me see that. I just did the same for you. I don't know what happened, but something is changing your memory, and since you all see something similar, I think what you really experienced was more like this ballgame than the darkness you were remembering before you came back. But even that is made up. Because of the diamond, and whoever was behind it, I think this *someone* manipulated you, all of you."

"Shit," I said uselessly. "What the hell?"

Jason was very pensive. He said to the kids, "Someone was playing with your minds. And knowing that, maybe we should not assume that you can't connect with your minds anymore."

Sam asked, "You mean we might be okay?"

"We need to try something."

I said, "Fucking coyotes."

Jason nodded to me, then announced to the crowd, "Everyone, please. Can I get your help on this? We need to do an Iter Anima with the children. Sam, are you guys okay with this?"

"Yes."

We shuffled within the circle, and everyone found a place from which to face the fire. Sam's story had taken quite a while for him to tell, and the sun was reaching down to the mountains.

I called over to Terry and the other soldiers, "Hey, if you guys want to join us, you might figure out what those voices were that you heard. You can see what we do."

They came over and found places to sit. They looked grateful for the invitation, and I was pleased to bring them into the group.

Aiden threw multiple packaged bundles of firewood onto the fire, not bothering to remove the plastic wrapping. I thought of the parallels between Jason and Sam, the similarities with our situation now. Ben had helped Jason see through the clouds in his memory, and Jason had helped Sam do the same. The kids had retreated to a Walmart, and here we were at our own Walmart. Jason was taking the reins to lead our group, and Sam was doing the same with the children. And we all had made connections around the world.

As we settled into another Iter Anima, it all felt familiar. The energy was already radiating throughout our collection of groups, our big composite group. I sat on a large blanket that Aiden offered to share. Jason didn't stand in front of us or by the fire, but instead, he sat halfway back in the crowd. We had no drums or items to use as drums.

Jason called out, "Sam? What did you do when you didn't need the fire anymore and found another way to connect?"

"At first it was just me, following sparks or lights. But later, with everyone, Avery sang."

"Avery? Can you take this?" Jason asked.

"Okay . . . "

We were looking at a different start, a new start. The Family were practiced in finding the flow into Iter Anima. I fell in easily, with some tiredness becoming a part of my experience.

Avery's voice slid across my ears and pulled me into streaming colors and light. She didn't sing with words, but notes that wavered above and around, growing, expanding, reaching, pulling us along, bringing us with her. I briefly thought of the elevating and inspiring female voice in Pink Floyd's song, "Great Gig in the Sky," and then Avery's voice became unlike any other.

I felt an orchestra join Avery's voice, and I saw my thoughts fly away.

We have more people physically close together than ever before when we begin this Iter Anima. I know where we are going before the wide dark greenery flies beneath us, endlessly disappearing to distant black among brilliant stars. Trickles of light touch the leaves as we dive deeper into the jungle.

Jaguar waits for us at the base of a tree that reaches up so wide and tall that it touches the stars. Her tribe surrounds the tree, all of them peacefully sitting, legs crossed, arms relaxed outward. The elder, Chianawookwook, sits near Jaguar. We arrive in their circle. Jaguar's eyes reflect the stars as if they are brighter inside her than they were in space. The leaves and the trunk of the tree glow with their own luminescence. I see the energy of us all, light peering out of the darkness. Our group remains behind my vision but inside me as well.

Sam and the other children hover in the distance, a small spot far from the rest of us. But Avery's voice encompasses our being. Jaguar raises her hands among soft streamers of light and brings them together slowly. In a quiet, seeping flow of energy, all the children join us, moving in close.

Jaguar speaks in us, and we all hear: "See together and become blind to lies. Look wide and know the truth. Trust each other and realize the world. Hold your minds in one and defeat evil. Want more than yourself and become God."

It is the last line that reaches deepest into me. *Something more than yourself*, I think. Isn't that God? And if so, how can we *become* God?

Avery's voice resounds a single, final note that carries through with Jaguar's message. It echoes, diminishing, diminishing, to silence. I hear my own breathing. The glow of the tree lessens to join with the dimmest collective of all starlight that filters to the forest floor in this moonless darkness. The jungle is there around us, and I can see it, but I cannot see the light directly that allows us to see. The soft illumination just exists. The warmth of us together and the forest itself hold me, and I know this is real. This is our presence.

Jaguar is showing us how to see with more than our eyes. Jason leads us where we have to go.

I am surprised at Jaguar's use of the "God." At least that is what I take her meaning to be. Trying to understand the whole concept, or her intention of meaning from what she says, will take some contemplation.

I now hear the calls of the jungle rising again, having not noticed their absence until their return, the rich, deep sounds of night animals and insects declaring their own presence. This is their place and their world. And we are also welcome here.

I may have slept. I lose track of whatever I may have been tracking, if anything. We are still with Jaguar, and I am glad of this, not wanting to return completely to myself yet. This feels like a more normal gathering now, though there is nothing "normal" about it, and I know normal is changing.

I sigh in satisfaction and say to Jaguar, "Good to see you again."

She smiles and says, "And you, too."

Jason has brought us here on Avery's voice and on flames from our fire. The children came here, too, discovering that their loss of mental connections has been a deception, and that they still can connect as before. The four soldiers witness this as well and are discovering that the voices they had heard are related to their new-found ability to see into the mind, what we know as reaching into the Cosmic Consciousness. Jason now stays back so I can converse with Jaguar for all of us.

I say, "You never cease to amaze me. You drew us here, didn't you?"

"We all drew each other."

"I understand that you connected with these children before."

"Yes. The children are unique, and we're coming together around the world."

"Do you know about what happened with Sam's group of children and Raya?"

"I do now. We lost them for a while after we sent the waves around the world. Someone else was there, too, and there always will be someone trying to break in. That's why we are leaving the jungle. We need to bring the jungle with us, bring it to the world, not bring the world to the jungle. The *physical* matters. If we only needed mind, the Earth would not be needed. And if we only lived in mind, we would be subject to deception with little ability to resist."

Because our communication is one of ideas rather than words and sentences, I often wonder what is lost in translation as we interpret each other's concepts. I don't know what subtleties are lost or misunderstood. Really, we could be misunderstanding more than subtleties. That certainly happens in seemingly-straightforward conversations, so in this situation, misunderstandings can be very likely.

I thought of what I had seen with Jaguar when I had experienced her meeting with the Kapok tree. That's when she appeared to have seen, even *traveled*, down to the level of DNA, which connects living (and possibly non-living) things throughout the world. She had been receiving information and understanding from the tree. And I had been trying to grasp her understanding. Now, she is trying to communicate more specific ideas to us. Not only am I trying to understand what she wants us to know, but I am also trying to accept that these ideas are coming from a child.

She is telling us that the impetus of her tribe's journey is physical as well as mental. Existential might best describe it. By implication, the journeys of us all are similar. And success on these journeys will require confronting evil. That is what we had been facing and discussing when Jason took the Family on this Iter Anima to Jaguar. Clearly, this is a primary concern for Jaguar.

I ask her, "Do you plan to come into what is left of the modern world and work to create a better harmony for survivors? To discover what you spoke about, that 'something more than yourself?'"

"Yes, that is our intention. And we have to work together to do this, especially to fight what hides behind that diamond, as the children saw it."

Again, she demonstrates that she knows more than I assume she does. "Do you know how we can fight it?" I ask.

"Hold our minds together as one but fight as many."

Jason comes forward and says, "I have been seeing this upcoming fight not as a fight that leads to a final singular victory, but one that involves many, relentless, small wins that take and take from the evil powers until nothing is left. Let's give it . . . give *them* death by a thousand cuts."

Jaguar says, "That is what is meant by many."

"We need to make this happen," Jason says. "I think we should continue solidifying the Iter Anima connections with as many people as possible.

We've already touched so many, and Sam's group has done the same. We need a way to keep the lines open, so to speak. That way, we can involve more and more people who can make those little cuts. Sam was already finding a way for the connections to become quicker and easier. And Jaguar, you're obviously doing the same."

Growls. A howling sound. Shouting. More howls spring out, breaking into our conversation. I feel Jason shudder, and I begin to sweat as my body reacts to something. The visions we see in our minds spin, and we are thrown back into ourselves by the fire in the parking lot.

I stood, startled into action. Others did the same.

Coyotes now surrounded us, dozens of them, very close.

Chapter 22
Repel

We all moved into defensive positions, drawing weapons, trying to evaluate the situation and decide what to do about it. Daisy growled, very agitated, but she didn't bark. The coyotes were already standing near our people on the outside of our circle. Other than a yip here and there, they weren't moving much and didn't appear to be on the verge of attacking now.

The soldiers were ready to start shooting the animals, but their line of fire included people, so they held off. Through my only clear view past people in the circle, I aimed my pistol at one of the coyotes and prepared to fire.

Jason said, "Stop."

I lifted my aim off the target and looked at him.

He said, "This is like what happened to Raya. Can you see it?"

I studied the coyotes more. They certainly weren't acting like the wild animals I knew them to be. Coyotes were great at working together, but these were surrounding our group with an apparent purpose other than hunting. If they wanted to attack, they should have done it already, and they should have attacked by picking off someone on the edge of the circle. Why would they surround us and just stand there, staring at us?

Shit! Jason was right. They weren't acting like typical coyotes. They were being controlled. If these people had the power to control Raya, it could be possible for them to control animals, too. Shit! That must be what was happening.

I felt the essence of something emanating from Jason and expanding to become an intense invisible wave coming from all of us, a wave that moved so slowly it seemed to hang in the air. It broke and touched the coyotes, immediately changing their disposition. Their purposeful intensity became surprise and confusion, shattering their stances. They bounded backwards and sideways, and then scattered and ran.

In a disorganized retreat they ran in various crisscrossing directions and disappeared into the distance, drummed away by our wave as it finished its single beat and dissipated. I felt the wave's completion like a low sound that thudded through us but wasn't a sound at all. It was a message that Jason sent, repelling the possessed spies that the coyotes were manipulated to become, breaking their connections to the nefarious fucks who hid behind them.

Jason said, for all to hear, "Next time, we're following the connection back to its source. We'll go right through and have a look at who these people are. This time, we needed to divert the threat. Next time, we'll be more ready. I'm getting an idea of what they're up to now."

We weren't confused by what had happened. We all had felt it and were part of it. Though we didn't have as much insight as Jason, we did feel like a team working toward the same goal, with Jason as the coach.

My adrenaline had jolted me upright, but the let-down in the aftermath of that jolt was creeping into me. Sleep was calling, even though I knew we had things to do. I wanted to think about what Jaguar had just said and revealed, including what she had shown me before the children arrived at the lab. I also needed time to clear my head after so much activity. But all I could think to do was sleep.

Jason and Glenda were talking to some of the new people who I had not met yet. Sam walked over to Jason and Glenda, so Daisy and I went over to them as well.

Jason introduced five new people to me, three men and two women. They were survivors, but obviously hadn't been typical crashed. They looked too healthy and well-nourished for that. I was too tired to interact with them much, so after greetings, I said, "I need to sleep. I'm pretty dead."

They understood and continued their conversation without me. As I walked toward the store, I heard Sam saying that his tribe's connections had returned and that he was amazed at how easy the Iter Anima had gone, bringing back what they thought had been lost. Jason praised Avery for her singing, which I thought was chillingly transcendent, myself. Though nobody was in the store, I knew they would come in to sleep eventually, so, carrying my rifle and pack, I went inside using my flashlight to see through the darkness. I grabbed the pillow and blanket I had planned to sleep on, and went into a back storeroom. There, I threw my stuff onto a stack of disassembled cardboard boxes, fell into the pile, exhausted, and shut off my light. Daisy lay on the floor beside me. I thought about taking out Lauren's phone, wanting to find the songs she had stored there. Then, I thought briefly about how I might bypass her phone's access PIN or figure out what it is. That's as far as my thoughts went as my mind sought sleep.

Blackness overtook me until I was somewhere else.

Chapter 23
Between

I don't know how long I slept, or when I stopped sleeping. I'm moving with Kallik, the shaman grandmother, and her family in Siberia. The sun hangs high above. I feel as though we've been talking already, and I had jumped into the middle of my own conversation. They walk on mossy tundra. Clusters of small yellow, white, and purple flowers are speckled among the rocks and lichens. More of her tribe are traveling with her than I have seen before, possibly 40 or so, all of them wearing reindeer-hide clothing, some mixed with colorful fabrics. Her core family are close to her. They all walk among their reindeer herds that are traveling in loose clusters, hundreds of the antlered animals, domesticated dogs among them, too. Some of the reindeer carry packs, including the tribe's yarangas – their portable tents – and other possessions.

I ask, "Are you going somewhere specific?"

"Krasnoyarsk."

"Why?"

"We need to come back to what is left of modern civilization so we can find other survivors and do what we can for the human world. Some people must still exist there, just as they do where you are. It is a big city."

"Is this Russia?"

"Yes. Our ancestors lived much farther north, but we have moved closer in recent times. The reindeer will do well enough outside the city."

"That's what Jaguar and her Zo'é tribe are doing, too, heading toward what is left of civilization."

"Yes, many separate tribes are coming out of the wilderness. Some who are in the wilderness that is within cities. You have helped connect us in new ways. Most had not known each other until now. This is the time for all of us to fight what has disturbed the world, what has disrupted our Cosmic Consciousness. And, as Jaguar said, we need physical interaction as well as the power that runs through our minds."

I'm not surprised that Kallik is aware of Jaguar and her determination to enter modern civilization's remains.

I ask, "Do you have contact with some of the groups who helped push the waves around the world?"

"We do, in a way. Most do not communicate like this. But talking as you and I do is unique. That will change, too, as more people understand what is happening. The awareness of the bigger threat exists in very few, though it is growing."

"Do you mean what is happening with the shadow behind the diamond?"

"That is one way to see it. It is the lie you have been told. There are endless lies told in different ways to deceive different people, but the liars we must fight are the same. They are evil."

I recall Jaguar's and Jason's exchange about how we might fight this evil. I say, "We are thinking that each of us can make cuts in these shadows. It's a Chinese concept of 'Death by a Thousand Cuts.' Or millions of cuts. That's what we're planning, anyway. But I don't know how we'll do it."

"That too, is a good idea. We will use *different* kinds of knives for cutting. Knives they do not expect."

I like her positive attitude, but it isn't giving me any idea how we can accomplish this abstract goal of cutting without *actually* cutting, and even worse, what we are going to cut isn't something we know how to find or identify. I'm glad to talk to Kallik, but at the same time, I'm annoyed that I jumped here when I was trying to sleep. My brain feels full. I want rest. I need to talk to Jason about getting more control of this. He seems to have a handle on it. Why am I getting thrown around without a plan?

I want to know what triggered this seemingly spontaneous Iter Anima so that I might control it. But . . . if I am *already* floating around, I figure I could try going somewhere else after talking to Kallik. *I should go see the climbers*, I think. They had been there for the BBs, but we hadn't talked in a while.

I'm still with Kallik, though, so I ask her, "How do you think this will work? These thousand cuts?"

We continue our southward trek. Kallik carries a thin stick for herding the reindeer, which she is not using at the moment, because they all are progressing well.

At length, she says, "We do have instruments for use in travels of the spirit. You will need to learn. I can teach you."

"This *shadow behind the diamond* came to us by taking over a girl's body,"

I say. "It did the same with a pack of coyotes. Is it using some instrument to do this? We had not considered taking over anyone's body, so we don't know how they did it."

Kallik is quiet again, though this time it's for another reason. I sense a drop in her positivity, a shrinking in her confidence.

"I have been feeling an uneasiness, which is why I persuaded my tribe to go south early. We needed to move. But I did not know about this. I do not believe that The Crash or your BBs could unleash that kind of ability. What you describe would not come from a chance occurrence. This comes from a different power, something with deeper roots and more experience. More maliciousness. You and I should perform a ceremony of our own, so we can find who is doing this. It will be too dangerous to take other people with us until we understand better. This is *very* dangerous."

Great! She wants us to do this alone. At least I know why I showed up here. The Family's affinities for going to particular places and people have done well for us thus far. I need to trust it now, so I mentally shake myself in order to get ready for what I know will be a deep experience. Kallik will want to do this immediately; she doesn't seem to be one for procrastination.

She tells her family, the herders, and a man who appears to be a leader, that she will be stopping here but that they can continue on without her. She pulls aside a reindeer with a large skin-wrapped bundle on its back and walks it over to a small rock outcropping. She unleashes the bundle and brings it down to the ground, revealing clothing, smaller wrapped bundles, and a *baubin*, a ceremonial drum much like Craig's drum that he had used in our ceremonies, but this one is considerably bigger.

She gathers rocks and arranges them to make a small fire circle, then unties a skin-bound bundle with fire-making materials, along with a larger bundle containing sticks for firewood. Soon, she has the fire flickering under the afternoon sun. She prepares her mind for what is to come. I do the same.

By the time the fire is stable and burning deeply, the tribe and the reindeer are dwindling in the distance. Kallik spreads out a woven blanket that has red, tan, and turquoise patterns radiating out from its center, and she sits on it, cross legged. From a skin pouch, she removes herbs that she places in a hand-sized metal bowl, along with water from another pouch. She places the bowl on the edge of the fire.

She takes hold of her baubin ring drum and rests one side of it in her lap, balancing it upright with her right hand. With her left hand, she picks up a long stick wrapped on one end with soft, pale animal skin. With it, she hits the drum once. Its deep sound spreads across the tundra.

I watch and wait, then find myself thinking of our situation, the things we want to accomplish, both here, ourselves, and with our extended tribe, the Family.

The enemy. *Who the hell are these people who are still trying to control the world? How do we find them? How do we stop them?*

I think of when I first met Ben on the street with his parachute. He was being chased by a well-trained soldier who was also a hitman. I try to trace this man's connections back to the source of the altered Stoffer Solution. He worked for Upstream Security, the enforcement arm of the larger company Ben teamed up with, Genetrix. It was this company that altered the Stoffer Solution. And, as we discovered, it had connections with the Chinese Communist Party, connections that surely went beyond the state itself. I had not been political, and I generally had not bothered to pay much attention to world politics. I wish I would have. I'm sure that our malevolent shadow people are the very ones behind Genetrix, the ones we need to find and stop now.

When I first met Kallik, I experienced insight into her and her family. I just *knew* things about her history, as I had with Chianawookwook and Jaguar. It had taken more interaction with them in order for me to learn details, but some of their history's essence had somehow become known to me.

I had come to believe that the *glitch* that happened when I tested the first Beep Jeep pulse had tweaked my brain differently than any of the others. Since that happened, I had experienced the ability to understand things about people and their pasts that before would have been impossible. Even at the time, during the Beep glitch, I had seen and understood things I still have yet to process. It seemed to have given me new knowledge. My first experience of this new insight revealing itself in physical application was when I had walked down the tunnel with some of the Family, before our destructive explosion, and I had suddenly known all of their names.

Maybe if we can get close to these malicious fucks, I can know more about them, too, I thought.

What kind of organization can span national borders and heavily influence or even control those who run countries? I'd heard hints of conspiracy theories that told of trans-national organizations bent on controlling the world. Something being part of a conspiracy theory wouldn't necessarily preclude it from actually being true. Is that what we're dealing with here? And if The Crash were not completely under their control, if it were really a *backfire* reaction to their altering of the Stoffer Solution, then wouldn't they have lost people to The Crash, too? How strong could their organization be now?

Kallik sips the contents of the bowl she had been warming in the fire. I continue thinking about Ben and the Genetrix connections. And I also feel a sense of Kallik's thoughts. The two split me. She searches while not searching, like being awake and not awake, or asleep and not asleep, at the same time. A state *between* thinking and not thinking.

The overhead sun rains light outward in drops that arch over us like an umbrella, but really the opposite of an umbrella, not protecting us from the raining sun, but becoming the source of it. I hear the baubin drum, the slow beats making waves that expand in circles reacting with the raining sundrops, rising against them. The tiny, colorful flowers that extend to every horizon jump with the drum beats. They begin to dance, and the raining sundrops flare brighter, while the fierce blue sky deepens to an ocean, becoming a yawning mouth that turns and swallows Kallik and me.

We fall down the throat, or we are swallowed, and the music I hear evolves from drum beats to wide voices calling in chorus, singing the greatness of who we can become. Other drums tap lightly with the singing. The sounds carry us, and I feel myself losing time again.

In the trance, we fall (*or fly?*) for however long or short in time. I see Raya's soft face and then another, a man's face. We turn inside him and pull away to see what he sees. It's Kallik and me! We stand before him, outside him, and inside, too, flipping back and forth until we stop, and we look into his eyes. He is fully aware of us and not surprised at our presence. The room is dark wood, reminding me of Ben's library but in a contrary way. This room has no books. It holds centuries of black energy, carved panels of historic battles, portraits in relief, menacing faces, arrogant confidence, unrelenting power, a darkly beating heart. Others stand alongside this man. Men and women, they are six in all, each dressed as if in celebration of a formal, landmark occasion, or in preparation for war. Their dress varies to match their ethnic backgrounds, from ancient oriental regalia to formal American attire.

I feel Kallik pulling me away, but I stop her.

She understands. And I *see* into this first man, something he can not do with me, though he knows that I am there. It is here that I come to know who he is, and he realizes my dawning knowledge. I see just a fleeting thought of worry in his expression before he flicks it away to show his typical arrogance.

I hear the voices of a funeral dirge, a death march in bitter winter, the drumbeats killing life by pounding it into the icy, frozen ground. This march of death is driven by his close ancestors whose thrones of strength were used for oppression. These are the offices he has inherited and heralded as Truth for humanity, while he pushes for and succeeds in achieving more control and power. The voices continue like a choir of the dead, lamenting lost potential, the defiling of life, and crimes against humanity.

Snow falls in the wood-adorned room in the form of disbursed tiny fragments, and soon becomes a deluge of heavy flakes swarming in whirling wind, collecting on the shelves, in the curves of the portraits, and on the six men and women standing before us. They do not react to the white storm amid the dark heart of this room. Their expressions stand cold and uncaring. I go inside them.

I learn more and more about these people while they act as if they have nothing to hide, as though their recent deceptions were mere diversion tactics for them, and they were ready to return to the more direct oppression their ancestors undertook, knowing in their black hearts that the opposition to them, if any, would be feeble and ineffective.

The information coming to me about these people accumulates like the heavy snow in the dark room. I commit their faces to memory, along with what I have discovered about them. And I also realize that I have a much better memory than I ever knew before.

When I feel I have learned what I can, I relax my hold, and Kallik lifts us out of the room. We fly above the buildings. We are in Cologny, Switzerland, a tiny municipality along a lake outside Geneva.

We know where you are now, you fucks, I tell them, though they cannot hear me. *And we'll find a way to use that against you.*

As with the Family's Iter Anima that had taken us around the world, allowing us to see the globe from afar, Kallik and I feel the forces spinning us along the curvature of the planet. We come back down in the Siberian tundra where we began. The sun recedes from its massive swell that surrounded us, and we're again in the bright quiet of moss, lichens, rocks, and flowers. Kallik's reindeer stands a few yards away, munching on whatever it finds edible in this low-to-the-ground vegetation.

The fire is embers now, and a breeze rushes across it, brightening its glow and whisking away the slight smoke that puffs from the ashes. Kallik sets her drum at her side and stretches. Suddenly, the reindeer trots over to her and across the fire, bucking its head up, pushing its antlers forward and toward her face. She throws herself backward and away from the animal. I do the same in her head. It snorts, tossing its head again, then realizes it's in the fire and jumps out, stomping its feet and running a few dozen yards away.

Kallik stands and says to me, "A friendly message from the shadows."

The reindeer, mostly unharmed except for a few singed hairs, twitches its tail, shakes its head, and begins to calm itself from the surprising agitation that had invaded it.

I say to Kallik, "These people are sick!"

"What did you learn?"

She understands that my new-found "gift" or ability is to receive information about people. It just comes, as it had with Jaguar's tribe and with Kallik, herself. This is why we went to find these people. We had hoped I would learn something, and it worked.

I reply, "It was kind of like the way I saw some of your past. I do know a bit of history, and these people have ancestors going back into some of the worst of it. They've embraced what their ancestors did, and they're doing the same things now, only worse in many ways. That first guy we encountered is the one who took Raya. He's now the head of an organization, whatever's left of them, that has been pushing a one-world government for decades. His father was a construction contractor for the Nazis.

"One woman's lineage goes deep into Russia. Most recently, they were involved in running the Gulags, the prison camps during World War Two. Another's lineage goes into the big money behind the American Industrial Revolution, with the gains they made having been used for founding banking institutions that still (for what it's worth) control most of the world's money supply. One is a Chinese man who traces his roots directly to Genghis Khan and who chose to emulate the horrible side of that terrifying ruler. The other woman is also an American from big money, and the last man is a tech billionaire with a German heritage.

"All of them work together through what they simply call *The Organization*."

"They orchestrated The Crash? They're the ones who are invading people's minds?"

"Yes. They controlled Genetrix, which was responsible for distributing Ben's Stoffer Solution, but worse, they altered the Stoffer Solution. And *that's* what caused The Crash. The first German man, whose name is Reinhard, actually told us through Raya that they had been close to making all these manipulations of the Stoffer Solution work the way they wanted them to work. They just needed a little more time to refine it. And they plan to come take Ben's technology so we won't get in their way.

"That's what they were doing with the Upstream troops all along. They never wanted to use the Beep or BBs to help anyone. They just wanted us to stop what we were doing."

On the one hand, it is good to know all this for sure, but on the other, I'm pissed! I think about what these people have done. "Nothing but lies and manipulation. All the time we spent trying to negotiate with these pieces of shit. Possibly our only saving grace was that they didn't know how close we were to setting off the BBs. Probably, they had no idea we could do what we did. Maybe that's their egos interfering with their thinking. We have to use those egos against them in every way possible."

Kallik says, "I'm going to contemplate the thousand cuts we need to give them. These people are a huge threat with their ability to directly control people."

"As if they weren't controlling society for decades anyway," I reply. "And I also think we need to worry about them sending more people to stop us. That's what they'll need to do if they're going to take Ben's technology. Though there isn't anything to take."

"It's gone?"

"We destroyed it after Ben died."

"That was a good choice. Do you worry that they might have other ways of getting what they need?"

"Only through the heads of—"

Fuck! I thought. *Only through the heads . . . the minds . . . of Craig and Elizabeth.*

Kallik heard me as I had my realization. She says, "The minds, yes. Maybe a bigger threat."

"I need to get back to the Family," I say. "We've been protecting against them taking the technology directly. That's not the only problem. Raya and the coyotes were a distraction. Not a show of force or even spying, but a distraction. Thank you for your help. I'll . . . we'll be back."

Kallik nodded. "I will prepare those *knives* as best I can."

Steven S. Patchin

Chapter 24
Threat

I flung myself awake, or *away*, startling Daisy. I fumbled around until I found my flashlight and ran out of the storeroom. No other lights were on as I wound my way over toward where I thought Jason and Glenda would be sleeping. Then, I decided I wanted to find Craig and Elizabeth first, so I began looking for them down the aisles where everyone had set up bedding and places to sleep. The store was quiet, and I didn't see anyone awake. The sight was eerily foreboding. Everyone lying in the aisles looked like they were dead, and I couldn't tell who was who.

Finally, I stopped my hunt and yelled, "Hey! Everybody! Hey, wake up. It's important. Craig! Elizabeth! Where are you?"

This stirred most everyone, and many began sitting up and turning on flashlights and other portable lights to see who was yelling. I heard a shout from Craig: "Here. Over here."

By the time I walked around to his aisle, Craig was standing at the back, shining his flashlight toward me. I picked my way around people in their sleeping bags and blankets to reach him.

Out of breath, I said, "They're not coming for just the technology. They're coming for your minds! Yours and Elizabeth's."

"What?"

Elizabeth shuffled over to us. Jason and Glenda arrived behind her.

I said, "These people, these people in the shadows, behind Raya and the coyotes, they're not coming just to physically take Ben's technology. They could be coming for Craig and Elizabeth, at least they will when they figure out what happened, and that Ben's dead. Maybe they already know."

Jason asked, "Weren't you asleep? How did you find out?"

"Iter Anima. I traveled by myself. I didn't want to, but it just happened. I went to Kallik, and then she took me farther. We found where the shadows are. I know who they are. But then we realized what their next step would be. Going into . . . controlling Raya and the coyotes was a distraction. Coyotes, see? The tricksters. We should have known sooner. They'll come for your minds next. That's how they'll get the technology."

"Distraction and misdirection are important tools in magic performance. I should have suspected their strategy sooner," Glenda said.

"How do we protect against attacks on our minds?" Jason asked.

"Man, I don't know," I said. "These people are more fucked up than we thought. And I'm starting to think that they could have found a way to make mind connections before we did, before The Crash. Just look at how they took over Raya and the coyotes. We couldn't do that."

"Are you sure?" Glenda asked.

"That we couldn't do that? Well . . . ."

"Didn't you feel like you were almost able to make the climbers move when you jumped perspectives in them? They fell to the ground, didn't they?"

"Uh, I wasn't trying to control them. I just made them dizzy with how I entered their minds."

"She's right," Jason said. "You were on the verge but backed away."

"No, I–" I stopped and thought about it. "I didn't see it that way, but Jason, isn't that what you did when we fought the soldiers in the stairwell?"

"It felt more like a video game to me. But yes, I did have some control."

Glenda said, "That's what I mean. We've been touching on that ability already. I wouldn't ignore it. I think we have it in us too."

"I did that, too," said Sam, who had stepped up next to Jason and Glenda. "I was definitely making some of my tribe move when we had to kill a bunch of crazies at the stadium. I felt like I had arms and legs everywhere, with a gun and sticks and stuff."

"That's right," I replied. "What you described was like what Jason did, right?" I looked at Jason.

"It sounded like it," Jason said. "But a little different. I think the kids are doing even more than we did, in some ways. Especially when they help other kids in different places. We should try to combine what we can do with what the kids can do and see how far we can take it."

"We should," Glenda said. "For defense and for offense."

"Then maybe we really can fight these shadow people. *The Organization*, that's what they call their group," I said. "They had members around the world. I'm not sure how many survived, but we have to assume there are more than just the six I saw."

I described my experience to them in more detail.

"Why don't they just attack us now?" asked Craig. "It sounds like they could kill us if they want to."

"Maybe they don't want to push us too much," said Glenda. "Maybe they don't want us to find out what *we* can do to *them*."

"Exactly," Jason said. "Maybe they're actually afraid of us."

"Then, let's make sure we're ready for them," Glenda said.

"I'm all for that," I said. "And I think we should be careful about our physical space as well. Those coyotes could have done a lot of damage if they had attacked someone. And, we don't know if the plane that bombed the base and the lab is still around, if they can load more bombs and come back. We have a lot to prepare for."

"At least if they really want to get what's in Craig's and Elizabeth's heads, they aren't likely to try to kill us at once," Jason said. "They'll need to be selective."

"I think so too," I replied. "So, we need some defensive plans, but like Glenda said, we also need to take the offensive. And for that, we need our own coyotes. Or, we can be the coyotes, ourselves. We've got to get into their heads and learn more about them. Kallik is working on some ideas for helping us make those thousand cuts you spoke about. She says there are *tools* we might use to make this happen. So first, let's figure out how we can send our own spies."

"Do you think there's a way to spy on them and not get caught?" asked Elizabeth.

"And how might they come for our minds?" asked Craig.

I recalled the first time we did an Iter Anima with the intention of recruiting someone new. It was Gabriel, the climber. We reached him as he was actually climbing on a high pitch in Squamish, British Columbia. I didn't want to startle him during the climb, so I watched and waited until he was in his bivy before I "spoke" to him. He hadn't known I was there until then.

"I think it's possible to target them and spy on them. *Maybe.*" I said. "We've been able to hang back in people's minds without them knowing. But these *Organization* people are different, so we can't be sure. As for how they might do the same to us, we can only guess. If they can get into our minds, especially Craig's and Elizabeth's, they could be able to learn what they need to learn. We have to be on guard. I wonder if we can actually guard ourselves. Can we hang back and watch each other's minds?"

"I think we can," Sam said. "We're already doing it with other kids."

"I've been thinking about that since you described it," said Jason. "We've reached out with our Iter Animas, but we had different aims. Although I do recall when we warned Jaguar about an incoming threat from the crashed, but we didn't do anything about it directly. It was up to them to respond . . . and man, did they respond. What you kids were doing is different. You're actually participating in those situations with other kids. I'd like to get with you and talk about that, and understand what's happening when you travel."

"I think that just having this awareness of the threat will help us defend against it," said Glenda. "Now that we know they're out there, that they can spy on us, we should be able to notice if they come around."

"You could be right," Jason said. "As we become more aware of what's happening out there, and become more in tune with our own abilities to *see*, we can watch each other. And we can learn to fight."

"And if we're to fight well," Glenda said, "we need to stop running, stop hiding, stop planning our defenses. Just for a time. First, to make our enemies think we're not watching, so we can catch them off guard. But second, so we can remember something of what life is *supposed* to be. We have a lot of people here, and we call ourselves the Family, but we're always on the run or reacting to what's happening. We were settling down a bit when we got to this store, but now we're back to planning offense and defense like we're an army. Can we stop for a time and just be people? And maybe let our enemies come to us?"

"We haven't had much choice . . ." Jason responded, starting to justify what we'd been doing.

Glenda cut back in: "I'm not saying we shouldn't make sure we're safe. I'm not *complaining*."

Jason and Glenda exchanged a glance that seemed to involve an understanding.

Glenda continued, "It's just that I think part of what's important is to remember to *live*. It's a horror what has happened to us, what has happened to the world. We're lucky to be alive at all. And we've done a lot as we've tried to put things right. So, can we stop for a minute and get to know each other, *especially* because our connections with each other could be the most important part of our strength? The better we know each other, the better we can work together."

We stood in silence as we contemplated what Glenda said. I knew she was right to an extent. Sure, some of us had gotten to know each other during all this insanity. Lauren and I had lived through an entire relationship in this time. But mostly, what we did as a group always revolved around some goal, however important. Survival, yes, but also trying to reset the minds of everyone. Maybe the goal now should be to take a break and not have a goal, or simply do nothing and see what happens. And maybe we're more prepared for our enemies than we think we are.

Socializing, for me, back in my former life, mostly had been limited to a few people at a time. I didn't like socializing in big groups, and when I found myself in group situations, I always kept to the fringes, maybe having a conversation with one or two people. But I also knew that *society* meant socializing. Civilization was about people. And we shouldn't be fighting only for survival. Really, we were fighting so we could discover what it meant *to live*.

Without Lauren, what I had been discovering was shattered pieces of what could have been. Jaguar had shown me that my life wasn't hopeless, and I had carried on with doing what had to be done, but I was afraid to stop and think about it. We had only buried Lauren yesterday. And yet, it seemed so long ago. Yes, Glenda was right, but it still scared me to stop moving.

Glenda asked, "We don't believe anyone will come for us or attack us immediately, do we? We can't know for sure, but can we take the risk for a little bit of time and just stop for a moment?"

"We don't know for sure," Jason said. "But I don't get the impression that something is going to happen right now." He looked over to me. "Do you?"

"I don't think so," I said. "But the thought of it sure as hell made me panic."

Jason said, "Maybe it's not the best thing to just jump into this without some more thought, anyway."

Elizabeth said, "I agree with Glenda. Let's take some time to be people. We're fairly safe here, and if we're not, we can deal with it."

I hadn't expected Elizabeth to say something like this. She had been mostly quiet, and I had seen her as an intense, dedicated worker, maybe even a loner. She did what was needed, and obviously cared about doing things right, but I hadn't thought of her as having any interest in social affairs. And while I had this realization, I also laughed to myself about the fact that I had just learned something personal about her. Yes, Glenda was right that we should get to know each other, and Elizabeth was right that we should remember to be people.

Jason dropped his arms to his sides as if he were letting go of some task he had wound himself up for. He even smiled. "Yes, yes. Okay. You're both right. How about we have a barbecue?"

At first, I thought he was being facetious, but I quickly realized he wasn't. *Fine with me*, I thought.

Glenda and Elizabeth both smiled in response to Jason's suggestion, and the others who had gathered nearby nodded in agreement. I glanced at my watch and saw that it was 5:36 a.m. So much for getting more sleep. It was a new day. Daisy rounded the corner of the aisle where we stood and sat lazily, evaluating us. If she could have spoken, I imagined her saying, "Are you people finally settling down?"

To which I would have answered, "No, but we're trying."

Chapter 25
Magic

The idea of having a barbecue sounded good, but actually having a barbecue in the precise traditional sense was not possible in our present situation. There was no fresh meat or vegetables. There were, however, grills for cooking and propane tanks for fuel, but no food that would have been typical for a barbecue in the past. The meat and vegetable sections of the store had become horrors of fetid decay.

But we could raid the canned and packaged food sections for alternatives. Here, we found an extensive variety of pre-cooked beef, chicken, and fish, including Spam. We also found a good variety of vegetables. Jon, who had cooked breakfast for us before we did the BB Iter Anima, took charge again, obviously enthusiastic about cooking. Even though it was morning, previously an unusual time to have a barbecue, we soon had everything arranged on tables in the parking lot to cook for and feed 67 people in our ragged and resilient group.

After cutting the anti-theft cables on the grills, we lined them up and fired them up. Lots of non-fresh food remained available on the shelves. We had our pick of spices, condiments, and sides. Within a couple hours, the parking lot became the place for a tailgate party without tailgates. Using bluetooth speakers they found in the store, a couple people played music from their phones. I thought of Lauren's phone with her music that I had retrieved from the lab, and a feeling of relief and comfort spread through me. At least I had that. But I would need to figure out how to get into it, considering it required a PIN for access.

As Jon and Ginny served varieties of seasoned and unseasoned meat from the grills, and others served side dishes, the group spread out, forming smaller cliques, everyone finding a place to feel welcome. The social occasion gained a life of its own, with smiles, laughter, tears, and conversations flexing organically across the blacktop of the parking lot.

Elizabeth, Aiden, and Ellen got together with the children to see what the kids might need or want. Mitchell, a crashed survivor himself, went to the new people who had arrived just before I had gone back to the lab, and began chatting with them. I really liked that guy, always so pleasant and positive, and not even a bother when I had found him barely surviving in his house. Javier and Nasir were speaking to the four soldiers I had brought back with me, and Jason was walking over to them, too. I saw Renzo talking to Craig, and Sophia eating with Glenda. Daisy wandered from group to group, depending on which one was most generous in feeding her scraps.

If I had a social direction I wanted to follow during this barbecue, I realized that it would involve talking to Glenda. We had a very difficult start to what would become an important friendship. When she had been lost deep in The Crash, and Ben and I had first approached her and Jason's group, who were already becoming the Family, she saw me only as a threat, and I saw her as an insane bitch who attacked me. I later realized, after seeing her fight Upstream troops, that she had been protecting her Family, and especially Jason, just as a mother and spouse would do naturally. I found a lot of respect for her then. When Glenda was wounded, Sophia had been instrumental in nursing her back to health.

I took my plate of barbecue-flavored canned beef, canned corn, and olives over to where Glenda and Sophia were sitting on lawn chairs in the shade of the store. I also carried a warm can of Guinness, which, being a stout beer, wasn't too bad warm. I noticed that they each had what looked like red wine in clear plastic cups, another beverage that could be tolerable while unchilled.

I greeted them and asked, "May I join you?"

They both smiled and indicated a nearby folded lawn chair which I could use. I grabbed it and settled in next to them. They even had a small patio table that was big enough that all three of us could put our plates and drinks on it.

I said, "It's really nice not to be fighting, traveling, or planning anything."

"Very true," said Glenda.

"And nobody seems to have any major ailments at the moment, either, so it's a good time to relax a bit," said Sophia.

She had taken up the mantle of caregiver for anyone who needed it. She was also the first person in the crashed Family to see through some of the insanity by recalling her profession and using her knowledge to help others. It showed Ben and me that purpose was a good way to pull some of the Family out of their crashed fog enough that they might have hope for some level of recovery.

"I don't know how you do it," I said to Sophia. "You've become the nurse for dozens of people."

"I love it. I think I was born to do this."

"I guess when it comes to aspirations, yours are being fulfilled right here and now."

She smiled. "I think you're right."

"That's great. It's good for all of us then."

"Very much so," Glenda said, looking at Sophia. "I wouldn't be here if it weren't for you."

Sophia blushed and turned to get a drink of her wine.

I addressed Glenda: "And you. You're keeping us all in check enough that we don't forget to live a little. I'm really glad you brought that up. I was starting to break down, and I don't know if I could have kept going much further. And with Lauren . . . ."

Glenda touched my hand. "We miss her. And I know it's even more difficult for you."

She didn't need to say more. We understood. I felt solace that she cared.

I didn't want to think about Lauren's death too much at the moment, so I said, "But you know something that's surprising to me? I feel I know you because of what we've been through together, but I really don't know anything about your background, what you did *before*. At least I know Sophia was a nurse or nurse's assistant, right? And I think you know that I was a motorcycle mechanic and hunter. What about you?"

Sophia stared at Glenda along with me, both of us with questioning grins on our faces. I wondered if Sophia already knew Glenda's background.

Sophia said, "Tell him."

Glenda sat up straighter in her chair and took on a formal persona, her hands in her lap and her expression one of such proper confidence that she appeared on the verge of making some sort of presentation or announcement.

She raised her hands above her head, palms upward, and tilted her head such that I saw the real depth of her beauty for the first time. She seemed to radiate an air of showmanship, too. It was a transformation that shocked me, or maybe it was my own realization that shocked me.

Her eyes actually twinkled. "I'm a magician," she said.

"What?" I blurted.

"I'm a performing magician . . . or was."

"Wow! I would not have guessed that, but I can see it in you quite clearly now. That's amazing."

"It was my passion, as I recall. A recollection I've only had recently, slowly starting in my dreams. But it's coming back, and I rather like it, the magic part at least. Some of the rest is disturbing."

"I can understand that," I said, "I know how you met Jason, but what happened to you before you met? Do you remember much from when The Crash took you? How you wound up on a baseball field?"

I was aware of Jason's story because I had heard a lot of it through his Memory Scribe sessions. His MS story included his first meeting with Glenda. But I didn't know Glenda's side of the story at all.

She said, "I don't yet remember how I arrived at the baseball field where I met Jason. I do remember meeting him, though, and what we did together." She looked embarrassed and troubled.

Like all of us, I supposed, we had done things we would prefer to forget, or at least keep private. I knew about a lot of what she and Jason had done, starting with their killing people while living in their crashed delusions. And the wild, crazed sex they had in the dugout at the baseball field. In the context of The Crash, they couldn't be faulted for their violent actions. And as for the wild sex, well . . . .

"Hey," I said. "We all know what The Crash did to us, what it made us do. We'll be dealing with that all our lives. We can't let it eat at our minds. Eventually, we have to accept what happened and keep living."

Hell, I had killed my fiancé, and I was grateful I didn't remember much of that.

Glenda began her story: "My parents were performers and musicians. They both sang and played multiple instruments. Before I was born, they lived in Las Vegas and had a successful celebrity impersonation show. And before that, they traveled with a larger group of performers. I guess you could say it was like a traveling circus. They went all around the world. When they settled down in Vegas, their show had a twelve-year run.

"Things changed in Vegas in the nineties, and a lot of the shows stopped using live musicians in lieu of recorded music. My parents moved to Denver in the mid-nineties and opened a costume shop, which became the go-to place for other performers. They never gave up performing, themselves, and did small gigs for events and parties here and there, sometimes even out of town. When my older brother, Jimmy, and I were old enough to sit at a piano, they began teaching us music. I took to the piano naturally and learned quickly. Jimmy was good at it, too, but his favorite instrument was guitar.

"What got me into magic was a friend of my parents named Lawrence Lane. He was a lot older than them, and he was a very successful designer and maker of magic props. He was a great magician, too, who was world famous in the sixties and seventies. He showed me a card trick when I was five, and I became obsessed with magic."

. . . .

Lawrence taught Glenda simple card tricks at first, and when she showed an aptitude for performing the tricks with flare and showmanship, he began teaching Glenda more fancy effects with props. By the time she was a teenager, Glenda was doing shows at her school. When she was in high school, she picked up gigs through her parents' contacts. Sometimes, she and Lawrence even did shows together. Jimmy sometimes joined them, but by then, he had his own local rock band, and Glenda didn't see much of him.

Two years after high school, she joined a small group of magicians who each specialized in a different type of magic performance. One did card tricks, another concentrated on hypnosis, and the third was into psychic mind reading. Glenda, who became the youngest of the group at 20, brought prop effects to their show, with her collection of tricks that included a disappearing rabbit, moving ropes through a box, large spot cards, and a shattering bottle, among others. All of these tricks were designed and built by Lawrence, who by then was 86 and suffering from dementia.

Her touring magic company, which they called Solo Collective, spent most of their time practicing, but they were also picking up gigs around town, and finally did a two-month tour with a larger illusionist act that traveled around the west. When that ended, Glenda taught an after-school magic class for elementary and middle school kids. It made her realize that she wanted to teach professionally, so she signed up for her first college classes at the community college, with the intention of getting a degree in teaching. After her first semester in community college, she still roomed with one of the magicians from her touring company, Mary Anne Heart.

The start of The Crash for Glenda was coming home to a disaster at her parents' house.   Until Lawrence developed dementia, he visited them often. When his memory began to fade, they would pick him up from the assisted living facility where he lived, and bring him to stay at their house, sometimes for the whole weekend. That happened less and less as Lawrence's dementia worsened. Because Lawrence's wife had died in the early 2000s, and his friends had either died of old age or become incapacitated themselves, he didn't have anyone close to him but Glenda and her parents. He'd never had children, and he saw Glenda as a daughter. They were really close, especially because of their love of magic. She deeply adored the gentle and thoughtful man every bit as much as she did her parents, with whom she had a very close and loving relationship.

Her loving relationships with the three of them made The Crash's intrusion into her life a nightmare beyond anything she could have imagined.

It began when she went to visit her parents while Lawrence was at their house. She heard the screaming before she opened their front door. She saw the blood immediately when she stepped through the doorway. She'd been feeling agitated during the prior couple days, and hadn't felt like visiting, but she went anyway, because it was the right thing to do. The agitation escalated when she heard the screams and saw the blood. It triggered her nerves and jolted her brain. It was The Crash jumping into her mind, but it had infected her loved ones first.

Lawrence sat in the big orange chair beside the dark fireplace, his legs pulled up and his arms wrapped around them. He was screaming repeatedly to nobody in particular, short, huffing, "UHH, UHH, UHH!" Very loud. The seat of his chair was soaked, apparently from urine, and Lawrence's hands were bleeding.

Glenda's parents stood in front of the fireplace, yelling at each other. Her mother held the fire poker out toward her father, whose face was red, his fists clenched.

He shouted, "You know I had nothing to do with that. It was canceled because you didn't get the deposit. They would have paid. And Lawrence would have gotten us everything we needed. But you fucked it up."

Her mother screamed, "Lawrence, Lawrence. What, are you sucking his dick?" She noticed Glenda in the doorway and directed her ire toward her daughter. "Maybe *you're* sucking his dick, you little whore."

Glenda slammed the door and added her own screaming to the mire, The Crash now fully invested in her mind. "You're jealous? Why're you yelling about dicks?"

Her father grabbed for the fire poker, but it was a feeble attempt, and her mother wrenched it away and swung it at the man's head. It cracked across his face, sending him falling onto Lawrence, who now jumped up and stood in the chair, shrieking. Her father rolled sideways and landed on his feet. He rushed at his wife who shoved the fire poker toward his stomach. He stumbled, and she rammed the long tool deep into him. He fell, pulling the poker down with himself as he tried to wrench it out of his stomach.

This sent Glenda into a rage. She charged her mother, hands flailing clumsily. Her mother took up another tool from next to the fireplace, the ash shovel. Glenda hit her before the woman could raise the weapon. They both fell onto the bricks at the base of the hearth and struggled with each other until the woman hit Glenda on the leg.

Glenda backed away and stood, yelling at her mother, "You fucking bitch! You wouldn't know what to do with a dick! I'll bet you're not even my mother!"

"Who would have you anyway? You're not my kid." She swung the shovel and missed, hitting Lawrence on the legs.

Now Lawrence heaved himself into the mix by jumping toward Glenda's mother, but instead of hitting her, he fell off the chair and bounced onto Glenda's father on the floor. With the poker in his stomach, the younger man was struggling in the slickness of his own blood. Lawrence tried to push himself up but was unable to find the strength. He turned sideways, his back resting on Glenda's father.

Her mother raised the shovel, ready to bring it down on Lawrence, but Glenda intervened, ripping it from her mom's hands and throwing it across the room. Glenda slammed herself into her mother and drove the woman's head into the fireplace mantel. That ended it. Her mother dropped on top of her father and Lawrence, not moving again. Her father didn't react, himself no longer moving either. Lawrence wormed himself away from the two bodies and leaned against the orange chair, panting.

Glenda stepped out of her dad's blood and stared down at Lawrence. Rather than feeling relief that the yelling had stopped, Glenda began to feel rage toward Lawrence.

He said, apparently thinking clearly, "Glenda, I'm sorry. It's terrible."

Reaching over her parents, she picked up the fire tool stand, knocking out the remaining tools and lifting the base above her head.

Lawrence said, lifting his hands toward her, "Glenda, you—"

. . . .

Glenda was bent over in her lawn chair, head down, arms around her head, crying. Sophia rubbed her back, trying to comfort her.

I said, "My God, Glenda. I didn't want to make you relive that. I'm so sorry."

Glenda mumbled from within her hunched-over position, "It's not your fault." I barely heard her when she said, "It was something that had to come out. I think this was starting to haunt my dreams."

I felt like shit, knowing that I had triggered this memory with my questions. I reached over and held her shoulder. She put her hand on mine so I wouldn't feel so badly, which made me feel worse, but I appreciated the gesture. The three of us remained in our triangle for a while, until Glenda sat up and wiped the tears from her face.

She said, "So, I'm a magician, or illusionist, as we like to be called. And I had been planning to become a teacher."

I said, "Maybe you could bring some magic to the children here. You've already brought magic to the Family."

"We wanted to take a break. Stop constantly thinking about how to open up the Family to more people. Stop thinking about fighting the ones who caused The Crash," Glenda said, "but it's impossible to let it go. What they've caused is an atrocity, not just a mistake, not a reaction to a miscalculation. *This was on purpose!*"

I couldn't disagree with her. As much as we wanted to believe or pretend that The Crash wasn't intentional, in one way or another, people had gotten together and had made the choices that caused it. I couldn't imagine this apocalypse happening without those who made these decisions knowing at least *something* about the potential consequences. What Glenda was saying was that she believed it was *fully* intentional. I saw no evidence to contradict her.

"Here's what I'm thinking," Glenda said, angry and determined. "With these thousand cuts we need to inflict on the people in The Organization, we'll have to use some magic. Sleight of hand, misdirection. We can use their egos against them. I have an idea about how we can do that."

"I'm glad to hear it. I don't know much more than the direct approach," I said. "If I could, I would charge straight at them and grind them into the ground, or scatter them into the ether, or whatever material works to eliminate them forever."

"Let me think about this some more," she said. "We really should enjoy this barbecue, too. And I do want to go talk to the kids."

"Sounds good to me," I replied.

I left Glenda and Sophia to collect themselves. I didn't feel like finishing my food then, so I threw it away and picked up another Guinness. Sipping the warm beer, I wandered around the parking lot and at least greeted almost everyone there. I managed to get a little more in depth into conversations with some of those I didn't know well, and by the time the party began breaking up, I realized that I had *socialized* at a very respectable level. The thought of that made me laugh. And the thought of what we had yet to do made me get another Guinness.

Chapter 26
Playground

After everyone had eaten enough, and the grills were turned off, nobody wanted to go back inside the store. It was barely past noon and comfortably warm, but not too hot, considering that it was mid-July. Elizabeth, Ellen, and Aiden decided to take the children up to a small playground that was across from the back of the store. I asked the four soldiers to come along as protection, and we joined the group, carrying our rifles. Sam didn't think it was necessary to bring the soldiers, but I wanted to talk to them, anyway. Glenda saw us gathering to leave and came along, too, though she was very quiet as we walked the couple blocks to the playground.

I noticed a coyote pretty far behind, following us. I didn't say anything, but I kept a surreptitious eye on it.

When we got there, Aiden jumped in with the kids, and soon, the tribe of children swarmed the three short slides that made up the bulk of the playground equipment. A couple of them wanted to play with Daisy, who was happy to oblige, and they took off running in the grass. The entire area around the Walmart was master-planned neighborhoods. Matching two-story houses overlooked the open playground and park.

I wondered if there were any formerly-crashed survivors left in these houses. We had planned to search for survivors and try to help them, but dealing with our own survival had prevented us from doing anything yet. I didn't know what we could have done, anyway, and I couldn't imagine there would be too many people left alive if they had been severely crashed. It had been more than three weeks since we did the first Beep in the neighborhood.

With the crashed who didn't join the migration to the center of the city, but stayed in their homes, if they hadn't eaten, they likely would have starved already. If they knew enough to eat, then they already would have the ability to survive, and they could come out into the world of their own accord. Sam told us that the ones who piled up in the city had mostly died by the time his group left.

It still seemed like a futile task for us to search for survivors from house to house. I hadn't spoken much to the new people who had arrived before

I went back to the lab. They didn't seem like they had ever been crashed. There were degrees of being crashed, with symptoms ranging from severe to almost unnoticeable. I was coming to the conclusion that those who were left would have to work things out on their own. Over time, we wanted to find a way to mentally connect with them and invite them into the Family, but for now, we had a lot to deal with ourselves.

We adults stood back from the play area and watched what seemed like a normal scene from our past lives. Children being children: climbing on the equipment and inventing games, pretending they were characters from books and movies, defending their small territory, and simply having fun. Knowing that this was now unusual added a level of sadness to it, but also some hope that it could be a normal part of regular life again one day.

I had already introduced Terry, Gerald, Moore, and Santiago to Elizabeth, Ellen, Glenda, and Aiden when we walked to the park. Now, Sam broke away from the other kids and came over to us. I introduced him to the soldiers.

He asked us, "What do you think we should do next? We were talking about teaching each other what we've figured out inside the . . . Iter Anima. Like guarding each other or something. Helping others fight."

This kid couldn't settle down any better than I could, or Jason. We'd come here to let the children play, but he was on task already. I could certainly relate to that. I felt that the break of having the barbecue had been enough to get me motivated again, and I imagined that we wouldn't have another time like that for a long time.

Terry replied to what Sam said, "We've only seen these mind travels the one time, and we don't know much about how it's done. If you're talking about setting up some kind of security perimeter in your minds, you're going to have to let us in on how the hell this works."

I said, "I don't see why we couldn't bring you into it more. Jason's the one who connects everyone, and Sam's doing it with his tribe, too. We think that our BBs helped solidify the connection pathways as if they were already universal in our heads but needed a kick to get going again. It looks like we've opened up the human mind, or more likely, re-opened it. And now we have to do something about the fuckers who are still fucking around and trying to control everyone."

"I sure got a dose of that when Ben and Kenner decided to make me a lab rat," said Terry. "That was some fucked up shit."

I couldn't disagree. I didn't like what they did, making him and some other soldiers test subjects against their will. But I couldn't have stopped it, either.

"I thought it was fucked up, too," I said. "How did you get away from the place where they cuffed you, anyway?"

Terry laughed. "That was from a trick I learned and practiced when I was in my teens. I can dislocate my thumbs and slip out. I was into magic tricks when I was younger."

Magic? I thought. I looked at Glenda but decided not to say anything. She was lost in her own thoughts, not paying attention to our conversation.

I said, "That's funny. I had wondered what happened to you, how you could have escaped. Turns out it was such a simple solution for you but a mystery to us. Do you think you caught the test wave anyway? It would have had a big pulse radius."

"Yeah, it still hit me, and I did feel different after it. I probably had The Crash. And the pulse likely did me some good. I hate to admit it."

"Did you feel the next ones we did from the B-52? It included some things we added through our Iter Anima."

"Yes, we all felt that one." He grimaced and then changed his expression to one of resignation. "Apparently, you actually *were* helping us."

"Even though Ben started losing it toward the end," I said, "he was always trying to make things right. That's all he cared about. When he used you and the other soldiers, he wasn't thinking clearly. I know . . . that's not an excuse . . ."

"No, but we do have to let it go. We're here now, and we have to make the best of it."

The other three soldiers appeared to agree, slight nods and thoughtful expressions showing assent.

Sam said, "Okay so, what I was asking was if we can set up some kind of guards or something in the Iter Anima." He looked directly at Terry. "You're soldiers. Can you do it?"

Terry seemed irritated at this directness from the kid, but he sucked it up and answered, "Yes, we can do it, if you show us this mind-fuck thing. Get what I'm saying?" He was throwing the directness back at Sam.

"Uh huh," said Sam. "I can show you what we do or maybe take you in. And if we bring in more people as guards, we can do even more to help. We're not letting these jerks tell us what to do . . . or take over one of us again."

"We can work on this with Jason," I said. "I'm glad you're all on board. But maybe we can relax a bit while we're out here at the playground. I think we're safe at the moment."

Terry sighed, and Sam frowned. I watched the kids play.

Sam couldn't relax, though. He addressed me with intensity. "Jason leads you in, but you do the talking, right?"

"Mostly, yes."

"I do both."

"I know. That's how you described it." I could see that he didn't want to go play. Or, he wanted to play too much. Was there a difference?

I said, "And I've also taken to keeping track of what's been happening with us, as best as I can. That includes Jaguar's story, and yours, too. Kind of a chronicle of things."

"Because you think it will be important later?"

"That's what I'm thinking, yes. It sure looks like we're either at the end of humanity or the beginning of a new humanity. If this is the end, it won't matter. But if it's the beginning, keeping track of what happened will be important someday. I've been taking notes, and I've been writing out some of the narratives in notebooks when I can find the time."

"Like in the Bible?"

I hadn't thought of it that way. *I wasn't writing a bible, was I?*

"I wouldn't say it's like that. The Bible was written by many people about what God did and later what Jesus did."

"What's the difference?" Sam asked.

Was he looking for a theological discussion? I wasn't the guy for that.

"Man, I don't see anything now like what happened in the Bible. I guess we could get with Javier and see what he thinks. He seems to know some things about Christianity. I'm a novice, really."

"I didn't go to church either. But it sounds like what we're doing is important. And you're writing it down. That's all I mean."

"Yeah, okay. That's why I'm writing about it."

"What if everything is ending and beginning at the same time?" he asked very thoughtfully.

"How do you mean?"

"You said that if humanity is ending, it won't matter if you write about it. But how can there be a new humanity if the old one doesn't end?"

Ah, he had me there. I didn't have an answer to that. I had been seeing the end and the beginning as separate, either/or, not as one leading to the other. Hadn't Jaguar shown me *The Eternal Now*? Wouldn't it mean that the end and beginning weren't separate? That they needed each other? *Damn!* What was with these kids? How did they think of this stuff?

I said, "Man, I don't know. Where did you get that idea from?"

"Jaguar . . . and I've been thinking about it anyway. It's like stories in movies. The good ones have a beginning, a middle, and an ending, all in one movie. And I guess the Bible, too. But I don't think we know the end of that yet."

"I see what you're saying, that with everything in one story, it's like the beginning needs the ending, and the ending needs the beginning. And humanity is one story, too."

"Yeah, something like that. I was just thinking about it."

"Okay then, want to tell me more about how you connected with Jaguar so I can write about that part of the story?"

Sam was anxious to continue telling his story. He said, "After we left that skyscraper, we started going farther away from downtown. We left because the bodies stunk a lot there, and we couldn't find much food after a while. We only stayed in the skyscraper for a few days.

"I found Jaguar . . . I guess she found us, when we went up by the river, but that was a long time later. We just kept checking out different places, and we were finding more kids in our minds the whole time. But no more here in the city. Once, we saw some army trucks on the streets. Maybe they were yours, but they were too far away for us to see where they went. Another time, when we saw you drive into the neighborhoods close to the big park, we saw helicopters, too, the next day. We were pretty close, then. You stayed overnight with your trucks. We thought the helicopters were yours, but after we got closer and saw one of them crash, and you were taking all those soldiers and putting them into your truck, we knew you were different. But we still stayed away from you. Until our connections cut out."

. . . .

The tribe left downtown Denver on the morning of a windy day in early June, more than three weeks before the Family ran the first Beep in a neighborhood and six weeks before the two BBs dropped from the B-52. They survived by avoiding the crashed as much as possible. Sam didn't want to fight them as they had fought the crazies at the stadium, unless there wasn't a choice. The tribe were ready when needed, but they didn't get into any situations that required all of them to fight. A few times, they had to stop some attackers, but overall, they avoided the crazies, and as the weeks wore on, the crazies that they did see were becoming weaker. Sometimes, they saw adults who Sam thought might not be crazy at all, but he still kept the tribe away.

They created a routine which began with finding stores, offices, or other larger buildings where they could stay safe for a while and where they could find food nearby, but they rarely stayed for long. Often, they would have to drag a dead body or two outside so they didn't have to smell it, or they would have to create a distraction in order to get a crazy to chase one of them so they could get it out of the building. Each night, Sam focused on the mind travels, either with the whole group, or with a select few when others were too tired or restless to participate.

After staying in one place for a couple days, they would set out to find something different. Along the way, they stopped in stores to get things they needed or wanted, usually the latter, such as electronic games and sports equipment. A few kids carried sports balls and other equipment: softballs, baseballs, bats, mitts, basketballs, and soccer balls. They took the time to play every day, and if they saw a field or court, they would stop there to play. This became their routine.

Though they didn't know the term, they had become *nomads*, wandering and searching for sustenance, safety, comfort, and even enjoyment.

The evenings were important times for Sam, and Theo always joined him as they went on their mind trips, regardless of how many others went with them. When they had stayed at the skyscraper and did their explorations that began around fires on the roof, the third time they had a fire, Sam had asked Avery to sing. He'd heard her singing inside when she and Raya had organized games for the smaller kids. He thought she could add something to how the tribe came together in their minds so that he could try to focus more on where they went and who they contacted, rather than keeping the tribe together. It worked beautifully. Her singing became like a sound wave they all rode together.

The first time she sang for them, Sam had asked her not to sing words but just sounds. She knew what to do naturally. She began by humming quietly, then stretching the humming to more open vocalizations. Her vocal range went from low to high, unlike anything Sam had heard from one person before. He didn't know the words to describe it, but he loved to hear it, and so did the rest of the tribe.

Avery joined Sam and Theo every night. Anthony and Raya participated most of the time, too. The other kids rotated in and out of the rituals. During the weeks of nightly mind travels, Sam counted 47 groups that he contacted.

One morning as the sun rose, they saw two helicopters flying low a few blocks from where they had spent the night in an office building. Sam grabbed some of the older kids to go with him, and they ran through the streets to get closer. One helicopter landed in the middle of the street. Military troops were lining up by the helicopter on the ground, and more of them had deployed on opposite sides of that street. They appeared to be waiting for something.

The children watched from a smaller side street as a group of two large moving trucks and two Jeeps approached the troops. The other helicopter flew above the small convoy, and from a loudspeaker, a voice ordered the approaching vehicles to stop. It hovered as the troops surrounded the convoy. The kids couldn't tell what was going on, and they stayed back along the side street so they wouldn't be seen. After a few minutes, a Jeep approached from near the landed helicopter. A couple minutes after that, they heard a whining sound and a deep boom.

Sam felt dizzy when the boom reverberated around them, and he watched as all the troops fell to the ground, and then the hovering helicopter crashed. After that, the people in the Jeeps got out and took the weapons from the dropped soldiers. When the soldiers woke up, the people from the Jeeps, who were obviously not friends with the soldiers, forced all the soldiers into one of the trucks. Packed them tightly inside, so tight that they barely fit, then, they all drove away.

The small group of kids ran behind, trying to follow the small convoy, but they couldn't keep up. The vehicles drove east into the sun. When they had driven out of sight, the kids kept walking along the path they had taken. They had walked a couple miles when they came to a wider street and saw open prairie on the other side. Something told Sam that the vehicles had gone past the fence and into that park area. He decided not to follow them farther.

A couple weeks after that, they saw a small fighter jet circle over the city, fly east just beyond the park area, and then come back over the city before circling south again and disappearing beyond the park. They heard other sounds of planes from that direction during the next few days. They didn't know what was going on, but Sam wanted to find out, though he didn't want any of these adults to see the tribe. He couldn't trust those people, whoever they were.

On this day, they saw the coyotes for the first time, three of them. The animals walked along with the tribe through neighborhood streets, just one street over, pacing the tribe, appearing a block away from them at every intersection for a mile or so. And then they were gone. Once in a while, they saw even more coyotes, a whole pack of them, but they kept a good distance away. Sam told the tribe to be ready to defend themselves if the coyotes approached.

On the day they saw the fighter jet, Raya disappeared. They searched for her but couldn't find her. After waiting overnight, in case she returned, Sam decided they had no choice but to continue doing what they had been doing, moving through the city. Sam didn't want to stay in one place for long because they would run out of food, and staying made him uneasy.

That night is when they connected with Jaguar. It was different from all the previous mind trips the tribe did. They were staying in a cafe by the South Platte River, not far from the neighborhood where the Family had run the BEMP from their Jeep and had taken the soldiers hostage. This was two days before the BBs were dropped from the B-52.

For reasons Sam could not articulate or understand, on this particular evening, he had a desire to build a fire by the river and include the whole tribe in their mind journey. His ambition felt stronger than usual, as though something important were coming, and they had to be ready. He was also trusting that no crazies would come after them while they were outside. They hadn't seen a live one in at least a week, so Sam felt that the risk of one approaching was small, especially down by the water, away from buildings.

A bunch of the children worked together to find wood for the fire and get it started. They found most of it under a cottonwood tree, where plenty of dead branches waited to be put to use. They built the fire in an open area close to a small drop in the river where the water gurgled over a rock slope. The fire burned strong and high, and the tribe gathered around it while the sun shone low to the northwest.

Sam was used to concentrating on interior lights or flashlights to start most of their travels, and they hadn't had a fire since the ones on top of the skyscraper. The warmth and intensity of the healthy flames gave him more inspiration than he usually had, and when Avery began her soft, haunting humming, Sam heard some of the other children join her, showing their increased enthusiasm, too. It all worked to give him an unusual perspective on finding the lines in the light of the flames, to open his mind and join all of the tribe into the one vision.

But this time, the lines of light did not travel down tunnels and pull them along. The streamers of colorful illumination twisted together, spun toward the sun, and erupted back away from the sun in a flash of brilliant white. When the white dissipated slowly, the sun was a hazy glare above the mountains, and the rest of the stars in the sky shone onto the tribe like the dazzling suns that they were, individual points of light much brighter than in a typical night sky. All the children looked above them from their places by the fire. The stars lit their world, giving them a brighter day. Avery stopped singing, leaving everything in silence as if the world were covered in snow.

A figure appeared from within the low sun's glare. It walked by the river next to the cottonwood tree. A young girl. She seemed to be only eight years old or so, tiny and wearing what looked like a short animal-skin skirt and a thin orange snakeskin wrap across her chest. Her eyes glowed like the reflection of blue sky, and her dark hair hung below her shoulders in relaxed strands. She wore no shoes and walked toward the tribe and the fire with all confidence.

In the way of communication Sam already knew, she said, "I'm known as Jaguar." Her expression was calm and curious. Her lips didn't move as she talked.

"I'm Sam."

"I'm not really here with you in this place," she said. "I wanted to meet you, so now you see me here."

"We've been meeting lots of kids all over."

"It's what we all can do now if we let ourselves see," she said. "You are different. You seek it out. Others where you are will send waves soon. The waves will reach around the world. They will change us more. Look for them. Go into the waves. You are needed there."

"But who are you? Where are you?"

"My tribe are the Zo'é. We are coming out of the jungle. We will help, too. We are far away from the rest of the world, though we are all together. You are closer. Our tribe needs time to get out. You are there now. It is the beginning for the children while it is the ending for the older ones. This is the change for all humans. And we will come together because of this."

Sam already had some idea of what Jaguar was saying, so it wasn't completely surprising to him, and he understood most of it. He knew that something was different with children, and the adults were mostly dead or dying. But this little girl, who seemed old, not a little girl at all, was also saying that something much bigger was coming, a change for all humans that was more than what already had happened. Sam hadn't been thinking of anything this big. He had been reaching out to other kids because they needed his help. And these other kids were starting to handle a lot of the problems without his tribe's help, partly because the crazies weren't attacking as much anymore.

This girl, Jaguar, was giving him a larger feeling of connectedness and purpose.

"You told me that I was different," he said, "You're pretty different, too."

"I can see," she replied. "I wanted to show you that we are together in this."

"You've definitely shown us. That's a pretty badass trick, coming here so we can see you."

"I would not say it is a trick. A trick is deception. You are seeing me as truth. There are others who play tricks. Those are their lies. You will learn the difference. That is when you will see."

"Okay then. I'm glad you showed us . . . you? That you let us see you. Good to meet you."

"Good it is. We will meet in person one day. Until then, we will work together as you have been working with the other groups. We are connected now. That is what matters most."

"Is there something else we should be doing?"

"Keep your minds open so you can see the difference. They will not stop with their lies. They are dangerous."

"Who?"

"Those who have destroyed themselves but do not know it yet."

"What about the waves that are coming?"

"Go with them if you can. They will help you see," she replied.

"We will look for them."

"Good. I will go back to my tribe now."

Jaguar abruptly turned and walked away. She became the glare again, and the light winked out. The suns dimmed to distant stars, and the day turned to night. The fire was old and hot, orange embers glowing inside.

Sam took a deep breath, and he knew, yet again, that he was in the right place, that what they were doing was what they were supposed to do. He felt proud of his tribe and what they had accomplished. He knew he could keep going with them, keep reaching the other kids. And he knew that the change in the world that they had experienced was only part of what was to come.

He wondered if his idea of all this being part of an alien invasion wasn't so far off after all. He'd imagined the invasion because it was the easiest thing for him to do in the moment. The craziness had invaded the world. He had wanted to keep the kids together so they could survive. Now, their purpose was much bigger than just survival. And Jaguar had warned him that people were out there who were responsible for what had happened. Whoever they were, he needed to be ready for their tricks, their lies.

How do I get ready for lies? He wondered.

No one spoke. Even the fire remained quiet. Sam gazed up at the stars while thinking about what he had learned from Jaguar.

After a while, he stood and addressed the tribe. "There are waves coming that we need to catch, go into them, or ride them. They will be waves that travel around the world to deliver something that is supposed to help people. It's best for us to be there to see who is making the waves, learn things that we need to know. I'm not sure how soon this will happen, but we want to be ready. I think it will be soon."

Theo said, "We're on it!"

The rest of them nodded in agreement. The tribe was unified and strong.

In the darkness down by the river, a movement caught Sam's eye. Three coyotes watched the tribe and then turned away to disappear into the night.

The group stayed at the fire until it burned to little more than ash. They had found some packaged food at the cafe where they had already stayed the previous night, and they returned there for dinner.

. . . .

I said to Sam, "That's amazing how Jaguar came to you. It's nothing like anything we've experienced. But it might be what others experience when we go to them."

"It sort of made sense to me. I figured, *if I can go see other people, why can't they come to me?* And Jaguar did."

Chapter 27
Pursuit

Sam continued his story:

The next night, he chose to skip having a mind travel session of the kind they were used to. But he didn't want to miss the waves that were coming. What he did instead was a meditation of sorts, not too different from what he did for their Iter Anima, but this time, he tried to reach out and find those who Jaguar had described as people who were close to the tribe, in Denver, he guessed.

He thought they might have something to do with the group of people who they had seen take those soldiers away a few weeks before. Those people had done something strange that had knocked out the troops. And then, Sam guessed, based on their direction of travel, they had driven into that big park area. *Could that booming sound they made be what would cause the waves Jaguar was talking about? Could he find these people through his mind?*

When his mind travels had begun, Sam had been in the Walmart, thinking about their situation. The lights on the ceiling had flared, and he was off. It just happened. After that, he had brought the tribe with him, and they had learned to travel with purpose. Now, he had another purpose in mind, but his approach felt forced. *How could he expect to sit down and find these people without knowing anything about them?* But he hadn't known anything about the other children around the world before he had found them, either. His intention now was different, though.

He started to question himself, mainly questioning his own doubts about what he wanted to do. *Was he sure that his approach was forced?* Could it be that the fact he was sitting alone outside under a cottonwood tree – with the intention of finding a group of people who knew how to send a wave around the world – was proof that what he wanted to do *wasn't* forced? Could it be that things happened for a reason? Was this how the energy of the world worked?

He decided to stop thinking about it, stop questioning and doubting himself. He held a small black flashlight. He twisted the top of it to turn it on, and he stared into its light. He soon found that he felt a pulling sensation, something telling him that he needed to go somewhere, that this was the exact time when he needed to go, and he was supposed to go there through his mind.

The light grew out and around him, and he fell into it. No streamers of colors this time, only bright light that flared and then faded quickly. He spun with fire around him and saw faces lit by the flames. They were in the middle of a dark baseball field, the beating of drums thrumming around them. He felt himself falling into the fire amid a warm embrace.

Now, these people he sought were ahead of him, though he couldn't see them anymore. Haze, smoke, clouds. He heard the thoughts of others in fragments, saw images in flickering pieces, sounds and sights in the distance, becoming clear.

He couldn't understand what the people were communicating to each other, but he began to see that they were building connections, spiders jumping from place to place with endless silky threads sticking and trailing, building a web, a giant undulating web, growing more and more complex.

Deserts and mountains, oceans and forests, ice and rain, towering buildings and open fields, glorious cities and distressing slums. In all of these places, he saw groups of people, endless varieties of faces, the colors and shapes of the cultures of the world. He knew they were joining each other, forming a unified understanding and intention. It was like the mind travels his tribe had experienced, but with many more people collected together and linked through this web, expanding, joining with everyone who wanted to join.

Except children. There were no children among them. Sam understood that the separation continued around the world, adults and children torn from each other, kept apart. But this web held humanity in its own sphere that encompassed the world. They were trying to hold together what remained of people everywhere and also bind them in a new way.

These ideas came to him as he witnessed the meetings of many groups in many locations around the globe. It was dizzying, and spectacular. Fast streaking, spinning, and brief stops. Connections forming, the web expanding. It was like a timeless flight, and he took the ride, forgetting any purpose, taking in the sensations with growing understanding.

Sam understood the essence of what they were doing, but not the details. He was pulled along behind them, these people around the fire, the first people he had seen after the light had brought him to them, and now they were returning to their fire at the baseball field.

He heard gunshots. He snapped back to his place, and his flashlight stared at him, the only light shining now except the stars in the night sky. He was back sitting under the tree.

Across from him, not 10 yards away, sat a single coyote, also staring at him. He had prepared for this possibility, and he reached for his pistol that lay at his side. Before he could bring the gun up to aim it, the coyote twitched and spun, and was gone.

Sam could feel that the people at the baseball field were here in the city somewhere, that they were close. They were the group Jaguar had told him about and the same ones he had seen with the soldiers. What they had just done by jumping around the world was beyond what he had been doing with his tribe. It was part of something even bigger than he could understand, the beginning of a change he couldn't comprehend. But children were not part of it, directly.

Why were children separate? Didn't these grownups know that children were still alive? Didn't they care? And what about the waves Jaguar had told him about? He hadn't seen waves. They had been making a web. Was it in preparation for something else? He had felt an urgency to this web building, as though they were rushing to complete it, and the web wasn't all they were trying to accomplish. He decided he would bring the whole tribe on a journey to find these people again the next night.

He didn't sleep much, thoughts flying in and out of his head. The next day, the only thing on his mind was making sure the tribe were there for the waves he knew were coming. He sensed that it would be this night. He would take them to the people he had seen, and they would see the waves, know how the waves worked with the web that reached around the world, and maybe show the grownups that kids were here.

As they sat around a new fire, preparing to travel, Sam realized how unlikely it was that a group of kids could come together and work toward these goals without bickering and fighting among themselves. Even the littlest ones, such as Henry, accepted their places and worked with the tribe, at least when they did their mind travels. In other situations, the kids were still kids, arguing and tussling.

They began their process. The light and heat of the fire joined with Avery's voice, and the light from the stars above, blue to red, shifted around them, blended together, and became a whiteness that lifted them into the growing Cosmic Consciousness.

Sam brought them to a gathering of adults around a fire on the baseball field, all the same as he had witnessed the night before. A large, loud, jet plane took off from a runway nearby, its running lights blinking and diminishing into the dark sky. This group were following the plane with their minds, reaching within something greater than their minds, moving into a wider consciousness that included them and many more, much more. But Sam felt that his tribe were outside this unified mind, apart from it, as though they could not reach it.

It was like a bad dream he'd had many times, with him fighting through rooms filled with things he didn't need, things that were getting in the way as he reached for a door, opened it, and found more of the same, more obstructions to push aside and wade through, until he reached the next door and opened it to find more of the same, never getting where he wanted to go.

The tribe drifted behind these adults and their expanding consciousness. They flew up to join the plane on an arm of smoke, and Sam saw the two bombs that were held in its belly. A fear crept into him, a *wrongness* that filled him like a dark mist. He heard the deep droning of the jet engines, the ominous thunder of air buffeting the plane. He started to feel his own body again, sweat forming on his face. *Something else* was there, a shadow among the stars.

He became afraid of the bombs and saw a woman, or the form of a woman, and he wanted to talk to her. He wanted to tell her that the bombs weren't good, that they would hurt people. He kept trying to reach her, but the bombs dropped away from the plane, and they all fell with them, the tribe, too.

Explosions erupted through the atmosphere, and Sam knew what the waves were. They came from the bombs and from the *people* all at once.

He prepared to grab the waves with his tribe, go with these people, but a new vision overtook him, what could best be described as a polished and gleaming diamond, though massive in size.

It is here that the memories of Sam, his tribe, and Raya had been jumbled and distorted until Jason had helped reveal something closer to the truth than what they had initially remembered. At first, they thought they had only seen the glowing diamond, but later, they remembered deeper and came to understand that they had been distracted, led to believe they were playing a baseball game. More accurately, what they had really experienced was a *shadow*.

The shadow clouded near them, barely there, growing stronger. Sam again sensed the form of the woman they had seen earlier, and he wanted to reach her. The shadow grew darker and crossed between them, and the woman was gone.

Sam heard a deafening hissing sound and felt an impact, as if someone had hit him in the face, and the tribe were back to themselves by the fire. All of them had been thrown outward, away from the fire, and they lay on the ground like petals fallen from a dead flower. His head hurt severely, and he rolled sideways, his arms up around his head. The others were doing the same, moaning, some crying. Coyotes yipped and howled from every direction around them.

Sam felt sick, but sat up and looked around. Slowly, all of the children sat up. After some time, Sam felt his nausea and the pain in his head subsiding a little. It appeared that the others were feeling better, too, as the groaning sounds tapered off, and they began to talk to each other, asking questions, comparing perspectives on what they had just seen and experienced. The coyote voices diminished and disappeared.

All the kids were sitting up, most of them talking, so Sam didn't think anyone was hurt too badly. He thought about what had happened and began to conclude that something was very wrong with those bombs and the waves. Why had the tribe been thrown out, thrown back here? He didn't get the sense that Jaguar had steered him wrong. It must have been something else. Maybe the bombs didn't work right. He couldn't know.

The fire hadn't been burning for long, so there was a lot of wood still to burn. Sam tried to calm the ones who were still upset, and eventually they all just chatted until they felt well enough to head back to the cafe.

They didn't know they had lost their ability to mind travel until Sam brought the tribe back out the next night to do one of their "regular" explorations. The fire crackled, Avery sang, Sam reached for the light, but nothing else happened. They went nowhere. Sam didn't feel anything like what he had felt every other time. He couldn't take the tribe away from there. He knew quickly that something had happened when those bombs exploded, and he felt his worry growing as he wondered if they had lost their mind connections. The tribe looked to him for answers, but he had none, until he decided that they needed to find the people who set off the bombs and get them to fix what they had broken.

· · · ·

Sam said to us, "I thought it was the bombs, until Jason showed us that I was wrong, that we were following lies. Now, Jaguar and Jason have brought us back so we can do the mind travels again. They showed us that we had been lost in lies. That the ones who took Raya were the ones who created the lies."

He looked up at me so I would know that he understood. "They took Lauren from you. That's who we saw in the shadows. They took Raya from us. They are trying to take the whole world from us. We're ready to fight them with you."

In the way he said this, I felt his dedication to work with us to make a difference. At that moment, it meant as much to me as anything could. I tried to stop the tears, but they fell anyway, and I let them. I was sad and angry and ready to fight. Fighting was all I wanted to do.

Glenda had listened to the whole story and our exchanges with careful attention. Now she spoke. "I had a daughter. She died in The Crash. She was five." It was a statement of fact with no emotion.

This brought me to my knees. I had no idea she had any children. I heard her words that said her daughter had died, and I couldn't process it. She hadn't said anything when she told me about her parents' deaths.

She continued coldly, "They have taken from us, and we will take from them."

She turned and addressed Sam, and with dawning warmth said, "You don't know me yet, and it's obvious that you and the tribe have handled things really well in all this madness, but I also believe that adults could help you, just as you can help us." I observed through my own tears that he was having trouble holding her emotions in check.

She closed her eyes briefly, opened them, and said, "That's what I'm saying. I'm saying that I want to be there for you however I can."

Rather than being offended by what could have been seen as presumptuousness, Sam seemed relieved. He said, "The littles could use an adult to look up to. Raya and Avery are good with them, but it's not easy. It would be great if you could get to know all the kids."

Now Glenda cried, standing straight and still. Ellen hugged her, and Elizabeth looked down at me as I leaned on my knee. She showed indecision, not knowing if she should say something to me or not. Somehow, that snapped me out of my sadness.

I stood up grinning, even trying not to laugh, and said to Elizabeth, "I'm okay. It's okay."

This kind of stuff was awkward to a lot of us, especially me. The soldiers looked uncomfortable, too, so I patted Terry on the back and turned to watch the children play. Elizabeth and the soldiers did the same. Ellen continued holding Glenda, and Glenda cried silently.

Steven S. Patchin

Chapter 28
Precedence

As we returned from the playground to the Walmart, we discussed how some of The Crash experiences of the Family and the tribe were similar. Both groups rallied around a leader: Jason for the Family, and Sam for the tribe. Both had discovered a way to connect with other people around the world through Iter Anima, though the tribe did not use a Latin term for it. The tribe had organized themselves in a Walmart, and now everyone was together at a Walmart. Just some items of note, I guess, as I had been thinking about them before. I don't know what it means, if anything.

When we entered the parking lot, we saw that Jason was leading a discussion with the Family and the new people. They had gathered in a loose congregation with Jason sitting on a pallet of fertilizer outside the garden section of the store, and everyone else having set up things to sit on, such as chairs, blankets, and pillows. It was similar to what we had seen when the soldiers and I had arrived here the day before, except there was no fire. It appeared that they had been talking for quite a while, maybe as long as we had been listening to Sam's story.

Our group stepped up behind everyone so we could listen but not interrupt. Even the children looked interested, so they kept quiet. Douglas, the engineer who had been instrumental in helping build the Beep and the BBs, and who had been one of the five who had been forgotten in quarantine and left behind by Upstream, was calmly explaining what his life had been like and what he wanted for the future. His gray hair and long white beard had helped give me the impression that he was a wise sage, and his technical skills had been impeccable.

Douglas said, "I liked the routine. I liked doing my job, until we got locked up by Upstream and left down there to die." He sought out the other scientists in the crowd who had been isolated with him and made eye contact with them.

I spotted all four: Danielle, Arthur, Kim, and Jennings.

He continued, "That was a big mistake, falling for their con. We had no idea what was going to happen. I never would have left my wife alone for that long if I had known. She was understanding when I wanted to join the experiment, and we thought it would only be thirty days. I don't know what I was thinking. I didn't need to do it. My life was fine without the adventure. And now my wife's gone. I just know it."

Sophia asked, "How do you know? Could you go look for her?"

"I just know she's gone. I can feel it. And my son was in New York. He could be alive, but I don't have a way to reach him."

"Some of us here want to go look for our loved ones, those of us who don't remember what happened to them." she said.

"I don't blame them. Nobody's had a chance to do that until now. I may go look one day, but I don't want to see her dead. I'm thinking I'll just find somewhere quiet to live and spend my time reading. That's about all I want after we do whatever it is we're going to do here. Someday I could help if people want to get the electrical grid started again, but for now, I imagine myself going to bookstores and libraries and reading."

Jason said, "I hope you can stay a while, at least until we finish this fight we have coming up. But I don't want to talk about the details of that, yet, for a few reasons, one of which is the possibility of them spying on us. I don't want them to know what we're going to do. And I think it's important for us to understand what we want first. That's why I asked you to all join me in this discussion. We don't all want the same things, and even though we've been working together really well as the Family, we're still different people. We're sharing our stories and desires for the future so we know what we want, what kind of society we want to build."

He gazed around at the group. "Who else wants to tell their story?"

"I agree with you, Jason," Craig said. "Our stories are important. I think my story's pretty simple. I've never been married, and I didn't have kids. I was married to my work with Ben. I loved everything about it. And I also love history and learning about different cultures. The Iter Anima is going to provide an avenue for me to explore as many cultures as I can. I'd like to write about the people and places we've been encountering, too. Make something to leave for those who follow us."

He looked back at me, and I knew he was also referring to our working together on the chronicle of the Family's experiences and all that had happened to us, *all that was still happening*. I liked the idea of that. We'd already discussed it in passing because I'd been keeping notes for a few weeks and had needed some background information that he was able to provide.

He said, "I think telling our stories, telling the stories of everyone, could be the most important thing we can do after taking out the psychopaths who caused The Crash. And I also believe that one of the factors in making The Crash worse was the degradation of our heritage that had been happening for decades, at least here in America. Our culture was founded on certain traditions, and they had been under attack from many directions. I'm not saying they're all religious traditions, either. But a lot of them were. I wouldn't call myself religious, but I have studied theology. Even from a layman's perspective, any reasonable person would have to admit that, *at least*, the structure of religious practice was an overall good influence on our society, even if they don't like the religious teachings.

"So much of that structure had been pushed out in favor of . . . well, nothing. In favor of hedonism, the idea that whatever we wanted, whatever gave us the most pleasure, took priority. Anti-theology, or atheism, was overtaking religious practice and replacing it with self-centeredness. The idea that each individual was the center of the universe became en vogue. And we began to forget that there are things greater than ourselves." Craig looked a little embarrassed and abruptly stopped talking. He was getting worked up, and it was obvious that he was passionate about this.

"Regardless of what religion someone might believe," Jason said. "Or even if people don't believe in any religion, it seems to me that we can't deny its importance in American culture. Not to mention other cultures around the world. Look at all the different groups we met in our Iter Animas. So many had religious foundations, and even those with traditions older than most religions practiced a spirituality that transcended any individual."

Craig was getting his composure back. "Sorry to go off on that," he said. "It's been bothering me for a long time. We've been learning that what Genetrix was after by altering the Stoffer Solution was to control people's desires for *things*. Ben's invention was intended to help people organize themselves better, become more efficient so that they could accomplish what they had to accomplish, and thus they would have more time to devote to things they wanted to do at their leisure. It was supposed to free them.

"But what Genetrix did was try to enslave them even more, quite the opposite of leisure. And they triggered The Crash by doing this. Now, these idiots with The Organization, who were really the ones behind what Genetrix did, want to continue with their push for more control. It was easier for them to take control because of the loss of our traditions and institutions. Churches, schools, and universities. They were either declining in attendance and affiliation or they had become places for guilting people into believing that humanity was bad, and that the world would be better off without people. What insanity!

"Sure, there's nothing wrong with respecting our planet and taking care of it – who could argue against that? – but doing this to the point of hating ourselves for our very existence? They were using those lies to control people. And it was pretty damn effective. Then, add the altered Stoffer Solution to the mix, and The Crash almost took out everyone.

"I think that Jason is doing something really important in bringing up our need to tell our own stories. Not the distortions that had people thinking we were better off dead, but the hope, excitement, and wonder that exists in our hearts. What made us feel most alive? What do we want for each other and ourselves going forward? What we have now is a new start, with new ways of interacting with each other.

"For each of us personally, whether it's what Douglas just mentioned, or it's the stories and desires others talked about earlier today, we've also discovered a new community throughout the world. It is not one that has to be a single entity, just as the Family doesn't have to be only one thing. It can be many different things with people who see the value of working together while also embracing traditions that have made them who they are.

"But as we go forward with creating our own stories and seeking to save civilization, we should also remember that there is something more."

He finished with a quote: "C. S. Lewis said, 'We shall never save civilisation as long as civilisation is our main object. We must learn to want something else even more.'"

I didn't know how many in our Family or our extended group were religious, so I didn't know how many might get the message in what he quoted. My guess, which I confirmed with Craig later, was that he meant we must want a power even greater than ourselves. And what C.S. Lewis meant was that this power was God.

I wasn't fully ready to accept the idea of God, myself. I didn't know who God was or what he might represent for us humans. I was one of the people who Craig referred to when he said that we had lost so many of our traditions. I had few traditions except for drinking, fixing motorcycles, and riding them. Craig wasn't religious, either. I would need to talk to him about this more when we could spend some time discussing it. But I already had accepted the idea that religions were important to people, not only as traditions and sources of structure, but also as inspiration for life, even if I didn't embrace the existence of God. I also understood that those who maintained their faiths could not envision their religions without their deities. For them, religion *was* God.

"Points well taken," Jason said to Craig. "Thank you." He paused and looked around at all of us before continuing. "We're getting some good perspectives here today. Craig, I don't have any practical or academic background in religion. I read some of the Bible when I was a child, but I only know a few of the stories, certainly those pertaining to Adam and Eve, Moses, and Jesus. But I'd imagine that my understanding is superficial. I know nothing at all about other religions, except what we witnessed with the groups we found around the world. I do get your point about needing to create our own story as a people, while also keeping in mind that there is something beyond ourselves. What we've found in the Cosmic Consciousness has allowed us to see things on a much bigger scale, at least to those of us not familiar with any religion.

"If we are to write our own story, while also being mindful of our *human* traditions and the stories some of you have shared today, I do get the feeling that most everyone here wants to stay together, at least long enough for this fight. The story of *us* has already begun. We've already accomplished many things of great significance. We have a good idea of how The Crash happened. And now, we want to join together for a different kind of fight. A fight against what almost anyone would define as an *evil* enemy. And a very *dangerous* enemy, at that.

"What will it look like to fight an enemy most of us have not seen? To fight an enemy who we can not see standing physically in front of us? To fight an enemy whose strength we don't know. To fight an enemy who has a long *tradition* of manipulation and lies. To fight an enemy whose story and ambitions are so foreign to all of us here that we can't comprehend the kind of thinking that leads them to do what they do, that lead them to cause The Crash.

"To call them psychopaths and narcissists is not precise enough. That's why I use the term *evil*. They don't think like us. And we can't really think like them. But we might be able to analyze their weaknesses, react to their personality traits, and give them responses that cut deeply into them.

"We first need to learn more about them. We know of six primary people who we need to target. These people are the enemy. They are the enemy to us, to the planet, and to humanity. I don't need to demonize them. We all know what they have done. And we know what they still want to do. So, first, we'll learn more about them. That's something only a few of us will be doing to begin with. They have already killed one of us directly, Lauren. Taken one of us, Raya. And spied on us through the coyotes, and maybe other methods, too.

"When all of us work together, it will be for the fight itself. And what that looks like depends on what we find when we spy on them ourselves. As for the story of us going forward, what does it look like? I think you already have a picture of that in your minds, a *narrative* that carries us through, based on what we've been talking about here today and based on what we've already done, together and apart. It is what brought us here together. You might say we're an army, or a congregation, or crusaders, or just people who want reasonable freedoms for humanity. We're the Family.

"You've felt our connections, even those of you who have not been with us for our Iter Animas yet. As the Family, we don't promise entertainment, comfort, safety, free food, or shelter. Our enemy might promise all of these things. No, we don't promise that. What we do promise is that we are here for each other, that we will do our best for each other, that we can trust each other, and that we want freedom for humanity.

"As Craig suggested, I would ask the question: 'can we promise that we are learning to want something even more than ourselves?' Please consider that.

"Our story is our freedom. It is the freedom to live among each other in places we choose. It is the freedom to associate with those who bring meaning and purpose to our lives. It is the freedom to say what we believe and believe what we say. It is the freedom to fight for what we believe. It is the freedom to leave, as well.

"Nobody here is obligated to stay and fight. You have the freedom to decide. Leaving does not make you an enemy. And if you stay, I hope that you will embrace the possibilities that this unified endeavor can bring to your soul. For me, it's the purpose and the camaraderie that gives me the greatest reward. It could be different for each of you.

"We're finding our way. We're doing what we believe is best. We're writing our own story. Soon, we'll be ready for our fight. We have some preparation to do first, and I'll keep you informed. Does anyone have questions or something to say?"

We all stood enraptured by his words. Nobody had anything else to say. I glanced around toward the edges of the parking lot, thinking about the coyotes. I didn't see any. Jason slid off the fertilizer bags and put his hands together. The gathering was concluded.

He walked around to Glenda, noticing that her face and eyes were red, likely realizing that she had been crying. He put his arms around her, and they strolled off in the direction of the playground, the sun backlighting them. The rest of the group began to stand up, but nobody walked away. We stood and talked about all manner of things that people friendly with each other talk about. I noticed certain couples now, relationships that had been developing for some time. Ellen and Javier. Jon and Ginny. Trong and Kim. Danielle and Jennings. There likely were others, but I didn't want to continue matching up people. I wanted to enjoy being there and feeling that I was part of something bigger than myself and bigger than my thoughts. So I did.

Steven S. Patchin

Chapter 29
Spies

When Jason returned hours later, walking into the store from the darkness, Glenda was not with him. The rest of us had eaten dinner, and we had separated into our different areas of the store, most of us relaxing in some way, or chatting in small groups. The children were playing together, throwing balls down aisles in some new game that appeared to be a cross between bowling and soccer. The four soldiers guarded the entrances and were planning to set up their watches in shifts.

I had thought about how I might open Lauren's phone, but I couldn't think of anything that would work, so I left it turned off. I was cleaning my M4 when Jason came up to me and said, very quietly, "Can we go outside?"

"Of course."

"I want to get Craig and Elizabeth, too."

We found them talking together and waved them over. The four of us went outside and stood by the fire mound, which contained only ashes at the moment. Clouds had come in since sunset. The sky was dull and dark, no stars or moon.

Jason said with a low voice, "Glenda is gone."

"What do you mean, gone?" Elizabeth asked in surprise.

"I have to leave it at that. It's best to avoid details."

"Is she okay?" I asked.

Jason just stared at me and didn't reply. I was bewildered at first, but began to realize what Jason was implying. I didn't think it meant that any harm had come to Glenda, but I did assume she wouldn't be back anytime soon. I knew to trust Jason and let it go at that. I did wonder, however, if this would affect what Glenda had said to the children about wanting to be a mother figure to them. I had thought that interacting with the kids was going to become her priority.

"When you saw those people with The Organization," Jason said to me, "did you get any impression of how they might have been able to spy on us? Do you think it's anything like what we do with our Iter Animas?"

"I don't really know. They did follow Kallik and me back though when we left them. They took over a reindeer and made it jump into our fire. They didn't do that by sitting around their own fire beating drums. At least one of them just followed us back to Siberia, seemingly with ease. And they were aware of me when I dug through their minds to learn about their pasts. I told you about being in that dark room and it snowing in there. I don't think it really snowed, of course, and I don't believe those six people were really standing in that room, either. It would have been too much of a coincidence for them to have been lined up like that, ready for me to see them. But then, I don't know. I think they were ready for me on some level, but I don't know *how* ready."

Jason closed his eyes and thought for a while. He said, "That's why we need our own spies. And we don't want them to know we're there. Can Kallik help with this?"

"She certainly wants to, but I'm not sure what she can do. I get the impression that these people have a pretty good handle on jumping around in others' minds. Including taking control of people and animals. At least one of them does. What can we do against that kind of ability?"

Craig said, "We have to focus on what we do best more than what they do best. We're good at bringing together all our strengths and connecting people. We do this most powerfully with our big group. It sounds like these Organization people are more agile, as if they might operate individually. Does that seem right?"

"Possibly," I said. "I didn't see them working together in the same way we do. And when Raya and the children saw someone in our Iter Anima, they saw what they thought was only one person . . . Actually, nobody has seen more than one at a time do anything. We don't know if they were different people. We do know that the coyotes were following the kids. But that could have been only one person controlling the leader of the pack."

"We can't assume much," said Craig. "But this gives us a starting point. If there are only six of them, and we have dozens, we could have an advantage."

"We need to find out more first," said Elizabeth. "Should we send just one person to spy on them?" She meant me.

"If we want to dig deeper, as of now, I'm the only one who can get into their minds to get information," I said.

"What do we want to know?" she asked.

"Where they really are, for one," said Jason. "And how big The Organization still is, and who else might be involved. They still had access to a bomber from somewhere else and managed to bomb us. It was a hell of an undertaking for Kenner and Shen to find, load, crew, and fly the B-52 for our BB event. And yet, these people managed to do almost the same thing, apparently by giving orders from overseas."

"And Taylor was ultimately working with them, too," Craig said. "Though we don't know how closely. They might have more people like her out there."

"I wonder if our BB reached some of them and calmed their brains, even if they had been isolated from The Crash before," said Elizabeth. "How dedicated are their people after all that has happened? Would they still want to follow orders?"

"Shen was pretty damn dedicated," I said. "She wouldn't let up for anything. That's the added problem of the Chinese Communist Party, itself. They've been great at building their own army of brainwashed soldiers. Who knows how many are left? And how do they work with the other Organization leaders? How unified are these people?"

"These are the things we need to find out," Jason said. "That will help us come up with a way to attack them." He looked at Craig and Elizabeth. "And we have to keep them out of your minds. So, we'll want to bring everyone else into the Iter Anima, everyone who wants to, the soldiers and the new people. Then pick a few who can serve as mental guards, who we can teach to hang back and watch. Sam can help with his perspective on that."

"What about the rest of the children?" I asked.

"They're going to be key to our fight. But let's not get into the specifics of that right now. We're assuming The Organization aren't spying on us at the moment, but we can't be one hundred percent sure. Let's get you into the heads of these fucks and see what we can see first."

"Then an Iter Anima," I said.

"Yes, but a different kind than we've been doing before. We have to become more agile, like they are, so we need to do this without a fire, like what you just did with Kallik last night. And when we send you, I think we should use only a few of us to make it happen, not the whole group."

"Okay, that makes sense," I said. "When?"

"How about now? Let's go inside and set up in the back where we can be out of the way of everyone else."

"Who else do you want to bring?" Craig asked.

Jason was quick to reply, "Aiden, Sam, and Avery. But you two need to sit this one out. We should also have someone watching over you. We don't know if they can get to you in your sleep."

Shit! I thought. It would be very easy to fall into paranoia, curl up into a fetal ball, and not get back up. I said, "At least they might not know that Craig and Elizabeth are the only ones who have the knowledge they're after. They still think they can get to Ben, and even get the technology itself."

"That's why we have to move on this now with a small group. We'll work with the bigger group later."

Chapter 30
Reinhard

We went back inside the store. Jason rounded up the other three while I found Sophia. I asked her to keep an eye on Craig and Elizabeth, saying that I didn't know what she might be watching out for, but that someone might mess with their heads like they did with Raya. I then asked Raya to watch Daisy.

Our small group of five met in the stockroom where I had slept. Jason placed a battery-powered lantern on the short stack of unassembled cardboard boxes. We sat on other pieces of cardboard and faced the lantern as if it were a campfire. Jason had already explained to the younger three what we were planning to do. We'd decided to do this with Avery's singing alone.

My job was to find the people leading The Organization without letting them know we were there. When we had first found Jaguar's tribe and when we had found the first climber, I'd held back and watched them, apparently unobserved. Could I do it with people who already knew about mind traveling?

I said to Sam, "Can you show me what you did when you distracted some of the crashed who were attacking other groups of kids? How you could change the perspective of what you saw?"

"Yeah. I can show you, but I can't explain it."

"That's what we're after. We have to stay hidden, though. So don't do anything to make them aware that we're there."

"I won't."

Avery began humming, soft and low. I began relaxing and thinking of these Organization people, while trying not to think of them *too* much, because there is a delicate balance needed in the mind to ride the Cosmic Consciousness. This was something I had been realizing. I couldn't force my way through. When we had started our Iter Animas, I didn't know what I was doing, and I just "thought" my way around without *too much* thought. It's like the first time I tried hitting a golf ball on the driving range. I just hit it, and the thing went 340 yards. Then, my friend who had brought me to the range began showing me techniques to control my swing. He began "teaching" me how to adjust. After that, I barely could break 200 yards.

Now, as Avery began to sing those jeweled, wandering notes, I needed to trust myself to make it work the way we wanted. I was also thinking about how we might streamline this even more, that we could try doing it without Avery or try without the light as a focus. I've seen a lot in dreams. How could we do it faster? But then again, I wasn't going alone, so why was I wanting it to be faster? I realized I was thinking in circles. What we were doing was like a form of meditation, though I knew nothing about meditation. And I wondered if other people meditated. And I told myself to stop thinking so much, but I wasn't listening to myself.

I opened my eyes. The others sat calmly with their eyes still closed. Avery continued singing. Why was my mind wandering? I needed to focus. In the darkness at the edge of the lantern's light, Daisy stepped out from around a pallet of laundry soap and peered at us.

No! It wasn't Daisy. It was a coyote! Its large ears locked forward, watching us, the ears more menacing than the animal's yellow eyes. I tried to shout, but I couldn't make a sound. I tried to stand, but I couldn't move. I felt the anger boiling in me. Not fear but anger. I took hold of the anger and focused it on the coyote. My vision rushed at the animal, and the darkness swelled like a blanket of tar rising up over us. It smothered us. I thought I couldn't breathe, but I realized it wasn't really tar covering us, but only darkness, and the coyote wasn't there, and my mind was actually doing what I had wanted it to do in the first place. It was letting go and taking me directly to Reinhard, the man who I had assumed was the senior controlling-authority in The Organization.

. . . .

My anger dissipates, and I relax. The sensation of being surrounded by tar continues even though I know there is no tar. It muffles Avery's singing. The thick blackness warps like a dark lava lamp, and it lets go. I feel as though I have become a drop of the ooze, and I drip off the larger mass to find myself in the room of dark wood again, where I had seen the six Organization people when I traveled with Kallik.

The inky wooden walls and carvings begin to turn from saturated, warm tones to cracked, ashy gray. The woodgrain starts splitting apart, as though the room is drying and decomposing through time. The cracked aging accelerates. The room becomes a cave, an elongated sphere, and I stand at its base, at the brain stem. It is a skull, an empty cranium. Sparks burst in the emptiness, neurons firing, slowly at first, then faster and faster, a firework show, and with each spark, gray matter appears briefly, as if it only exists in the light, and then it disappears. The whole display dazzles me, and I turn within this massive cavern, seeing the open eye sockets that look out to a dim scene of old buildings, centuries weathered, abandoned. A neighborhood of various Queen Anne-style homes scattered into the distance.

Now I'm outside, and the skull is gone. A town sits in grayness but with no dark shadows, no bright highlights. The buildings are incomplete, not as if they had fallen apart, not as if they had never been fully constructed, but as if they are pieces of a jigsaw puzzle in three dimensions, partly assembled. It's too quiet, though not muffled like dampened sound, but open with the absence of sound waiting for something to happen.

I'm experiencing a partly-formed, frozen thought. Not mine, but someone else's. Time is stopped, except for me.

Sam is there, and so is Jason. They are *live*, too. I hear Avery, her voice echoing briefly in the far distance. She stops singing and watches us.

I realize we can communicate among ourselves, without being heard in the place where we seem to be, without being heard by the one who holds this frozen, partial thought. And I know it is Reinhard whose head we have penetrated.

"Okay, this is different," I say.

"I felt someone out there in the black," says Sam. "I was trying to turn us to a different place, so we weren't in front of anyone. So nobody sees us. It kind of jumped us here."

"Yes," Jason says. "We were headed straight, and I felt your pull that turned us. I let go. Is this what you felt when you were distracting the crashed people from other kids?"

"Sort of. It's how I turned when I needed to. And then seeing from inside someone's head. It's like this, but I don't know why everything's frozen."

"I do," I say. "It's the fragments of a thought, caught in time."

"What do you mean?" Jason asks.

"This is Reinhard's head, a thought anyway. A frozen thought, not complete, only part of it."

"I won't ask how you know this," Jason says. "Let's just go with it."

"I think this is the result of the three of us combining our *methods,* so to speak. You gathered energy and directed the Iter Anima based on my 'compass' directions, my affinity to go to a certain person or place. Sam took the wheel and turned it so we didn't hit our target and crash. *Meaning that he kept us from letting Reinhard see us.* And now, we're stopped in the road, figuring out where to go from here. We're stopped in a partial thought."

"That's a good enough analogy for me. It's like we're passing through his mind, and we need to sidetrack just a little so we can see his thoughts, and he can't see us."

"I think so," I say. "Maybe we just tune the car radio a bit. Change the frequency but keep the windows rolled up while we listen."

Sam says, "I don't know what you guys are talking about. All we have to do is let go and move. You don't have to make such a big deal of it."

"Should we let off the brake?" I ask, feeling a little amused with myself.

"If that's what you want to call it," Sam says, a little irritated.

I feel us turning, and the puzzle-houses snap together, all the pieces filling in. I really do have to let go as Sam said, and I feel him guiding us. He obviously doesn't need as much analysis as Jason and me. Likely, we need to let go of the analysis, ourselves. But I would have great difficulty explaining how this feels to us if I don't make comparisons to things we know. I don't want to say we just jumped somewhere, as though it were that simple, either. There are nuanced subtleties involved, because we're not looking at an earthen landscape, flying over it. This is a *mental* landscape.

The turning takes us into a view that's like what I'd seen in my limited experience with virtual reality video games, the kind with VR headsets. This landscape feels artificial as we fly over it. But I begin to do my thing, and the information comes to me. Now, it's more like what I'd already experienced as I learned things about people through their minds. This is more intense and visual, however.

Peter Horst Reinhard, now in his mid 80s. I see his German heritage threading into history. Lots of names and faces, but I'm searching for things that are relevant to our purposes. A construction site appears.

His father was a Nazi contractor, an expert in building bridges and industrial buildings. Horst, or Reinhard, as he was more commonly called after his father died in 1978, went to job sites with his father during World War II. His father's name was Otto. The bulk of Otto's construction crews were Jewish prisoners, and the man didn't see them as people, but rather, they were a means to his construction ends. Horst, only ten when he first began visiting the job sites, was impressed by the efficiency of his father's systems for completing projects, especially his labor systems. The Jews weren't particularly hard-working, but they were steady and predictable when the German foremen made them follow very strict rules. This helped Otto keep his set schedules.

Seeing what his father had set up on these job sites gave Horst an appreciation for efficiency. He grew to love efficiency in all aspects of life, so much so that he became obsessed with it, to the detriment of all other considerations, most notably the physical and mental limitations of the human labor force. Efficiency was more important than the people themselves. His father had taught him this perspective, but Horst would take the concept to extremes his father never would have dreamed possible.

Horst attended a very strict boarding school until the war ended in 1945, when he was 10. He loved the cold brutality of the teachers and staff of the school, as well as the bulky stone and brick architecture. They suited him perfectly. He was happy to fight for every social position, whether it be for those in the sports clubs or for status in the social hierarchy of the school. And if needed, he would fight to prove his worth. After the war, the family struggled, and Horst had to move from school to school as his family moved to various cities where his father could find work. His mother died of consumption when he was 18, and his older sister died under mysterious circumstances when he was 20. Having a very high IQ, he finished his formal university education in 1955 at the age of 20. His specialty was maths and engineering.

By then, his father had rebuilt his construction business enough to support the two of them, and Horst took a leading role in overseeing the business. During the next two decades, Horst expanded the business and branched out with new ventures, most of them initially related to engineering, but later specializing in providing staffing for other businesses, an industry that would become what we call human resources today. These, along with investments in growing technologies, made Horst very wealthy. By the time his father died, Horst, then known simply as Reinhard, was one of the wealthiest men in Europe.

Combining his experience and expertise in engineering and labor resources, in 1972, Reinhard formed a company whose task it was to conduct research and make recommendations for engineering a better society. The goal was to create global, cultural movements that would become accepted throughout the world and would eventually become compulsory. This company was Global Initiative One, or GI-1. It would later evolve to become The Organization, which was referred to among the inner circle as The Org.

To institute their social movements, they first needed the cooperation of wealthy corporate executives and well-connected government authorities from around the world. They accomplished this through elaborate and enticing conferences where attendees were pampered and treated to the best accommodations, food, and leisure activities. The Organization became more than a research company, and by the end of the 90s, it held annual meetings where the most powerful people in the world attended, including popular celebrities and those who remained out of the public eye. By then, the Organization had developed a public persona of being concerned about the environment and the rights of repressed people and minorities throughout the world. Only a few "conspiracy-theory nuts" knew that the goal of the Organization was not to help the planet and oppressed people, but rather to socially engineer a global network of controlling authorities who would implement strict rules of behavior, limit human rights, and destroy freedoms until The Organization controlled everything.

Those outside the inner circle who thought they belonged to The Organization, powerful people who ran governments and massive conglomerates, and who believed they would be leading humanity under their own unified world government, didn't realize that only a few, 10 people, actually held all the power. These 10 were The Org, the core of the larger Organization. Six of those 10 still remained after The Crash.

These six were behind their own "final solution," which they intended to implement through Ben's altered Stoffer Solution. They intended to take control of the world's population by affecting everyone's mind, seemingly giving all people what they wanted, while in reality, taking away what it meant to be human.

This would have been Reinhard's ultimate application of efficiency: pacifying everyone's mind, making slaves of humanity, and ruling over the world. But it didn't work. Instead, it caused The Crash and led to the deaths of more than 90% of humanity. Those deaths resulted from starvation and from the crashed people murdering others. Even while facing this disaster, The Org still sought a way to resurrect the core brain-changing technology behind the Stoffer Solution, so they could finish the work they started.

They had not anticipated Ben's response to The Crash, however. Ben had found a way to correct what The Crash had caused, and we in the Family, along with many others who joined us, had sent Ben's BB waves around the world, resetting the brains of those who still survived. Now, The Org desperately wants to use this adapted technology to jump right back into their original goal, only now using a different method. They had destroyed the Space Force Base, and had bombed the entrances to Ben's lab. Their intention had been to trap those of us who remained underground, not caring whether or not we lived or died, and later to send crews to dig out the lab and take control of the newest technology that Ben had developed.

But we had gotten out of the lab, and The Org had hesitated sending crews to dig into the lab, apparently not sure what to do with us, especially if Ben was among us.

They had known early about the smaller Beep that Ben had created and that we had built into the Jeep. They had tried to take it from us, but they hadn't expected the resistance we put up against them. Then, they had been surprised by the existence of the far-reaching BBs, and further, they had been shocked by our Iter Anima method of distributing the BB waves around the world, even though they had discovered their own version of Iter Anima.

After decades of planning, social engineering, finding ways of influencing and even controlling national governments, and gaining control of large masses of the world's population through social movements supposedly created to save the world, they had been faced with the personal disaster of everything they had worked for being destroyed.

Now, they see one final hope for fulfilling the goals of their narcissistic, psychopathic, sociopathic egos, and they are not going to let that slip away. That hope is to seize Ben's technology and use it for mass mind control. I know, to the core of my soul, that simply stopping them from getting the technology is not enough. These people and anyone else around them who support their efforts must be destroyed.

This "spying" has given us a background understanding of who we're dealing with. Next, we need to understand how this man of high efficiency has set up his network of people and who might remain running that network. Seeing into Reinhard's mind shows us his ambitions, and it's clear that he has no intention of stopping his mad, murderous rampage through human decency and freedom without eliminating the five others who still exist in The Org. They, too, are tools for his desires. The other five are *almost* as dangerous as Reinhard. We need to deal with all of them using our own solutions. They are part of Reinhard's systems and structures. It is against these people that we will begin applying our million cuts.

All of this information has come to me in the form of images and ideas, sometimes as complete concepts, sometimes as statistics. It was a flood that overtook me and that I had to swim through while continuing to breathe. All the while, I remained aware of Jason, Aiden, and Sam in the distance, and Avery even farther back. I know they have witnessed some of this, but to them, it likely has been an assault on their own ability to think.

I turn along with them again, turning inside Reinhard's mind, and we see a new direction, the present. I am grasping for the structure of The Organization, looking for who we should attack first and where they are. This time, the information comes in the form of a map and a list, as if it were someone's memory, not like a picture placed in front of me. I see highlights and names: Cologny, Switzerland; Davos, Switzerland; Beijing; Tokyo; New York; and the closest to us, San Francisco.

These are locations of The Organization offices. I focus on San Francisco, but I don't get any sense of who might be there. I glimpse a dark place with dozens, maybe hundreds of people lying on mattresses. And then I hear laughter. We're immediately in the room of dark wood again, in front of Reinhard as he laughs. He stands alone in this dark space.

He says, "Having a nice tour?"

So much for not being noticed. I jump right into a response. "We wanted to see who you were. Maybe figure out a way we could work together. But we were worried because of what you did using Raya, the way you controlled her."

"Yes, I know you didn't like that. But it was the most efficient way for me to talk to you. Not to worry, though. I'm sending troops to get Ben's new designs and equipment. Genetrix were his partners, afterall. And we funded that partnership. So, we will be working together again soon. I hope you give our troops a friendly and proper welcome."

"I'm sure we can give them a proper welcome," I say. "Sorry you can't be with them in person."

"That is being arranged." He changes subjects. "So, I see you didn't take my advice to stop these mind travels. It really is causing discord in the consciousness of the world. Maybe the troops can do a more efficient job of persuading you. I'll have a talk with their commander."

"That's why we wanted to find a way to work with you. Maybe we can make things more . . . *efficient* in our exchange. Maybe this doesn't have to be so difficult."

"We'll need to talk to Ben about that. It seems that some of the *settings* on the Beep could be *altered* a bit, so it gives the proper result. We could try it on your people, your *family*, and you'll see how much it will help you. That's how we can work together."

Fuck this guy! He thinks he's going to turn us into zombie minds to help him take control of this wasted world. Hell fucking no. But I have to string him along so he keeps talking. I say, "Yes, Ben's the one you need to talk to about that. I'm just here to help. Are you coming to meet him in person?"

"Soon, but first, he can meet with the troop commander. I'll send instructions to Commander Orlinsky."

I want to ask him questions, but I don't want to antagonize him. I also wish that I could pummel him into the ground. I wonder how we might break into his mind or his body and start making our cuts. I'm fairly sure he can't see into our minds, without our knowledge at least. But he certainly had the ability to get into Raya's mind deeply enough to manipulate her.

I decide I'll ask questions and see how it goes. I say, "Are you flying troops here? It seems that you killed all the soldiers at the base."

"That was necessary. We had to stop you from making any more of those waves. I've already told you how damaging that is to the world."

"I'm just a grunt, here. I'm not in charge of the settings. Maybe you're right. Maybe some adjustments are needed to the BBs."

"Yes, the BBs. We'll need to make better versions of those. Commander Orlinsky can work that out with Ben. We already sent another B-52, as you're well aware. We also have a 747 coming in. Those troops will be there presently."

Presently, I thought. That must be pretty soon. They had bombed the runway at the base, so they would have to land at Denver International Airport. And we wouldn't necessarily hear a plane fly over, on its way to landing. They could be on us anytime.

"Okay then," I say. "We'll go prepare to meet your troops. Nice office you have here, by the way."

"Thank you. Our whole facility is shielded. Though not from your rude intrusion, apparently. It *is* a nice office. Maybe you'll visit in person here one day."

"Maybe so."

We pull away, and I signal for Sam to watch our backs, however it is that he can do that. We don't want to be followed or watched.

.   .   .   .

We came together and faded out of the black, back into the stockroom where we sat around the battery-powered lantern. We stayed quiet for a while, all of us trying to make sure we hadn't been followed. I started to believe that Reinhard and his people weren't too concerned with spying on us at the moment, considering they were sending troops anyway. None of us got a sense that we had been followed, so we relaxed a little, as much as we could, knowing that we were back in a situation of dealing with troops again.

Jason said, "If they want Ben, then we will give them Ben."

"How would we do that?" I asked.

"Magic."

I thought I understood his likely reference. "Do you mean something Glenda can do?"

He didn't answer directly. "If they're looking somewhere they expect to see Ben, then they will see Ben there. And what Ben tells them about the technology will be up to us. Can you get with the Family and our soldiers and prepare for the visitors? I'm taking the kids away from here."

"Absolutely," I said.

Part III
Annihilation

"Bleating and babbling we fell on his neck with a scream
Wave upon wave of demented avengers
Marched cheerfully out of obscurity into the dream"

– Roger Waters

Steven S. Patchin

Chapter 31
Separation

I trusted that Jason had a plan for the children, and I focused my attention on telling everyone else that more troops were coming to cause us problems. I didn't think that they were coming to kill us immediately, but there was no way to predict what they would do, what Reinhard would order them to do.

The kids and Jason gathered to leave after stocking up on food that they could carry.

Sam stepped over to me near the front of the store and said, "We're going to reconnect with the groups of kids we found before and get ready for what you guys plan to do. Jason wants us to stay separated for now."

"He's right. We don't know when these troops will show up. It's best you get away from here."

"I'll see you later, then," he said.

"One way or another," I replied.

After all his standoffishness, this was the first time Sam had shown me any hint of friendly consideration. I really liked him, with his cautiousness and his unwillingness to back down. I doubted I could have had that much strength and determination if I were his age during The Crash. He was very smart, too.

The group started filing out the front entrance and into the darkness. Jason stopped and said to me, "I take it that you'll make whatever preparations you see fit. It's starting."

"I will."

We shook hands, and I watched them leave. I approached Terry and Moore, who were standing next to the open doorway. I asked them, "Do you have any suggestions for how we might deal with these troops coming our way?"

"We don't know how many there will be," Terry replied, "but I doubt they'd only send a few. So, we can't fight them with guns. From what you said, it sounds like they could be sending a whole platoon, maybe sixty soldiers or more. I don't know how they'll get here because they won't have military vehicles. From Denver International, they'll have to use regular cars and trucks. It should be interesting to see what they do. At least if they come at night, we'll see their headlights."

"You're right about that. And I don't believe there are any more Genetrix troops already here. Those ones you killed are likely the last of them or we would have seen them already. Reinhard didn't seem to indicate that anyone else from his team was coming here except for those he was sending on the 747."

"Why is he sending them at all? What does he want?"

"Their aim is to get Ben and his technology," I replied. "We know they can't do that. But I don't see why we should just sit here and wait for them. And if we stay in a big group, I think they'll track us down too easily. Maybe we should disburse. Just scatter in all directions, so they can't surround us."

Terry shook his head and shrugged his shoulders. "Why can't you and the Family get together and take them all out, like you did back at the lab? How did that work?"

"I still don't know exactly how we did that. It was a funneling of energy through all of us. But this time, we're not looking at killing everyone. We don't think that will be useful, and we really don't know how dedicated these troops are anyway. Were they shielded? Or did our BBs reach them and reset their minds? The Org people who sent them won't quit, either." I pondered this for a moment. "No, we can't just kill them as a group, even if we had a way to do it. We have to approach it differently. We need to be sure we get every single person who is behind this."

"What then?"

"We have something that we're working on. And we do need to guard ourselves physically. I think we should split up and be prepared to fight. But let's not give them a tidy target. How about we go off in small groups and make sure at least one of us who can shoot is near each group?"

"We can do that," Terry replied. "Okay, we have five of us here. I assume you can shoot."

I nodded. Yes, I could shoot.

He continued, "How many more?"

"I taught all of the original Family how to use M4s, the basics, and we all have guns, but as for how many can really fight . . ." I thought of how we had defeated those soldiers at the parking garage, which seemed so long ago. I had been able to set them up in defensive positions while I did most of the killing. "I would say that Aiden can fight. Maybe Javier and

Nassir. That's eight. How about we divide into that many groups? There are less than forty of us here now, so that's five per group."

"Okay," said Terry. "Then we'll just split off and head out wherever each group wants to go."

"And not tell each other where," I added. "We can work out how to join back up later." I didn't want to get into how we would deal with giving them Ben. I didn't know, myself.

"Why did this guy, Reinhard, tell you in advance that the troops were coming? Seems pretty stupid," Moore asked.

"Oh, he's not stupid. His ego might get in his way, but he's used to being in control. He expects that we'll hand over Ben."

"Well, *that's* a problem."

"We're working on that problem."

Inside, we divided into groups with designated shooters, or defenders, in each one. Thus we separated into eight groups individually led by Terry, Moore, Gerald, Santiago, Aiden, Javier, Nassir, and myself. I asked Craig and Elizabeth to come with me, along with Mitchell and Ginny. We all left the Walmart, going our separate ways with our groups.

I started us out heading north, and then began taking streets east and north through residential neighborhoods. The light from our flashlights lit our path. I didn't know this area of town, so we just Gumped our way along with no particular destination in mind. The silence was soothing, except for the sounds of our footsteps and Daisy's toenails clicking on the pavement. Even the surrounding darkness, with no lights but our flashlights, was comforting to me. We weren't worried about an attack from people at the moment. We knew the coyotes could be following us, but there wasn't anything we could do about that unless they attacked, so I began to enjoy the walk.

Mitchell, who had spent a lot of time soaking in the peacefulness outside the tunnel at the park, was also appreciating our walk. I had wanted him in our group because I found his calm demeanor to be a positive influence on my own wildly fluctuating psyche.

He said, "I don't remember the last time I took a walk and felt so relaxed. I know we're supposed to be on guard, but this quiet is really nice."

"Yep," I said. "I was thinking the same thing."

Craig said, "If only this were a casual stroll after dinner, instead of a retreat to escape an advancing army in the middle of the night."

"Oh, come on. Don't spoil it," Elizabeth replied.

"Sorry. This has me a little wired."

We didn't talk again for a long time. We walked for more than an hour, arrived at a private, gated community, hopped over the closed entry gate (Daisy squeezed under), navigated around some abandoned cars, and soon found ourselves at a golf club. I figured it would be a good place to stay, considering the closed community gate and the open views from the golf course.

We used a small landscape boulder to break open the front door of the clubhouse and found the inside to be free of obnoxious odors and free of other people. We could settle here and wait a while before we tried to contact Jason. We chose a big meeting room in the back that overlooked the golf course, now completely dark. Tables and chairs filled half the room.

We would need to do an Iter Anima to reach some of the others and figure out how we wanted to present Ben to the troops when they arrived. That would be later. I was confident we could make the mind connections, given what had happened in the past two days. But I didn't know what Jason meant when he said we would use magic. I also hadn't thought much about it yet. From almost any standpoint, one would view some of the things that Jaguar had done as magic. She had made herself appear in multiple places at once, and more powerfully, she had made attackers see a jaguar that wasn't there. This had led to my giving her the name *Jaguar*, an obvious name which she had accepted because she had yet to be named, even at her age of 10 or 11, and she saw it as appropriate.

When compared to our human abilities before The Crash, what we were able to do now would seem like magic. But, even though I had found a way to read minds and even read deeply into a person's DNA enough to know some of that person's history, I still didn't equate that to magic.

Sam and the kids could shout at people in far-away places, and those people would hear their shouts. Reinhard could manipulate people and coyotes. But none of these things seemed like magic to me. I understood – as much as I could without a scientific analysis – how some of these abilities had arisen in us recently. But magic? *Wasn't magic inexplicable?*

We were fairly relaxed after the walk, except for Craig, who said, as we all sat at one of the round dining tables, "How are we going to deal with these people if they think they can get Ben and his technology from us?"

"I was just thinking about that," I said. "We're going to have an Iter Anima, or at least a mind connection, just before dawn. We'll figure it out then."

Craig drummed his fingers on the table and said, "Okay. I need to relax, I know."

Elizabeth patted his hand to show she understood how he felt. I wanted to get some sleep, which likely wouldn't be more than a couple hours. I excused myself and made a place to lie down along a wall in the open half of the room. I rolled out a simple mat that I had found at Walmart. Daisy lay next to it. I didn't even remember sitting on the mat before I heard Jason in my head.

Steven S. Patchin

Chapter 32
Coordination

My eyes shot open when I heard him. The blue-gray light of dawn approaching revealed the golf course outside the window.

This was the first time I had been "called" in my mind by anyone other than Jaguar. I'd called others this way, especially when we connected with so many people around the world before we did the BBs, and now I knew what it felt like to be called. Not as intrusive as I'd expected it could be. It really was like a whisper from nearby, but I knew it was in my head.

Jason said, "Hello. We're coming together now." This was very like someone talking to me, no visions, just a voice.

I saw the others in the room sit up, even Mitchell, who hadn't yet been drawn deeply into one of these connections, though he had gotten some feel for it the day before the barbecue. The four of them were looking around and quickly realizing they were hearing Jason in their heads. I sensed a lot of the Family here, but not our soldiers or the children. Not Glenda, either.

Jason said, "I'm back at the Walmart. No sign of any troops yet. I'm waiting here with Ben."

"What?" I heard Craig say out loud, and then heard the same from others within the connection.

Jason didn't answer the responses of surprise, but instead carried on. "We need to bring Jaguar and Kallik into this. Can we do that?"

He was talking to me, so I said, "I can reach out to them."

"Please do."

He wanted me to do this immediately. I was usually pretty good at waking up quickly, but this was like having ice thrown in my face and being told I needed to name all the presidents. Well, it wasn't *that* bad. I didn't know all the presidents' names, but I did know how to channel an Iter Anima.

I took a few breaths, closed my eyes, and thought of Jaguar, thought of visiting Jaguar, thought of the deep green jungle and her Zo'é tribe. And I found her. The tribe are combing through dense foliage, very big leaves at waist level and tangled vegetation on the ground. I feel their toil, and also feel guilty at my abrupt entrance interrupting them.

Jaguar takes my presence in stride. I say, "A lot of us are here. We're beginning this fight."

"Yes, it's time," she says.

Jason says, "Hello."

Jaguar replies, "I'm ready."

They are ahead of me in communicating our purpose. Jaguar stops and sits below some massive leaves. The rest of her tribe stop where they are in their long line and set down their burdens, then sit to rest, themselves.

Jason says, "We need to prepare The Org for Ben. They need to see him, and they need to hear what we tell them, but they also need to hear what they want to hear. And it has to come from Ben. This will require a coordinated presentation. I propose that you, Jaguar, help them see Ben. And that you, Craig and Elizabeth, provide the information Reinhard wants to hear. And we also need Kallik's help."

To me, Jason says, "Can you contact her?"

As serious as this is, and as really wild and almost unbelievable as well, I can't help but think of making a conference call. I'd never made an actual conference call using a phone, but I had done something like it with the climbers. Our big unifying Iter Anima had been more like touching points on a web to connect people, and the BB had been riding waves. This connection now would be more like a conference call.

I look for Kallik. It is still dark in Siberia, and I find her sitting calmly by a fire in her yaranga, like she was when I first met her. She hasn't been sleeping and is aware that I would be calling.

"Kallik," I say, "The fight is beginning."

"I have thought about this, and I do have something that will help."

"Thank you. And Jason is here. You have not spoken directly to him yet. And Jaguar is here, too."

Jaguar stands. Kallik stands. My thoughts of phone technology disappear, and this conversation changes into something without words. I had not considered the fact that Kallik and Jaguar had not conversed before, at least as far as I knew. They had participated together with our bigger group and had been there for our recent funerals, but, apparently, they had not met formally.

Low vibrations tremble through us, not in our minds, but physically *through* us. The vibrations overtake my surface thoughts and what functions like a conversation. I had been seeing where I was, where Jaguar was, and where Kallik was, depending on my focus. It was like turning my head and seeing different pictures. What I see now is overwhelming white light that expands with the vibrations. Two hazy forms of warmer light, bright amber, circle each other within the wider whiteness. They are Kallik and Jaguar.

I see only this and hear only the vibrations. All of it penetrates me, the others, too. The colors of light mix and turn pale. A blueness prevails as all movement slows and stops. I see the two of them now, and they speak to each other.

Jaguar bows and says, "Kallik, I honor you. Your presence has touched us. Your reach has changed us. Your sight has allowed us to see."

Kallik bows and says, "Young one, you live beyond your years. You see farther than your eyes. You reach farther than your thoughts. You will bring us forward."

They remain still, both bowed. They have said what they wanted to say. The vibrations subside, and I feel the surface connections again, an indication that we can return to a more standard conversation. Kallik and Jaguar lift their heads.

After a polite silence, Jason says, "Kallik, I am honored to meet you."

"And I you, Jason."

"That you and Jaguar are with us now is of ultimate importance," Jason says. "We have a task, a *performance*, that we must present. I believe you can help, though I do not know how exactly. I apologize that I do not know what I do not know. My hope is that you will see what is needed and that you will contribute."

"I will. What is this performance?"

Jason says, "Please allow me to explain." He first addresses Jaguar. "Jaguar, I believe I understand your place in this performance, however, I do not know enough to be specific. You are Jaguar because you have shown the world Jaguar. The animal was there and not there all at once, even while you remained throughout. You made people see a jaguar. For our performance, we need people to see Ben."

Jaguar says, "A person is more than outward appearance, as is an animal. I understand who a Jaguar is. Can you show me who Ben was?"

"Together we can." Jason means all of us who were close to Ben.

I'm starting to see what he is orchestrating here. But I can't imagine how an image of Ben would mean anything to Reinhard. An image is not enough. That is what Jaguar is referring to. How can we re-create a person? How can we re-create Ben?

Jason says, "Craig, you in particular knew Ben better than the rest of us. And Elizabeth, too. I believe you can bring those deeper parts of Ben to bear. We can make Ben live enough to tell Reinhard what we need to tell him. Especially if we communicate through his surrogate, who is likely to be the commander of the troops that are headed this way."

Craig says, "I'm not like Ben was, but I do know his work thoroughly. And Elizabeth knows really well how to operate all the devices. Perhaps we can get together with Kallik and Jaguar and give them some insight."

Elizabeth says, "We've been working with Ben for many years. We can help."

"I believe Reinhard will be looking to change the backend of the BBs," Jason says. "He wants to make adjustments that meet his ends. We will need to string him along for a while, long enough so that we can get to them and break apart their Org. This is the sleight of hand that allows us to accomplish our own ends. This is our magic."

"Why not just tell him that Ben is dead?" Craig asked.

"I fear that if he knows Ben is dead, he won't hesitate to take us all into custody, even kill the Family. He'd likely send his troops out to hunt us down because he'll have nothing to lose. He would have no problem torturing us to get information. These people are brutal. Don't be deceived by his politeness. If Ben cooperates willingly, Reinhard's best play is to keep Ben happy. I don't think he'll resort to force if Ben works with him."

Elizabeth says, "Most all the equipment and devices for making the BBs was at the base. We don't know if that part of Ben's tech survived the bombing or not."

"That's a problem," I say. "When we went to the base to get the explosives, I saw some bomb damage to the hangar where you built the BBs, but I don't know if the damage was enough to destroy what might have been left of Ben's equipment. Are you saying he left something there that could lead to making another BB?"

Craig says, "I saw the damage, too. I wasn't thinking about the BBs then. Ben hadn't planned on making more BBs. There isn't another device ready to go, but his laptop could still be there. Elizabeth, do you recall if Ben's laptop was at the lab when we destroyed everything with the grenades?"

"It wasn't," she says.

"Then, it's still at the base," Craig replies.

"Or, more likely, Ben brought it with him," Elizabeth says. "He didn't bring it down into the lab, though. It could be sitting in the Jeep. Javier moved the Jeep into a crater, didn't he?"

"Yes," I say.

"Okay," Jason says. "We need to check that. Wherever the laptop is, we can't let Reinhard's people get hold of it. And for our performance, you're right. You two can get together with Jaguar and Kallik and figure out what will work to fool Reinhard and his lackeys."

Craig and Elizabeth agree.

"Now," says Jason, "What do we want to show Reinhard about Ben's tech if we can't actually give him the real tech?"

"It seems that he intends to control the BEMP settings in such a way that he can finish what they started before The Crash," I say.

"That would mean he wants to go back to what they did with the altered Stoffer Solution," Craig replies. "Only with some change that he thinks will give them the results they want."

Jason says, "And we have to make him believe that we can program those adjustments and provide a delivery method like the BBs."

"Right," says Craig.

"That seems to be the gist of it," I say.

"That brings us to our presentation," says Jason. "Let's let Kallik and Jaguar get with Craig and Elizabeth to work out Ben's backstory and personality. We'll call them Ben's Team." Jason says to me, "I think you should go with them."

"I agree. They can use my perspective with seeing into minds."

"Okay, let's talk for a moment, first."

We bid everyone else farewell. I tell Ben's Team I'll catch up with them. And yes, I do notice that this Iter Anima communication is becoming surprisingly casual.

Jason says to me, "Sam is taking his tribe to confirm all the connections they have made already, and to start making new ones. They should be safe where they are. And Glenda has been working on the performance."

I am relieved to hear mention of Glenda, but I don't press for more information. I say, "Okay, where do you want to give this performance?"

"That will be part of the performance. We'll start at Walmart, where we are waiting for the troops to arrive."

"Then, I'll go join Ben's Team, and we'll prepare as best we can. Be careful, Jason."

"You, too. I'll let Glenda know she should join you now. Please bring her in."

Chapter 33
Timeline

I search my mind for the five who we now call Ben's Team. I find four of them easily. I think of the mind connections and Iter Animas the Family have had, and I resolve to let go of analysis enough to allow my mind the freedom to *be*.

We have been realizing that the mental limitations we had created for ourselves as a species were a big factor in humans losing mental connections and abilities throughout history. We don't know how much of what we can do now with our minds is a result of re-discovering what we had lost, but I do know that over-analysis can lead to self-imposed limitations. Now is not a time to create my own limitations. Now is a time for me to let it all go and expand my reach until something else stops me. I need to say *Fuck It*, so I do.

I will be joining a conversation with two people who reasonably could be called shamans, and two who are among the smartest people I've ever met, and one who is an illusionist. Myself, I have the ability to see into minds and into history. The six of us are meeting to contemplate and understand the man who changed the world: Benjamin Lee Stoffer.

My connection with the others has begun with sensing their voices. The sounds swell around me, and I see a place that four of them have created together, likely directed by Kallik. It's a comfortable place where we can speak freely without worry of anyone spying on us. All at once, it is forest, tundra, ocean, and mountains, with stars overhead, and a slight orange glow orbiting slowly around us beyond the mountains. We sit in a circle with a small fire beating in the center, all but Glenda, who is not here yet.

Beneath us and around us are the elements and objects of our natural world, and they shift, never staying still. Forest leaves, tundra grasses, mountain rocks, ocean water. They flow into each other, always changing. The sky mixes all of it with transforming colors flowing and reflecting throughout.

I feel calm immediately. We present ourselves dressed in the clothes and styles we identify with the most. Kallik wears her elaborately-patterned combination of colorful woven cloth and reindeer skins. Jaguar wears her orange animal-skin skirt with a snakeskin wrapped around her chest. Craig wears brown slacks and a black turtleneck sweater. Elizabeth wears a rose-colored knee-length dress with a thick turquoise necklace. And without thinking about it in advance, I find that I'm wearing black motorcycle leathers and a red flannel shirt.

I don't know how all this has come to be, and I tell myself to stop thinking about the how. *Fuck it!*

The sound of wind through trees blends with the sound of ocean waves. Ben's Team – of which I am also a member, but more like a floater – now are waiting quietly. Whispers of small flames fly upward from the fire to the stars.

I reach out to Glenda, knowing she needs to be here, and that I need to bring her to us. She appears from within the fire, waves of heat and bright dancing flames. She is fully prepared to work with us. I'm stunned at her beauty and powerful presence. It's as though I am seeing her for the first time. She rises, turns, and steps out of the fire, her flowing green dress spinning as she sits down next to me.

"Hello," she says, as if this is a casual meeting, rather than the origins of an impossible illusion.

All of us acknowledge her arrival, and I'm particularly relieved and happy to see her.

Kallik says, "This is a meeting place where shamans throughout time have come to know each other and to know themselves. We are here now to find the essence of Ben. What can be told of him?"

Craig answers, knowing that he has the deepest knowledge of Ben. "Ben was both complex and straightforward. Complex in his extensive interests and aptitudes. Straightforward in his approach to life. There was little that he did not want to learn about, and much that made his life exciting and enjoyable. His intensity and concentration could be so deep that he noticed nothing other than his work, but his curiosity also could make his mind sing like a hundred-piece orchestra. He believed that technology could make human endeavors more successful and make the human mind farther-reaching. To Ben, humanity had limitless potential, and his life's purpose was to improve the human condition."

Elizabeth says, "He was able to see and understand the smallest details in his projects, and fix problems that I often didn't even notice. I loved working with him. I felt like I was making a difference by helping him realize his ideas and create his inventions. None of my boyfriends through the years was too impressed with my devotion to Ben, though."

I ask her, "Did Ben have relationships outside of his work?"

"He was married when he was in his early twenties, and they had a daughter. His wife took their daughter and left him when the girl was two. As far as I know, he didn't have any close romantic relationships after that. From what I understand, I think his wife left him because he didn't pay enough attention to her and their daughter. Knowing how much Ben lost himself in his work, I think it's surprising that he ever had time to date, much less get married. Maybe he realized after their divorce that he shouldn't even try again. To my knowledge, he never had contact with his daughter after that, either."

"It must have been rough on him," I say.

"Other than telling me that he had an ex-wife and a daughter, he didn't talk about them to me."

I ask, "When did you go to work for Ben?"

"I joined the team nineteen years ago, in 2001. Craig had already been there for more than 17 years when I came on board."

Craig says, "Elizabeth was exactly the person we needed, and she became invaluable very quickly after that."

Jaguar says, "I have no close relationships with anyone." She's just stating what she knows. I don't sense regret or yearning in her tone. "I feel my connections with people in different ways than what you describe."

"I wonder how different you are from most people," I say. "Whether or not it has more to do with your age than your unique natural connections."

"Both," she says. "And I like learning about what other people do. I know our tribe's ways are different from what you experience. This is good, too. We all can be unified in our differences if we are careful."

Careful, I think. She's right about that. Our unity is more important than our differences, and those differences can be the sources of our unity, rather than the characteristics that divide us. Our differences do not need to be leverage for psychopaths. As we had been discovering, there was a lot of divisiveness in our world during recent times, most of it coming from governments trying to divide people. Some of it had been used to exacerbate The Crash. She is right about our need to be careful.

Glenda remains silent, paying close attention to our conversation, absorbing everything we say with great concentration.

"I can give some perspective on Ben's life, if you want," Craig says. "Through all my years working with Ben, I have learned a lot about him."

"Please do," I reply.

Craig begins his narrative:

. . . .

Ben was born in 1952 in Colorado Springs, Colorado. His father worked at an equipment manufacturing facility close to home, and his mother took care of the household, as well as baby Ben. They never had other children.

By the time Ben started elementary school, his father began having mental health problems, which worsened through the years. He became more impatient in every personal or business interaction. Eventually, when Ben entered high school, his father's disturbing behavior caused the man to lose his job. Ben's mom, who was a very smart woman, but who had no work experience that she could put on a resume, was forced to find work. She got a job in a secretary pool, starting as a trainee, because she was not initially a good typist. She learned quickly, did her job exceptionally well, and kept the job until she died in 1979 at age 48.

During high school, Ben chipped in by getting odd jobs, one as a janitor and errand boy in a machine shop similar to the business where his father had worked. After graduating high school two years early at age 16, in 1968, Ben attended the University of Colorado, Boulder, on a full academic scholarship, majoring in physics. He completed all of his course work within three years, but did not officially complete his degree. The situation with his father's mental health problems led him in a different direction.

Instead of moving to a higher degree in physics, he transferred to Oxford in the United Kingdom, majoring in psychology. This, too, was under a full academic scholarship, including housing and transportation, which was a testament to Ben's extraordinary intellect and academic achievements. He completed his psychology degree in 1974 at age 22, earning a PhD in psychology which was called a Doctorate in Psychology, or DPhil in the U.K.

Before Ben completed his degree, and while he still attended college in Boulder, his father's mental health deteriorated so much that the man could barely deal with feeding himself. It was a good day if he could avoid having an emotional episode. These episodes would cause his father to sit on the floor at his bedside, talking to himself for hours, and they happened a few times a week.

The medical and mental health industries offered no practical help for his father. His mother financially supported the family while also taking care of her husband during this time. When Ben graduated high school, and was awarded the university scholarship in physics, his mother insisted he take advantage of it, even though he would have to leave home and move to Boulder, Colorado. It was an hour and a half drive from his house, and this would mean that he typically only came home on weekends and holidays.

Ben became more interested in psychology because of his father's problems. He wanted to find ways of understanding the human brain so that he could find a cure for his father's mental illness. It may have been a naive aspiration, but it was an important goal to strive for, anyway. He began studying psychology and psychiatry while he worked toward his physics degree. When he was admitted to Oxford in their psychology program, his mother insisted that he go, even though she knew this would mean he would be away in England throughout the school terms.

Leaving his mother alone with his father worried Ben considerably because his father's condition seemed to be getting worse. The man hadn't been locked up since being committed to an asylum when Ben was a freshman in high school. That didn't mean his mother was safe from her husband's outbursts, however.

Doctors had let his father come back home after a few weeks in the asylum. Ben and his mother settled the man back into their home, hoping he had recovered. He seemed okay for a few years, even making his own meals during the day for a while, but it didn't last. As he worsened over time, his mother's only reprieve from taking care of him was when she went to work. But she came home during her lunchtime to make lunch for him. Mostly, his father just sat in their bedroom all day talking to himself or watching TV.

His mother kept her struggles to herself, to shield Ben from the difficulties of her everyday life. She wanted Ben to focus on his education and ultimately help advance the field of psychology. Ben realized years later, in hindsight, that he had pretended his mother could handle things, and he had pretended his father wasn't that incapacitated. Ben focused on his education, and had hoped everything at home would be okay. His mother wanted it that way, and Ben didn't let himself acknowledge how big her sacrifice was.

His father committed suicide the day before Ben graduated from Oxford. Ben returned home to a mother who was distraught but also somewhat relieved that her burden had been lifted. Ben felt guilty for not having been there for his parents, and this weighed on him throughout his life. It also affected the choices he made later in his career.

With his degree in psychology, he joined an existing psychology practice in Colorado Springs, in order to gain the experience required to get a license to practice psychology in Colorado. His education focused on evolutionary psychology, but he had always intended to practice clinical psychology so he could help people with mental ailments.

Helping patients work through their problems gave him a lot of satisfaction. These experiences also were invaluable in improving his understanding of human behavior. He enjoyed it so much that he stayed in the clinical practice for more than a year after he got his license in psychology.

During this time, Ben met the woman who would become his wife. They married in 1976 and had a daughter the following year. In 1979, after Ben started his own practice, his wife left him, taking their daughter with her. The girl was barely two then.

Also during this time, Ben teamed up with a manufacturing company and a medical equipment company in order to re-design and improve existing technologies that related to understanding the human brain.

As an offshoot of his clinical practice, he formed Stoffer Enterprises in 1978. His first breakthrough was the invention of an advanced version of an electroencephalogram machine, or EEG, which he called EEG^2. It facilitated the recording of much deeper and more detailed brain scans that, through the years, eventually included multiple types of neural pathway tracing.

He and his mother grew very close in these later years. Though he worked most of the time, he made sure to have dinner with her at least every other day. Only a few weeks before his EEG^2 breakthrough, Ben's mother died from a brain aneurysm at age 48. This was in 1979, the same year his family left him. Ben was 27. Her death hurt him deeply, and he channeled his grief into his work.

From this time forward, his closest relationships would be with people he employed. By the time of The Crash, the most important people in his life were Fitz, Elizabeth, and me. It was Ben and Fitz who invented the

Stoffer Solution together. Fitz died when the plane Ben parachuted out of was shot down by Ronnie, the relentless piece of shit who was head of Upstream Security. Ronnie captured Ben in order to take him to Genetrix authorities. We now know that they were really working for The Org and Reinhard. Fortunately for all of us, Ronnie was killed, and Ben was saved from being dragged to Reinhard and forced to do their bidding. (Craig looks pointedly at me.)

It was in 1980 that Fitz joined Stoffer Enterprises. His education and experience was in electrical and mechanical engineering. Fitz and Ben collaborated on a number of improvements to devices and systems designed to better understand human brains. What ultimately led to the Stoffer Solution was technology that was based on the transcranial magnetic stimulator, TMS, which was an old technology that evolved from the study of electrical brain stimulation. It had not become viable for practical use until 1980, when Merton and Morton successfully used transcranial electrical stimulation, TES, to stimulate the motor cortex. TMS devices, magnetic instead of electrical, were not developed until 1985, and they were not approved by the FDA for use in brain stimulation until 2008.

Ben and Fitz began their studies of TMS in 1985, and they persisted in their research for more than 30 years. It was not until 2014 when they got their breakthrough that allowed them to translate the bulky TMS technology into what would become the tiny, personal Stoffer Transcranial Device or STD. This – combined with an elaborate system designed to improve the efficiency with which people manage their lives – became the Stoffer Solution.

The Stoffer Solution's appeal to Reinhard is obvious. His primary impetus for controlling people had revolved around efficiency. No wonder he wanted to control the Stoffer Solution!

It was Ben's mistake of partnering with Genetrix in 2016 that changed everything. He made the decision because his own company was organized to distribute medical technology to other companies, not directly to the general public. Genetrix maintained manufacturing and distribution channels which would work well for distributing the Stoffer Solution to as many people as possible, as quickly as possible. Ben knew nothing about The Org, or that The Org owned Genetrix. He had never heard of Reinhard, either. But it was this partnership, ultimately a partnership with Reinhard, that led to the alteration of the Stoffer Solution, which then led to The Crash.

Years before they invented the Stoffer Solution, Ben and Fitz built Stoffer Enterprises into a hugely successful company that primarily supplied technology and systems to the mental health and medical industries. They expanded, building facilities in six countries with multiple locations in each. This allowed for coordinating international research and provided psychological and technological treatment to thousands of people. We lost contact with all but a few of those facilities two months into The Crash. By the time we assembled the BBs, we had lost the last of those contacts.

None of Stoffer Enterprises' peripheral labs and clinics outside of the Denver facility held any of Ben's sensitive technology such that someone could steal it. Those locations were used for research and treatment. But they also served as hubs for the distribution of some of his less sensitive and refined tech, such as EEG[2] and a few smaller diagnostic devices.

I joined the team in 1983. Elizabeth joined in 2001. The company began construction of the underground lab facility at Rocky Mountain National Arsenal Wildlife Refuge in 2007 and moved most of their operations there in 2011.

Perhaps Ben's greatest invention was Memory Scribe, with its ability to record memories that were induced by hypnosis. It was soon overshadowed by the Stoffer Solution, partly because Ben did not distribute Memory Scribe to the general public. He kept that invention close, and he allowed only a few loans of the system to particular institutions. Even those were allowed to operate MS only under strict supervision. With a different situation, Memory Scribe could have caused its own apocalypse. Ben recognized this, and kept it close, never allowing anyone to see schematics or specs. He feared that the technology would get out and be used in harmful ways.

The Stoffer Solution experienced a much different distribution because Ben's goal was to manufacture it cheaply and distribute it to everyone who had a smartphone. He did not consider the device or his system to be dangerous in any way. He also did not imagine that someone would alter it in order to control people.

The Stoffer Transcranial Device was approved by the FCC in 2016, and the full Stoffer Solution was approved by the FDA the same year. Both of these approvals had been expedited so quickly that, in hindsight, it seems obvious that someone was pulling the strings for fast distribution of the product. One might question who in the U.S. government could have been behind altering Ben's device and been connected to The Org.

In 2016, Stoffer Enterprises partnered with Genetrix for the manufacture and distribution of the Stoffer Solution. The first Stoffer Solution devices were released to the public in November of 2019. By February of 2020, The Crash was already out of control, and Ben was on his way to becoming the most hated man in the world since Hitler.

This hatred was not because people blamed him for the damage his invention was causing; few understood that the Stoffer Solution had anything to do with The Crash. It was because Ben was the most famous person in the world at the time, having created the immensely useful and world-changing Stoffer Solution, the system that helped so many. People initially loved him for improving their lives. It was as if his invention had given them more time in the day, or it had sped up their ability to think and get things done. All of this led to better productivity throughout the world, and, along with the improved productivity, more leisure time for most people. They were achieving more, earning more money, and finding more time to enjoy themselves outside of work. The world was becoming a better place because of the Stoffer Solution.

Within only two months of the Stoffer Solution's release, the alterations in the STDs began adversely affecting people in noticeable ways. In what is possibly the strangest effect of The Crash, people began to hate Ben. This led to their quitting the Stoffer Solution. And their disconnecting from the Stoffer Transcranial Device caused short circuits in people's brains. It also gave them withdrawal symptoms similar to those caused by withdrawal from heroin. But for The Crash, there was no treatment until Ben invented a new solution using the Beep and then the BBs for distributing the waves of the pulses.

Ironically, something about The Crash, the purely illogical insanity of it, had led people to blame Ben for their troubles. There he was, visible on all standard and social media, every day. They saw him and hated him. The hatred was an amplification of a negative aspect of human nature, that of looking up to what is held high and wanting to tear it down. In many ways, people's hatred for Ben had become the catalyst for the ballooning insanity that led to the global scale of The Crash. But conversely, The Crash itself had already begun in people's brains, and it led to their hatred of Ben. It was a vicious cycle, a fiery, voracious monster feeding on itself and birthing itself all at once. And if we didn't know better, we would say that none of this made any sense.

Chapter 34
Physics

Craig finishes his narrative, a timeline of Ben's life and the events that led to The Crash. It's very enlightening. Hearing it all put together in a continuous account is quite sobering as well. Figuring out the events and people involved in causing The Crash has taken a lot of effort, and our stepping back to understand this allows us to see just how much we have done to fight The Crash and those trying to perpetuate it. Given the forces and resources devoted to civilization's destruction, it's amazing we're still here to fight.

Kallik says, "Now, we need to go deeper into who Ben was. We need to find his emotional connections and the inspirations that led him to his great accomplishments."

I know it's my turn to lead the way. I feel the slowing of the surface-talk, which is our conversation. Kallik lifts her hands. As if under her command, sparks twirl out of the fire. The sparks become small birds that fly so fast in a spinning circle that I can't identify their features. The birds fly into our heads. I feel the six of us close together, seeing as one.

I think of Ben and the experiences we went through together. These thoughts overtake me and swell. The rest of the team are there as these images and experiences come to me. They are there in them just as I am.

I see Ben as he was the last time I saw him alive, standing in front of the Family, announcing that we would need to leave the lab. Then, I see him next to the bombed-out ground where the tunnel entrance used to be. I'm joyous to see him alive. My memories are flowing backwards and touching on events surrounding Ben.

Next, Ben is saying, "I'm sorry," to me after Lauren's death. We're on the baseball field, having just delivered the BBs. We skip to a time before we launched the BBs, and Ben is saying to the Family, "Now go do what you do." And then he's lying on the floor after having been shot. Next, he's standing, getting shot.

I see various times when he's working on the BBs. Then, he's talking to our group. Now, he's saying, "There's more than one setting on the Beep," after he knocked out the soldiers in the street. He's showing delight at the success of the Beep test, working on the Beep tech, running other tests on me, tests on members of the Family, getting us into his locked underground lab, fighting with us to cross the city, talking to a crashed Jason in the street, seeing Jason for the first time standing among the crashed who would become the Family. Then Ben is telling me the story of jumping out of the plane. We're escaping from Ronnie after I shot the man, then running through the woods after Ben caused a helicopter to crash, now he's riding with me on my motorcycle. Next, standing in my apartment, using a tiny phone to call his people to come get him.

I see Ben in the street with his parachute strung over a car. He is trying to untangle himself from the lines. This is when I first met him. His briefcase lies open and empty. He tells me to help him, rather than asking me. I want to turn away and go back to my apartment, because I recognize him, and I also hate him, just as most people did. But I help him, instead. A choice that would change everything.

Now I dive down a spinning tunnel to things that happened before I met Ben. I see glimpses of moments I can't identify. I see faces and situations, sense dates and times, feel places, until . . . the movement stops.

Ben is eight years old on a warm summer night. He hears thunder. The family have finished dinner, and his mother sits at her sewing machine that she has set up at the back of the living room. She is taking-in a dress that she will wear next week at a party. Ben's parents are excited about attending this fancy party with their friends who live three doors down. Ben's mother is very adept at sewing and has always enjoyed tailoring her own clothes, especially if she's taking them in because she has lost weight.

"Where's Dad?" Ben asks her.

"He's in the garage doing something," she replies with a smile.

Ben goes through the kitchen to the door that leads to the garage and opens it. He sees his father sitting in an orange woven lawn chair. The full garage door is open, and the lights are off. The man's back is to Ben as he stares out toward the wet street. A lightning flash shoots through the distant clouds above the houses, silhouetting his father and giving Ben a jolt of excitement.

"Wow!" he says.

Thunder cracks toward them and rumbles away.

"Grab a chair," his father tells him, without turning around. He takes a puff of his cigarette.

Ben unfolds a green woven chair like the one his dad sits in, and hops onto it, legs swinging. He asks, "Is the storm coming?"

"I think so."

Another lightning bolt zips through the clouds. It takes a few seconds before he hears the thunder again.

Ben asks, "How come the sound doesn't happen at the same time as the lightning?"

His father chuckles. "That's because sound is slower than lightning. Lightning is as fast as light, and light is the fastest thing we know. But sound is much slower. So, the lightning makes the sound, but it's far enough away that we don't hear the sound for a few seconds."

Ben has never considered that sound could be fast or slow. As he thinks about how sound has to travel in a line, it makes sense to him that it would have a speed. Otherwise, he would hear everything all at once. A song on the radio comes out through time. And thunder that is far away has to take time to reach them.

"It must be really far away, then," he says.

"Only a couple miles."

"But aren't radio stations even farther away? Does it take a long time for their sounds to get to us?"

His father chuckles again. "Actually, those sounds travel as fast as light, because they aren't really sounds at all. They're transmissions that get converted to sound when they come out of the radio. To us, they don't take any time to travel through the air to our radios. But their sounds do travel slowly from radio speakers to our ears. We're so close to the radios that we don't notice."

"Holy cow!" Ben says. It makes sense to him. His father is telling him about something he's never thought about, but it all makes sense. This excites him in ways he's never felt before.

More lightning and delayed thunder flicker and crack around them, lighting up the whole neighborhood. Huge raindrops begin to speckle the driveway, bouncing as they hit. The scents of rain and wet pavement mist into Ben's nose, and this moment embeds itself into his psyche. It makes him feel as if his whole future is out there in the clouds and lightning, and it's waiting for him. He wants to run out to it and learn more!

But he also wants to sit here with his father all night. The rain splashes up from the driveway, hitting his bare feet, but otherwise, Ben stays dry. A cool breeze shifts across them and into the garage, whipping back out and tousling their hair from behind, as if a prankster ran inside and then ran out laughing.

Ben laughs.

His father laughs.

The rain falls, and the storm approaches.

We rush through memories again, forward this time.

Ben is 13. He has come home from high school for the day. He hears his father crying, or actually whining very loudly as though he is in pain. Ben knows the sounds. It's another emotional attack that his father, Victor, is experiencing.

Ben's mother, Pamela, steps out of her bedroom as Ben walks through their front door. Her face is pale, and she is holding a white towel that is soiled with what Ben can smell is feces. She stops when she sees Ben. Her hands fall to her sides, and tears flood her eyes.

She says to Ben, her voice shaking, "We have to call someone."

Ben hears Victor scream from in the bedroom, followed by the sound of shattering glass. Ben runs past his mother and into the bedroom to find his father standing, facing out a broken window. His hand is cut and bleeding. He moans.

Ben shouts, "Dad!"

Victor turns and sees his son. His eyes are wide, his hair matted, and blood is already smeared on his cheek. He wears only baggy white underwear with wet brown stains. Poop is smeared on his legs. On seeing Ben, Victor's crazed expression flickers and turns to a sad pout. His head drops, but he leans and picks up a piece of glass from the window sill.

"Oh Ben," Victor says. "If you only knew what it really looks like outside. You'd know it was hopeless."

"What are you doing, Dad?"

"I need to leave. Maybe you'll understand one day. Maybe you can stop it."

"What do you mean?"

"Victor, this is your son you're talking to," Pamela says from behind Ben. "You're scaring him."

"What do *you* know?" Victor says with disdain.

"Let's just get you in the shower," she says. "You'll feel better."

"What's the matter, you don't like the smell of shit?"

"We can clean it up. It's okay."

"No, Pamela, it's not okay. Why don't you two just leave me the hell alone?"

"Victor, we want to help you."

"You can help . . ." He faces her with anger and yells, ". . . by getting the fuck out of here!" He throws the piece of glass in Pamela's direction. It bounces off her arm, leaving a gash, and hits the nightstand next to her.

Pamela screams, drops the soiled towel, and grabs her arm, covering the wound.

Ben turns to his mother and pushes her out of the room. Victor continues moaning. Pamela cries and trembles.

"What do we do?" Ben asks.

"Call the operator. Tell them to send an ambulance or something."

Ben escorts his mother over to the kitchen entryway where their phone hangs on the wall. He dials "O," and waits.

"Hello, number please," a female voice asks.

"Uh, my father hurt himself. He needs a doctor . . ."

"I'll connect you to the hospital."

Another female voice answers, "County Hospital, how can I direct your call?"

Ben responds, "Hello? We need a doctor?"

"What seems to be the problem?"

"My father broke a window and cut himself."

"Can't you drive him to the hospital?"

"Uh, no. He doesn't want us near him."

"Is he dangerous?"

"Uh, I don't know. Uh . . . he threw–"

Victor screams from the bedroom. The sound tears through the house, giving Ben chills.

The voice on the phone says, "Is that him? You need to call the police."

"He needs a doctor. Can you send a doctor . . . an ambulance?"

"I don't know if anyone is available, but if he's dangerous, you'll need the police. We can't bring him here."

"Okay, I'll call the police. But can you send someone, too?"

"I'll see what I can do. What's the address?"

Ben gives her the address, hangs up, and again dials "O" for the operator. This time he asks for the police. He tells the woman who answers at the police station what the situation is and gives her the address.

Ben hangs up and ushers his mother over to the kitchen table where they sit and wait. They can hear Victor as he continues moaning and begins talking to himself. The sounds come to them muffled, and they can't make out what he's saying.

Pamela lifts her hand away from the wound and looks at the cut. It's bleeding, but it's not extremely bad. Ben gets up, wets a paper towel from the faucet, and hands it to his mother. She wipes the blood and holds the towel against her arm.

She says, "I don't know what to do anymore. I don't know what happened to him. Did I do something?" She begins to cry and covers her face with her hands, dropping the bloody paper towel on the table.

Ben doesn't know what he should say. He tries to console her. "Mom . . . it's not your fault. He needs help. Maybe the doctors will know what to do."

"I hope so. Victor didn't want to go to the hospital when I offered to take him before. He got mad."

"He has to go to the hospital. They'll know what to do."

Her crying tapers off, and she stares out the kitchen doorway. Her bedroom doorway is across the living room. From this angle, they can't see Victor in there, but they do hear his continued moaning and mumbling. They wait for what seems to Ben like a long time, but finally they hear a siren, and then the doorbell. Ben goes to answer the door, and when he opens it, he sees two police officers on the porch, wearing their official mortarboard hats. He begins to comprehend the severity of the situation as he notices their uniforms and their guns. He pushes the screen door open to let them in.

The taller one says, "Someone called about a problem at this residence?"

"Yes," says Ben. "That was me. My dad needs help. He's upset, and he needs to go to the hospital."

The officers step into the living room and shut the door behind them. The more muscular officer says, "We're not a taxi service."

Victor moans loudly from the bedroom and shouts, "Is somebody out there? I didn't say anyone could come in."

"It's okay, Dad," Ben calls back.

"What's the problem?" the taller officer asks.

"I don't know. He cut himself. He's been angry lately. We just want him to get help."

"Is he a danger to anyone?"

Pamela steps into the living room, dazed. Her arm is bleeding more, and blood drips onto the floor. She barely registers that the officers are there.

The muscular officer notices the blood and says, "Did *he* do that?" He points toward the bedroom.

"He wasn't trying to hurt her," Ben replies, pleadingly.

"That's assault," the officer says. He looks at his partner, and they both draw their guns. "I need you two to go into the kitchen."

"He's—" Ben begins, but gets cut off.

"Now, son. Take your mom into the kitchen."

Ben does what he's told and guides his mother back to the kitchen table. She won't sit down. She stands by the table without saying anything. Ben watches the officers through the doorway. With guns drawn and ready, they stand outside the bedroom on both sides of the doorway, away from the opening.

The tall officer calls into the bedroom, "Hey in there. This is the police. We need you to come out here, and hold your hands up. Do what you're told, and we won't have any problems."

"Oh yeah?" Victor responds. "This is my house! You don't tell me what to do in my house."

The officer takes a quick peek into the room and stands back. He shakes his head at the other officer, and says to Victor, "What's your name?"

"Get the hell away from me!"

"We need you to come out. You're scaring your family. Let's get you some help."

Ben calls to the officers, "His name's Victor."

"Victor, let us help you. Just come out here and we can work it out."

"Get the hell out of here. I told you to get away from me," Victor yells.

The muscular officer says to Victor, "I'm going to step inside. You need to back up. We don't want to shoot you, so just do what we say."

He nods to his partner, holsters his gun, and steps into the doorway. The taller officer moves out with his gun still drawn and ready.

Victor yells, "Ahhhh. Get out of my house!"

Muscular Man charges into the bedroom, and the other officer follows quickly, the equipment on their belts jingling. Ben can hear scuffling. The doorbell rings. More scuffling, and now groaning, too. Victor yells. The officers give orders. Metal clings together.

Victor grunts and yells obscenities, one atop the other, "You fucks, you fuckers, goddamn it, you can't do this, it's my house, sons of bitches, motherfuckers . . . Who sent you? How did they know? What's the idea here?"

The doorbell rings again. Ben can tell from the sounds in the bedroom that his father has been restrained. Ben steps cautiously out of the kitchen and walks to the front door. He opens the door to find two men standing on the porch, wearing white coats.

One of the men says, "You called the hospital?"

"Yeah, the police are here, too. Come in. Can you tell them that my dad just needs help?"

Ben opens the screen door and lets them in. They enter cautiously, looking around with worried expressions.

The first one says, "We don't—"

The two police officers emerge from the bedroom with Victor, handcuffed, walking in front of them. They each hold one of his arms as they push him forward.

Victor looks at his son and says, "You did this. You brought them here. You just don't listen. You could stop it. You don't know what's out there. You have to look, damn it! Look at what's out there. It's all going to change!" He turns away from Ben and says to the muscular officer, "You fucker!"

The second man in a white coat asks the officers, "Are you taking him to jail?"

"You from the hospital?" the tall officer asks.

"That's why we're wearing white coats."

The officer regards him with irritation for a moment. He says, "His hand's cut pretty bad. How about you take him to the hospital, and we'll come along?"

"You guys have him cuffed. You take him."

"We don't need blood all over the squad car."

"You think we want it in our van? Everything's white inside."

"For shit's sake! Don't you have some towels in there or something?"

"Look, if he's dangerous, we'll have to put him in a straight jacket. And he'll get blood all over that, too."

"Goddamn it! We'll take him. But you might have to put him in the loony bin, anyway. So you're gonna have to get your straitjacket ready."

The two continue arguing as they walk Victor outside toward the squad car in the driveway. Victor has calmed down and isn't saying anything now. Ben stands on the porch watching the exchange.

Ben says, "Are you taking him to the hospital?"

They don't respond and continue arguing. The tall police officer opens the backdoor of the squad car, preparing to shove Victor inside.

Ben yells, "Hey! Are you taking him to the hospital? Are you going to help him?"

The muscular officer shouts back, "Yeah, yeah. We're taking him to the hospital. Taxi service! Then we might take him to jail because of his filthy mouth."

"He needs help!" Ben yells back.

"Take it easy, son. We know what we're doing."

They shove Victor onto the backseat of the car and slam the door. They get into the front, and the tall officer starts the engine, then realizes the white van is behind them.

He rolls down the window and yells, "Are you going to move the damn van? Or what?"

"We're going. Just hold your horses," the first white-coated man yells back.

They get into their van, and the two vehicles drive away. Ben stands on the porch, watching them go. His mother stands inside on the other side of the screen door. He hears a short inhale and crying as she tries to hold in her emotions but can't. She lets it out, and Ben goes inside to try to comfort her. He's shaking, himself.

Now I feel something new, an empathy that runs so deep that it feels like my own emotions. But what I'm feeling is Ben's emotions. The pain of what has just happened, what Ben is feeling, stabs me like my loss of Lauren had stabbed me. It's a trauma that is very difficult for thirteen-year-old Ben to understand or handle. The way the so-called professionals dealt with the situation, arguing about who would take Victor to the hospital, made it worse. Didn't they care that they were dealing with a person?

Until this moment, his family had been experiencing difficulties, but Ben had believed that everything would work out, that his father would get better, that it was all just temporary. Now, Ben stands in the doorway with his mother, who doesn't have it in herself to comfort Ben, so he finds himself comforting her. He hugs her.

Ben searches his mind for a way to understand what has just happened. He realizes that these things are not in his control, and that his father's mental health isn't something that can be "fixed" like a squeaky door. Victor has been taken away by people who don't seem to know how to help him. And Ben is not sure where his father will wind up. This makes him distrust the doctors, and he wonders why the doctors don't know what to do. It comes to him then, that he will need to learn more about people and how their brains work.

These thoughts will first lead him toward physics, which is where he thinks the answers lie. *The brain is physical*, Ben thinks. *And science is physical.* So, Ben decides right then to learn more about science. This will lead him to an interest in physics, which will become his obsession during high school. *To fix the brain,* he thinks, *you need to understand the smallest particles in the brain. The smallest particles are cells*, he thinks. His guess as a thirteen-year-old is not even close to correct. But it sets him on his course to learning about science, more specifically physics.

Ultimately, it will lead to a discipline that isn't generally accepted as a field in the physical sciences in 1965: Psychology.

Chapter 35
Psychology

We rush forward through more memories. Ben has attended high school, and he's attending college at the University of Colorado in Boulder, working toward a physics degree. He's desperately searching for ways to understand the brain, but he's losing patience with the course work, which involves too much math and chemistry that doesn't seem to relate to understanding people's behavior. He's spending most of his time studying tiny particles, yes, and he's happy to have discovered that the smallest particles aren't the parts of cells, but particles so small that some of them can't even be seen with regular microscopes. But he's finding out that physics isn't taking him where he had wanted to go in the direction of the mind. And it certainly isn't leading him toward understanding why people's brains sometimes don't work right. He is no closer to finding anything that can help his father.

It is not until he discovers the works of Carl Jung, the founder of analytical psychology, that he sees a new direction that might take him where he wants to go. By now, he is halfway through completing his physics degree. He begins studying Jung, Freud, Rogers, James, Piaget, Pavlov, and others. A year before his graduation, he applies for a scholarship to Oxford in the field of psychology. He gets accepted two months before the end of the term. He's so excited about the prospects that he doesn't bother to apply for graduation in his physics degree, even though he has completed all the course work. Instead, he prepares to move to England. He's 19.

I feel these emotional threads as though I have been the one experiencing the anxieties and desires and that I am the one finding a better direction for learning. Ben knows that Oxford will give him something important that he needs. But he's also torn between his desire and his need to help his parents. He doesn't want to leave them, but he can't go to Oxford without leaving. And he still believes that he can find a way to help his father by learning about psychology.

Victor has been relatively calm during this time. Ben makes himself believe that things are okay at home and that his mother can handle it. He doesn't want to face the reality that his mother is barely hanging on and that his father is headed for a crash. He comes home from Boulder on a Friday afternoon after skipping a statistics class and leaving campus early. He has news that he's been accepted to attend Oxford under a full scholarship, and the thought of telling his mom turns his stomach.

She's in the kitchen washing vegetables in the sink when he gets home. Ben hasn't told her he was coming, so she's surprised when he walks through the front door and marches directly into the kitchen. He kisses her on the cheek.

"Ben! I thought you weren't coming until tomorrow morning."

She smiles with great joy, which makes Ben hurt even more.

"I wanted to get out of school and come home early. How are you doing? How's Dad?"

Her brightness drops a few shades, and she says, "He's okay. He's been really quiet lately. He's taken to watching "Bonanza" and "Mayberry." Those are his favorite shows. But he also watches daytime soaps. Boy, I hate those things, but it makes him calmer, so I'm glad he can watch them. He's in the bedroom in his recliner right now watching something."

Ben forces a smile. "But how about you? Are you handling work and making lunches for Dad okay?"

"Oh sure. It's not too bad. He likes bologna sandwiches. They're easy to make. I don't mind coming home for lunch. But I'm tired of bologna sandwiches, if you want to know the truth."

Ben knows that this is her way of skirting his question about how she's doing. He also knows that neither of them want to say the truth out loud, that Victor is getting worse, and it's wearing on her.

Ben takes a deep breath and comes out with it. "Mom, I got a scholarship to Oxford."

She looks confused but immediately composes herself. "Oxford! England, right?"

"Yes, it's in their psychology program, and it could lead to a PhD."

She sees the apprehension on his face. "Ben, if you think I'm going to talk you out of this, you don't know me."

"Mom, I–"

"This is your calling. This is what you were meant to do. I know what psychology has come to mean to you in the past couple years. You think you can find the answers you're looking for through psychology, don't you?"

He relaxes. "Yes. I think I can make a difference through psychology.

And there isn't a better place for me to learn, either."

She smiles sincerely. "Then congratulations! I couldn't be happier."

Ben breaks down and struggles to keep from crying. "Mom, I'm so sorry. I want to be here to help. I just didn't know what else to do. I could just stay and help–"

"No! You'd be wasting your time. We'll be fine here. I have friends on our block. They'll help. It's all going to be okay. You have things you need to accomplish. I want you out there doing them."

He hugs her and doesn't let go until she pulls back and says, "I'm making pork chops. I know they're not your favorite, but I can make some sauce for you . . . ."

He laughs. "That will be great, Mom. That will be perfect."

I know that Ben's father will kill himself before Ben gets his PhD, and I know that Victor's suicide will haunt Ben his whole life. But it will also inspire him never to give up. That attitude is what I witnessed in Ben, myself. And this makes Ben an inspiration to me.

I feel exhausted from the wild turbulence of the emotions we've been through. The kitchen spins away, and we come out of these experiences of Ben's life. I become aware of our calm nature-sphere again, with our fire and us at the center. We are emotionally shaken by what we have witnessed. We sit for a while in this peaceful place. I continue trying to sort through all of it.

Eventually, I ask Craig, "What was Ben thinking that led him and Fitz to invent The Stoffer Solution? What was he trying to accomplish?"

Craig replies, "It all started with their trying to understand the human brain and trying to find ways to fix neural pathways that were not working correctly. Ben was still seeking ways to help people like his father. Time and again, however, they discovered that people with severe mental illnesses could not be cured with their technology.

"What is broken in damaged brains involves more than unscrambling poorly routed neural pathways. And their research revolved around training the brain to use better neural pathways for thinking. Kind of like apps used to find the best ways for people to drive from one place to another. That's a lot of what the Stoffer Solution was designed to do.

"They discovered progress in using their technology on people who appeared relatively normal. The brain stimulations they tried on these people indicated improved clarity of thinking and improved motivation to accomplish tasks.

"Ben believed that the brain and the mind behind the brain were not exactly the same. To him, the mind represented the real person, and the brain was the interface between that person and the physical world. A broken brain did not necessarily equal a broken person. So, he believed that if he could improve brain processing efficiency, he could improve human functionality, and thus make people's lives better.

"Their original focus with the full-sized Transcranial Magnetic Stimulator was to stimulate areas of the brain that he believed could function more efficiently. Ben and Fitz achieved a lot of early success in helping people think more clearly. But they knew that people couldn't all come to a lab for TMS treatment. It took them decades to get similar results with smaller devices. Those devices would evolve to become the Stoffer Transcranial Device, the STD. But the device alone didn't do what Ben had envisioned. From his psychological studies and from his experience in his clinical practice, he developed the structures and systems that would integrate with the STD, and this was his greatest breakthrough, putting these things together. This is what became the Stoffer Solution."

"You make it seem so straightforward and obvious."

"Oh, it's neither of those. And we now know that it was still too complicated for Ben to think of everything and keep it in check."

"True," I reply. "But everything Ben started was initially inspired by his wanting to help his father, which he was unable to do. This left him wanting to help everyone, and thus led to the creation of the Stoffer Solution."

"That's the simple explanation, yes," Craig replies.

"A boy's desire to help his father . . . . From that to changing humanity," I say.

Craig nods and asks quietly, "So, what I would ask now is, *how do we use all this information and insight to help us in our present situation?*"

Kallik replies, "When we interact with The Org or Reinhard himself, the more we use Ben's real history, the more we believe what we project about Ben, the more successful our performance can be, the more real it will be."

Elizabeth asks, "But how will making Ben live in our minds help us stop The Org?"

Kallik says, "We have discussed needing to find ways to inflict damage on the people running The Org, a thousand or a million cuts. There are *airshots*, which can be fired by shamans. For us now, I believe we can make our airshots into *fireshots*. Each of us is made of many spirits, and each of us has spirits that can go forth and help us. The opposite is also true: others can send their helping spirits to fight against us. It is these spirits that can send and receive the fireshots. We can make our own fireshots that can go into the spirits of The Org. And this is how we can steal their strength. This is how we can break apart the essence of their bodies and minds."

DNA, I realize. She's talking about DNA, which to her is the many spirits that make up each of us. Is she proposing that we attack the DNA of The Org with fire, by using our own DNA to channel these fireshots?

I say out loud, mostly to Craig and Elizabeth, "DNA! That's what creates the physical essence of our bodies. Is she saying that we can tear that essence down with these fireshots?"

"Attacking the very DNA that holds them together?" Craig replies. "Are these your spirits? Are they DNA?" he asks Kallik.

"It is true that the spirits hold us together, and it is the spirits in everything that connect us. In them, we are joined. Through them we can help each other. And we can also do harm through them. You call some of these spirits DNA. There are many spirits in number and in kind."

Semantics! Who cares what it's called?

Craig asks, "And we can break down the spirits, the DNA, with these fireshots?"

"It is possible," Kallik replies. "But fireshots are not fired as if from a gun. Direct attacks can be seen and blocked. It is the attack from within a deception, from within a *performance*, that has the best chance of working. A fireshot cannot be too big, and it cannot be too obvious. A single fireshot must not be felt. Each shot alone must be invisible so that, all together, they can produce the desired effect: death from a thousand cuts."

Jaguar says, "Our performance is making them see Ben. As they see Ben, through us, others can send their fireshots. The Org will not notice until it is too late."

One of the many amazing things I like about Jaguar is her directness. She doesn't ask questions; she makes statements. She never appears unsure in how she perceives things or what she does. She sees clearly and acts succinctly.

Kallik says, "Yes. Our performance will distract them and enthrall them. But someone must *be* Ben."

We all look at Glenda, and she smiles. She will be the performer. She will *be* Ben.

"And who will send the fireshots so they won't be felt?" asks Elizabeth.
"The children!" I declare, yet another realization on my part.
But of course, Jason and Glenda had already figured out most of this.

Chapter 36
Ben

Reinhard's troops arrived at the Walmart the next morning, a couple hours after sunrise. They pulled up in a random collection of everyday cars and trucks, and commercial airport vehicles, including shuttles and vans. They entered the parking lot from three different directions. Jason estimated three dozen vehicles in all. The troops who got out of the vehicles all carried rifles and handguns. They wore backpacks of varying sizes, each for specific military equipment.

We were looking at more than 120 troops dressed in fatigues and spreading out around the grounds of the supermarket. They took up defensive and offensive positions in the parking lot, along the streets, and near the building. We witnessed this deployment through Jason, who was the only person outside the store to greet these soldiers.

We, the Family, remained separated in our physical groups but mentally unified through Iter Anima. It was a delicate operation for us, considering the coordination necessary. I felt the presence of our different groups except for the children. Most were observers rather than participants for this initial interaction with our adversaries.

Jason stood in front of the fertilizer pallet, arms crossed. He waited to see who would approach him. When the soldiers settled into their places, a tall bald man with deep brown eyes got out of a black Ford truck and marched over to Jason, stopping only two feet from him.

"I am Commander Orlinsky," the man said, keeping his hands to his sides. "You are?"

"Jason," said Jason, holding his hand out for a handshake.

Orlinsky ignored the gesture and said, "Where are your people?"

"Oh, they didn't want to get in the way here. They're off entertaining themselves elsewhere."

Orlinsky ignored Jason's flippant reply. "I understand that you know why we are here." He had a thick Eastern European accent that Jason could not identify. Not German. Maybe Russian, but Jason wasn't sure.

"You're here for Ben Stoffer's technology," Jason said.

"And Ben Stoffer, himself."

"Then let me introduce you to him. He's inside."

Orlinsky gave an order in his language, which I understood to be Polish, though I did not understand the language itself. Eight troops followed their building-entry, military protocol, and carefully went inside the store, one at a time through the main entrance. I heard shouts from within that likely were along the lines of "clear." After almost ten minutes, one soldier exited the store and reported to Orlinsky in Polish.

The Commander said to Jason, "There is nobody inside."

"I'm sorry, Commander. It's a big store. And we also don't want Ben to be harmed. We weren't going to let him be grabbed by reckless soldiers. No offense intended." He indicated the entrance with his left hand. "Please, allow me to introduce you to Ben."

Orlinsky nodded to another group of soldiers, who then entered the store. Jason and Orlinsky followed them inside. The soldiers all shined flashlights in the darkness, most of them very powerful, and the entryway became well illuminated with moving beams of light.

Jason stepped through the cluster of soldiers and said, "Follow me."

He marched directly down the central aisle. Orlinsky and a few soldiers followed. Jason stopped before the double doors that led to the back of the store where stock is kept. He pushed on one of the doors, leaned inside, and said, "Ben, we have visitors." Then, he backed up to allow Ben space to exit.

Ben pushed open both doors at once and strode out, all confidence and determination.

.   .   .   .

We saw Glenda. The soldiers and Orlinsky saw Ben, our genius inventor, leader, and friend.

For this *Illusion of Ben*, Glenda was the main performer, the magician, the illusionist creating the core illusion. She became the physical person of Ben. But it took the whole team to make the illusion work. Jaguar projected the mental image of Ben around Glenda. Craig and Elizabeth provided the specifics of Ben, the knowledge and background of the man so that he could speak. And Kallik worked to hold them all together and provide some distractions when needed, some sleight of hand.

Lit by multiple flashlights from the soldiers, Ben marched directly to

Orlinsky and thrust his hand forward. Orlinsky, briefly off guard, shook Ben's hand.

"Commander Orlinsky," Ben said. "We have some work to do."

Orlinsky composes himself and says, "That is correct."

"I believe we have misunderstood what you wanted to achieve. We had been under the impression that you wanted us dead. Your people destroyed our lab. Destroyed our devices that we used to help the crashed. We only have a few pieces of our tech left undamaged. Was I wrong in thinking that you wanted to destroy everything?"

Orlinsky said, "I am sure you make new machines. You are inventor, after all. And if you have machines still working to help our objective, we will use them."

Ben smiled. "I do have something that will be useful. It's back at our main lab that you bombed. You didn't destroy everything. In fact, a laptop is still there that will make things a lot easier."

Brief panic rose in me at the mention of the laptop. I had not expected Glenda to tell these people about what was left of the lab, especially the laptop. I had to calm myself and stay focused.

"I know where your lab is located. We will go there now," said Orlinsky.

"Of course," said Ben. "Will Reinhard be joining us?"

Orlinsky hesitated at the mention of Reinhard. He could see that Ben knew Reinhard was already in Denver. He decided not to lie, and said, "This is his choice. It is none of your business."

Ben smiled. "Then shall we go?"

Orlinsky turned and marched out of the store, followed by Ben, Jason, and the soldiers. A lieutenant-level soldier whistled and swung his arm above his head in a circular motion. The troops all returned to their vehicles, and soon, a convoy wormed through the streets toward the park and the lab. Orlinsky had insisted that Ben go with him in his truck. He had a driver, so Orlinsky and Ben got into the backseat. Jason rode in another truck directly behind Orlinsky's truck. He had already removed his weapons before the troops arrived, but they had searched him so they could make sure he was unarmed. Both of the vehicles took positions a quarter of the way from the front of the convoy.

The rest of us stayed with Glenda in her illusion of Ben.

Orlinsky said, "I do not see people on streets, except the dead. Where are the people who received your wave?"

"There were very few remaining throughout the world. I wouldn't expect to see anyone wandering here outside. They would have barely survived The Crash after having the affliction this long," *Ben* replied.

"And yet, you went to all the trouble of turning their minds."

"Yes."

"That will give us more people to work with," Orlinsky said offhandedly.

"How do you plan to work with them?"

"That is up to The Org. Reinhard will let us know what he wants to do."

"So, how exactly do you want me to configure the tech? Are you looking to make another BEMP?"

"BEMP? That's your pulse, or wave, correct? It's not up to me what to do with it. I'm not a scientist."

"Sorry to ask so many questions," Ben said. "I just want to make sure we can do what's needed."

"We will get to your laptop and then see what else is there. We will go to the Space Force Base, too."

"Do you have someone on your team that I can work with, or will that be Reinhard?"

Orlinsky was getting irritated with the questions, which, I believed, was part of what they intended, keeping the man distracted and off balance.

He rubbed his face and said, "We will stop with questions. You will tell me where you get food."

"Our food was destroyed in the lab. We eat what we find in the stores."

"It smelled spoiled in store," Orlinsky said.

"Meat and vegetables in the store, yes. Those were spoiled. Our food in the lab was refrigerated until the lab was bombed."

Orlinsky smiled. "Maybe better if you not fuck with Org." He laughed.

A hand radio mounted on Orlinsky's belt crackled, and a voice said something in Polish. Orlinsky pulled the microphone off its shoulder mount, responded briefly, and then turned back to Ben.

"Where is laptop?" he asked Ben.

"It's in a Jeep outside the park. I believe I left it there."

"You're not sure?"

"No. Sorry."

He looked at Ben with distrust.

Ben said, "I didn't need to say anything to you about the laptop. I could have kept quiet. But it can help us. I'm pretty sure it's there."

The long line of vehicles continued its slow progress through the semi-obstructed streets. After a half hour, they arrived outside the park gate that we had used ourselves, the familiar small warehouse just inside. Lots of open space along the road here allowed plenty of room for the convoy to park.

"Where?" Orlinsky asked.

"It's all the way inside a crater close to where the south entrance to the lab used to be. Straight through there." Ben pointed toward the eastbound road.

"We will send your Jason ahead."

Orlinsky got out and walked to the truck behind them where Jason sat, said something to Jason and the driver, and returned.

Jason's Jeep moved ahead of everyone else and entered the open gate. The rest of the vehicles followed for most of the way until we were across from the hidden air vent access. Ben's Jeep was parked where Javier and Ellen had left it after Ben returned to the lab for the last time. The convoy stopped as Jason's truck drove out and down to the Jeep, which was a couple hundred yards away. Jason searched through the Jeep as two soldiers held rifles on him. He climbed out of the passenger-side backseat holding a black bag, presumably with the laptop inside.

The soldiers motioned for him to place the bag on the hood of the Jeep and open it, which he did. He slid out a silver laptop, and I worried again. This was no trick. It was really Ben's laptop where he would have saved detailed files related to his research, especially those for the recent Beep and BBs.

Orlinsky said, "Let's go."

He exited the truck, and Ben followed him down to where Jason stood at the Jeep with the laptop. I wondered how Glenda would know the code that unlocked the computer. Jason had already turned it on, and it sat waiting for unlocking, the cursor blinking at the beginning of six empty boxes. Ben stepped up to it and swiped the lock screen. The desktop screen opened. There was no need to enter anything. The password was nonexistent.

Orlinsky said to Ben, "Show me."

Ben opened an app interface that I knew to be the settings controller for the Beep and BBs. This was how he programmed the BEMPs when the laptop was directly connected to the devices.

"We use this for BEMP programming," Ben said. "I'll need to know your objective so I can configure the settings and create an algorithm. That will mean a lot of calculations to analyze and configure. But that's only a small part of it. Our bigger problem is that we don't have a BEMP device."

"We will have to remedy that," a voice says from behind them in clear English with a slight German accent.

Ben turned to see Reinhard approaching from a dozen yards away. He walked over from the distant convoy. His piercing, blue eyes were his most noticeable feature. He wore black slacks and a brown leather jacket. He stood out from the troops with his clothes, his demeanor, and his intensity. He was in his 80s but looked much younger. His thick hair was close-cropped and white.

He said, "Ben, it's good to finally meet you. I'm glad to see that you are ready to work with us."

"The moment is quite overdue," Ben replies.

Reinhard extended his hand to Ben, who shook it confidently. Heavy wind gusted across the plains, buffeting them briefly before dying down.

Reinhard turned toward Jason. "Jason. Good to meet you, too."

"I feel like we've already met," Jason said. They didn't shake hands.

"Yes, I know the feeling." Reinhard clapped once and said, "So, where to start . . . ."

Ben said, "Now that I have the laptop back, I can use it to program whatever we need. But knowing what to program is complicated. To start, you'll have to tell me your objective."

Reinhard raised his hand and said, "In good time, my friend. Let's take a walk."

Ben and Reinhard stepped across some of the rough, bombed ground and worked their way toward the dirt road that ran north and south. Jason and the troops stayed behind. We in the Family remained with Glenda. They turned south and began walking toward the graves of Family members and of Upstream troops, Lauren's grave, too. I didn't see any bison out in the open. They likely were hiding among the cottonwood trees, staying out of the sun which was making this mid-July morning very hot.

"Your people, you call them the Family," Reinhard stated, and began to say more, but Ben answered him as if it were a question.

"Yes, they are the Family."

"They were pretty upset with me when I spoke to them through that girl, Raya," Reinhard said, as though he was hurt by this.

"You have to understand that they have been through a lot," Ben said. "We worked hard to help the crashed. And you were telling them that their Iter Anima was a problem, that it was causing harm."

"You're a scientist. You can see that what they were doing was dangerous. It disrupts the natural order. You stayed out of it, yourself."

"That's only because I was busy making the BBs," Ben replied. "And there's nothing natural about *those*, either. What would you have them do?"

"Ah, you're right. What's done is done. They just need to stay out of it, now."

Ben let that statement float for a while. "Actually," he said, "If you want to send another BB wave, you'll need the Family. The bomb and BEMP alone aren't enough. The BBs needed the help of the Family."

"That's going to be a problem. Perhaps we will teach the soldiers how to do this Iter Anima."

At this point, I was struggling with my anger toward this man who I knew had killed Lauren somehow. Why did he do it? To what end? He was very casual about manipulating people and using them however he wanted with no regard for their humanity or their rights to pursue their own desires. Even worse, he did not care about their rights to live. I wanted to tear him apart. But he was not the only one involved in The Org. And I was not physically there to tear him apart, anyway.

We all knew that our Iter Anima connections went deeper than just connecting as if we were on a cell phone conference call. What we didn't know was how deep Reinhard and his people were able to go into their mind connections. Certainly, Reinhard had found a way to control Raya. He also had found his way into our Iter Anima with the BBs. But, he had not stopped us while he was there. Was that because he couldn't? He had managed to deceive the children into thinking they had lost their mind connections. And he'd killed Lauren. Had that been an attempt at stopping us?

We knew that arguing with Reinhard would not help our cause, and pushing him to defend his position would not help, either. We had to carry on with our performance. And I had to keep my thoughts to myself, not that the others would disagree with me.

Ben said, "How can I help you, Mr. Reinhard?"

Reinhard laughed. "You are very down to business, Mr. Stoffer. Why have you done all this?"

"Because I was stupid. I thought I could advance human thinking by making people more efficient. And look what it led to."

Reinhard laughed louder. "People, themselves, do not want to be more efficient. That's why your Stoffer Solution didn't work. They would rather be told what to do, knowing that someone will take care of them. *That's* your big mistake. They didn't want more time to make their lives better. They only wanted a quick and entertaining way to fill the time they already had. What we programmed into your devices would have given them that. It would have helped them make all the choices in their lives *easier*. And then, we could have given them their entertainment, their distractions, and their products, all based on what we dictated. From there, we could have directed the rest of their time to whatever tasks we saw fit. They would have been a perpetual army of happy workers.

"*That*, Mr. Stoffer, is how we could have made humanity more efficient. They needed fewer choices, not more. Just imagine what we could have accomplished with all those minds focused on what we wanted. The things we could have accomplished. The inventions we could have built. We could have flown to the stars.

"And maybe we still can. Maybe there are enough people left so that we can reach the stars, expand ourselves into the universe."

I don't know how Glenda refrained from pummeling him to death upon hearing this. But if she tried, I think Reinhard would have physically crushed her like an aluminum can.

Ben said, "You are right about my mistake. I don't want to do that again. With the BBs, I tried to fix what I had broken. But now, I have a chance to accomplish what I set out to do with the Stoffer Solution. If you'll help me."

Reinhard stared at Ben as they walked. "It is possible that the mistake we made was in not consulting you about the changes we were implementing in your STDs. If we had worked directly with you in the first place, it could be that The Crash would not have happened."

Ben laughed. They arrived at the Family's graves where the laughter fell into irony, but it was only ironic to the Family who were with Glenda then. For Reinhard, Ben's laughter was an acknowledgement that Ben wanted to work with him and The Org. This had been our objective all along.

Ben said, "I think you are right, there. So, now we have a chance to fix our mistakes. Are you telling me that your objective is to give people what they want?"

Reinhard patted Ben on the back. "Yes, my friend. That is what we have been trying to do all along. You and I have wasted a lot of time with this misunderstanding. I will take responsibility for that. And now that you understand, does this give you an idea of what our objective is?"

"Yes. I believe I can look closer at the data we have from the altered Stoffer Transcranial Devices and find a way to ferret out the errors, fix them, and create a clean solution that will work."

Reinhard smiled. "Ah, you see? We are both working toward the same ends."

"It does appear to be so. But you destroyed . . . but the base has been destroyed. Do you have a way to get more bombs so we can make and deploy another BB?"

"Yes, the base's runway is not functional. But we have an entire airport not far from here. The B-52 is there right now. And we can get more bombs."

"Very good, Mr. Reinhard. I believe we have a plan. And I agree that we should go to the Space Force Base and see if any of my equipment survived the bombing. There could be something of use that wasn't destroyed."

"We will go there, Mr. Stoffer. Yes, we will go there. And now, maybe we will reach the stars as well."

I heard in my mind what I realized were screams from certain people in our Iter Anima. Glenda heard them too. Ben and Reinhard already had turned and begun walking back toward the cars and trucks. Glenda was left trying to ignore the screams so Reinhard didn't notice a reaction from Ben.

I looked for and found Moore's group which included Douglas, the engineer; Renzo, the lab tech; Kim, an associate of Douglas; and Jackson, a lab tech who had been so severely crashed that he had been either locked up or ill for almost the whole time I was at the lab.

Douglas said through Iter Anima, "They've found us—"

And I didn't hear him anymore. All five of them were cut off from our Iter Anima.

Chapter 37
Assurance

I tried to reach Moore's group, but I couldn't find them. Upon returning to the convoy, Reinhard gave orders to head for the Space Force Base. They traveled in the vehicles as they had before, and the Family came along for the ride. I wondered how long Glenda and the others could maintain the illusion of Ben. I also wondered what had happened to Moore's group, but I didn't have to wonder about that for long.

Reinhard said to Ben, "It seems that some of your *Family* didn't want to cooperate. My men found them in a library and had to kill one before the others complied. Are you sure we'll be able to work with this Family of yours?"

Glenda fought to maintain composure, and Ben replied, "That wasn't necessary. I'm working with you already."

"Maybe it wasn't necessary, but it was prudent. Just a reminder that I will not tolerate any more resistance. You will contact all of your people and let them know about our agreement, unless you want more reminders."

"I don't have any way to contact them. I don't even know where they are."

Reinhard laughed. "I'm sure you will find a remedy for this, too. Perhaps Jason can help."

Ben couldn't say more about this. We knew it would not be useful to argue with Reinhard. They rode in silence through streets that were familiar to us. At the base, they headed directly for the warehouse building where Ben had built the BBs. Part of one wall still stood, but all of the structure had been severely damaged by a bomb. Orlinsky sent a couple soldiers to have a look in the wreckage. They could not get under any of the rubble and came away saying that there was nothing salvageable in sight.

Reinhard, Ben, Orlinsky, and Jason gazed across the wreckage. Ben said, "I'll make a shopping list, and you can send some guys to get the electronics and other equipment that I need. We found it before in a few stores around here. Are we going to do the BB manufacturing at Denver International?"

"Yes, we should be able to find the tools we need in their machine shops."

"What about power?"

"My crew have been working on re-fueling the backup generator and getting it running. They'll have that taken care of."

Ben said, "Good. But another issue is that we won't be able to take the bombs out of the plane without the loader. It was in that building."

"Can you do the modifications in the belly of the B-52?"

"If there's room for me to open one of the bombs in there."

"We'll work it out. I have enough men that they should be able to work together and move things so you can get the access you need. What is the specific type of bomb you used?"

"It was a Mark 84."

He gave an order to Orlinsky: "Have the pilots take the B-52 back down to Kirtland in New Mexico and load two MK 84 bombs."

"Yes, sir." Orlinsky walked away from the group to speak into his radio.

"You will make your list," said Reinhard.

One of the soldiers handed Ben a notebook and a pen. Ben spent some time making his list and handed it to the soldier. Reinhard then ordered four soldiers to go get the items on the list. They drove away in a truck and a van.

"We will go to the airport now," Reinhard said. "They can meet us there."

The company of soldiers with their civilian vehicles headed out, including Jason and Ben. They worked their way up to I-70 and then onto the toll road, E-470, and finally onto Peña Boulevard to get to the airport. On the way to the boulevard, they had to move some abandoned vehicles using a couple of the larger trucks in their convoy, but when they were on the boulevard, a clear path remained from when they had traveled from the airport to Denver in the westbound lanes. Now, they took that route to the airport using the westbound lanes to go east.

They arrived at the airport more than two hours after leaving Buckley Space Force Base and entered the tarmac area through a gate that they had previously broken open. The convoy drove northward along part of a runway that ran parallel to the east side of the airport terminal. Airport vehicles and equipment were scattered throughout the area, along with planes in various positions of abandonment, some parked at the terminal and some askew in open areas. A few had crashed into each other, wings and engines locked together during some sort of road rage with airplanes. *Tarmac rage?* I wondered.

Halfway down the second row of gates, a fire had destroyed a big portion of the building. A few bodies lay here and there against luggage carts, below extended runways, and in the open. Compared to what we ad seen in the city, the human carnage here was minimal. To the east, the skeleton of a large burned-out plane lay like a decayed animal between two sections of runway.

After traveling for about a half mile, the convoy pulled onto the open tarmac next to the United Airlines hangar. Parked nearby was a white 747 with "LOT Polish Airlines" on the side, Reinhard's plane. We didn't see a B-52 anywhere, so I assumed it had taken off already, as ordered, to get more bombs.

The main entry door to the hangar was open, allowing enough room for a plane to enter. Inside the expansive open space, a 737 waited for its engines to be reassembled after maintenance, something that likely never would happen. Overhead lights illuminated everything evenly. This space would serve well as Ben's lab. Ben and Jason began checking to see which tools were available. Reinhard introduced them to a couple soldiers who were mechanics. Clearly, Reinhard had come prepared.

The four of them organized and prepared a section of the hangar for modifying and assembling the parts to make a BB from an MK 84 bomb when it arrived. Meanwhile, Orlinsky called the troops to attention in a parking lot at the north of the hangar, where they then set up a command center using supplies they had brought on the 747. Soon they had a few tents erected with weapons and ammunition laid out under them. They set up another tent and served meals to the whole company. Soldiers spread out around the parking lot eating and talking. None entered the hangar except for the two mechanics.

The four working on preparations for the BB continued gathering the tools they would need and arranging them on rolling carts. They checked a scissor lift, found that it had power, and brought that over to the work area.

As Ben plugged in his laptop to charge, Reinhard patiently strode up to him and said, "It will be sometime tomorrow, late morning, before the

B-52 returns. You'll have your parts this afternoon. Is there anything else you need?"

"Yes, as I said before, this won't work without the Family helping carry the pulse wave around the world. We will need to prepare them for an Iter Anima like what we did with the other BBs."

Reinhard stared at him for a while before saying, "*Not* like that Iter Anima with your first BB. That is when you caused the most problems around the world. That is what you are going to fix. And we will bring The Org into your wave, too. There can be no mistakes, I assure you Mr. Stoffer. This will be done my way or everyone in The Family dies."

"I understand. I thought we already worked this out."

"Just a reminder, Mr. Stoffer."

"Okay, then I need to program the software. We'll also have to connect with your people so they understand what to do. That's Jason's department."

Reinhard called out to Jason, who was clearing a cart on the other side of the hangar. "Jason, we need you over here."

Jason crossed the open space and stood next to them but said nothing, just waited to see what Reinhard wanted.

Reinhard said, "We will be having an Iter Anima with The Org. This is something you will set up to prepare for the new BB."

"Okay," Jason replied. "Can you tell me who will be joining us and how we can reach them?"

Reinhard leaned toward Jason and spoke softly and slowly. "There will be six people from The Org, and they will know how to reach you when you are ready. I want you to understand what Ben already understands. You will not fuck with me or the whole Family dies. Is that clear?"

Jason maintained a cold shield and said, "Understood."

Reinhard straightened his stance and said, almost cheerily, "Good! Now, how will you go about this Iter Anima, Mr. . . . ."

"Worthington," Jason replied.

"Mr. Worthington, how will you go about this Iter Anima?"

"It requires a fire and some drumming. With just me doing it . . . or are you joining us, Mr. Reinhard?"

"Yes, I will be joining you."

"Okay. We drum next to a fire. From there, I find my way in. So, if your people have their own methods, and you as well, you're welcome to reach out however you want. I will find the Family, and we will make our connections."

"And then what?"

"It depends what you want to do. If we're going to send another wave, we'll need the BB pulse. But before that, are you just looking for a proof of concept?"

"For now, yes. We will connect the Family and The Org. This afternoon. There are plenty of places around here for your fire. I suggest you go find something to burn, Mr. Worthington."

"Okay," said Jason. "I'll get it ready."

Jason headed out of the hangar, and Reinhard watched him carefully.

Ben said, "I have a lot of programming to do. I need to work through the data and determine the settings we'll need. Do you mind if I go inside this plane here, so I can concentrate? It's going to take a while."

Reinhard said, "If that's what you need, Mr. Stoffer. But I'm sending a babysitter with you. Mr. Nowak, here," Reinhard indicates one of the mechanics, "will join you."

Ben now stood straighter and stared at Reinhard. "Look, I understand you don't want to trust me. But I need to work. This is not a matter of flipping some switches. I need my space, and that's all there is to it. I cannot have someone looming over me. If you want this done right, you'll have to leave me alone to do my job. Your people can check my work afterward. Is that okay with you, Mr. Reinhard?"

The man grinned slightly, as if he was pleased with Ben's response. He said, "Agreed."

Ben gathered his laptop, its case, and a notebook, and carried them up the portable stairs to the 737's front entrance. He entered through the hatch and marched all the way to the back of the plane. He took a middle seat in a row second from the last and set everything down in the window seat. There, he sighed briefly and disappeared, becoming Glenda again. She leaned her head down between her knees and fought to keep from vomiting.

"Can you keep this up?" I asked Glenda.

"The show must go on," she replied. "How are the kids?" she asked.

"I don't know. I want to go check on them."

I was more worried about Glenda, and I had no idea how all this could be affecting her body and mind. But she was right. We couldn't stop.

All of us relaxed a little and immediately felt the exhaustion of the extended effort, especially those involved in maintaining the illusion. I felt Jaguar take a few breaths, herself mostly unfazed, but Kallik fell onto her back, having remained sitting throughout. I experienced some dizziness from Craig and Elizabeth. For my part, I felt physically okay, but I realized how tense I had become under the stress of this high-wire act they had been performing.

Jason was not connected with us at that moment. I asked Aiden to stay alert through Glenda in case someone entered the plane. I sought out Moore's group and discovered that he had been the one the soldiers had killed. That group weren't connected either, as they were being held prisoner, but I could tell that the others were alive. I felt sadness at Moore's death. He had helped me carry Lauren up the stairs and out of the lab. I had found him to be someone I likely would have wanted to know better. There was something calming about his disposition, and I had appreciated his help.

I looked around for the others and asked Jaguar, "How are you holding up through this?"

"It is not a problem. I need to eat now, and then we have someplace to be."

"Yes, please eat," I said. "But be ready in case you need to jump back in."

"I am here."

"Kallik, are you okay?"

"It is hard on my old skin. I can keep going anyway. But we do have someplace else to be soon."

"Okay, please rest as much as you can."

"I am doing just that."

I didn't know, at first, what they meant by having someplace else to be. Then a sense of it came over me like an urge, a need to go to a particular place. For the moment, I held it in check.

Some of the Family maintained the connections while I pulled away to check on Craig and Elizabeth in person. I sat up, and seeing me, Daisy did the same. I felt groggy as though I had been asleep for a while but needed more sleep. I went over to Craig and Elizabeth and sat down. They remained on their backs with their eyes open.

"That went far smoother than I expected," I said to them.

"I'm glad the illusion worked so well," Elizabeth said. "It was a long time to concentrate that hard, though."

"It was really something," Craig said. "I was worried a few times there, that I couldn't keep up. Good thing we didn't need to answer questions that were too specific. Keeping my presence in Ben was taking almost everything I had. And we still need to program the BB app."

"Come on, old man," Elizabeth said. "You act like you've never done telepathy and chewed gum at the same time."

"Actually, it was my first time."

"Hey, we're both virgins then. Who would have thought?"

"For virgins, you two did an impressive job of fooling them," I said. "With Glenda, of course."

"I think Ben rubbed off on us," Craig said.

"More than a little bit," said Elizabeth.

I asked, "How will you deal with the app programming? Do you think they'll know what they're looking at when they see the settings on the laptop?"

Craig sat up. "We're giving them exactly what they're asking for. We'll be able to show them why we . . . eh, Ben, is using what settings. It will all be based on what went wrong with their adjusted STDs. We'll show them how the errors that Ben found can be straightened out, and other parameters can be changed to achieve the results they want, which is controlling people's minds."

"But what happens when we send the BB?"

Elizabeth sat up, too. "Everything on the Laptop is mirrored but not actually functional when the computer is opened without a PIN. Nothing on it that is opened without the PIN will function for real. It will only appear to be working. On the surface, everything is the same. But the apps only *simulate* the BB controller programming and interface. When the BB goes off, no BEMP will be sent. Only a harmless wave."

"Holy shit," I said.

"Ben set up all his equipment that way years ago, in case someone tried to hack it," Craig said. "He kept that protocol ever since then."

"Okay," I said. "Then we'll have to pull off whatever we're going to do before the BB is dropped."

"Yes, we will," Craig said. "More precisely, *during* the BB drop."

Chapter 38
Adolescence

I fed Daisy and went to a different room so I could let the others talk and so I could seek out the children. I felt a need to do this as if it were a calling that could not be denied. I also thought that I should have been resting after being "under" for a few hours, but I really wanted to see what the children were doing. It had been a day and a half since I had heard anything from them, and we were intentionally avoiding talking about them or involving them with Reinhard, out of an abundance of caution. I knew that with Reinhard, we couldn't be too cautious. But considering that Jason was preparing for an Iter Anima with The Org, and Aiden was watching over Glenda, I figured there was enough going on that I could slip away without being found out or followed by Reinhard's people. We assumed they didn't know where the rest of us were.

After fluffing my pillow, I lay down in a small empty room with tall windows that faced west. Sunlight crept toward me almost imperceptibly across the gold patterns on the burgundy floor. I closed my eyes and sought the children.

. . . .

I find Sam quickly. But I hadn't imagined the situation I would find. Sam has been busy. I see a mindscape akin to what they had just created when we met to discuss how to present Ben to Reinhard. They had made a sphere of nature where we could exist safely and explore time. This place feels like a spherical space, though why it feels that way to me, I don't know. I cannot see a boundary. And in this space are not just a few small groups of children, but thousands upon thousands of them.

I can barely think. I float above them, directly over Sam, who grows smaller and smaller as I reach toward him. The mass of children blanket every direction throughout the space, lichens and flowers reaching endlessly like Kallik's summer tundra. Light rays stream down from all directions, focused toward the center of the children. Clouds whisk by overhead as they do among high mountains. Waves ripple through the children as if they are the ocean itself. The sounds of singing, Avery's singing, carry across everything and back again, echoing and compounding on top of themselves, more voices joining with hers, harmonizing. It is these sounds that give me the impression of a boundary, because of the echo, but I still don't see an end to this expansive space and the crowds of children.

The energy of everyone builds beyond the collective, reaching out exponentially. I feel it deep inside. Sam's Iter Animas have broken open and become a single form, a single entity with its own strength and per-spective. Avery's voice warbles in a high soprano, and the crowds underlie this with their own sounds, much deeper, a bass hum that rumbles below, supporting the higher notes. It's an improvised chorus of exultation mixed with desire and anger, determination and intention.

I know that I am not here by accident, but by invitation. The motions and sounds slow to that of a giant beast breathing. A calm overtakes the children, and the focus turns to Sam while the breathing continues.

Sam says clearly so everyone can hear, "We know why we are here. We know what we have to do. There are three others who have joined us and who will show us how, together."

The breathing remains steady and healthy. Its sounds permeate the open space.

To me, Sam says, "You know the way." And I realize that I do. "So you can show us." And I know that I will. I now stand next to Sam.

He continues, "Jaguar will give us cover." He is silent for a while.

Jaguar walks through the crowd, a powerful, muscular jaguar with dark spots, intricate patterns within the spots like organelles in cells. I see her from above, muscles rippling and stretching as she approaches Sam and stops next to him. A guttural rumble emanates from her throat.

"And Kallik brings our weapons."

Steaming fire billows in Jaguar's open path. Kallik walks amidst the brilliance. Small darts of flame burst away from her and disappear above. She stops next to Jaguar, and her fires diminish to a hazy glow. Sam, Jag-uar, Kallik, and I stand together at the heart of it all, Jaguar showing her human form now.

Kallik says, "We all have the fire in us, and that fire can be controlled. Look inside yourselves now. See the fire. Feel its core. Bring it forth and pull it out. Hold it in your hands."

Like the flames of lighters at a concert, fire begins to glow above the hands of a few children, sporadically here and there. The numbers of flames grow, the faces of the children lit orange by these small fires glowing under the heavenly light from above. The flames become as numerous as the children themselves, and the whole crowd shines like a single amber sun.

"Now pull it back until it is but an ember, smaller, smaller, but not gone. Keep that ember glowing and hold back the flames."

The sun dims to speckled cinders in the hands of thousands.

Kallik says, "Feel your control of the fire. You are children who are leaving childhood behind. Today, you find your adolescence as you grow stronger and reach for adulthood. When you go forth, you will bring with you a new humanity, one born from the ashes of destruction. A new existence that will carry you into the future.

"But you cannot go forward without cutting the bonds that have held back so much of the human race. Those who have imprisoned minds and bodies for generations still fight for control. Do not underestimate them. They did not reach their level quickly or easily. The prisons they have built were made slowly, with much patience, and many of those whom they imprisoned never knew they were prisoners.

"*This* is what we are here to defeat. They are *who* we are here to defeat. But we will not assume they can be cut down easily or without cost. They have reigned for generations. They came close to completing the full circle of control. But The Crash got in the way. Now, they seek to fix their mistake, as if the death of most of humanity was but a kink in an otherwise tight and straight thread that leads to the control of every living human.

"We know The Crash was not just a kink. It did cause destruction, but it also caused a shift in the evolution of humankind. All at once, The Crash came close to destroying humanity, while also providing our path to salvation. We are changed by it. More importantly, you, the children, are changed by it so that you can direct the evolution of humanity itself.

"First we need to finish off the old humanity, those who made the prisons. And to do this, we will break them down from the inside, burn the very essence of who they are. Killing these people is not enough, for they also have found themselves changed by The Crash. Destroying their bodies alone will not destroy their essence. So you will use your fire. We will use our fireshots to sever their essential forms, burn away the tiniest parts of them, piece by piece until their bodies and minds fall to ash.

"And this we will do from every direction, each using the softest of touches with our fireshots, so that no single one will be felt by them, but each will add to the other until together they become an undefeatable firestorm. Your fireshots will be the slightest flame that forms from the embers you now hold, and they will be shot down into the smallest parts of these people, the particles that they cannot feel separately. And you will burn these small pieces of them until nothing is left.

"The moment is near. I will help guide your fireshots. And others here will lead in different ways." Kallik finishes her speech and looks toward Jaguar.

Jaguar says to everyone, "As Kallik told us, we can not attack them directly. That is why we must hide in their minds among what is already there, and hide in the world among what they already see, just as a hunter hides among the trees in the jungle.

"What is in their minds? We know that they see force and control as their means to everything. And so, what they see in their minds are prisoners and slaves. Those real from the past and those imagined in the future. We will be those prisoners and slaves. We have someone who will show us the way inside."

She has said her piece, briefly as always. And I know that she now refers to me. It's my turn to speak. I was not specifically prepared for this, but I am ready.

I say, "We will be attacking The Org with fireshots. We will hide among the prisoners in their minds. I will show you who they are and where they are. They are called The Org, and some of you have already experienced their evil manipulations, especially the machinations of Reinhard.

"We are creating another bomb with waves to travel around the world, something they are forcing us to do. Our healing wave from the recent bomb, the BB, required the help of the Family to push the waves along. This one is no different. But this time, The Org will be there in the Iter Anima. And you will be there too. We've already found them once, and Jason is bringing them into an Iter Anima this evening to prepare them for the new BB. I'll know more after that.

"What we don't know yet is the extent of their connection to the Cosmic Consciousness and the depth of their ability to use Iter Anima. Kallik suspects that they can do things we haven't thought of. We do know that they can control people from inside their minds because of what they did to Raya. And if they can do that, they could have other abilities we don't know about.

"While I can show you the way to them, Jason will help organize your assault. Jason and Sam." And that was my speech.

Sam takes over: "Yes, Jason will organize our assault and lead us. I will help. So, now we have the details. I've brought you here for this reason. All of you have arrived here through the mind. But not all of you know how to control your directions and movements. You have your separate group leaders to guide you. The first of those who I met were Himari and Mateo. I have since met many, many more. But I have not met most of you or your leaders because you did not find your connections directly through me. At least all of you know your own groups and your own leaders. You can work together, and we will lead you."

I add, "But there is something more that we all need. We need to remember where we came from, and we need to know where we are going. All of us have been through the nightmare of The Crash. We have lost parents, family, and friends. Remember that this happened because of The Crash, and The Crash happened because of The Org. They will not stop trying to control everyone who is left. The world in their eyes is the enslavement of everyone. We know this for sure now, but it was not that clear for those who came before us. Most did not even know they were being controlled. And if The Org survives to carry on, the same things will happen again."

Sam says, "So, it is up to us to stop them if we want a better world. Remember everyone who died. Remember why they died. And know what we want for our future. We want the freedom to decide how to live in our new world. *That* is worth fighting for."

Sam turns to Avery, who is precisely in tune with him and knows what to do next.   She calls out with her melodious voice, an agonizing and wild cry, "Hayaaaa ha!"

The children return her call in unison. "Hayaaaa ha!" It overtakes everything.

Avery sings out again, and the crowd responds. Their fires flare to an overwhelming pure white. We feel the exaltation of the moment and our determination to fight. The light and sound ring true.

From within this, I begin to hear Aiden shouting: "Where *are* you? You need to come back! You need to come back now! Can't you hear me?"

Steven S. Patchin

Chapter 39
Org

I snapped away and over to Glenda where she had remained inside the plane. The others got there before me and brought out Ben. *How long had we been gone? 20 minutes?* Two soldiers were walking up to Ben's row of seats while calling his name.

"I'm here already! What the hell is it?" Ben said, flipping open the laptop.

One of the men said, "You are needed outside."

Ben closed the laptop and slid it into its case. Taking everything with him, he followed them out of the plane and out of the hangar. Around the corner, Reinhard stood with his hands on his waist, watching Jason, who was arranging items to make a fire. Jason had stacked various pieces of scrap wood, along with a box of papers, at the edge of the grassy field and was positioning some metal rails to make a square for the fire pit. Commander Orlinsky stood nearby, also watching.

Reinhard said, "Ah, Mr. Stoffer. We're going to make some *adjustments.*" He then called out to Jason: "Mr. Worthington. If you would . . . ." and indicated that he wanted Jason to come over to where he and Ben stood.

Jason complied, and with a quizzical expression hiding his disdain, came up and faced Reinhard.

Reinhard said to him, "You will be sitting this one out. We will have Ben oversee this Iter Anima."

Jason could not conceal his worried expression but did not say anything.

Ben said, "I've never done an Iter Anima. I have no idea how to make the connections . . . how to find anyone . . . how to do any of it."

Reinhard smiled a mischievous smile that I knew was not an indication of playfulness but evidence of his calculated manipulations. He replied, "You're a smart man. I'm sure you'll figure it out. We need Jason to keep his fingers – his thoughts, really – out of this."

Jason couldn't argue about it. We all knew it wouldn't be of any use. But Glenda would need to find some way to control the situation so that whoever was with The Org, whoever would be making contact with us in the Iter Anima, could not see what was behind the illusion of Ben. At the worst, they could see the man behind the curtain only to discover that the man behind the curtain was the same man who stood on the stage. An illusion behind the illusion. *How the hell could Glenda pull that off?*

Ben said to Reinhard, "The Org must be more versed in Iter Animas than I thought. Will they know how to find me and connect? Are you going to guide everything yourself?"

"As you know, it shouldn't matter who is physically present. Some of your people have already paid me a visit. A couple visits, actually. I expect they can manage to find us again, even without Mr. Worthington's help."

It seemed that Reinhard might be looking for a way to locate the Family, and he wanted to keep Jason out of it. He obviously knew a good deal about us. I wondered what he had seen when he had followed us and killed Lauren, how much he knew about us as individuals. He certainly knew enough to separate Jason.

Ben said, "Again, I really don't know anything about this. I've never participated in an Iter Anima."

"Then, you will have to rely on your *Family* to come and help you. Isn't that what family is for?"

"I'll try."

"I know you will."

"When do you want to do this?"

"Now will be good. Mr. Worthington can finish making your fire."

Jason had no choice but to do what Reinhard wanted. He went about making the fire pit, placing the wood scraps and paper in the center. With a lighter he already had, he lit the paper carefully and shifted the wood until it began to burn. He stood up and watched the fire's progress, then glanced at Reinhard.

"That's it, then. Your magic porthole into the mind," Reinhard said. He looked at Ben. "Shall we?" He gestured in the direction of the growing fire.

The two of them strode over to Jason. Soon, two soldiers marched up to Jason and escorted him past the hangar and into another building. The hangar's shadow reached the fire pit as the sun glared above it in the clear blue sky. Reinhard and Ben sat down in the grass on opposite sides of the fire pit. Ben laid his laptop next to himself and stared across at Reinhard.

This one would be on me, but Ben would have to get it started as part of the show. He stared at Reinhard. The man was along for the ride now, at least until he made whatever move he had planned. We would be starting with our core of Glenda, Craig, Elizabeth, Jaguar, Kallik, and me. I didn't want to involve anyone else except Aiden.

Inside, I said to everyone, "I'm sure Reinhard plans to look for the Family. He obviously knows Jason is important and strong in the Iter Animas. That's why he's blocked him out now. So, let's keep this group small. Everyone who is not working with Ben, please pull back, except Aiden, who I want to stay here but in the background. I'll guide us after Ben gets it going, and I'll try to make it all about The Org. Reinhard has been aware of my presence before. I'll talk to him if I have to. As for Ben, I'll leave that to you."

Our core and Aiden all acknowledged what I said, and they agreed. I felt the other Family members back away.

Ben said to Reinhard, "They drum in order to do the Iter Animas."

"That is no longer necessary," Reinhard replied.

Ben stared at Reinhard for a while and finally closed his eyes. I wanted to take charge and maintain as much control of the situation as possible so the others could concentrate on being Ben. This had to start with Ben, though, to keep the illusion alive.

I also concentrated on seeing Ben.

.   .   .   .

I need to get my own perception together before Reinhard jumps in. In my mind, I wrangle Glenda, Craig, Elizabeth, Jaguar, and Kallik. They are like spinning sparks to me, and I twist them into a single stream to hold them as one, see them as Ben.

Now I turn to Reinhard and wait. Ben concentrates on Reinhard and moves his consciousness toward him to find the direction of The Org. Ben and Reinhard both become shadows in gray inside the Iter Anima.

Reinhard immediately pulls Ben as though he's grabbing him by the lapels so he can bring him closer and strangle him. The motion whips Ben away, and Ben seems to separate into different layers for a moment, then snaps back. I realize that this is Ben's team coming apart and going back together, a wobble in my perception. Reinhard is very close and doesn't seem to notice as the team keep Ben together.

The stage is now set as simple grayness and shadows. After the violent move, everything is calm again. Ben and Reinhard walk side by side, Reinhard leading Ben, who has to regroup himself.

Distant hazy shadows begin to take form, becoming distinct shapes. They separate into five people. I know they are the other surviving Org members, and I'm surprised at how quickly they showed up. Reinhard had made us believe that Ben would lead the Iter Anima, but now we see that Reinhard is fully in charge. The five are just as I remember them from the first time I saw them, each wearing formal regalia from their cultural origins or just their personal preferences. Even Reinhard now wears a gray tailored suit.

They seem ageless in the sense that they are older than middle age, but they are not withering on their deathbeds. I assume their ages are similar to Reinhard's because he had formed The Organization of people from his generation. They likely are in their 80s, but what I see are vibrant adults with sophisticated, confident expressions and handsome good looks. Their images could be what they want us to see, or they could be a reflection of who they are. Likely they are both.

I know their names now, and some of their background and heritage, even before Reinhard introduces each to Ben. None were ever married. All were extremely wealthy. Reinhard makes the introductions, but I fill in the descriptions.

Valentina Blakin: Russian with gray hair and blue eyes. She wears an elaborate full-length coat of deep aqua, embroidered in fancy gold patterns like something the tsars and their families would have worn before World War I. Her family, not related to any tsars, were deeply involved in creating and running the Gulags where millions were imprisoned and killed before World War II, and even more during and after the war.

Ezra Oberman: Polish Jew with salt-and-pepper hair. He wears a simple black suit and black tie, though not that of orthodox traditions. He wears no hat or kippah. His family were involved in the diamond trade for generations and expanded into banking, eventually moving to New York after World War II and gaining substantial financial power.

Li Fu: Chinese man with conservatively-cut black hair. His family descend directly from Kublai Khan, who ruled China in the mid-1200s. He wears a black robe with a red belt tied around his waist. His family had embraced Khan's governing style of horrible brutality, and they maintained power in the Chinese government as well as the Triads.

Golnar Tousi: Tall, thin woman of Persian descent, deep green eyes, long black hair, hints of gray. She wears a long burgundy robe with gold piping and large, layered sleeves. Her family were connected with Iranian nobility for generations, and maintained their power in modern Iran. She moved to America in 1994 to expand her family's banking business, which grew to enormous wealth and influence in recent years.

Armin Stein: American man of German descent with black eyes and thick brown hair. He wears a light blue suit with thin, gray pinstripes. His family were instrumental for generations in developing mechanical technologies. Their tech empire kept its fingers in diverse holdings throughout the world and became one of the wealthiest and most powerful conglomerates in history after they took over three of the biggest advertising and media companies in the 80s.

Ben greets each person in turn and says, when the introductions are finished, "I never imagined we could meet like this, all of us in a room that doesn't exist except in our minds. And yet, here we are. The Crash has triggered our brains in unique ways."

"Remember," Reinhard says, "None of us are crashed in the same way you understand. Our brain alterations were much more controlled. We used our own version of the altered STD to give ourselves a little boost."

"Interesting. Then you do have control of the STD."

"You could say that, however, almost everyone else who survived received your BBs. *That part* of the process is what we need to correct."

"Okay then," Ben said. "We discussed the need to relay the new BB wave with the Family. Can you do that with us?"

Armin responds, "Yes. And we won't need the Family for this." Arrogance drifts along with his words like sewer gas over waste water. "We have our own . . . *family*, so to speak. They can relay the wave. Mr. Li and Ms. Blakin have done an outstanding job of arranging this for us and getting our people up to speed."

"Are you saying you have a network of people who can help with the relay?" Ben asks.

"They do not need to help with the relay. They will do the job," says Mr. Li.

"Just so I understand," Ben says. "You have people who were *isolated* from The Crash and who then received a pulse from the STD? They can actually do these mind travels?"

"Precisely," says Golnar Tousi. "We actually do know what we are doing, Mr. Stoffer."

"Then what do you need me for?"

Reinhard laughs.

Valentina Blakin says, "You are here to correct your mistake. Your target will be the same as your BB was: Everyone, except us, of course. We will provide the means through our people, and you will provide the exact settings that will fix the problems you created."

"And who will run the Iter Anima for this BB?" Ben asks, trying to dig for more information.

Ezra, the Jewish-American responds, "It sounds like you want a tour. How about we give you one?"

"That's up to you. I'm just trying to understand what has to be done. Then, I need to get back to the programming for the BB," Ben says.

Reinhard puts his right arm around Ben and raises his left, as if to indicate a direction. Ben's illusion wobbles. I fear that they won't keep him together. All six of The Org turn, and the graynes becomes twisting darkness. I've already decided not to interact with them, so I'm along for the ride with Aiden trailing behind. We stay silent.

A smell hits me through the dark before I see anything. It is the stench of unwashed bodies, urine, and feces. Then we see rows and rows of people sitting on the floor, each one shackled in place an arm's length from those nearby. Hundreds of these prisoners form rows throughout this space, which is as large as a high school gymnasium. It is also a sweltering cinder block structure dimly lit by yellowish-green fluorescent lights, many of which flicker.

On a raised stage stands a metal platform with short legs. A pile of wood waits to be lit on the platform. The ceiling of the room is black from previous fires and smoke. This is a place made for campfires and Iter Animas that are designed around coercion with no consideration for the people involved. They are physical and mental slaves. Surrounding them, along the walls, dozens of soldiers stand as prison guards, though they look only slightly better off than the prisoners themselves.

None of us are able to experience this without feeling horrified. Ben's team are not prepared to respond, and apparently what The Org people see on Ben's face is enough of a reaction to satisfy their intentions. Every one of them smiles with gloating gratification.

We all know that slavery has existed throughout history, but the thought that hits me now is to wonder how Ezra, a Jewish person, could accept this, and even worse, gladly participate. What has led him to facilitate this horror? How can anyone do this?

Reinhard laughs and says, "Yes, I know. You are not a fan of compulsory tasks."

"Slavery, you mean," Ben spits back at Reinhard. "How does this help you?"

"We do not have the luxury of asking nicely. Time is of the essence, as you know, Mr. Stoffer."

"How many of these places do you have?"

"Enough to do the job."

"My God."

"Certainly not mine," says Mr. Li.

Valentina says, "So you see why we do not need your Family for this. But we will need someone from your group to synchronize these people with the BB. This will not be your Jason. There is another among you who has been poking around in our business. He'll suit our needs."

I know she means me.

Reinhard says to me, "So, if you're done hiding, you can take us on a little trip right now. Or, you can keep pretending, and we'll say goodbye to Jason."

I wasn't worried about myself or even Jason as much as I was worried about Ben's team. Did The Org know about them? Were they playing a deeper game than us?

I said to them, "Where would you like to go?"

Reinhard smiled. "Ah ha! That's more like it. You can take these people here on a spin around the block, visit some of their compatriots. Didn't Ben say that we need a worldwide network? Let's see if you are a good driver."

I feel the imprisoned people in this room even more strongly. I hear them coughing from previous smoke inhalation and from illness. I notice their weakness, and I sense their pain. We have to do this. I have to use them if there is any chance of following through on our plans. They're already deep in this, and I imagine The Org will likely kill them regardless of the outcome. I search for a way to do the Iter Anima without coercion. I can't understand how The Org have done anything like that without willing cooperation from the participants.

I look up at the fire platform. We don't need fire, either.

Ben says, "How about I sit this one out?"

"I think not," says Reinhard. "You can ride in the back seat."

Fucking driving analogy. Sam was right about that silliness, too.

I begin by thinking about these people shackled to the floor. I have to forget about their situation and concentrate on the Iter Anima. I'm understanding more and more that these mind travels work in layers. We're already within an Iter Anima, and we will now go deeper, just as I had done with Kallik when we sought out The Org the first time. Without having a fire or drums or singing, I can only think of the pathways of our minds, how patterns everywhere lead us where we want to go. Even the apparent chaos of fire has its patterns. But music is more obvious. I imagine Avery's singing. I "play" her voice to these prisoners and let its effects do as they will.

I look at each person, dozens upon dozens of them. I bring them together as one, and think of other groups like theirs. I touch the Org people and Ben. I let Aiden hang back. Everyone is with me now, so I reach to another room, not knowing where it will be or who will be there. The grayness returns briefly but breaks open to white, and then we're in another room of The Org's prisoners. I throw away the thought of their prisoner status. They react to our presence, realizing all of us are here, and they join us.

We jump from room to room doing the same thing in each one, collecting more and more people. Just as I begin to think the numbers of people will reach high into the thousands, we stop. We're out of rooms. We've reached only ten in all, and though this means more than a thousand people are enslaved for the mind travels, it also means The Org's reach is not as extensive as I feared it might be. This does not come close to the numbers we had for our BBs. It gives me hope.

I relax my hold on everyone and return to the first room. I hadn't been paying attention to The Org people during all this, so I'm somewhat surprised to hear awe in the voice of Reinhard.

"Well then," he says. "That worked, didn't it?"

The prisoners appear less miserable as they react to the Iter Anima, themselves. I see awe in their faces, too, and I wonder how deeply they have traveled with Reinhard. *Not very deep*, I think.

"Right," I say. "That did work. Are you satisfied?"

"I believe so."

"Proof of concept," Valentina says.

"Alright," Reinhard says. "Ben, you can go get that programming done. The B-52 will be here before sunrise. We'll get this BB together quickly after that. And we'll run the Iter Anima with it just as we did right now. I *expect* that we won't have any problems from anyone. Remember, we can say goodbye to Jason and some other Family members at any time."

We are whipped out of the room and back to the unnecessary fire by the hangar. The movement happens so quickly that I'm stunned. So are Ben's team. Ben sways for a moment.

.   .   .   .

Reinhard jumped up as though he had just finished doing ten easy push-ups and wanted to go for a run. He was trying to appear invigorated. I thought that he looked more his age out here than he had in the Iter Anima. Ben stood slowly.

Reinhard said, "You can get back to it."

Ben returned to the inside of the 737, and we all relaxed a little. I hadn't liked that Reinhard knew I was there, but I also found out that they weren't as in control as they made themselves out to be.

Glenda slumped in the same plane seat as she had before. We now saw each other as our separate selves again. Aiden came forward, too.

I said, "They wanted us to believe they had control of the tech they used, their own STD. But I don't think they do. Those prisoners weren't in any condition to be controlled easily by mental force. If they were, The Org wouldn't have kept them chained up. And if The Org knew how to program the STDs, they wouldn't need us. No, they're not as in control as they say. And I think that test drive scared them a little."

I could tell that Craig and Elizabeth were exhausted. They acknowledged what I said and agreed with my evaluation, but didn't have much more to say right then.

Kallik said, "I see an opening for attack. I hope the children can handle it."

"I will help them," Jaguar replied.

"I will, too," Aiden said.

"We have a day or so before you can get the BB ready, at the fastest," I said.

"I want to get Jason's help with it," Glenda said. "Let's ask Reinhard. Maybe he'll see the advantage in terms of getting it done quicker."

"He's practical. I think he'll get it," I said. "He just didn't want Jason in the Iter Anima. I can't blame him, there."

"Okay," Glenda said. "Let's get this programming done so they accept what we set up the BB to do. I'm going to need some sleep soon, though."

"Us, too," Craig added.

"I'll leave you to it, then," I said. "Amazing work today, everyone. I really think we can pull this off."

They all agreed.

Aiden and I traded off throughout the night, keeping an eye on Glenda and sleeping a little. The team finished the programming on the laptop a couple hours before dawn and then slept until the B-52 approached the airport.

Ben came out of the 737 to watch the B-52 land, and I watched along with them. I recalled how impressed I had been upon seeing the other B-52 at the Space Force Base. I was still impressed. The morning darkness barely yielded a glow on the horizon as the hulking plane landed with its screaming engines and taxied over to the hangar. Many of the troops watched it come in, too.

Orlinsky ordered specifically-trained troops over to the big jet, and everyone got to work quickly. The mechanics had already organized the supplies that Ben had requested and that had been brought in during the night. Soon, everything they needed was in place under the plane, and the bomb bay doors were open.

Ben went up inside the plane to inspect the bombs, and some techs set up a workspace on the bomb bay walkway for him. Reinhard agreed to allow Jason to help, and Jason came out to have a look, too. They went to work making the new BBs from the two bombs just as they had for the previous two, but with one big exception. The plan involved using only one BB, with the other as a potential backup if needed.

Chapter 40
Aim

I seek out the children. They are ready and waiting in the same meeting place where everyone had recently assembled. I am here to lead the children to The Org.

They sit in their massive space, facing the center where Sam stands. Thousands of them have assembled here, and they're already humming, getting into the right mind patterns for the arduous journey and tasks ahead. Because of their ages, many of the youngest children are not here. Sam decided, wisely, that what he had planned would be too intense for the youngest ones.

I stand beside Sam to address everyone. The expanse grows quiet, and they look at me. "There are six leaders in The Org," I say. "They are old psychopaths continuing with their plans to control humanity. They have come dangerously close to accomplishing their goals. The central figure among them is Reinhard. He's in charge of running this operation with the bomb, and he's also at the airport with Ben. I know you're familiar with the situation, and you know who Ben is. I'm going to lead you to the other five in The Org, and when you know who and where they are, you can start using your fireshots against them and Reinhard."

The humming begins again. The children know what to do. The sounds grow louder and louder until I feel them reverberating and overwhelming any distracting thoughts. The mass of children start to sway so that the giant circle of these children first becomes waves and then a turning wheel. The space around us spins with the wheel, and all I have to do is guide the turning, show everyone who and where these evil people are.

The Org members are in different places. I only want to give the children a look, not much more than a glimpse so that we are not detected. In this situation, I don't get a sense of distances or exact places where The Org people are located, though I know I'm creating a thread for the children to follow later.

I find Li Fu first. We see his Chinese face in close-up. His previous facade is gone, no war regalia like what he wore the night before, only everyday casual clothes. He's simply washing his face, a mundane task performed by people every day. He's nothing more than human, though I think that he's considerably less than human. He has no idea we are looking in on him, and neither will the others.

Next is Valentina Blakin. She stares out a window to a quiet garden, her old and tired face reflecting back with only her lonely self for company in this dull room. She touches her chin and sighs.

We move on to Golnar Tousi. She, too, is alone. She lies in bed wearing her bedclothes. She stares at the ceiling, her frail body sunken into the plush bed like a worm in the mud. A single light casts pale yellow across her pallor skin.

Elsewhere, Ezra Oberman lays his head across his right arm as he stretches it out over a dark wood dining room table. Papers are stacked around him, and they dominate his existence.

Armin Stein looks across a parking lot from within his car. He stares out at the other vehicles, nobody else in sight. Some of the cars and trucks are left askew, having bumped into or crashed into the others. He rests his hands on the steering wheel, showing no signs of going anywhere anytime soon.

And Reinhard. He's the only one of The Org who appears to have immediate purpose, and we all know what that is. He stands inside the hangar staring out at the B-52 as the crews work on assembling the BB that he wants to use against everyone who survived The Crash.

I am bewildered that all of these Org people, except Reinhard, are alone inside themselves. They show no outward connections to anyone. I can't imagine they would have had that kind of orientation when they were building their empires. They must have been very different earlier in their lives, having had deep desires to accomplish what they eventually did, and the misplaced fortitude to create The Org.

It must have taken great effort, I think, for *them to have presented themselves as having such overriding power and assurance when we met them, if this is their real condition.*

Even so, we don't want to underestimate either the people themselves or their abilities. *What else would old people do when they aren't actively working, anyway, besides sitting around waiting for their next big moments?* I wonder. Regardless, I find them to be pathetic.

I have accomplished what I needed to do here, providing the children with connections that will lead them to The Org. The rest will be up to them. We all hope that the fireshots will wear down whatever power The Org wields. Reinhard likely will be the biggest challenge.

We return to our enormous spinning wheel. I do not want to stop their momentum, so I depart from the children, intending to check on the Family. Those in the Family not held captive by soldiers will bring their own front to bear against The Org and their army of prisoners.

I first retreated back to my room at the golf course so I could clear my mind. After a few minutes, I reached out to the groups of Family, except for Moore's group that includes Douglas, Renzo, Kim, and Jackson. They were still held captive by Reinhard's soldiers.

The other groups remain in good spirits, and most of the Family are well-rested. I hadn't previously thought of this in detail, but I cannot imagine anyone better than Aiden to lead the Family's Iter Anima in this upcoming battle. With me doing Reinhard's bidding, Jason out of commission, and Ben's team maintaining the illusion, the person I want in charge is Aiden. He was the barrel of the gun for Jason's and the Family's tunnel explosion. He's been with me whenever I've needed him, and he knows how to handle himself. At 14, he's not one of the children, and he's not an adult, either. He can contribute to all of our groups. When I ask him, he accepts the challenge enthusiastically.

"You know I'll do my best," he says.

"Yes, I do."

I talk to everyone briefly, and confirm that the plans are set. We all have to believe in each other to do what needs to be done. I go back to rest for a while and wait for things to begin.

. . . .

It was approaching sunset before the work was done, and surprisingly, Reinhard did nothing more to check Ben's programming on the laptop. The two techs assigned to work with Ben went through the app settings, and apparently, that was all Reinhard required. Ben's team had gone through such extensive effort to make it believable, and now it seemed to be for nothing. But we all knew that the details in the show mattered.

The main BB was ready, as well as the backup BB. Reinhard, Ben, Jason, Orlinsky, and the B-52 crew stood in front of the plane. The setting sun reflected across the metal fuselage.

Reinhard asked, "Is everyone ready for this?"

The plane's captain said, "Yes, sir. We have our flight plan and the timing for the drop. We're ready to go when you give the order."

Reinhard looked at Ben, who said, "It's all set. Programmed as you wanted, correcting for the errors of the altered STDs and counteracting the changes we made with our previous BBs. This will give you the results you wanted, easing people's minds and helping them want what is best for them, just as you originally intended. Once armed, the BB will detonate at the set altitude. I've done everything I can."

"Alright. I'll prep our people. Tell your man to get ready for the Iter Anima. We're going to go through you again to get this started, and then let him connect everyone else." To Captain Piotr Nowak, Reinhard said, "Thirty minutes to departure. We need to make sure of our timing with the Iter Anima. Have you coordinated with Ben?"

"Yes, sir. We'll set an exact time for the drop just before we take off, so you'll know how to direct the Iter Anima."

Reinhard clapped twice and ordered two soldiers to come over. He said to them, "Take Mr. Worthington back to the holding room and make sure he doesn't close his eyes until this operation is over."

As they took Jason away, Reinhard marched up to Orlinsky and gave more orders. Ben went into the hangar, and I tried to mentally prepare for what was to come.

Chapter 41
Fireshots

When everything is ready at the airport, dusk has stolen the day, leaving blue shadows around us. The B-52 bomber taxis to the closest runway beyond the field, on the other side of the burned-out plane. It takes off to the south, with its forward lights blazing into the distance and its running lights blinking on its wings and tail. It will circle above the city to gain altitude before dropping the BB over the park where Ben's lab lies buried. I think of Ben and the others who are also buried there.

Glenda has already gone out to where Reinhard waits. She presents herself as Ben, prepared for the BB. Ben and Reinhard sit in the same places they sat during the previous day's Iter Anima, though nobody has lit a fire this time. A pile of ashes rests between them, bits of the gray dust whisking upward in the breeze. Except for the two troops assigned to guard Jason, the entire company of soldiers stand in a wide circle around Ben and Reinhard like the teeth of a giant saw blade. Some face inward, some outward, all holding their rifles at the ready. The differences between this circle and the children's circle are striking. The children's circle appeared almost endless and filled with life. This circle feels like an instrument for cutting life to pieces.

Orlinsky stands a good distance outside the circle to oversee the troops. Reinhard expects me to be there to guide the Iter Anima. I certainly will be there. What he doesn't know is that the Family, children from around the world, and Sam's tribe will be there, too. Sam's tribe will also be here at the airport in person.

During the previous day, the children made the 20-mile trek on foot, following along the avenues, crossing through fields, and climbing over a barbed wire fence using heavy blankets to avoid getting cut by the barbs. In the early morning, around the time the loaded B-52 landed with the MK 84s, they arrived at the airport. They now hole up inside the Frontier Airlines hangar, just to the northwest of the United hangar. There, through their Iter Anima, the tribe of 27, along with the thousands of children they brought together to help with this battle, began their fireshot attacks on The Org.

Kallik and Jaguar can't be involved with them now because they are needed for the illusion of Ben. But they have prepared the children, and the fireshots have been underway for hours. Through Ben, I saw what I assumed were the effects of the fireshots starting to work on Reinhard. He had been constantly energetic and sharp. But as I watched him across the empty fire pit, he wavered a little, almost losing his balance while stooping down to sit. He recovered quickly and adopted a very straight posture of determination.

Ben and Reinhard sit, staring at each other, Ben through the efforts of five people trying to stop further destruction, and Reinhard with his psychotic plans to control the world. We wait briefly, knowing the B-52 has just taken off and that all of this comes down to timing.

We begin the Iter Anima with Ben closing his eyes. He searches for the connections. I follow him and prepare to lead the way.

Immediately, Reinhard takes charge. This is not what we had expected. I am ready to gather The Org's groups to concentrate on the BB before we divert everything in another direction.

Instead, we find Reinhard looming above our view like a winged devil descending from the sky. He is shadows and fire, deep blackness and striking reds, but I know it's him. The other Org people appear nearby, though not as harsh and extreme. Their bodies flow as dark whirling browns mixed with amber flames.

We have entered a howling tornado of violence and brute force.

What happened to the passive old Org people we saw a few hours earlier? What happened to the fireshots burning through the essence of these people, breaking them down into dying coals?

Ben dives into the storm, ready to fight. I move closer, too.

Reinhard feels my presence and screams at me as if through real wind: "You've got a job to do. Now get on with it. Everyone is waiting."

I was expecting to do the job we had planned, not what Reinhard demanded. But we're facing wild, unexpected power, and with this show of force, Reinhard requires me to follow *his* plans. *We really have underestimated him,* I think. *Where are the Family and the extended tribe of children?*

I will have to keep moving forward into the vision Reinhard wants until I can find a way out and maybe get some help. I follow Ben deeper. I reach toward the first room of The Org's prisoners so I can bring them into the Iter Anima. The prisoners are dozing, their shackles holding them in place. The soldiers guarding them are only slightly more alert. I throw a breath of acknowledgement at the captors to let them know we're beginning the process.

I take the prisoners along with me to the next room of prisoners, and the next, until I bring all 10 rooms of people together. Reinhard and The Org hover nearby, maintaining their monstrous personas, and I connect them with everyone else.

I'm not Jason, and I don't have the instincts for orchestrating these forces the way Jason can. I'm here because Reinhard has forced it, but my real purpose now is to create the appearance that we can carry the BB waves around the world the way we had delivered the waves of the previous BBs. To me, this first means we should encircle the bomb inside the B-52 to prepare for when it drops.

On my direction, hundreds of us come together around the plane. The prisoners have been told a simple version of what they would be doing, but they are lost and confused. The Org has worked with them, but I don't feel insight and open minds here. I feel fear. The Family are not here as I have expected, neither are the children, so I decide to use the prisoners in a different way.

I separate the prisoners from The Org and lie to them: "You are here to help carry a wave around the world. This wave comes from a bomb in this plane. Your job is to push the wave along when it reaches you, keep it going so that it continues around the world and reaches everyone. You are relays for the wave. You'll know it when it comes to you. Just help it along. This will make sense to you when you see the wave."

I channel the prisoners into lines like strands of cable that hold bridges together. I fan them out like a wide funnel, and set them spinning. I plan to move them near the BB and behind The Org. I want to keep The Org close to the BB.

To The Org I say, "You will be with the bomb when it detonates. You have to infuse your push with the strongest power you can, and put it all behind the wave to carry it along. That will throw the wave outward, sending it on its way. To begin, I will take you down with the bomb."

I realize my slight slip in phrasing, telling a little too much the truth of my intentions, but The Org people don't notice. I form an image that will bring them in, so they will want to follow me. I'm getting this idea from what happened with the other BBs.

I need something that will make sense to them, and I need to disarm their control of their own devilish apparitions. With Jaguar's help, I summon the vision, and The Org accept it, letting go of their winged devil images and making my vision their own.

The six of The Org and I become mighty birds that fly with the B-52. Our wings spread broadly, black and white, the tips curling up in the wind. Ben dives toward the bomb. We follow him through the plane's fuselage, into the plane, fly around the bomb that hangs ready to drop.

The bomb bay doors open. We spin round the bomb like protons orbiting an atom, our dizzy energy becoming a frenzy. We continue our motion as we wait for the bomb to drop. The time is near.

This either works and we see that the fireshots have broken The Org enough for us to take control, or we will expose our bellies and they will throw our guts to the coyotes.

I pull away from the bomb and leave the Org birds flying around it in their tight orbits, chasing the figure of Ben. I position the prisoners, their spinning funneling strands, just behind the Org birds to create a place for the children to hide. But I don't know where the children are. Without the rest of the Family and without Jason, there is little more I can do but let this play out.

Finally, Aiden approaches with the Family, leading them toward us. The Org birds respond by attacking the Family like mockingbirds driving away a cat. They burst forth toward the Family. Ben casts himself between them, a distraction. The Family spread out in response to the attack, separating and becoming disorganized, then backing off. Satisfied for the moment, the Org birds follow Ben back down and return to their business with the bomb.

The Family spin around the plane at a wide enough distance to avoid attracting The Org's attention.

The time for dropping the bomb looms closer. The birds dive and dart, in and out, through the plane, swarming around the bomb. I see a break in the birds' movement, a hesitation in their flight, a cinder flaming off the wing of one bird. And then another. Smoke trails drift in the air. The birds' flight becomes rough and wobbly. And I see what's happening now.

I see shots of flame rushing into them. I see the *fireshots*! And I see Ben holding The Org close to the bomb, positioning them as distinct targets for the children's fireshots. Sam leads the children in the attack like a warrior leading troops into battle. This is not the beginning of their efforts. It is the end.

They have been shooting their fireshots at The Org for hours, and now the children are becoming more visible in their battle as their attacks become more direct.

The prisoners spin behind the children, blocking The Org from seeing their attackers.

The children increase the power of their attacks, expanding the fireshots so that they are no longer imperceptible, tiny cuts. They become obvious balls of fire as they fly past the prisoners and hit The Org birds.

These balls of fire burn parts of the birds. Little burning spots accumulate in the birds' feathers. The fireshots burn The Org themselves. With each shot, I see the face of a different child, briefly flashing in the light of the fire.

The bomb drops.

Ben, The Org, and the children fall with the bomb. The funnel of the prisoners stays between The Org and the children. Fireshots follow the Org birds, smashing into them. The frequency and brilliance of the fireshots increases, and with it, the faces of the children glitter like a crowd watching fireworks. This crowd of children burst forth from the heavens like the stars themselves. I barely see the falling bomb now, amid all the children and their fireshots. The prisoners spin away and retreat back to their prisons.

The Org birds burn more and more, but don't react to their fate, as though they don't recognize that they are burning. They only see Ben and their goal. They never veer from their diving path. They exist only for the control they believe will be theirs when the bomb explodes.

We have maintained enough of our illusions for this attack to continue. We have distracted these enemies of humanity and exposed them to their own destruction.

We keep following them. Down goes the bomb, spinning into the darkness, spiraling toward the grassy plains below. Down goes Ben. Down go the children and their killing fireshots. Down goes The Org.

I feel Jason emerge among us suddenly, and Aiden hands him the reins of the Family. Jason pulls them together. The Family's unified force swells around me. They pull Ben out of the maelstrom.

The 2,000 pound bomb keeps falling. It does not detonate at a set altitude, but keeps dropping, dropping, the Org birds falling with it, burning, burning.

The bomb hits the ground, its long body compressing and compacting into a deep hole it creates as it crashes. But it does not explode. Jason had disarmed it before the plane took off.

The Org birds break apart on impact and evaporate, leaving smoke floating in the aftermath, their mental projections shattered and burnt, The Org themselves blown out of the Cosmic Consciousness, never to return.

The fireshots have done their job. Ben and the children have succeeded. At the impact site, two bison, responding to the crash, shudder and trot into the darkness. I feel excitement at our success, but we are not done yet.

Reinhard and Glenda jump back to the airport. The Family, the children, and I follow them. Reinhard's presence in the Iter Anima has been destroyed, but he is not dead.

Whether from instability in the illusion and fatigue from the effort, or maybe even the desire to reveal the truth, Glenda releases the illusion of Ben and stands opposite Reinhard, showing her real self, letting the psychopath see her.

Craig, Elizabeth, and I can only watch what happens through Glenda. Kallik and Jaguar also get disconnected from the illusion and can do nothing more than watch the situation through Glenda.

Reinhard gets up slowly, arms and legs shaking. The surrounding troops, some 120 of them, come to attention because of Reinhard's movements and because Glenda now stands where Ben was standing before. They are confused. Orlinsky marches over and squeezes between two soldiers to see what is happening inside the circle. He takes in the scene, looking from Reinhard to Glenda, back and forth, not understanding what has happened, and not knowing what to do without instructions from Reinhard. No instructions come.

Reinhard is stunned but not fully disabled. As his head clears somewhat, he begins to understand that things have not played out as he had wanted. He stares at Glenda, who is weak from the experience, battered yet triumphant. Dizzy, she struggles to avoid falling and shuffles slightly to find better footing.

Reinhard says to her, seething with a raspy voice, "Who the fuck are you? Where's Ben?"

Glenda says, coldly and bitterly, "Ben died days ago. And so did your ability to control people. We took that from you and your Org. You will die alone with nothing that matters."

I feel the Family and their energy growing stronger around us, channeling through Jason as he tries to focus their strength. He works with them from the room where he had been held, his two captors killed by a group of children who Sam sent to free him. Jason forms a mental circle of energy around the soldiers. It grows stronger as it spins up, gathering more force. I stay with Glenda and know that Jason intends to channel the power through her, create a protective shield and create something more.

Reinhard reaches down toward his holstered pistol.

I see movement in the darkness to the north. The soldiers notice too, and some turn with their rifles raised. It's Sam and the whole tribe approaching cautiously, no weapons drawn.

Orlinsky barks an order at them: "Hold it right there."

They stop. Orlinsky directs 20 or so troops over to surround them.

We, through Glenda, glance back to Reinhard just in time to see him fire his gun directly toward our view, directly toward Glenda. He empties the magazine. I feel Glenda fall, and I lose her.

I jump to the Family. Craig, Elizabeth, Kallik, and Jaguar do the same, and we see nothing but black. We rush out of the black toward the children and see through Sam, our perspective now outside the larger circle of soldiers. I feel and hear Jason scream in horror. We, the Family, along with the children, cry out.

Through Sam, past the troops surrounding the children, into the larger circle of soldiers, past Reinhard's back, I see Glenda lying on the ground. The sight of her and the realization of what this means slams into me like a physical punch that strips away my strength. As I feel the sickening panic begin to consume me, something else diverts my horror.

Violently, the Family's energy draws inward and explodes back out through Jason, away from the children, a blinding wave erupting and obliterating almost everyone nearby except the children. The wave expands outward from their circle, growing bigger and bigger, rolling forth in turbulence, throwing its own light across the landscape, electric lightning expanding farther and farther.

The Family follow the wave's leading edge, expanding with it, the massive widening circle spreading more and more rapidly over the ground, blowing across the planet, blasting over plains and cities, mountains and valleys, through oceans and clouds, into places where people barely survive, to where prisoners are shackled, right up to where evil crouches.

The prisoners' shackles break away, dissolving into the ether, releasing the imprisoned. People of The Org, not just the core, but more of them from the larger Organization, freeze in place. These few dozen of them, lesser powers, but scars on humanity nonetheless, feel the wave break into them, and they feel no more as they disintegrate.

The other five of The Org, now broken down from the fireshots, cower in corners, knowing what is coming, feeling the wave crash into them, seeing the faces of the children and the Family roaring through with the wave. It hits them, and these five wither to nothing, their essence dissolved, their existence no more.

The wave dies like an ocean wave spreading across pebbles and soaking into the sand. The explosive wind that crashed outward with the erupting energy spins back on itself and dissipates quietly.

Glenda still lies on the ground.

I see Reinhard still standing, his gun now lying at his feet. He doesn't move, his essence burned to a husk. His image remains as a shell floating in space.

All the soldiers are gone, nothing of them left, not even ashes. The children stand together in their group, the Family inside with them.

Sam steps away carefully and with cold intention. He strides over to Reinhard, draws his gun from his holster, and fires one shot into Reinhard's head. The shell of the old man drops to the ground and disappears as though it was never there. The sound of the shot echoes on and on until silence slowly takes back the night.

No lights shine except the stars. The Milky Way arcs above, stretching across the sky as it always has. The children gather around Sam and Glenda in the darkness. From behind the hangar, Jason emerges, walking slowly, hesitantly, not wanting to face his loss. But he continues until he stands above Glenda's body.

He sits down next to Glenda and gently touches her face.

Chapter 42
Nexus

The B-52 returned through the darkness, its lights flaring toward us as it banked in for a landing at the darkened airport. We weren't worried about the captain and the crew causing us problems. Jason had learned during the BB assembly that Captain Piotr Nowak and his five member crew had been forced into this mission by Orlinsky and that they previously had The Crash until our BBs cleared their minds. We knew that this crew likely would become part of the Family.

Jason sat quietly with Glenda's body for more than a half hour, until after the B-52 landed. The children joined him during this time, forming a circle, not crowding him too closely. The Family stayed with him, too, all of us feeling the loss and sadness, showing Jason that he was not alone and that we were there for him. But, as I knew well, this kind of grief cannot be shared fully. After giving our condolences, we also gave Jason space. And we mourned, too.

For Jason, Glenda had been strength. They survived the early days of The Crash together. But far beyond that, Glenda was Jason's lover, his partner, and his soul mate. They became much more together than they were apart. Their combined energy was the unifying force that brought the Family together.

We figured out that the Family's cleansing wave, started and directed by Jason, was selective, that it was somehow tuned so that it only took out obviously-dangerous threats, people whose minds indicated malice as well as those who Jason specifically targeted, such as the extended members of The Organization and the remnants of The Org itself.

Craig saw a parallel between this wave that took out the worst of humanity, and the Flood described in the Bible, which God sent for the same reasons, though Craig and Jason knew that Jason was no god.

Jason stood while the B-52 taxied toward the hangar, Sam strode over to him. They watched the beast approach.

Sam said to him, "I'm sorry about what happened to Glenda."

Jason couldn't reply, but he put his arm around Sam.

Sam said, "We will never forget what she did. We saw her there with the bomb, keeping The Org in place, making sure we had clear targets for our fireshots. We knew she was doing it for all of us. She told me that she wanted to be a mother to us kids, and that's how we'll remember her, as Mom."

Jason leaned on Sam as the plane stopped nearby and began powering down.

.   .   .   .

The next evening, Jason drove a utility truck to the park, carrying Glenda's body. Sam went with him. It was past sunset by then, and the B-52 crew drove a couple of the airport shuttles so the rest of the children could be there, too. They headed directly to the grave sites where we had buried our other Family members.

Our group at the golf course found a car and drove into the park to meet them, and the other groups did the same. On the way to the grave site, we passed the small crater where the unexploded bomb had impacted, not far from the former main tunnel entrance to the lab. The dark hole looked innocuous, just another feature in the park.

Everyone attended the service, including the children and all those Family who had hidden from Orlinsky's troops. As we gathered, I saw a lone bison not far away, staring at our big group, standing in silhouette against the deep blue starless sky. The waxing gibbous moon reached down toward the distant mountains.

Jason, Aiden, Craig and I dug Glenda's grave. Most of us shared our sadness mentally, through Iter Anima connections, almost not needing words. A few did speak out loud about their friendships with Glenda. Sophia had become especially close to her while she nursed the injured Glenda back to health during Glenda's recovery from gunshot wounds. All showed respect for Glenda as a person and acknowledgement for what she had done in posing as Ben for their fight.

Craig and Elizabeth had a difficult time maintaining their composure after having been woven so tightly into the illusion with Glenda. They stood close throughout the service, leaning on each other.

Through Iter Anima, Kallik and Jaguar paid their respects and gave their thanks, after also having been involved with Glenda in the Ben illusion.

With little light remaining in the evening, Jason stood at the head of the grave. He said, speaking to Glenda's spirit, "My love, you were everything to me. And you are still the world to everyone." He released a shovelful of soil onto her body.

As we joined him to bury her, Jason paused, looked around, and said, "This place has meaning."

I understood exactly what he meant.

We all took a moment to reflect on what we had been through. We had stopped The Org, and in the process, we created stronger connections with people around the world. We lost people in the fight, Glenda the most recent sacrifice. But we maintained great hope for the future with no more obvious threats looming in the shadows. After a while, our exhaustion caught up to us, and we drove out of the park to find somewhere to sleep.

We found a grouping of motels near 88th and I-76, a supermarket not far away. We set up temporary residence there, with plans to find a better homestead soon. The next day, as we searched for more appropriate accommodations, a few survivors approached us from their hiding places throughout the city.

During the following weeks, more people arrived from outside the Denver area, and we had thousands of survivors among us. All of them maintained some awareness of the turmoil their brains had experienced, and they felt a compulsion to come looking for others like themselves. What drove them to find us, we did not know. Their physical health varied from barely able to walk, to reasonably stable, but almost nobody was strong and healthy. They would need time to recover.

Groups of children arrived separately, all of them healthy, and all of them mentally acquainted with Sam and his tribe. They had participated in the attacks on The Org with their fireshots. They now integrated with the children's tribe very quickly.

We cleaned out houses where we could live and gathered food. We gave medical aid to those who needed it. And when things stabilized somewhat, we began to think about the bigger picture.

Jason, Craig, Elizabeth, and I discussed that the mind meeting place Sam and the children created – similar to the smaller mindscape Kallik had brought us to – was an important characteristic of the Cosmic Consciousness, and even the New Humanity, about which many of us were beginning to speculate. In keeping with the naming creativity that had led us to *Iter Anima*, and before that, had led Ben to the unintentionally poor acronym *STD*, standing for Stoffer Transcranial Device, Craig coined a new name for the mind meeting place, or place of collective thought. He suggested "Locus Logos Collective," and immediately shortened it to "Locus Logos." We liked the name immediately. It would come to mean the place *and* the meetings themselves.

Soon, we held our first Locus Logos since Jason's and the Family's explosive, cleansing wave. That wave had eliminated known evils incarnate and finished off The Org after they were broken down by the children's fireshots. Some of us had been reaching out to specific people through Iter Animas, a few wanting to practice this new-found ability, but we had not held a general meeting, so-to-speak. We started the first meeting with our core groups in the Denver area, and included Kallik and Jaguar. We did not immediately bring in the wider masses of adults and children who had been arriving during the few days following what we were now calling *The Wave*.

We couldn't just jump into an Iter Anima and have a meeting. We first had to "call" a meeting. For our close-by groups, we certainly could have had a physical gathering, but our goal was to expand our reach to what could be many thousands of people and more around the world. We chose a time, and I, in essence, mentally *broadcast* the invitation to the invitees. This first *Locus Logos* would include: the original Family, the children's tribe, the first Beeped survivors, the forgotten techs, the first four new arrivals, the troops we met above the lab complex, and the B-52 crew. This totaled more than 60 of us.

.   .   .   .

The mindscape, the Locus Logos, is a place that we mentally create together. It appears limitless and with boundaries at once. Easily accommodating our few dozen initial participants, the space fits us comfortably, not giving us the feeling that it is endless, but rather that it is specifically for this group. As we will eventually expand our scope, so will the space to accommodate us. Thus, we know it is limitless and feel its boundaries at the same time. Now, a thin veil of illuminated clouds whisk overhead, stars shining behind them. We present ourselves as we want to be seen, most of us looking no different than we do physically.

Jason starts the meeting without preamble: "All of us have been discussing our situation and what has happened these past many months.

Compared to what we knew before The Crash, we certainly have experienced things we never would have expected. Just the fact that we're meeting here, like this, is *almost* unbelievable. But it's not unbelievable.

"We *know* that this, and much more that seems impossible, is our new reality. We have discovered the Cosmic Consciousness. And we, ourselves, constitute a New Humanity, especially the children. Our overall state of being has changed. What we need, going forward, is an agreed-upon understanding of how we want to live, what we want our society to be, and how we should go about making this happen."

Jason stops speaking so we can consider what he said. A few of us already had discussed our need for defining the foundations for our society, or societies. The obvious practical needs, such as food, shelter, physical safety, shared duties, and much more are being handled individually, as-needed, thus far without detailed rules and procedures. But we know that complications can arise if we don't discuss and agree upon our core values.

Jason continues, "Before we get too far into the foundations of society, I'd like to bring up something of interest that we should think about. It's a question, really. Here in Denver, Ben invented The Stoffer Solution. Through good and bad, it led to The Crash throughout the world, and it also led to our New Humanity. Here in Denver, too, people came together and formed the Family. And also here in Denver, a key group of children came together and formed their tribe.

"In isolation, any of these occurrences would be considered highly unusual. One in a billion. But every one of them was necessary for the successful start of this New Humanity and the elimination of its most nefarious opposition. In light of this, I'd like you to consider that there is something more to these occurrences than what coincidence should cause. What each group contributed to changing the world was integral to the process and the results we achieved. The likelihood of each situation happening at the same time, in the same place, is so improbable as to be statistically impossible."

Jason pauses again so everyone can ponder what he is saying.

After a few moments, he resumes: "The invention of the Stoffer Solution, the formation of the Family, and formation of the tribe, could have happened in different places, but they didn't. They happened here in Denver. And all were necessary to bring us to where we are now. Many others contributed, including Kallik and Jaguar. None of this could have happened without them. But what changed the world originated here. It originated in Denver."

Thoughtful silence.

"Considering this a coincidence seems unreasonably unreasoned. You might compare it to the existence of life on Earth, as it has evolved. But I see a glaring difference. And that difference is long spans of time. Many highly improbable things had to happen for life to begin, and infinitely more improbable things had to happen for humans to evolve to what we became. But you could write off a lot of this progression, this evolution, to time, millions of years of time. Many do.

"What happened that brought us to our New Humanity, this rapid jump forward, did not involve long periods of time. It happened instantly. And it originated here in Denver. Are you starting to see my question?"

More thoughtful silence.

"Unless you accept it as a statistically impossible coincidence, you have to acknowledge that there is something unique about this place. And if you accept that our location here in Denver is something special, you might ask *why*."

Nobody wanted to speculate openly yet. They waited to hear Jason's point.

"Why did all this happen here? Why would this place matter? Why does it *still* matter? People are coming here from everywhere. We haven't invited them here. As far as I've heard, nobody has said that a dream is telling them to come here. Nobody has said that some sentient force, good or evil, is directing them to come here. And yet, they come.

"If not by coincidence, then what? I can only conclude that someone *caused* this to happen. And then I must ask, '*Who caused this to happen?*'"

Javier, an original Family member, asks, "Do you mean God?"

Jason doesn't respond immediately, letting the question ring for a while. Then he says, "In the loosest of definitions, at least someone greater than us. Maybe you could call it alien, but that seems trite or dismissive of a deeper understanding."

Javier replies, "I have no doubt that it is God."

Danielle, a previously-forgotten scientist we had found locked up in the Upstream section of the underground facility says, "I know it's not God." She does not say this as a challenge, but rather as a statement of her beliefs.

Now, the thoughts of individuals begin to flutter among all our minds.

They are questions, doubts, certanties, ideas of gods, beliefs in paganism, commitment to science, speculation about alien races, feelings of higher callings, deep fears of hell, and so on.

These thoughts are not becoming aggressive or antagonistic, nor are they conflicting with each other. There remains a unity among everyone, a respect, but Jason is not looking for a debate.

After a few minutes, Jason interrupts: "I did not bring this up because I believe we can solve this mystery or because I think we can come to an agreement on whether or not there is a higher power than us. But I do want to remind everyone of our connections around the world, those people who helped us carry the BBs and clear the minds of other survivors.

"The most poignant aspect of who we found naturally and who we found through our individual affinities is that we contacted a wide assortment of people and encountered the manifestations of their beliefs: people who represented agnostic or even atheistic ideals, along with those who had deeply religious backgrounds. All of them helped each other, helped the whole world, together. We did not need to fight over our differences.

"I bring up this question of who might have started us on this new path because I want us to consider that there could be something greater than us, *someone* greater than us. We don't need to argue over religion, paganism, or science. But if we take away the concept of a higher authority, people in governments and *organizations* present themselves as gods. They become accepted as gods. We have seen the disasters they have caused."

Jason remains silent for a while and then asks, "Can we at least agree that we, as humans, are neither the highest form of life that rules over all, nor a blight on the planet that should be exterminated?"

He again waits for a while before continuing.

"Even if we cannot agree that there is something greater than ourselves, something greater than civilization itself, can we agree that *acting* as though there is something greater will do us no harm? To act as though there is something greater would, at minimum, give us a goal for orienting our thinking and our deeds. It will help us make the best of ourselves and aim the future of humanity in a positive direction."

I feel everyone's thoughts dancing among us. Our smaller group had been speaking of these things for weeks, and I already agree with what Jason wants to accomplish. I hope that the others do, too.

Jason asks, "If nothing more, can we tilt ourselves upward toward heaven?"

Nobody openly opposes the concept or gives any comment, so Jason says, "I'm not asking for a definitive answer to this right now. I just wanted to pose the question and let you consider it."

He continues on a different topic: "From here, we do need to agree on the foundations of our society. We need to do this before we can get down to the specifics of how we should go about the business of civilization. A few of us have been discussing some initial ideas. They are not new. I'll start, and we can have a conversation. Feel free to propose other ideas, too.

"First, we believe that freedom of speech is a core value around which society should be structured. Free speech is the same as free thought, and without it, society can fall prey to narcissists and psychopaths who will manipulate others in any way they can. Free speech allows us to tell our stories about who we are, what we have done, and what we want to accomplish. Absent free speech, people can manipulate perceptions of truth because they can repress dissenting voices."

Jason pauses again before continuing: "Does anyone disagree with this? Agree? Have any comments?"

Phillips, once an ally of Upstream, says, "I think . . . ."

.   .   .   .

When we felt comfortable with some of our foundational ideas, and had a consensus to proceed, we held our first of many Locus Logos that were open to everyone. The number of people who attended was in the thousands. By then, the numbers of adults who came to live in Denver were also in the thousands. The children who had survived in Denver and who had arrived from other places numbered, we estimated, more than 10,000. We were deep into removing and burying the dead, cleaning houses, and fixing things so we could live more comfortably.

We found plenty of food in stores, but we soon would need a better plan for the long term. We began discussing ideas for how we might organize hunting in the surrounding areas and grow crops the following spring. We planned to look into getting the power grid working again, that and other infrastructure systems. Thus, we handled our immediate needs and sowed the seeds for a new civilization at the same time.

Next, we addressed our long-term objectives with a massive, open Locus Logos. I put out an invitation, and the attendance was more than promising.

. . . .

This gathering reveals the limitless feel of the place with the numbers who attend: tens of thousands from Denver and throughout the world. For the first time in an Iter Anima, I also retain a physical sense of where I am in Denver. Our feeling that this location has a special meaning, is really the *nexus* for the changes in humanity and the world, has grown so powerful, that we no longer speculate whether or not Denver is unique in this way.

The nexus is not only the place, but also the people who participated in causing the changes throughout the world. We don't see ourselves as above anyone because of this. To the contrary, we feel that our responsibility to humanity is greater.

I also wonder whether this nexus location can move with us, we who are the nexus people. *What could it mean as we reach for the stars?* But I have to put that thought aside for now. We have more practical matters to address, such as the foundations of our new civilization.

Beyond those we are meeting for the first time, some old friends are here, people dear to our hearts and souls. They are the ones who joined with us to create the BB wave that cleared the minds of crashed survivors throughout the world.

With joy, we acknowledge the presence of these people and their groups: Kallik and her whole tribe, Jaguar and her tribe, Tenzen Lama and his followers in Tibet, Omeo and his aboriginal people in Australia, Rabbi Boucher and her congregation in Paris, Amir Habib Muhammad and his congregation in Istanbul, Quang Jin and his gathering in China, Bhakti Bhagwan Swami and his followers in India, Lin Jing and his followers in a monastery in China, Deacon Isaac McCarthy and his congregation in New York. I feel a great warmth upon experiencing the re-connection with all of these groups.

I'm especially happy to see all three of the Squamish climbers here. Gabriel was the first I had met, and then he had helped bring in Audrey and Hudson. They had helped us get more control of our Iter Anima when we were just beginning to discover what it was. I had worried that Hudson didn't want to deal with what we were doing, and even that he might cause problems. But as it turned out, all three of them brought in more people who they felt akin to. They could be considered among the least religious of us, but they were spiritual, and ultimately, they embraced what we were doing, making big contributions to everything, themselves. Reconnecting with them made me want to visit Squamish, myself.

The minds of everyone in attendance hum among us, and I feel an expanse of feeling and understanding that I cannot describe. It is everyone at once and each individual separately. Even though we had already experienced our Iter Animas and the first Locus Logos, I had expected this to be something like a physical meeting with people talking, though purely mental. But there is no comparison I can provide to describe what it really is. Our level of communication has transcended beyond expectations. Our comprehension of each other is uplifting in ways I never imagined. We feel the possibilities of our lives and the future of humanity glowing in our souls.

Jason speaks to everyone: "Welcome. This is where and how we will maintain our expansive connections. I am excited to see what we can achieve together. I'll provide a brief introduction to some ideas we have been considering, and then we can discuss them. Feel free to take this wherever you want it to go."

.   .   .   .

The crew of the 747 that originally flew the plane to Denver had been killed with the other troops during the Family's Wave. Captain Nowak and his crew of the B-52 were fully trained and experienced in preparing and flying 747s. Their next destination was Krasnoyarsk in Russia to pick up Kallik and her tribe. They brought them to Denver. The tribe arrived on the plane two weeks after The Wave.

We had to wait almost a month for Jaguar's tribe to emerge from the jungle before the crew could fly to Macapá, Brazil to pick them up. It was late August when they landed in Denver. An early snow had dusted the tarmac, but it didn't interfere with us rolling stairs up to the big jet so the passengers could disembark.

A large crowd gathered to greet these Zo'é Family members in person, including Kallik, Jason, Craig, Elizabeth, Aiden, Sam, and hundreds more. I waited at the foot of the stairs and watched as Jaguar emerged from the plane and stood briefly, overlooking her new home. She descended the stairs and set foot on solid ground, her expression one of pure joy.

All I could do was throw my arms around her and cry.

Chapter 43
Apocalypsis

We have come to some tentative conclusions based on revelations that arose from our experiences with The Crash and our future:

The Family were formed because they were attracted by the animalistic focus of Jason and Glenda. Without being consciously aware of it, they rejected the conflicts that caused The Crash. They rejected the chaos and lies propagated by The Org and their associated government collaborators. They rejected the hedonistic attraction of freedom without responsibility. The Family brought back focus and purpose by embracing mutual cooperation for a greater good and doing this without force.

The core of society is family, and in this case, the core of this society will be the Family. It is not a commune; it is a cooperative spirit that lives in those who welcome it.

The effectiveness of Sam's tribe revolved around Sam's willingness to accept his calling to be a leader. Most other children did not hear the calling. It was a call to sacrifice the present for a better future. He accepted the risks and was willing to fight for what he believed was right. And even more important, his tribe were willing to follow him.

We believe that a pro-human, pro-civilization outlook is a foundational pillar of society, and that free speech and meritocracy are integral to a thriving civilization. Our daily actions affect who we are and how successful our society can be. With that in mind, we go about our daily activities, doing things with the intent of contributing to the greater good and the greatest realization of who we can be as individuals.

Our grandest revelations were the discovery of the Cosmic Consciousness and becoming part of a New Humanity.

In simplest terms, the Cosmic Consciousness is like a brain. The people within it are like neurons in the brain. The Cosmic Consciousness can be an interface for greater understanding and a way to connect individuals mentally, but without the need for physical contact. When we choose to meet through Iter Anima in the Locus Logos, we can grow closer, but we also know that physical proximity and direct contact are human necessities. Mind and body, both, make us human.

It could be millenia before people can claim to understand what this New Humanity means, if ever. There is no doubt, however, that The Crash changed children in different ways than it changed adults. We are realizing that the children work together differently than any groups did throughout history. They experience fewer conflicts and greater cooperation among themselves because of their mental connections. But this does not mean that we, the last adults from before The Crash, have become unnecessary or useless to society. As we found during our attacks on The Org, we all need each other.

Going forward in the New Humanity, we adults are teaching the children about the important things that made our civilizations great. If we were to take the approach that starting from scratch, disregarding all that came before, is the best way forward, we would be denying thousands of years of human development. We would be leaving the children as infants, naked in a field to be eaten by coyotes. Instead, we are working with them so they understand our past, so they continue learning, and so they continue making Humanity greater than it was before.

Kallik is one of the main teachers, always available to impart her wisdom to anyone who will listen. Jaguar, a child herself, enjoys discussions with Kallik. They both enthusiastically embrace their new home and our New Humanity, as well as their positions as leaders.

An interesting aspect of our Iter Animas showed itself when we wanted to actually talk, using our voices, with others who didn't know our language. Inside the Iter Animas, we had discovered a way of understanding each other that did not involve our voices. We thought in both ideas and words, and we communicated successfully through our minds. But in physical interactions when we used our voices, we experienced the difficulties of not knowing each others' languages.

We found that the mind connections helped us learn other languages very quickly. The Iter Anima abilities we developed in ourselves allowed us to understand and translate languages as we practiced them. But it was not instantaneous. As we heard other languages during conversations, we began to connect the underlying meanings of the words to the new words we heard. Instead of having to study and practice translations of these other languages, we could hear the words and know their meanings at the same time. But we still had to practice using the new words after hearing them. It became an accelerated way for us to learn each others' languages.

The children were much faster at picking up on these new language skills than we adults were.

Jaguar and Kallik joined together to organize classes for the children. Under an old oak tree in a grassy park, they held their first class. Jaguar brought together a small group of the youngest children, those who had been too young to participate in throwing the fireshots at The Org.

Kallik leaned toward them and said, "Let me tell you about the fearsome devilish birds that almost destroyed the world . . . and the one who led them away. Let me tell you about Mom and Old Man. Let me tell you about the children and their fireshots."

They stared at her with awe and excitement.

She whispered slowly, drawing them in: "There was a woman named Glenda. You will come to know her as Mom. She knew that the devilish birds were coming to attack all the survivors of The Crash. And so she . . . ."

We began rebuilding civilization and figuring out how we wanted to organize our societies. We adults in the Family strive to do what we think is right, and we remain open-minded about how humanity has changed, receptive to these new ways of existence. We accept that what the children do with this New Humanity will be up to them.

Steven S. Patchin

Afterword

Since I got hit with the Beep glitch many weeks ago during the first BEMP test, I have been keeping notes about all that has happened to us. Lately, I've been going over my notebooks, arranging their content for what could be a useful historical chronicle. I am determined to give my best effort in writing this narrative of our experiences so that I might do justice for the people involved. I have filled multiple notebooks with various stories that people told us, along with details that I remember.

Through discussions with Kallik and Craig, I came to realize that one of the most important tenets of civilization is our own stories. Those that have affected us the most have been told in the context of myths and religions, whether or not they actually happened. It is these stories that have provided the foundation for civilization. And I want to make sure our most recent, significant story is told as accurately as possible, not just in the details, but in its essence.

I have not, however, officially started a proper draft of a work that I would want to share with others. One thing in particular remains on my mind, and I finally find myself ready to address it.

I set out on foot with Daisy at my side to begin my pilgrimage to the downtown Denver Art Museum. It is close to where Sam and the children had resided in that highrise for a while, where nobody wants to go now. The walk takes a few hours, and it is late afternoon before we arrive amid the piles of dead and rotting people. We can do little more than climb over them at times. We reach the museum grounds after crossing a park to its north. We enter the concrete building on one side of the round glass section of the facility. The glass entry door has been shattered, and a few bodies lay inside. I do my best to ignore their stench. It has been a smell we've dealt with for months.

My trek to the museum was inspired by Lauren. We had discussed the importance of art and music during our short time together. I know little about art, and what I know about music is only what I had heard on the radio. I've always enjoyed music, but I had not experienced its transcendent potential until Lauren showed me how to feel music deeper. She had accomplished this by playing a song for me, "Rain Black, Reign Heavy," by Crippled Black Phoenix. That song has haunted me and inspired me since I heard it. The music and words played in my head during our tunnel explosion that first revealed the burning intensity the Family could produce when we work together. Later, we had used the song to demonstrate Jason's ability to channel information to the Family mentally.

On my trek to the museum, I thought about all that had happened on my journey that had begun with Ben.

I went from being pulled out of my alcohol and porn-induced stupor to finding a purpose through Ben. I was crashed at the time and didn't know it. Ben pushed me along, forcing me to use my skills, and then to expand on them. First, I had to get Ben away from Ronnie, the robot-like mercenary and dedicated soldier of Upstream Security. To do that, I had to kill him. After that, we found Jason and Glenda, along with the Family, and we all had to fight Upstream troops to get across Denver and reach Ben's underground lab. This involved my teaching some basic defensive and offensive firearm skills to the Family. Then, we actually battled and defeated a group of Upstream soldiers.

Along the way, I met Lauren, who changed how I saw the world, opening me to music and art on a level I had never considered. In a very short time, she had become extremely important to me, and I was falling in love with her.

At the lab, as Ben invented a way to reset the minds of the crashed, the whole Family pulled together to build his machine, which we called the Beep. It worked as intended. But immediately following this success, we had to face more troops. Ultimately, we negotiated our way out of the situation such that Ben could focus on a larger objective, which led to his creation of the BBs.

During the same time, some of us in the Family, at Craig's suggestion, got together and discovered that we could travel with our minds. At first, it was an elaborate undertaking, involving a fire and drumming in order to find the state of mind to take us deeper into the Cosmic Consciousness. Slowly, we experimented with ways of making deeper mental connections. Jason, almost by accident, already had discovered a method of channeling our energy in such a way that we obliterated a platoon of soldiers and their equipment when they prepared to attack us.

Our mental connections kept improving, and we found that Jason also could channel instructions to us and even cause us physically to move. We connected with thousands of people and groups around the world and sent Ben's BB waves to cure the crashed survivors. The cost of this, for me, was the loss of Lauren. But even with this loss, I was pulled further into a greater purpose than myself, and a greater purpose than that of human civilization. I found that there is something more, something higher.

With the help of the children and the examples they presented in their connections with each other, we realized that our Iter Animas could be started and controlled much easier than we had believed possible. Jaguar and Kallik also contributed greatly to our mental expansion. This allowed us to burn down the heartless body of The Org, including those who founded it and used it to control society.

We had gone from being crashed, to functioning as unified groups, to realizing we were forming a New Humanity. Our mental connections became easy and natural. This brought me back to what I had also discovered in myself. And that was my own heart and soul, along with something even greater. These revelations are for each individual to discover and embrace, and I was embracing mine.

For this moment at the museum, I am reconnecting with Lauren in the best way I know how. Inside the building, I see a myriad of options to explore. I want to start by viewing paintings, because Lauren was a painter. I follow signs that direct me upstairs to a gallery, Daisy stays near me. With no working lights, the rooms are dark, only small glints and glows of sunlight reach this far inside from the large windows in the lobby. I use my flashlight and allow it to lead me to the first painting I have seen in any museum.

I find this first picture apropos of our recent experiences. It is oil on canvas, approximately 20 by 40 inches mounted in a tasteful gold frame. It is titled "Herd of Buffalo," and was painted by William Jacob Hays in 1862. More than a dozen silhouetted buffalo move in cloudy dust, backlit by a very small, low sun. It reminds me of the bison in the park and how they had been present during everything we did there. I had even seen one of them at the Space Force Base during our first Iter Anima in the baseball field. Hunters had slaughtered buffalo across the plains during the 1800s and into the 20th Century, killing almost all of them. Now, it is humans who have been mostly wiped out.

I think that even if I don't see another painting in this museum except this one, my trip will have been well worth the effort. I feel as though I am standing in the haze along with these buffalo, and I begin to feel the power of art that Lauren tried to explain to me.

I skim more paintings, admiring the collection, appreciating the variety of subjects and styles. The next painting that takes hold of my attention is a small Monet titled "Waterloo Bridge, Sunlight Effect." I am so stunned by its depth that I get chills and feel tears in my eyes. Its impressionist style, with light blues and purples accented by yellows and oranges, depicts a scene of water and a bridge with smokestacks in the background. The fact that it is not photorealistic, using extreme details, but instead provides an *impression* of a place at one moment, makes me *feel* the sense of it instead of leading me to analyze it. And this is what makes all the difference. I had never thought that a painting could have this effect on me.

I am enthralled by painting after painting in these galleries, and I feel myself getting full, as if I am unable to see more paintings and still feel the way I should about them. But another painting catches my soul and turns me inside out.

This glorious work, four by five feet in size, dominates its own wall. It is "A Mountain Symphony" by Birger Sandzen, painted in 1927. Its colors are both unexpected and exactly right. Purple mountains behind orange and green trees reflect in a lake. It is unreal and hyper-real at once. It embodies eternal natural beauty, but its power reigns with the feelings that crash through me as it overtakes my psyche.

I try to consider it logically, and I imagine the patterns of a paint-by-numbers painting, something pre-set, made to be reproduced without much artistic effort. I realize I am seeing beyond this painting's surface to a deeply hidden structure, though nothing about this work of art is paint-by-numbers. In my attempt at applying logic to it, I have found a flaw in my thinking and also discovered a greater understanding of what depth feels like.

I imagine the artist witnessing a deep structure just as I had witnessed in Jaguar's vision, what I believed was DNA itself. Like me, this artist had been unable to forget what he had seen, unable to leave it unexpressed. I had used my experience to connect Jaguar and the Family. This artist had brought forth his insight by creating this painting. The colors seem to blend with what we had experienced through our Iter Animas: the greens and purples we had seen in DNA, and the bright orange of our real fires along with the fires in our hearts. Here I stand, facing a work of art that was created almost a hundred years before The Crash, before our transcendence as people into something we have yet to understand. It represents, in one image, the feelings I can not express fully.

I go to a different part of the room, find a leather bench, and drag it over so I can sit in contemplation of the painting and our new humanity. Daisy lies down on the floor next to the bench, and I scratch her ears, then pet her for a while.

I position my flashlight on the bench so it illuminates the whole landscape painting. From my backpack, I take out Lauren's smartphone. I hold its power button until it begins powering up. I have already charged it using a solar charger, so the battery level shows as 100%. I insert wired earbuds into my ears, plug the cable into the phone, and stare at its screen.

The device waits for me to enter the PIN. I had been wondering about solving this problem since I had picked up her phone from the desk in our room at the lab the day we buried Lauren. I will not be able to listen to the music Lauren has stored on this phone unless I can access the phone's apps. And I can't do that if I don't enter the PIN.

Without effort now, I see the number in my mind . . . along with Lauren's life and her personality. I enter that PIN, and the phone opens itself for me. I find the music app easily, select "random play," and let the music flood into me.

We sit on the bench, Lauren and I, to live this moment. The painting a symphony of Earth. The music a picture of us. We embrace our New Humanity.

I pull out a fresh notebook and open it to the first page. I begin writing:

"The sound of machine gun fire made me toss my old porn magazine onto the floor and roll off the couch, knocking over a half-empty bottle of vodka and spilling it on the carpet."

Steven S. Patchin

About the Author

Steven S. Patchin is an Emmy-winning photographer and artist living in Las Vegas, Nevada. He holds a B.A. in television production from UNLV. *Children of The Crash* is Steve's fourth novel, following *Backfire Crash* and *Beyond The Crash*. His first novel, *Derelict Dreams*, is an illustrated novel with more than 80 illustrations, each a work of art itself. All of the artwork in *Derelict Dreams* is available for sale in multiple sizes, as is Steve's other artwork. Steve has also published a collection of his short stories called *Burnt Ends, Fucked Up Stories*.

To stay up to date on *The Crash* series please visit the website:
BackfireCrash.com

For more information on Steve's artwork, please visit his website:
StevePatchinPhotography.com

For more information on the illustrated novel, *Derelict Dreams*, please visit the webste:
DerelictDreamsBook.com

In addition to creating his artwork and writing, Steve also owns and operates Patchin Pictures, which is a photography and video business he founded in 1996. For more information about Patchin Pictures, please visit the website:
PatchinPictures.com

Music is an important inspiration for Steve, especially when he writes. Below is a link to a **Spotify** playlist to accompany the trilogy "The Crash." It is hours of music that he loves. Enjoy!

Spotify Playlist: **StevenPatchin.com**

Made in the USA
Las Vegas, NV
05 May 2024

89466448R00195